QUEEN OF STORMS

FIREMANE: BOOK TWO

RAYMOND E. FEIST

HARPER Voyager
An Imprint of HarperCollinsPublishers

QUEEN OF STORMS. Copyright © 2020 by Raymond E. Feist. All rights reserved. Printed in the United States of America. No part of this book may be used or reproduced in any manner whatsoever without written permission except in the case of brief quotations embodied in critical articles and reviews. For information, address HarperCollins Publishers, 195 Broadway, New York, NY 10007.

First Harper Voyager mass market printing: May 2021
First Harper Voyager hardcover printing: July 2020

Print Edition ISBN: 978-0-06-231593-9
Digital Edition ISBN: 978-0-06-231587-8

Map by Jessica Feist
Sword graphic by VectorShop/Shutterstock, Inc.
Cover design by Richard L. Aquan
Cover illustration © Larry Rostant

Harper Voyager and the Harper Voyager logo are trademarks of HarperCollins Publishers in the United States of America and other countries.

HarperCollins is a registered trademark of HarperCollins Publishers in the United States of America and other countries.

23 24 25 BVGM 10 9 8 7 6 5 4 3 2

Also by Raymond E. Feist

To Rebecca and James,

This book is dedicated to the start of your great adventure together.

Love,

Dad

CONTENTS

The Ice Floes

Summer Passage

Westlands

Copper Hills

North T

Port Colos

Dangero
Passag

Barony of
Marquensas

Beran's
Hill

Wild Lands

Endless Depths

City of
Marquenet

KINGDOM
OF
ILCOMEN

Oncon

Narrow Strait

Covenant
Land

KINGDOM OF ZINDAROS

South T

Swamplands

Range of the Border Tribes

Abala

The Burni

Endless
Desert

Scorching Sea

Garn's Wound

Scorched Coast

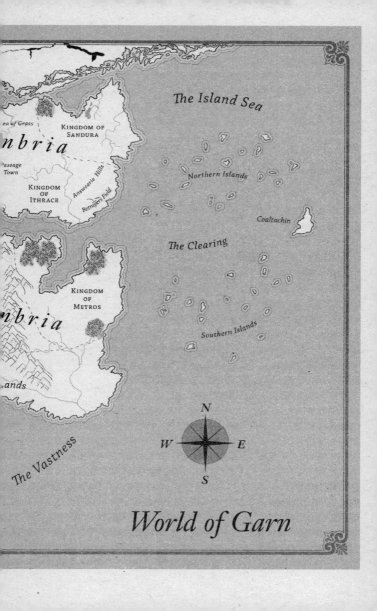

QUEEN
OF
STORMS

PROLOGUE
A VOICE FROM WITHIN SHADOWS

He was known as Bernardo Delnocio of Poberto, which was the first of many lies about him. His birth name had not been Bernardo, nor was he from a family named Delnocio. That family had been famous and powerful until a war took the last son; he claimed to be a distant cousin, from a lesser branch of the family, with no claim to any legacy but a once-noble name. Nor had he been born in Poberto, a prosperous town surrounded by the villas of the wealthy and powerful. That notable community rested just outside Brojues, the capital city of the Kingdom of Fondrak, home to the Church of the One. Instead, he had come from the poorest squalor of Aliestes, a minor city on the far continent of Enast many miles from the splendor of Brojues.

As a boy, the man calling himself Bernardo had been an abandoned guttersnipe, raised by a gang of urchins. He had grown up roaming the streets, surviving in a vicious world that provided few respites from struggle, living by his wits and a brutal determination to survive, until he had been recruited by the Church.

His natural combativeness and will to survive had been

recognized and his early training had been channeled effectively into serving the Church. He had spent nearly ten years as a member of the Order of the Church Adamant, the martial arm of the Servants of the One, soldiers willing to die unquestioningly to defend the faith and, more important, attack its enemies without hesitation.

His will to survive had elevated him above the other soldiers, first by avoiding duty that would have trapped him in a permanent role as a pioneer, engineer, or gynour, though he had been clever enough to learn a bit about building advanced entrenchments, rigging bridges, repairing roads, and operating siege engines, so he became as well-rounded as possible.

He had a knack for accents and quickly improved his speech so that his common origins faded as he learned to adopt more refined rhetoric and behavior. He soon became the youngest minor officer in the Church Adamant.

After only three years as a unit commander, he realized the true power wasn't in the army, but being a cleric in the Church, and that was when his urge to survive had been transformed into a desire to thrive, rise, and become more powerful at every turn. He had surprised, even shocked, his companions when, as a rising young officer, he had announced he was leaving the Church Adamant to take holy vows and become the lowest of the clergy.

He did not remain a minor priest for long. Bernardo was not the most overtly aggressive player in the deadly internal politics of the Church of the One, but he had an intuitive grasp of something few did: he could quickly recognize the true organization of any group, where the power actually resided as opposed to ostensible ranks and titles. He identified those who were public figures and those who moved quietly in the background. Above all, he had a lethal instinct for when an opponent was vulnerable and no hesitation in taking advantage of that recognition.

He immediately understood that while the Council of the Episkopos was the governing body of the Church of the One, there was a handful of men within the Council who controlled every aspect of the Church. The Church priesthood had as many barriers and dead ends as the army had, and picking a path to power had given him a challenge, but surviving in the streets had proved a harsh yet enlightening education.

His natural skills and intuition meant he knew the right moment to act, and more than once he had managed to convince someone else to be responsible for the fall of one of his rivals. He merely suggested something and other people acted, and he made sure they believed it was their own brilliance that had led to the targeted rival's downfall. Gang leader or powerful episkopos, he could apply his talents equally, discerning quickly who was truly loyal or easily manipulated or even bought, who might become an ally, and who must be neutralized or even destroyed.

On the streets he had learned early which boys were bullies full of bluster. They came and went, often to an early grave or a slave gang, but the truly clever, gifted, and thoughtful—they endured. Those were the ones he observed and listened to, as he sought to survive.

Over the years Bernardo had also found it convenient to shape the truth of his past to suit the fluid politics of the Church of the One. Those who knew the inconvenient facts of his early life were either his closest supporters or dead. Ridding himself of potential enemies had sharpened his naturally keen intellect and driven patience into the very fiber of his being. He had waited months, even years at times, to see a rival dead. His imperturbability was almost

legendary within the higher echelons of the Church in Brojues. He was now counted among the wisest of the rulers
of the Church and, by wide consensus, the most patient.
Today, he was approaching the end of that patience.

More than once he'd come close to death either in the
name of the One or in establishing his place in the hierarchy
of the Church, and right now he'd gladly return to those moments and embrace a quick death.

He sat silently in a large bedchamber in the castle of Lodavico, Most Holy Majesty of Sandura, ruler of the single
greatest power on the twin continents of North and South
Tembria. Getting Lodavico to sit motionless for hours had
proved impossible, but Bernardo had managed to get him
to sit for minutes at a time, a small but necessary step in
Bernardo establishing complete control over the king and,
through him, the Kingdom of Sandura.

The king sat as still as he could while a painter attempted
to capture his magnificence on a treated board of cured
wood. The artist was a captive from the city of Ithra, taken
by one of Lodavico's oathmen. He had managed to survive
the destruction of Ithrace's capital, avoiding death and slavery but not captivity. His name was Bantiago.

Bernardo watched closely as Bantiago deftly applied
color to the wood and, through some artistic magic, created
a likeness of Lodavico that was flattering but not overtly
false. Bernardo understood how the painter had survived
the destruction of Ithrace. His superb talents had kept him
from death.

Bantiago painted so well that he had been passed from
one noble to another over the years, building a reputation
and eventually living well by painting brilliant portraits of
his captors. Despite still being considered a captive, Bantiago traveled with servants, most of whom were strikingly
handsome young men; an apprentice, also handsome to the

point of being pretty; and a token guard. It was a captivity to be envied by most citizens of Sandura, thought Bernardo.

These portraits were an Ithraci thing, a vanity that rather offended Lodavico, but gradually Bernardo had convinced him to sit for a portrait to commemorate his glory. Bernardo had studied Lodavico for more than a year before they met, and he had now been a member of the king's court, his most trusted adviser, for a decade. He knew the monarch of Sandura had hated the way he looked his entire life.

The king knew he was often mocked for his appearance behind his back. His nose was slightly bent to the right, his left eye was marginally higher than the right, and his rare smile was noticeably lopsided. This asymmetrical visage, while not ugly, gave him an odd appearance that put people ill at ease for reasons they couldn't quite fathom. Coupled with his gaunt frame and a certain coiled energy that made it look as if he were on the verge of sudden violence, it meant few people were ever comfortable in his presence.

He had taken advantage of that discomfort his entire life, bullying his young siblings to the point of terror long before he took his father's throne. All of them gladly accepted distant fiefs or convenient marriages to be as far from the court in Sandura as possible.

He had agreed to a portrait only at Bernardo's quiet persistence. In all his life, Lodavico had not met anyone he felt more at ease with than Bernardo. This had been achieved over years of Bernardo's clever manipulation and the building of trust. There had been nights when Bernardo had simply wished to kill Lodavico, or possibly move to the other side of Garn, but in the end, he knew his persistence in winning Lodavico's trust would win out. Now that trust was almost absolute.

Something about his manner, his solid presence, calmed Lodavico no matter how stressful the situation that faced him. He counted the episkopos's counsel as vital, and after many years of having the cleric at his side in the king's chamber, it was clear that Lodavico couldn't imagine making important decisions without Bernardo's advice.

For Bernardo, persuading Lodavico to sit for a portrait was just one more tedious, tiny step in completely controlling the king without him being aware of it. The episkopos knew that by the time this portrait hung in the great gallery of the castle, amid the banners and crests of Lodavico's ancestors, the king would be convinced the portrait had been his idea, not Bernardo's, which was exactly what Bernardo wanted.

Growing tired of posing, Lodavico said, "That's enough." He stood and indicated for a servant to remove the heavy red cape with the ermine collar. He hated the vanity of the thing but had agreed with the artist that it made him look "regal." Lodavico had finally relented and seemed to be growing fonder of the pomp, which was also in keeping with Bernardo's plans.

Bernardo rose, feeling his joints protest slightly, reminding him that at his age, approximately fifty years (his exact date of birth was unknown), he needed to spend more time exercising. He had been lean and fit his entire life, adding muscle and sinew as a soldier, and had seen too many others of his rank let themselves run to fat. He would engage one of his retinue to spar with him early tomorrow morning; he was an episkopos, but he had been a soldier long enough to prefer dueling and wrestling to other forms of exercise. He was a tall, broad-shouldered man, and his dark hair was shot through with grey. He still looked as vital and energetic as a man half his age.

He wore the less formal clothing of his office, a black cassock with no trim, with black buttons down the front. His feet were clad in ankle-high boots of soft leather, and his only ornamentations were a silver circle brooch identifying him as a follower of the One and a ring of office that adorned his left hand, another simple circle of silver, though set in the center with a small ruby.

Vanity was not part of Bernardo's nature, so his appearance was not designed to please himself but to project an image he wished others to see. He wanted less to be noticed than to be a presence. More often than not it was a difficult feat.

He waited for servants to take away the heavy cloak Lodavico wore and for the king to move toward the door before falling in a half step behind, on his left, a position of slight deference. Bernardo remained silent; for he could see the king's mood was darker than usual for this time of the morning, even after one spent posing for his portrait.

Lodavico headed for his council chamber. As they approached down the long, gloomy hall, bereft of any windows as it had been cut through the heart of Lodavico's castle, shadows from torches in sconces flickered in grotesque parody of the king's naturally awkward walk. Bernardo was aware of the shadows annoying the king, even though he had endured it since he came to the throne thirty years before. He occasionally wondered why Lodavico hadn't ordered his architect to design some other type of lighting, but he didn't linger long on the question; it was possible that Lodavico endured the daily passage as a reminder of his own self-loathing.

Entering the chamber, they found a tray laden with fruit, cold meats and cheese, a loaf of warm bread, a bottle of wine, and a pitcher of cool water.

"Good," said Lodavico. "I'm famished."

"Anticipating Your Majesty's needs is always my aim," said the episkopos.

Lodavico indicated that Bernardo should sit in the chair

to his right hand at the end of the council table. The Privy Council had consisted of up to a dozen nobles of the kingdom from dim antiquity right up to his father's rule. Lodavico had named several nobles to various positions, but rarely convened the entire council, having done so only once after the war against Ithrace, just for public show. Most of the time he preferred to be in consultation with a few advisers, and lately with just one of them: Bernardo. The truth now was, for a little over ten years, the episkopos and the king made every decision in Sandura.

Lodavico said, "What news?"

Bernardo unfolded a leather portfolio he carried. He knew the king expected him not to discuss matters of state while his portrait was being painted, but now that they were alone, Lodavico was anxious to hear the day's reports.

Bernardo had long since come to understand the king's preferred order of reporting, and the usual accounts of trade, taxes, and other mundane matters were always subordinate to intelligence, news, and even rumors about anyone Lodavico considered a threat.

"Little new to report on, Majesty. Some of the companies of mercenaries who've been employed in the north are taking ship to come and join your campaigns." He paused. A tightening around Lodavico's eyes communicated clearly what the king desired to hear.

"No news from Marquensas, Majesty. Our agents report . . . everything is calm."

"What about that . . . company Daylon assembled in that town . . ."

"Beran's Hill," supplied Bernardo. "Not really a company, sire, rather a local militia of sheriff's men, though there is no proper sheriff. A young smith has been given command, a fellow named Declan."

Lodavico waved away the detail. "Beran's Hill is an invitation of sorts, I'm certain."

Bernardo had listened to this conjecture countless times, but knew his best course was to simply let the king continue his speculation without interruption and to reassure him that everything that could be done was being done.

"Daylon Dumarch has magnificent defenses in every port, garrisons of size in key locations, cities, trade route intersections, and active patrols everywhere but in the north, along one particular trade route. Why?"

Bernardo hesitated, waiting to see if the question was rhetorical. Seeing that the king expected an answer, he shrugged. "He faces very little real threat from the north. His only neighbor of consequence is Rodrigo of Copper Hills, and he is one of Baron Daylon's closest friends. Dumarch would as soon expect a brother to turn on him as Rodrigo Bavangine." He paused, gauging the king's reaction.

Lodavico nodded. "The governors and rulers of the northern ports are scattered and more prone to welcoming smugglers and traders than armies. Besides, none of the ports are large enough to accommodate a flotilla that could put a substantial force at Marquensas's rear. Port Colos is the largest, and it is so close to Marquensas's border it might as well belong to Daylon." He stroked his chin, a habit Bernardo had seen countless times when the king was lost in thought. "Daylon is . . ." He looked at the episkopos as if at a loss.

Gently, the cleric said, "I think he is taking care of what is his and guarding it."

Lodavico shook his head. "No, I know he is planning something. He's amassed wealth and has sway over many of the barons. He's making Marquensas the new Ithrace. I've read the reports . . ."

Seeing that the conversation was taking a familiar turn, the cleric sat back, keeping his features a mask as he resigned himself to another pointless harangue about Daylon Dumarch's close friendship with the dead king Steveren Langene, the ruler of Ithrace, real intelligence commingled with imagined slights and insults, turning into a rant invoking every possible reason to hate the most powerful baron in the twin continents.

When at last the king's ramblings tailed off, Bernardo gladly turned the conversation to other matters the king needed to consider, not urgent, but important, and called in a scribe to record the king's decision. As the meeting came to a close, the episkopos waited for the king's permission to rise—they had worked together so often, this amounted to the cleric inclining his head slightly and the king nodding—and as he stood, Bernardo said, "Majesty, I shall have the edicts recopied and returned before nightfall for your seal."

"I expect I should return to sit for that wretched artist. The sooner I'm done with this exercise in vanity, the better I'll like it."

Bernardo bowed slightly, and the king departed.

After the monarch was gone, the episkopos waved the scribe away, then lingered, enjoying the silence and solitude, if only for a few moments.

He refused to wallow in his transitory frustrations over dealing with a monarch who by any reasonable measure was on the fringe of madness. Bernardo Delnocio of Poberto had quickly recognized that Lodavico was a truly lonely man, hated even by his own family, surrounded by those who feigned loyalty and affection for him only out of fear. Rather than be another attention seeker, Bernardo had patiently provided counsel and the Church's support, ensuring that Lodavico became more dependent on him over each passing year.

Many times the king had asked the episkopos what he desired, to which Bernardo had always answered, "Only to serve," and every time a gift had been offered, Bernardo had declined it.

In truth, the gift came the other way; it was the cleric who gave the ruler what he most craved: Bernardo listened. No matter how preposterous or deranged Lodavico's rant, Bernardo listened, and the king needed this indulgence.

After Bernardo had spent almost two years on Lodavico's council, the monarch had come to view him as the only being on all of Garn who didn't hate him, fear him, or want anything from him, the only one who truly cared for his well-being. In short, Lodavico had decided that Bernardo was his only friend.

And this was when the manipulation had begun.

Over the last twenty years Bernardo had contrived to get rid of anyone who might prove an obstacle to his control of the king—a timely accident, an assignment to a particularly dangerous frontier post, a sudden illness. A great deal of patience had brought the cleric to almost complete mastery over the most powerful kingdom in North Tembria.

Bernardo could finally see his goal on the horizon: the Church's control of Sandura, and his control of the Church. These two aims were intertwined, and he knew the closer he got to his goal, the more his deadliest foe would be his own impatience.

Should the cathedral under construction next to the king's castle be completed in his lifetime, Bernardo already had plans to annex this monstrosity of a castle to it, tearing down walls, replacing dark corridors with passages of light, ancient dark stone with massive windows of the finest glass. He knew that would be completed years after he had left this existence but was content that whoever he appointed to follow him would share that view. When the Church was supreme, ruling over all Garn, there would be no need for castles, fortresses, or armies.

His plan extended beyond his own lifetime, which was more of a vainglorious desire to be remembered in the Church than for any personal gain. The rulers of Sandura would be so submerged in the culture of the Church that they would not realize this.

He heard the faintest rustle behind him and knew he was no longer alone. Only a handful of men could move that quietly and of those only one would dare approach him unbidden. Without looking around he asked, "What news, Belli?"

Marco Belli, Bernardo's most trusted and deadliest servant, spoke softly. "More rumors from the west."

"Marquensas?"

"Yes."

Bernardo turned to face him. Marco Belli, known as "Piccolo" for obscure reasons, stood motionless before his master. He was a smaller man than Bernardo, but of average height, wiry and agile. Belli's eyes were his most deceiving feature, for he could look innocent, or jovial, even while planning how best to kill you. He sported a red cap with a hawk's feather, a dark blue tunic, and leather leggings. At his side hung a short sword, but Bernardo knew he was an expert in many other weapons. Piccolo was the only man the cleric fully trusted and would permit in his presence alone and armed.

"Tell me about Marquensas," said Bernardo as he re-seated himself.

"For months now a town in the north of the barony, Beran's Hill, has been very busy."

"This I know," said the cleric. "Rumors, little more."

Piccolo nodded. "True, but persistent rumors, Your Eminence." He paused for a moment, as if gathering his thoughts. "There is no pattern, nor is there any one item worthy of serious consideration, but in total . . ."

"A design?"

"Not apparently, but . . . something is taking shape. Though if someone is behind it, it isn't obvious."

Bernardo nodded. "Something is going on in that town." He also organized his thoughts before adding, "It's where Lodavico and I expect the lure to be. If Baron Daylon expects Sandura's attack, with Copper Hills's aid, he could trap Lodavico's forces there."

"Lose the town, but win the war," agreed Piccolo.

"Exactly. Lodavico loses a huge number of his military, enrages allies expecting an easy victory, and convinces others of Sandura's perfidy when whatever excuse Lodavico dreams up is exposed as a lie, so it's a victory both militarily and politically. At worst, Sandura is wounded and weakened, perhaps enough for old enmity to rise and former allies to turn on Lodavico. At best, Dumarch has allies ready and launches a counteroffensive . . ." He spread his hands slowly and moved them outward, as if wiping away game pieces from a table. ". . . leaves Sandura much as Lodavico left Ithrace . . ." Bernardo let out an audible sigh. "And that we cannot have."

Piccolo glanced around the dark room. "Can't say I'd miss this castle."

"On that we agree. But when the cathedral is finished and blessed it will be the seat of the Church's power in the twin continents. And that must be protected.

"This war is inevitable, given our king's obsession with all things related to the fall of Ithrace. Even the suggestion that Daylon Dumarch is becoming the next King of Fire . . ." Bernardo paused. "I have little problem with them making war on each other. I just wish it to be on my terms, at a time of my choosing. Remember, the perfect plan executed at the wrong time has another name."

Piccolo raised an eyebrow. "A disaster?"

Bernardo chuckled. Piccolo was as lethal an agent as he could have wished for, but he was also clever and occasionally amusing. "Yes."

Piccolo nodded; then he asked, "Do you wish me to go?"

"I do not; I would rather keep you here, but I think there is a need. We have rumors of odd comings and goings. The agents of Coaltachin are apparently poking around, and they have no business we know of that far west. I've also received reports of . . . those who are best kept under watch."

"The Azhante?"

"I still employ their services. They are not a risk . . . yet. They are the ones sending me intelligence."

"Whom do they suspect?"

As if fearful of saying the name too loudly, Bernardo almost whispered, "The Flame Guard."

Piccolo's shoulders dropped slightly. "Is there no end to them?"

"Apparently not. Most we killed or captured when Ithrace fell. But . . ." He moved his hand again, this time in a vague sweeping gesture, wiggling his fingers. "Some seem to have been carried away on the wind."

"A few," observed Piccolo.

"But with . . . magic. Power. Whatever you wish to label it." Bernardo remained silent for a moment, then said, "I don't suppose there are any reports of a young man or woman with copper-and-gold hair, by chance?"

Piccolo shook his head. "Even if there were, that doesn't make them true. A Firemane heir conveniently landing in Marquensas, or even more so in Beran's Hill, would spur Lodavico to act rashly, I would wager. Even your influence would barely slow him. If that rumor suddenly sprouted up, it very well might be Dumarch's lure."

"Yes, agreed." Bernardo's brow furrowed slightly. Then

he said, "Not if we move first and look for the man or woman. Ensure the rumors are false."

"So, I should leave now?"

"Yes." Bernardo stood up. "Go, take a thorough look, then return with haste. I need to know if any of the rumors are true."

"If they are?"

"Do nothing. Observe, then come back and we shall consider our position. Send word by pigeon and courier, stating clearly the time you will arrive outside Beran's Hill. Take an armed escort, but look as if you're traveling mercenaries, then meet our agent outside the town; whoever arrives first must wait for the other. I'll leave it to you to work out the details. Now go." He made a dismissive gesture, hand held fingers downward, then a flip up toward the door.

Piccolo bowed and slipped through the hidden doorway. Bernardo was always slightly amused at his agent's use of ancient passages not known even to the king.

Alone again, he put his mind to matters of the day. In the end the Church would rule Sandura and he would rule the Church, but until that time, he was His Most Holy Majesty's loyal adviser. It was time to go and advise. Or at least sit feigning attention while watching a bored man pose for a portrait. And ponder this persistent rumor about a man or woman with copper-and-gold hair in a small town half a world away.

1

HUNTING AND
AN UNEXPECTED ENCOUNTER

———————✦———————

The sound of a twig cracking underfoot made the deer's head jerk upright from grazing, its ears moving as it looked around, seeking the source of the noise. Its nostrils flared as it tested the wind.

Hava froze, her bow halfway to a ready position, not wishing to startle the young buck. After a moment of sniffing the air, the deer started to wander away. Hava stole a glance at Molly Bowman, who looked back at Hava and, with an inclination of her head, indicated she would move off to her right, then, with her lifted chin, communicated that Hava should keep stalking the deer.

All this was new to the girl from Coaltachin: her home islands had no forests like this. Here the trees were so much bigger; the boles were massive compared with the smaller pines, balsams, and fir trees that littered the relatively small mountains on the islands. The lowlands had been cleared centuries earlier for farms and orchards.

She wended her way between massive oaks, while avoiding the sprawling beech trees and their multiple roots and low-hanging branches. Hava understood how easy it would be to get lost. This area, with its interlinked forests, woodlands, small hills with dells, and dead-end canyons, was called the Wild Lands and had once been a haven to savage tribes and outlaws. While the western half of the region was relatively peaceful, due to the Dumarch family's pacification of their demesne over generations, it was still a very wild place to navigate. To a girl raised in tiny villages and schools on small islands, it was a veritable maze filled with potentially lethal traps. Navigating was hard: she couldn't see the sun, and the shadows were confusing. All the tricks she knew for how to find her way from place to place in cities were useless in the densest forest she'd ever encountered.

Even the smells were different. There was a damp earthiness overlaid with something that was almost familiar, something like sandalwood, but not. Another floral note teased her, almost apple or pear, but not. The alien quality of this place both intrigued and intimidated her.

The deer started to drift away, and Hava glanced over to see that Molly was already moving. Hava tried to follow the deer as silently as possible, painfully aware that compared with Molly she was making enough noise to scare away half the wildlife in the forest.

Hava liked Molly. Of all the young women she had met since arriving at Beran's Hill, Molly was by far the most interesting. The others were much as she expected from her own experiences with town girls while traveling, as well as the girls she had known at home, people caught up in their day-to-day tedium, living predictable lives. They served their families, then got married, moved out, and served their husbands. Or served many men as barmaids, shopgirls, or whores.

Though Hava was not yet twenty years of age, she'd traveled, learned to sail, killed a man with a rock, and seen things these women couldn't dream of, let alone attempt.

She had observed their relationships over the years, but they had no meaning to her personally. The hardest thing for Hava to understand was their blind acceptance of such an ordinary existence.

When Hava left her father's house and joined the class at Master Facaria's school, she had been just another student, one who excelled, but unlike the town and farm girls she had met, she was her own person, not someone's daughter or wife.

Molly, too, was different, and she knew some things better than Hava did. Hava might be able to negotiate a dark alley and remain unseen, or enter a house without noise, but she was little more than an awkward child in this forest. She wasn't even certain how she would get back to the town if Molly wasn't there.

Then Hava realized Molly wasn't there. A tiny pang of concern twinged in the pit of her stomach: the first hint of fear. It needed to be ignored, lest it lead to panic. Immediately she employed part of her childhood training to prevent her imagination from running wild and leading her into poor choices.

She took stock of her position. What would she do in a city? She started looking for anything that made this location unique. All she saw were trees! A chiding voice from her memory echoed, from a crew boss named Hilsbek, "You look, but you do not see. Learn to see!"

Again she surveyed her surroundings and saw there was one tree with deep scratches in the bark at chest height, as if someone had used a blade or saw on it and then stopped. To the left of that tree was a stump, perhaps from timber felling, or a diseased tree falling, she didn't know, but it was old, covered in some sort of vine.

Quickly she inventoried more details: a small outcropping of rocks to her right, a half-broken bough hanging from a large spread of branches forming a sort of canopy behind her. After a moment, she had confidence that should she return, she'd recognize this spot.

She turned around, and was making every detail indelible in her mind, when she heard Molly say, "You coming?"

Looking toward the source of the voice, she could barely make out Molly between two trees growing close together. Hava jogged forward, circling the trees, then saw a hint of movement behind Molly.

Without hesitation, Hava drew and shot, sending a shaft past Molly's neck. The sound of the arrow striking and a slight grunt was followed by silence. Molly didn't flinch or even show surprise, but turned to see what Hava had loosed at.

Molly looked back at Hava. "I hope what you saw *was* a deer and not some fool wearing a deerskin jerkin!"

Hava smiled. "Hadn't thought of that."

She moved purposefully through the trees, pausing a couple of times to circumnavigate barriers of brush and tree trunks. Reaching the fallen animal, she knelt and saw it was still alive but motionless in shock, breathing rapidly and shallowly.

Molly knelt next to Hava and with a quick movement slit the deer's throat. "Best to put it out of its misery." Sitting back on her heels, she added, "Good shot." She glanced back. "You had maybe a foot of sight, through five, six trees?"

"I saw movement and took the shot," Hava said with a shrug.

Molly slid her pack off her shoulder and took out a large sack. "Waste nothing," she said to Hava, unfolding the sack. Then she drew a light rope out of the pack and in moments had the deer hanging from a branch. Gutting the animal, she gathered the offal into the sack and tied it off. She handed the bag to Hava. "Someone might want the liver or kidneys for pie, and Jarman will give me a few coppers for the rest for his hogs."

"What about skinning it?" asked Hava.

"When we get back to town." Molly cut down the deer and with Hava's help—though Hava thought Molly hardly needed it—she shouldered the carcass easily.

As Hava picked up the bag, Molly said, "Where did you learn to shoot like that?"

Falling into the almost unthinking default of lying about her past, Hava said, "My father taught us all. I was the oldest, so I had more time to learn." She paused, then added, "We all learned."

Molly said nothing for a few paces, then asked, "You didn't hunt much, did you?"

"A bit," replied Hava quickly, seeing where the conversation was heading. "It's different where I'm from. We don't have forests like these."

"Oh?" Molly sounded curious.

"My family lived on an island . . ." Hava let the thought trail off as she quickly realized she didn't know if Molly had met Master Bodai when he passed through Beran's Hill in the role of a horse trader. That had been before Hava and Hatu returned to purchase the burned-out inn Hatu was working at restoring while Hava hunted with Molly. The story then was that her "father" was a horse trader.

Hava resumed her story, making a mental note to speak with Hatu when they were alone so they could reconcile their false past history. "The island was small, but pirates and raiders came close sometimes. We had little of worth, so they rarely troubled us, but occasionally they would take food and, if they could, prisoners they could rape or sell to slavers.

"So we all learned the bow. We'd grab what we could and head up into the hills, leaving behind enough for the raiders so they wouldn't risk following us. Everyone in my village did this."

Molly glanced at Hava. "I was curious, because you're a very good—or lucky—archer, but you seem completely lost in the forest."

"We left the island when I was young," said Hava, which was close to the truth. She had been barely seven years of age when she was sent to Facaria's school. "Trading horses . . . you need to be able to defend yourself. Father didn't like paying for guards . . ." She shrugged as she let the explanation drop. One thing she had been taught in her training was not to volunteer too much information; it made keeping a false story consistent more difficult. She switched topics. "I admit I had just lost sight of you for a moment and was wondering how to get back to town."

"Most girls from town would get lost quickly . . . and a fair number of the boys, too.

"I was an only child, so my father took me hunting, despite my mother being furious. I tried to learn the things my mother wanted to teach me, cooking, baking, and all that."

Hava fell into stride with her as Molly went on. "I learned some of it. I can bake simple bread, cook a bit. I can't make . . . whatever they call that fruit . . . preserves, yes; I can't get that right. I recently opened a jar I'd stored away and it was nasty." She chuckled ruefully. "I never realized how much my mother knew until after she died."

Hava reflected on that for a moment, realizing she'd never thought much about her own mother, a woman constantly beset by the demands of four younger siblings when Hava left. As a child, Hava had taken her mother's efforts for granted. Then when she was at the school, those needs were met by the matrons, from wiping noses and bottoms to tending cuts and bruises, to occasionally comforting a crying child, until such time as the children learned not to cry.

Hava said, "My mother . . . I lost her before I was seven years old. I really don't remember too much about her . . ."

Molly turned slightly so she could glance at Hava, then returned her attention to where they were going. "See that dip ahead?"

"Yes."

"Follow me," she instructed, seemingly unburdened by the heavy deer she was carrying across her shoulders. When they reached the dip, Molly said, "This little rill here has been cut by runoff when it rains. Check and you'll see which end is lower. If you get lost up here, look for a stream and follow it downhill. There's a river on the other side of a road the baron's family cut through here years ago, and if you follow any of them it will lead you to that road. Turn west and in less than an hour you're back at Beran's Hill."

"If there's a road nearby, why aren't we taking it?"

Molly chuckled. "Roads mean people. People mean that animals only cross at night when people aren't around." She lifted her chin to her left and added, "That's a game trail. See how it's packed earth and rocks?"

Hava nodded.

"You follow those to find game or water." Molly grinned. "You're very good with a bow. We'll hunt again soon and I'll teach you some woodlore."

"I'd like that," Hava replied.

Molly took a step, then froze. Hava became motionless a second later, her training instinctively taking over so that she was ready for whatever came next. She put down the bag of entrails, silently drew an arrow from her hip quiver and nocked it to her bowstring.

Molly unloaded the deer carcass onto a small, flat rock outcropping, letting her shoulder pack drop next to it; then she pulled an arrow from her quiver and nodded approval at Hava already being ready for trouble.

Hava remained motionless and silent, waiting for Molly's instruction. Molly lifted her chin to show the direction she wished to move. Hava fell in behind her, glancing over her shoulder to see if anyone was following, an old city habit.

Molly moved with purpose, and Hava could tell from her posture and economy of motion that she was ready for a fight, though her quiet caution also told Hava that Molly wasn't looking for one.

Then Hava heard what had alerted Molly. Riders approaching: the sound of them growing noticeably louder. Molly headed down a slope, then knelt low.

Hava knelt beside her and saw there was a break in the trees a dozen yards or so ahead, and beyond that, the road. Within moments the riders came into view, moving at an easy canter, a gait designed to cover long distances quickly without ruining the horses. As they passed, the man in front raised his arm and reined in a bit, and the horses slowed to a trot.

As they rode out of view, Molly stood up and said, "Come on."

"We're going to follow them?" asked Hava. "What about the deer?"

Molly shouldered her bow. "Scavengers are already on it. There are more deer to hunt." She pointed up the road. "This is more interesting."

"A company of mercenaries on their way to Port Colos is interesting?"

"Did you see how they reined in on command?" Molly asked.

"Yes."

"Not mercenaries. Soldiers dressed like mercenaries. They rode in formation and reined in on a hand signal. Well-trained cavalry."

Hava chided herself; she should have noticed that. "The baron's?"

"If they turn south, they're the baron's."

"If they don't, they're someone else's."

"Interesting?"

Hava nodded, her expression conceding Molly's point. "Very."

Molly started to move up the road at a fast walk, and as Hava caught up they both broke into a jogging run.

THEY MANAGED TO STAY CLOSE enough to the riders to keep them in earshot, as the soldiers disguised as mercenaries were traveling at a modest trot and the women were alternately running and jogging. Finally, when the sound of hoofbeats stopped, Molly glanced at Hava and gestured that they should move into the trees and keep following out of sight.

After skirting the road for a few minutes, Hava glimpsed the riders through the trees. The two young women retreated upslope a little more, staying low behind brush and fallen tree trunks. When the baron had had the road cleared most of the timber not harvested—mainly mounds of branches and an occasional diseased bole—had simply been dragged uphill on either side, providing several convenient places for an ambush, or to spy.

Molly crouched, put her cheek next to Hava's, and asked, "What do you think?"

Hava observed how the riders organized themselves: two feeding horses out of nose bags while four others stood in a circle in discussion. One walked a short distance back down the road, apparently to see if they were being followed. Hava said, "They're meeting someone."

"How do you know?"

"If they were just pausing to rest the horses they'd walk them slowly and then feed them once they reached town. They don't know how long they have to wait for whoever is meeting them, and don't want the horses hungry and rest-less if they have to linger. If it was anything else, they'd be riding into town or finding a place to let them graze."

Molly raised a questioning eyebrow.

Hava grinned. "My father, a horse trader?"

Molly returned the smile. "Now?"

"We wait," said Hava, and Molly nodded.

Hava had endured enough stints of observation as part of her training that she ignored the urge to drift off into random thoughts: the many unanswered questions about the choices that would come, if not soon, eventually. About her loyalty to the Council on Coaltachin and her years spent with Hatu—and their lost friend Donte—coming into con-flict. She wrestled with that occasionally, electing to push it aside most times, content that when the time came for her to choose between a lifetime of friendship and love and a sense of duty instilled since childhood, she would make that choice.

Instead she turned her attention to the soldiers waiting at the verge of the road below, attempting to see as much as she could without being seen. Molly had been correct; these men were a poor excuse for a mercenary company. She'd seen a number of those in her travels, and they were at best a scruffy lot, given to all manner of choices in armor, weapons, sad-dles, and mounts. The men below had chosen to wear some unlike garments, but they were all too clean, not in need of mending, obviously little worn. More revealing, they all wore the same boots, and the horses had identical tack. She was convinced if she got closer the swords and any bows would be alike. This was a company of soldiers, should anyone take a few moments to study them, and not just any soldiers, for gar-rison soldiers had variations in armor, weapons, and boots. These were castellans: personal soldiers of a noble, the best of his army, whichever army that might be.

"Why are there so many of them?" Molly whispered.

Hava shrugged. "Maybe we'll find out."

The two young women waited in silence, as the men stood idly and rotated every so often to ensure the horses didn't wander off the road now that the feeding was over. Hava knew that sooner or later the horses would need water and she softly asked Molly, "How far to water?"

Molly pointed to the road and then beyond it. "That way. Not far."

Hava murmured, "They'll have to water the horses soon."

Molly nodded.

As Hava had predicted, two of the soldiers led half the horses off toward the small river that ran to the north of the road and, after a short while, returned and led off the other mounts.

Minutes passed slowly. As the sun lowered in the sky, the last of the freshly watered horses returned.

Hava leaned over and whispered, "See those two men, standing a little way off?"

Molly turned her attention to the indicated pair. One stood tall, a soldier by his bearing, but the other was a short man, apparently slender under his heavy cloak. Hava whispered, "The shorter one is not a soldier, but the tall one—their leader—seems respectful of him."

"How do you know?"

Hava again returned to the fabricated history she had concocted. "My father taught me early to study people; horse traders need to know whom they are bargaining with, even if they're strangers. You look at who jumps to follow instructions, or their faces when they're told something." As if to punctuate her observation, the tall man nodded and said something to the other soldiers, who immediately started inspecting the horses and making ready to ride soon.

"Someone is coming," said Molly.

As soon as she spoke, Hava heard hoofbeats and a rider came into view, followed by the soldier who had been stationed down the road. The rider jumped down from his mount and nodded a greeting to the two men Hava had observed. The tall man moved away, leaving the short fellow and the newcomer alone to speak.

Hava said suddenly, "I've seen him before."

"Keep your voice down!"

Hava silently chided herself for letting a moment of surprise break her discipline.

Molly asked, "Who?"

"The man who just arrived was at the inn two days ago seeking a room. Hatu said the repairs were not quite finished and sent him off."

Since the Inn of the Three Stars was still under repair, travelers were often referred to other quarters, to smaller inns and several farmers' barns. Their inn should be in a good enough state to allow travelers a place to stay by tomorrow, Hatu had told her.

"Do you know him?" whispered Molly.

"Just a traveler. I didn't pay attention after he asked about a room."

Molly said, "They're getting ready."

"Yes, but for what?"

"To leave, look." She pointed where the riders were inspecting their horses, tightening girths, checking bridles, ensuring saddle packs were secure, before restarting their journey.

Hava said, "We should go," and began to creep upslope.

Molly moved in beside her, and after they'd crested a ridge and were heading toward Beran's Hill down a gentle slope, Molly said, "What do you suppose all that was?"

"Nothing good," said Hava.

"Should we tell Declan?"

"Tell him what? That a man escorted by soldiers disguised as mercenaries met a man who came into town a couple of days ago and has been . . ." Hava shrugged. "What? Sneaking around town?"

Almost as one, they both said, "We should tell Declan."

Hava said, "You tell him when we get back. He knows you better and I need to . . ." She almost said "warn Hatu" but caught herself. ". . . let Hatu know to be careful with those two should they come by the inn."

They continued on until Hava realized she knew where they were, just as sound from the town drifted to them on the afternoon wind. As they neared, Hava made out the sounds of a hammer and smiled.

HATUSHALY PAUSED TO WIPE PERSPIRATION off his forehead and then resumed hammering another hardwood shingle into the supporting board. Summer was approaching and the days were getting hotter, especially when spent up on the roof of the inn. He and two workers he had hired were finishing all the repairs started by Declan Smith after raiders had tried to burn down the Inn of the Three Stars.

He'd purchased it from Gwen, the previous owner's daughter, the week before. He and Hava had discussed it at length before they made the offer. Hava had grown to like Gwen, who was to wed Declan, the smith. He had become Hatu's first "friend" in this town.

Hatu leaned back and caught his breath. The work was not exhausting, but it had been a week of very long days, up before dawn, engaging in tasks that challenged what he knew of several crafts; like most students from Coaltachin, he had spent time being exposed to many skills, for the most part to provide believable stories while acting as an agent for Coaltachin, but he was a master of none of them. This restoration had taught Hatu just how much he didn't know about carpentry, masonry, and other building trades.

He surveyed the town of Beran's Hill, taking the time to actually look at the sprawling, growing community. It still felt new to him, as the longest he had lived in any one place had been the school where he had first met Hava and their lost friend Donte, and he sensed his perspective on this place and the people who lived here was changing.

He was playing the part of a new husband and innkeeper, a first as either. He had trained all his life to be a member of the Quelli Nascosti, the secret assassins of Coaltachin, but in fact all of that had been a front contrived to keep him hidden from his true family's enemies.

Hatu's real name was Sefan Langene, or so Baron Daylon's body servant, Balven, had told him. He was the son of a dead king. That made Hatu king in name as well, except there was no kingdom, save one of ashes and ruin on the far side of this continent. As a baby, Hatu had been given over to Master Facaria to be raised as "one of his own," and the baron hadn't realized that didn't mean raised in the relative safety of a castle somewhere, surrounded by guards and retainers. One of the older masters, a onetime member of the Council of Masters of Coaltachin, Facaria had indeed raised Hatu as if he had been one of his own children. It had been a difficult, violent, and dangerous upbringing. Hatushaly had been reared to become a warrior, crew boss, even master assassin and spy for the Kingdom of Night, as Coaltachin was known. The irony of the dangers he'd faced growing up were not lost on him. Still, it all made sense in a convoluted way; Hatu considered himself as safe as he was ever likely to be, as there were few better students in combat than he.

He almost laughed at his situation, for if he remained a

simple innkeeper and kept his hair colored as a precaution, he was probably as safe as any man in the Barony of Marquensas. Short of being overcome by some mad desire to reclaim his lost heritage, he could spend the rest of his life in relative peace, assuming that his former masters didn't order his "wife" to kill him. That did cause him to laugh aloud and wonder what more convoluted fate awaited him as he returned to work.

He loved Hava more than he could say, for his schooling had taught little about matters of the heart. He had loved her his whole life but had recognized that only recently. She had always been there for him, a calming presence at the worst times in his childhood, an anchor to keep him from spinning off in rages, the one person who understood him, perhaps better than he understood himself. He also knew she loved him, but the question was: Did she love him enough to ignore orders from her masters to leave him or, worse, to kill him? Only time would tell.

He finished a section of the roof and stood up to regard his work and found it apparently sufficient—at least until the next rain, at which time his mistakes would reveal themselves. Then he lifted his eyes and saw Hava and Molly emerging from the woods on the other side of a field. Neither seemed burdened with game, so he wondered if they'd simply not found any or had used hunting as an excuse for Hava not working.

He doubted the latter, for avoiding work wasn't in her nature, though he knew she disliked carpentry and the general cleanup the inn required. As game was reputedly plentiful this time of year in the forest nearby, he assumed something else had arisen and that made him curious. He stepped higher up the roof ridge and waved as Hava and Molly cut across the fallow field. Hava spied him and returned the wave.

By the time he had climbed down the ladder, Hava had

reached the back gate to the stabling yard. "Anyone inside?" she asked.

"No," answered Hatu. "Samuel is on his way to Declan's to get another bucket of nails." He wiped his forehead. "And we're almost done."

She motioned him to follow her inside. "Where's Roary?"

"Something to do with helping his mother do something at her shop. He'll be back in an hour."

Hava glanced around the almost-restored common room of the Inn of the Three Stars. The day before they'd moved casks of ale, barrels and bottles of wine, and whisky into storage. They had also stocked the kitchen, which was why the roof was not quite finished. Hatu was determined that by tomorrow they would once again be open for business.

"You know that fellow who came around day before yesterday—dark hair, tall, looking for a room? The one you sent over to Jacob's barn?"

"Yes. Why?"

Hava recounted what she and Molly had observed, and when she finished Hatu said, "Sounds like something we may need to report to the masters."

"Almost certainly. Who will go?"

Hatu said, "It will have to be me."

Hava's frown indicated that she didn't understand why that was the case, so Hatu continued. "Haven't you noticed? None of the women here, except for Molly Bowman, travel alone."

"Odd, isn't it?" asked Hava.

"I gave up trying to understand why people do a lot of things since we started traveling with the masters," said Hatu softly.

Hava nodded. "What will you tell them?"

By "them," she meant the masters who would receive his report.

"I think I'll wait a day or two and see if that fellow and the man you said he met reveal anything." He glanced around the almost finished common room and said, "I think we were fortunate to have chosen this business. I can't imagine a better place in Beran's Hill to have information come to us."

Hava nodded. "I'm not sure how we'll do as an innkeeper and wife, but if those are the roles we need to play, so be it."

Hatu smiled, slipped his arm around her, and gave her a slight hug. "I'm enjoying the wife part."

She pushed him away with mock disdain. "None of that until you've bathed. You reek."

He laughed. "It was hot up on that roof." With a sigh, he added, "But I'm not quite done yet, and those shingles will not attach themselves."

"Off you go then," Hava said with a smile. "And do bathe before tonight." She looked him up and down slowly. "You still need more practice in bed."

He raised his eyebrows in mock shock. "Practice?"

"You're *almost* competent as a lover but your technique needs work," she said, turning her back and disappearing into the kitchen before he could respond.

Chuckling to himself, Hatu climbed back up the ladder. This roof would be finished before the evening meal. Then all that was left was to hang the sign above the door. He returned to where he had been, knelt and picked up a shingle, hammer, and nails, and resumed his labor.

MOLLY FINISHED SHARING WHAT SHE and Hava had seen with Declan, who silently listened. For a long moment he considered what she had told him and then said, "That does sound like something to fret over."

Molly nodded. "They weren't ordinary soldiers. They were guardsmen or something like that."

Declan nodded. He had seen enough men-at-arms pass through Oncon, the village where he had been raised, to appreciate what Molly meant. Household, honor guards, castellans—all tended to be the most accomplished of soldiers, and to see a company of such dispatched on an escort mission indicated that the person they escorted was of some consequence.

"Where can I get a glimpse of these fellows?"

"I think Jacob's barn is where the one fellow who was here slept, or maybe one of the other inns? Though Hava's inn is supposed to open again tomorrow. Maybe there?"

"I'll ask Gwen. She's over there now inspecting the place for Hatu and Hava . . ." He let the words trail off. Staring out the large open door of his blacksmith shop, he finally said, "She's still in mourning. She holds it in well, maybe too well. The tears were there at first, but . . ." He looked concerned. "I think perhaps she's trying too hard to be strong, you know?"

"I know," said Molly. Though she was usually a woman of few words, she added, "Once you get her with child, things will change."

Declan fought against smiling at the thought of children but couldn't help it. His life had taken some unexpected turns since his own childhood and he wondered how he had been so fortunate.

"If you find those men let me know," Molly said. "I'm curious." Without another word, she left the forge, leaving Declan alone with his thoughts.

Since returning from a visit with Baron Dumarch, Declan had informed everyone in town that he was authorized to organize a militia. Over the weeks since then, the able-bodied men of Beran's Hill had organized a bit of training here and there. Some grudgingly, some enthusiastically, but all understanding that since the raid on the town by a mercenary named Tyree and his band, who had burned the Inn of the Three Stars, killed Gwen's father, and abducted two women, it was necessary—and each man serving who didn't miss training received a few coins, which tipped the balance.

As a result, Declan found himself more and more inclined to think of himself as the party responsible for town defense, even though the baron's authorization of a militia was vague in terms of organization and mandate. The arrival of this mysterious man, escorted by elite troops, fully reinforced that sense of responsibility. It made him curious as to who the two men were and what they were about.

HATU FELT REFRESHED AFTER BATHING. His hair was still damp—and he had used the hair dye he had bought in Marquenet to keep the bright red toned down to a brownish red that was almost as dark as Hava's. Given his upbringing, regular bathing never occurred to him, but as he had a proper bathhouse just outside the rear entrance to the inn, he planned on using it regularly—once a week, perhaps more often.

Gwen's father had owned the Inn of the Three Stars, and she had literally been born here. Hatu and Hava stood quietly waiting for Gwen's judgment.

Gwen surveyed the common room and nodded. Her eyes had a slight sheen to them, but no tears. Softly she said, "Better than new. Da had some fixin' he never quite got around to, and the old bar was roughly used." She nodded toward the highly polished, massive oak bar. "Splinters, stains from spills, cracks here and there. This one's . . . beautiful."

Hatu smiled. The two women stood in stark contrast to each other, Gwen voluptuous, not quite stocky, with her pale skin and dark brown hair, and Hava with her slender, not quite boyish figure, her dark brown hair with a hint of red, her dark eyes. He recognized that most men would find Gwen more attractive, yet to him, Hava was the most perfect beauty he'd ever seen.

"Before I began traveling with Hava and her father, I was apprenticed for a time to a boatbuilder. He showed me how to seal wood and put a finish on it," Hatu said to Gwen, who let out a long sigh.

After a short pause, Gwen asked, "You two ready?"

"Not really," said Hatu jokingly.

Hava said, "We'd be helpless without you, Gwen. When we agreed to buy the inn and repair it . . . let's say there's a lot more to running an inn than either of us imagined. How to stock the supplies, and what keeps and what doesn't, which ale to buy . . ." She fell silent a moment, then added, "Just so much."

Hatu nodded in agreement. "Had I known, I might have changed my mind." He kept his tone light.

Gwen appeared to him to be on the verge of tears, but she took a deep breath, slowly let it out, and smiled. "No use pretending things aren't as they are." She crossed her arms and looked at Hava. "Whatever you need to know, ask. Da was a good man in many ways, but in truth he could be lax when it came to keeping the cold cellar stocked or ensuring fresh vegetables. We had our share of nights serving meats that hadn't quite turned, hard cheese, boiled potatoes, and day-old bread." She took another long look around the room, slowly turning as she added, "Some things you can buy easily, but others . . ." She again let out a sigh. "You'll manage as long as you don't run out of ale, wine, and whisky, but a well-stocked larder and clean beds will have the regular travelers always stopping here." She smiled. "Adding those two new rooms upstairs was . . . Da talked of more rooms for travelers, but never quite got around to it. Too much interest in finding the perfect whisky."

Hatu nodded. "That whisky takes a bit of getting used to."

Gwen laughed for the first time since Hava and Hatu had met her. "Did Declan give you that first taste?"

Hatu nodded, and tears gathered in Gwen's eyes. Then she laughed again, squeezing her eyes so the tears fell— but they were those of joy. "My father did that to him, leaving him to swallow that first taste without warning. The coughing and watery eyes, red face, and the rest seems an odd rite of passage, but there it is." She took another deep breath and said, "Now you have a legacy to carry on, Hatu." Then she turned and left. Hatu thought it was before he saw her weep in earnest.

"I'll do my best," Hatu said softly.

After she left, Hava said, "I find it strange."

"What?"

"Having feelings . . . for a place." She shrugged. "I don't think I understand."

"It's all she knows. Her parents both died here." Hatu reflected for a second that he had never known his parents, so he could barely imagine what it must feel like to have such bonds of affection. "I guess that leaves . . . memories? It seems important to her that this inn returns to what it was."

"Which is a good thing for us," admitted Hava. Looking around the empty common room, she added, "There are too many things we know nothing about . . ." She chuckled. "More things we never could have foreseen."

"Bedding," said Hatu, and Hava broke out laughing. "Wouldn't it have been wonderful to welcome our first traveler and have no place for him to sleep?"

"Well," said Hava, "what about . . . ?" She left the question unspoken, knowing he'd understand.

"Let's see what they do in the next few days. I can always claim to need something down in Marquenet."

She nodded in agreement, and the two of them set to work on those tiny details neither had anticipated. After the sun set, Hatu spent a quiet evening with Hava talking about mostly unimportant things—not having to constantly confront life-and-death issues was welcome—before she fell asleep in his arms.

Hatu had never been one to chase every girl he saw, unlike his friend Donte, and it had been Donte who had paid a whore to initiate Hatu into sex. Since being with Hava, he had felt no desire for other women; he could admire them, admit they were attractive, even have a passing thought that he might have been interested had Hava not existed, but Hava was his world.

It was a love he could hardly understand, let alone explain. He knew she cared for him, too, but he had lingering doubts that she was able to feel for him what he felt for her. One moment it was because he felt unworthy of her, and the next it was because of how she had been trained to deal with men. And still other times he had no idea how she felt. Neither of them was prone to speaking of feelings, as it was not the way of Coaltachin. He had been taught that feelings could interfere with duty, and as a result, he had rarely mentioned to the woman he loved—who now lay tightly against him, slowly breathing as she slept—how he felt; not since his first protestation of love. And she had spoken of feelings even less than he.

Was he still serving the Kingdom of Night and didn't know it, or was he to be a simple innkeeper until fate demanded otherwise of him? Or was he a prince of a fallen kingdom with duties and obligations to that heritage he couldn't remember, let alone understand? As sleep began to overtake him, he wondered which part of his life now was an act and which was real.

Questions without answers swirled around his head as he finally drifted off to sleep.

THE NEXT DAY SAW THE hanging of the repaired and repainted sign, a circle of black edged with white, with three golden stars set at the top and lower left and right.

Gwen nodded her approval. "I wasn't going to say anything, but I was worried you might wish to change the name."

Hava put her arms around Gwen's shoulders and squeezed. She felt no genuine urge to comfort the daughter of the former owner, but she knew it was the sort of gesture people in this part of the world expected.

"There was no good reason to change it, Gwen," said Hatu. "It's a familiar name, with a good reputation built by your father." A slight nod of approval from Hava led him to add, "Now all we have to do is live up to it."

Gwen smiled. "Thank you."

"Bring Declan by this evening and the first meal is on us."

Gwen grinned and headed back to the house behind the forge where Declan was working.

Hava said, "Well, we are now innkeepers."

"Given some of the places you and I have slept, this is a palace."

"Never seen a palace," replied Hava, "but I agree it's better than most of the inns we've seen."

They went back inside. "I guess now we just need some customers," Hatu said.

"I've made a list of a few things," said Hava, holding out her hand.

Hatu removed the coin purse from his belt and handed it to her. "Such as . . . ?"

"A loaf of bread, and some of those beef sausages Parter the butcher sells."

"We already—" Hatu interrupted himself. "Ah, yes,

of course." He knew she was going out to sniff around about the man who'd arrived yesterday with the escort of soldiers. The baker they used was close, but the butcher she mentioned was on the other side of town. As she was the "new woman" in town, the other women were interested enough in Hava to want to stop her and "gossip." Hatu wasn't sure what the difference was between gossip and rumors, but he assumed it was something the women of this barony did, or just another word for the same thing. Either way, it was useful for gathering intelligence on odd comings and goings.

Hava left, and Hatu suddenly felt abandoned. He found that very odd, then realized that it wasn't so much abandonment, but that with Hava here he had someone to talk to, something to do. Now he found himself presented with two choices: either sit and do nothing while waiting for a customer or repeat every inventory check, room inspection, and other task he had seen to repeatedly over the last two days. For the first time in his memory, Hatu found himself wide-awake with nothing obviously needing to be done. He found the situation wryly amusing. Most of his life had consisted of studying, working, or trying to sleep. He moved behind the newly restored bar and once again familiarized himself with his array of bottles and kegs. In coming to learn the innkeeper's trade, he realized that the previous owner, Leon, had stocked a wider variety of wine, spirits, and ale than most tavern keepers. It had not occurred to him to ask Gwen about that, and his best surmise was that it would attract travelers with varying tastes.

Well, he thought, best take advantage of the opportunity to rest. Hatu moved to a chair at the table closest to the open end of the bar and sat down. After a moment, he reached forward, pulled another chair out, and put his feet on it.

HATU WAS DOZING WHEN HAVA returned. He sat up and pushed away the chair on which he had placed his feet. "Sleeping?" she said, obviously amused.

"No," he said. "Just resting my eyes a little." Coming to full alertness as she put the bread and large sausage on the bar, he asked, "Discover anything?"

"Nothing important, though we seem to be the subject of some speculation, as we appear exotic to our neighbors."

"Well," said Hatu, "we are from about as far away from Marquensas as anyone is likely to be. I've seen a few travelers pass through here that are darker skinned than you, but no one who lives here."

"They're a fair-skinned lot around here, aren't they?" Hava sat in the chair opposite Hatu. "There is some talk that the number of travelers has gone up recently. Just a sense there's something going on that is causing more travelers than usual to pass through town."

"Business?" asked Hatu.

"The merchants are happy: they're selling more. Declan's busy repairing gear and horseshoes and the like." She fell silent a moment, considering. "It's the . . . type of people who are passing I . . . I think we need mention to . . ." Reflexively, she glanced around to make sure no one could overhear, but of course the only two people in the building were Hatu and herself. "When we send that message, we should make it clear that bands of armed men seem to be moving toward Port Colos. And some of the trade goods . . . Barons Dumarch and Bavangine aren't the only ones having weapons made. Armor, swords, and who knows what else in those tarp-covered wagons."

Hatu nodded. "If you care to make notes, I'll memorize them and pass them along."

"When are you going to Marquenet?"

"Next week or the week after, I'm thinking." He stood

up. "If we don't have a customer soon, I think I'll . . ." He shrugged. "I don't know what I'll do."

"You have never known how to simply sit and . . . just be!"

He was forced to return her laugh. "I suppose so. Donte always knew how to find something fun to do, didn't he?"

She lost her smile at the mention of their friend's name. The last they had seen of him, he had been hanging from chains in a cave beneath the waves, a prisoner of a coven of witches called the Sisters of the Deep. "He did, didn't he?" Looking at Hatu, she said, "I know one thing you can do."

"What?"

"Run upstairs and open those little windows at each end of the landing. Now that the roof is done, it's getting hot up there. Get a breeze going through and we'll shut them at sunset."

He laughed. "That will certainly keep me busy for a few minutes."

He went upstairs and moved to the window at the far end of the landing. He had made some improvements at the suggestion of the carpenter Declan had hired to start the repairs—Hatu had enough carpentry experience to see the man knew his trade. He'd added two new rooms overlooking the rear of the inn, which would increase profits once the inn filled up, and these windows, which created a breeze through the upper floor to help keep the rooms from getting too hot in summer, which was now quickly approaching. He swung the hinged window inward, four panes cleverly separated by a wooden grille that could be removed should the glass break, allowing him to slip unbroken glass into the grooves set into the larger frame. The configuration would keep costs down, as only a broken piece of glass would need to be replaced, rather than the entire window.

He also judged that should the weather turn cold, he might need to put heavy shutters on the outside. He'd wait until he saw what winters were like, assuming he was still here then. Every plan was plagued by unknowns, something that had bothered him since childhood.

He opened the window at the opposite end of the landing and was heading back down the stairs when he heard a voice. A man said, ". . . heard you'd reopened, so we hurried over. Sleeping in a barn is . . ." The man stopped speaking as Hatu came into view and nodded a greeting. Returning his gaze to Hava, he said, "So if you have a room and a bath, it would be welcome."

Hava seemed slightly wooden in her posture to Hatu, but the two men seemed unaware of it. Hatu required all his self-control to maintain his easy manner. The first man was the one who had been seen around town for the last few days, the one Hava was seeking information about, which meant the other man had to be the one who arrived with the armed escort the day before.

What caused Hatu's chest to tighten was that he recognized the second man. He was the man Hatu had spied while investigating the cathedral in Sandura, the one who had been speaking to the assassins known as Azhante, dangerous men somehow related to the sicari of Coaltachin.

Hava said, "This is my husband, Hatu."

Both men nodded, and Hatu said, "We have a bathing room out back. I'll heat up some water while my wife shows you to your room."

"Two rooms," said the second man.

Hatu nodded.

After a few minutes of hauling water from the well to an iron kettle and starting a small fire beneath it, Hatu heard Hava enter the bathhouse. She held some folded cotton towels and hung them over a wooden bar next to the tub. "Well," she said, "I guess we'll find out what those two are up to."

"I have to travel in the morning," he replied.

Her eyebrows shot up. "Why?"

Master Bodai had given firm instructions after Hatu had seen those assassins speaking with this man, who had worn the clothing of a soldier of the One Church. Slowly he said, "I cannot tell you."

Hava's face remained impassive, but her eyes searched Hatu's face, seeking a clue about what was happening. Her training took over and she nodded slightly. "I'll tell them the bathwater will be hot in a few minutes." She left him alone in the bathhouse.

Hatu watched her vanish through the door and wondered if he should have said more. Again he considered how the line between truth and lies could be blurred, and the fact that she was his wife—or would be once their marriage took place at the midsummer festival—only because she was ordered to play the role. That made him painfully aware that he had been told his obligation to Coaltachin was over with his return to Baron Daylon Dumarch, yet at the same time he was to continue as an agent for the Kingdom of Night. If his duty to Coaltachin was over, why did Master Bodai order him to continue as if it were not?

Hatu had no ready answer to this conflict he knew would only grow inside him. He knew a time might come when he would have to elect one side or the other. Whichever choice he made might end his relationship with the woman he loved.

2

AN UNPLANNED EVENT
AND A SURPRISE REUNION

Gwen entered the forge and Declan asked, "How is it?"
She didn't need to ask what "it" was. She nodded
and smiled. "Fine. To be truthful, Hatu's fixed up the place
far better than Da ever did." She fell silent, looking puzzled.

"What?"

"There's something about that man."

"Hatu?"

"Yes. Hatushaly. It is a bit of a foreign name, isn't it?"

Declan crossed to the forge and began putting his tools
away. "Well, I expect there are places where Declan sounds
foreign."

She nodded. "I like him, in a way. I also like Hava;
she's been kind." She let out a slow breath. "And as I said,
the inn has never looked this good. They even cleaned out
the cold cellar and completely organized the bathhouse.
I'd bathe there myself."

Declan had never used the bathhouse, having the luxury
of a tub of his own in the house that came with the smithy.
But he'd heard stories, and judged Leon, Gwen's father, to
be a less than fastidious innkeeper. Given how run-down

the place that passed for an inn in his home village of On-con was, Declan hadn't been put off by the condition of the Three Stars. He rather enjoyed it there, but the truth was that what he had enjoyed was Gwen's company, and it didn't matter much where that was.

"Speaking of bathing," he said, "I could do with a wash. Would you mind heating some water while I clean up?" He glanced out the door where the afternoon light was starting to fail. "Or if you need the time to get supper ready, I'll bathe when I've finished."

"Supper?" she said as if remembering something. "Actually, we've been invited to dine at the inn tonight, as Hava and Hatu's guests."

"That's kind of them," said Declan. He smiled broadly. "So, if you'd please heat up some water for me, I'll be as clean as that new inn!"

She laughed, one of the few times he'd heard a sound of genuine amusement from her since the murder of her father. "I'll do that." And off she went.

Declan continued to put things away and wished Jusan was there to help, but he was down at Ratigan's new freight yard arranging for a wagon to ship more swords south to Baron Dumarch. The order had surprised the young smith, for the baron had his own weapons smith in his keep. Still, it was a good order and would settle all of Declan's costs for the coming half year, perhaps longer. For a moment Declan wondered if there was enough trade coming his way to take on another smith. Jusan was now a journeyman, and they didn't have a proper apprentice . . . perhaps it was time.

He finished up just as Jusan appeared at the door. Declan said, "So, are we set?"

Jusan nodded. "Ratigan's fellow . . . ah, Randal? I don't know why I have a problem remembering names."

Declan frowned. It was something about Jusan that annoyed him—one of the few things—that he seemed almost unable to remember names of people until he'd met them several times.

Jusan said, "Anyway, we have a wagon ready to leave the day after tomorrow."

"Not tomorrow?" asked Declan.

"No," said Jusan. "Seems Ratigan had only two in the yard, both due to leave at first light, and . . . Randal said there were more wagons bringing up goods from Marquenet late today, and as they've just made the trip and back, he's going to rest the horses for a day before they make it again, so they'll be free the day after."

Clapping Jusan on the shoulder, Declan said, "Business is good all over, it seems." Jusan smiled at that. "It's time to bring in an apprentice, I'm thinking."

Jusan paused, then nodded. "I wouldn't say no to an extra pair of hands to do the work around here."

"Well, you were a poor apprentice," Declan said jokingly, "but perhaps you can train up a better one."

"Funny," said Jusan, showing he didn't think so.

"I'll spend a bit of time in the city when I get there and ask Gildy if he or the other smiths have a boy who's ready to train. If not, we'll ask around here."

"Jacob Berry's son, Callum, seems a likely lad. He turns up now and again and asks questions."

Declan said, "Curious type, then?"

"A bit scrawny."

"So were you when you first arrived," said Declan, amused. "Solid work and good food will put some muscle on him."

Jusan nodded. "When you get back, then."

"If I haven't found a more likely boy, we'll have a word

with Callum Berry. Now I'm off for a bath, and Gwen and I are going to eat at the inn."

"It's open then," said Jusan with a satisfied nod. "I'll tell Millie we're on our own."

"Where is she?"

"Down at the market, I think," said Jusan. Millie had been the other barmaid at the inn when it had burned down and had been terrified to the point of refusing to leave the house Declan and Gwen shared with Jusan and her. She was slowly recovering, and her being at the market alone was a good sign that healing was under way.

"That's good," said Declan. "Now finish closing up: I'm off for a hot bath."

Jusan smiled and started on the work, while Declan walked briskly toward the house, as if truly eager for a bath. Then Jusan realized Declan would be alone with Gwen for a while and chuckled softly. Two young couples sharing close quarters had put a strain on privacy, so the journeyman smith decided he'd take some time organizing the smithy and wait until Millie returned from the market before entering the house.

THE COMMON ROOM WAS BUSY. Word had spread that the Inn of the Three Stars was again open, and many townspeople had decided to stop in and see how the repairs had turned out.

Hatu was learning quickly that working behind the bar was a great deal more demanding than he had anticipated, for while a few folks had just dropped in to look around and then departed, many decided to have at least one ale before heading home.

Gwen and Declan entered the chaotic common room, and Gwen had taken one look before motioning Declan to take a seat, then hurrying over to Hava's side. The new proprietors of the inn appeared overwhelmed, and Gwen saved Hava from dropping a large platter of food on the floor. A quick consultation ended with Hava handing the tray to Gwen, who turned and carried it to a corner table where four men waited to be served, while Hava disappeared back into the kitchen.

Declan observed the commotion and saw his wife enter the kitchen. He waited a minute, then rose and worked his way through the growing crowd as more people entered and finally got behind the bar next to Hatu. "Lend a hand?" he asked.

Hatu looked at him with gratitude. "Where did they all come from?"

Declan chuckled. "We should have expected this." Without another word to Hatu, he turned to three men clamoring for attention and took their orders. Within a few minutes the pace at which drink orders were filled increased noticeably. After the demand for service died down, Hatu exclaimed, "Thank you!" He grinned. "I'd still be swamped had you not joined in."

Declan smiled. "I came here so often courting Gwen, I often lent a hand behind the bar. So, you've never tended a bar before?"

"No," said Hatu with a rueful tone, drying his hands on a bar rag. "I thought it would be simple. I've not frequented many taverns, and I've never seen one this crowded."

"They get like this once in a while in a big city," said Declan as he started piling up empty mugs next to a big wash pan, sunk into a counter behind where they stood. "Today, it was curiosity. You may see a bit of a rush tomorrow when those who couldn't come tonight decide to see how it is, but it'll die down. Once in a while, if a large trading company—eight, ten wagons with teamsters and helpers—or a company of soldiers comes through, it will get very busy, but most days you'll be bored. Still, even when Leon owned it, as run-down as it was, it was the most popular inn with the local folk. With all the talk of your opening, people have started calling the road outside 'Three Stars Road.' That's a thing, right?"

Hatu looked amazed and nodded slightly. "Indeed."

Without thinking, Declan started washing mugs and stacking them on a draining board. Hatu realized he was just standing there and took his rag and began wiping down the bar, just as another group entered the tavern and pushed its way through the crowd to order drinks. Hatu turned to Declan and said, "I think we'll be eating late tonight."

Declan laughed.

MORE THAN TWO HOURS WENT by before the majority of the townspeople departed, leaving the four friends alone in the common room with only the two strangers who had arrived earlier quietly occupying a table in the corner. Declan and Hatu had marked them earlier in the evening, and both had seen them quietly observe everyone who entered and departed. Neither spoke of it.

As they cleared the empty tables and piled up plates, bowls, and mugs, Hatu looked at the mess and reckoned he'd be cleaning for a couple of hours after his guests left.

Gwen and Hava entered from the kitchen carrying plates of bread, fruit, a bit of sliced pork, and a sliver of cheese. Setting them down on the table, Hava said, "I need to go to the market early tomorrow. We have barely enough for the four of us!" She sighed. "Is it always like this?" she asked Gwen, her tone somewhere between amusement and concern.

Gwen smiled and shook her head.

Declan said, "As I told Hatu, the town turned out to see how things stood." Glancing around at the room with chairs out of place, some tables pushed aside, and a few dishes on the floor, he added, "This was special. It'll start calming down tomorrow."

"Still," said Hava, as she sat and motioned for Declan and Gwen to do likewise, while Hatu returned with a pitcher of wine and four glasses, "we need food."

Hatu said, "I was planning on riding down to Marquenet in a few days to pick up some things, but I think I made four . . . no, five trips to the cold cellar. We are out of cheese, have no sausages, no fruit except oranges, and I think our spices could use a bit of restocking as well."

Gwen held up her goblet and said, "You did well enough for the madness that descended on you tonight."

"If you and Declan hadn't pitched in, we'd still be serving, assuming people didn't leave in disgust over the wait." Hava looked at Hatu. "I think we need to hire someone."

Gwen glanced at Declan and said, "Well, with Millie doing most of the work around our house, I could spend a little time here and help until you find someone."

Hava reached out and squeezed Gwen's shoulder. "That would be appreciated more than I can say."

Declan said to Hatu, "I'm shipping a wagon of swords down to the baron the day after tomorrow. Why don't you ride with me and get everything you need and bring it back, rather than order it and wait for it to be shipped up?"

Hatu glanced at Hava, and, as he did so, let his gaze pass over the two men who were sitting opposite him behind his wife and Gwen. He considered a day's delay in sending word to Coaltachin of these two men's arrival and thought he also might learn a thing or two more. "That's a welcome idea. Yes, I'll ride down and back with you, and I'll pay the freight back."

Declan smiled. "I was hoping you'd say that."

All four of them chuckled.

As they ate and chatted, the two men in the corner rose and went upstairs, and both Hatu and Declan tried to observe them without looking obvious.

Hava noticed Hatu's intense expression. "What?"

Hatu whispered, "Just watching our last guests going up."

Hava instantly understood. "Fine. When we've eaten we can finish cleaning down here."

"Unless someone else shows up for a drink." Glancing at Gwen, Hatu asked, "When did your father close up for the night?"

Gwen laughed. "As long as someone had the coin to pay for another drink, we were open. Da would close up after the last customer left."

"So, sometimes late," observed Hava.

"Sometimes when the sun was coming up," answered Declan. "There were nights I was supposed to spend time with Gwen after she finished, but I'd have to give up and go home so I wouldn't be useless at the forge the next day."

Gwen gave him a mock disapproving look and said, "Faint heart."

As Declan and Gwen began to stand, a familiar voice from the doorway shouted, "Declan!"

All four turned to see Ratigan entering the inn. "Look who I found!"

He was accompanied by a tall woman with light brown hair, her suntanned face set in a broad grin. Despite grey dusting her hair, and age lines in her sun-darkened face, she moved vigorously as she ran forward to throw her arms around the smith, hugging him tightly for a long moment.

Gwen's expression became very still: this woman's greeting was clearly one born of close familiarity.

Declan said, "Roz!" He gripped her shoulders, but

then caught a glimpse of Gwen's face and stepped back. "How . . . What are you doing here?"

Rozalee smiled broadly at his clumsily hidden embarrassment. "Which of these pretty girls is your betrothed?" she asked, poking him playfully in the chest.

Flushing with embarrassment, Declan beckoned Gwen to his side. "Gwen, this is an old friend from Oncon, Rozalee. Roz, this is my fiancée, Gwen!"

Roz smiled and gave Gwen a hug. Gwen looked uncomfortable.

Declan glanced at Ratigan, who grinned at him. He'd thank the teamster when they were alone for telling Roz that Declan was now betrothed. He could see that Gwen was already wondering, so it was just as well that Roz had not given him her usual greeting of a bear hug while grabbing his ass or a deep kiss, let alone saying some of the things she used to say to him in public, or he might not have a fiancée after tonight.

Roz let go of Gwen and held her at arm's length. "You're a beauty, for certain." She glanced sidelong at Declan. "You know you can do better than him, don't you?" she said, grinning.

Hava and Hatu watched the meeting with barely contained amusement, and at last Hatu said, "Welcome to the Inn of the Three Stars. Ale?"

"Never thought you'd offer," said Ratigan, grabbing two chairs from another table and moving them around so they could all sit in a semicircle.

As Hatu filled six flagons with ale, Declan said, "How's Jack?" Quickly he explained to Gwen, "Roz's husband."

"Dead," said Roz in a matter-of-fact tone.

Declan's expression instantly changed from a self-conscious smile to one of shock and disbelief. After a moment, he regained his composure and asked, "What happened?"

Roz turned to Gwen and said, "Your lad here saved my life. I got into it with a bunch of bandits working for that bastard Lodavico, and after I gutted a couple, they got me. Declan came out and found me, nursed me a bit, and he and Ratigan loaded me up into my wagon and took me back to my husband. Did you know that?"

Softly Gwen said, "No, he never said."

"That's like him," replied Roz. "It's funny, but there I was hanging by a thread for a bit and finally got some strength back, and just as I was getting up and about, old Jack dies in bed. Heart gave out, I expect." To Declan she added, "It was the way he would have wanted it. I was starting to catch up on the business, but he was . . . in the company of his most devoted servant."

Suddenly Declan realized that Jack had died in the arms of the pretty maid he had met. The unexpected image of the fat old man dying on top of that young girl almost caused Declan to burst out laughing, and only by an act of pure will did he stop himself. He gulped air and let out a long breath, his eyes watering a tiny bit. Finally he was able to say, "I expect you're absolutely right, Roz. That's the way he would have wanted it."

Seeing Declan fighting for control, Roz looked at Gwen. "Jack and I had an . . . unusual marriage. We had no children, and I ran the shipping, drove the wagons—did all the bargaining out of town—while Jack took the orders from merchants in Ilagan," she said, naming the capital city of the neighboring kingdom of Ilcomen. "Anyway, I expect it'll be different with you and this lout. Children underfoot in no time, I'm sure."

"It's not that I'm not pleased to see you, Roz, but what brings you to Beran's Hill?" Declan said. "Certainly not just to visit me and Ratigan."

For a second her expression turned serious. "I do owe

you two my life, and I'll never forget that, but I'll let my partner explain."

"Partner?" asked Declan, looking at Ratigan.

Hatu had placed an ale in front of each of the other five and sat next to Hava, the two of them content to silently watch the others, though Hatu occasionally glanced at the stairs against the possibility one of their two guests might appear.

Ratigan said, "I ran into Roz in a town called Amberly, halfway between Ilagan and Marquenet; you take a little road a few hours up into the hills and down to a nice little valley. I was delivering some freight but mostly picking up a big load of fabric from the wool fair." Looking at Declan, he said, "Remember, I told you about it when we left Ilagan on our way here?"

Declan nodded.

"After dropping off my cargo, I ran into Roz at the west freight yard in town, and we had a drink and talked. One of my wagons had broken a spoke, and . . ." He looked to Roz and said, "You finish."

She grinned. "I was going back to Ilagan empty, and Ratigan didn't want to wait for his second wagon to be fixed, so I agreed to haul a load of cloth to Marquenet for a fee, see what I might pick up there heading back to Ilagan, and . . . with Jack gone and things turning nasty in the east, I wanted to find more business to the west and north, and Ratigan had more business than he could handle."

"I needed more wagons," added Ratigan, "but couldn't afford to invest in new ones, so I was losing business."

"So we decided to team up. I have no reason to stay in one place, as you know," she said to Declan.

"So now you're partners," said Declan, shaking his head in wonder.

"Yes," said Ratigan with a grin. "I now have new wagons and Roz has new markets."

Hatu asked, "What do you mean 'things turning nasty in the east'?"

Roz said, "Sandura has claimed Passage Town, so the last free city in the east is gone."

Declan's brow furrowed. "Passage Town? I thought that was in the Covenant, sort of. Not in Sandura, not in Ithrace, so people could come and trade freely. Was I wrong?"

"It was," said Roz, "but not anymore. Sandura hoisted its banner over it a few months ago, according to what traders from the east tell us."

Ratigan said, "Sandura has been fighting two barons on its northern border, and rumors abound it's going to claim that land when the fighting's done."

Declan said, "So what's next—Ilcomen?"

"Maybe," said Roz. "No one knows, but everyone is arming as if it's coming west."

"A fair number of free cities and small baronies are stuck between the two kingdoms, and the nomads of the Sea of Grass aren't going to take kindly to an army marching across what they claim as their people's lands."

"So everyone is buying weapons," said Declan. "I keep getting orders from Copper Hills and the baron here. I'm thinking about taking on another smith."

Gwen said, "Really?" Her tone implied more than curiosity.

Hatu looked at Hava, who gave a slight nod. Both understood that Declan might be in a bit of trouble. Hava tried hard not to smile and almost succeeded.

Declan also understood at once. "Just thinking about an apprentice," he said quickly.

Gwen seemed to accept that at face value.

"Anyway," Ratigan said, "we're going to organize ourselves and set up a larger yard here and get Randal some help."

"I've got good people in Ilagan, so we'll both operate out of Marquenet."

"So we'll be seeing more of you," said Gwen, her tone flat.

Roz smiled. "I think a little. Most of my contacts are to the east of Ilcomen, so mostly I'll try to keep business out that way going as long as I can."

"Well," said Declan, standing and nodding in Gwen's direction, "I'm glad to see you again and pleased you met Gwen and our hosts. If you need a wagon fixed or a horse shod, you know where to come."

"Good to see you again, Declan." Roz gave him a light buss on the cheek, then surprised Gwen a little by doing the same to her. In a mock whisper, she said, "Don't tell him I said so, but you found yourself a solid lad there."

As he turned to leave, Declan asked, "One thing, have you word of Edvalt?"

Roz shook her head. "Those slavers returned and fired the town. A few fisherfolk came back and rebuilt their huts, but what you knew of Oncon is gone, Declan. Where Edvalt and Mila landed, I don't know. Perhaps with their daughter in . . . whatever that place was she moved to."

"It didn't have a proper name, but they call it Riverside Village, as it's on the banks of the Tohon River."

"Well, they may be there. Not much business for a good smith that far from the road. Next time I'm down that way I'll ask around."

They said their good nights, and after Declan and Gwen departed, Roz smiled and said, "He picked a good one."

Hava said, "I like Gwen."

"She knows I used to have my way with Declan," Roz admitted with a smile. "It's an intuition some women have."

Hava shrugged. "I wouldn't have guessed."

"Some don't," admitted Roz.

Hatu looked at Ratigan, who grinned broadly. "So, he's in trouble?"

"For something he did before they met?" said Roz. "Not likely, unless she's meaner than I think. But she'll let him know those days are past."

"I don't think she needs to," suggested Hatu. "I haven't known Declan for long, but he doesn't seem the type."

"He's not," agreed Roz. "I've known him since he was barely able to grow a hair on his chin, and he'll never break a vow. He's a good and gentle man in his way, but he's got more steel in him than any sword he's made. If he makes a promise, he'll keep it or die trying."

Hava said to Roz, "Do you need a room?"

"No," she answered. "I'm bedding down over at Ratigan's little house."

"I've got an extra room," said Ratigan quickly.

Roz chuckled. Walking to the door, she said, "The poor lad fears I have evil desires on him."

Ratigan laughed and said, "There was a day I wouldn't have objected, but there's a girl down in Marquenet I've got my eye on, and I'd not want her to think ill of me."

"A girl?" said Hatu. He didn't know the wiry teamster well, but had spent enough time with him to think this a highly improbable turn of events. "Tell us more."

Ratigan smiled, waved his hand, and said, "Some other time. Good night." The two wagoners departed.

Alone with Hava, Hatu said, "Well, as I now have a day before I must travel, and we have guests who may wish to eat upon arising, we'd better clean up."

"Yes," agreed Hava. "This is harder work than I imagined."

They entered the kitchen and Hatu looked around. "Less to do than I thought."

"Gwen showed me how to do some bits here and there along the way, rinsing mugs and letting them dry." Hava pointed to a ridged wooden rack next to a tub of slightly dingy washing-up water.

"Oh, that's what that is for," observed Hatu. "Very clever."

They set about cleaning, and less than an hour later Hatu said, "Fair enough."

"The windows," said Hava.

Hatu smiled and nodded. "I would have forgotten. I'll be back."

He moved quietly up the stairs, not wishing to disturb his two guests, and went to the far end of the landing and closed the window. As he passed one of the closed doors he heard faint voices. This was a little odd, since each man had his own room, but he assumed they had something to discuss.

He caught a word and froze, listening carefully to what little he could hear through the door, then silently hurried away, thanking his years of training, which enabled him to tread quietly enough to avoid alerting the two men to his presence. He reached the near end of the landing, closed the window, and hurried down the stairs to where Hava waited.

One look at his face and she said, "What's wrong?"

"Now I'm certain I know that man who arrived earlier today. There is no doubt I must send word to the . . . to our grandfather."

Hava nodded. Old habits of secrecy were unlikely to be put aside just because there was no one in this entire town who would understand what he meant. Both also knew that his need to report was born out of habit, as he no longer had any obligation to the Kingdom of Night, and that he was doing this partially so Hava wouldn't have to explain why he was traveling to Marquenet without her.

They retired to their room next to the kitchen and Hava

quickly fell asleep: she had done more physical work than Hatu, carrying platters in and out of the kitchen all night.

Hatu lay awake, staring at the ceiling. Who were these men and why did hearing that one word fill him with an undefined sense of dread? Weaving in and out of this question, that word echoed in his mind: *Azhante*.

3

MORE MYSTERIES
AND A SHORT JOURNEY

Hava was boiling eggs, slicing what was left of a ham, and simmering a pot of grain porridge. Somewhere between buying the inn and this morning, Hava and Gwen had discussed what to serve at each meal, and the consensus was to cook the meal and if the travelers didn't care for it, they could seek a meal somewhere else.

Hatu had decided, for no other reason than needing to be behind the bar when the two men upstairs came down, to keep reorganizing the collection of whisky he had inherited from Leon. There was also something about this process that intrigued him, and he was now doing it for the third time since he had awoken and gotten dressed.

He had almost choked and vomited the first time he'd drunk whisky. Declan had convinced him the proper way to drink it was to "toss it down." He wasn't sure if some of the liquid had gone down the "wrong pipe," as Declan said, or whether it was just inhaling the strong fumes that had done the trick, but he'd ended up coughing and spitting before regaining his composure.

He had been barely more than a child the first time he

was introduced to ale and wine, and he remembered having a similar reaction, though not as severe. Each alcoholic beverage seemed to require a different approach. Ale and beer could be simply drunk down, and one of the things he had been taught was how to appear to drink copious amounts of "brew" without really drinking that much. Wine was trickier: the knack to staying sober was to dilute it with water, which was difficult with red wine, easier with white. Hatu had no idea how to drink whisky and stay sober; maybe with some water, but even then . . . Declan had told him it was an acquired taste, and Hatu now was doing his best to acquire it.

Each had interesting properties. Some whiskies had a hint of this or that flavor that others lacked. All he knew at this point was that not only were there "good" and "not good" whiskies, but that within a certain limit of "good" there was an unexpected variety.

So, trying to organize his thoughts on the matter, he managed to avoid total boredom while awaiting the appearance of the two lodgers upstairs. He had six different bottles of whisky, ranging from what he considered undrinkable to pretty good, and was considering his thoughts on cost when his two guests appeared.

They moved directly to the bar and Hatu asked, "Something to eat, gentlemen?"

"What do you have?" asked the man who had arrived first in town.

"We have eggs—some are hard-boiled—and a few slices of ham. So today it's eggs, ham, porridge, and oranges. In Marquensas we always have oranges."

"I could smell them on the air," said the second man, who had been the one Hatu recognized from Sandura.

"Lots of groves to the west, and when the breeze is right, you can smell them all the time," said Hatu. He had heard that from the locals, and repeating it made him sound more like one of them. He didn't know why, but he worried about the man whom he had seen before, sensing there was little chance it was mere coincidence that had brought him to this town so soon after Hatu himself had arrived.

"Hard-boiled eggs," said the first man. "We can stick them in our pockets and eat them as we go."

"Busy day?" asked Hatu.

"Depends," said the second man.

Hatu nodded, saying nothing. Part of his training as a boy had been how to withstand questioning, as well as how to glean information; silence was a far more useful tool than most people realized.

The first said, "We're looking for someone, and . . ." He stopped, looked at Hatu, and said, "Maybe you've seen . . . ?"

"Lots of people pass through town, and quite a few stop here for a drink or room," said Hatu encouragingly.

The second man said, "We're looking for a family, but perhaps they're not all together."

"Cousins, actually," interjected the first man. "My family really. They fled some troubles in the east and I got word they might be here, or have recently passed through."

Hatu shrugged. Hava came out of the kitchen and put a bowl of freshly boiled eggs down on the bar. She had poured cold water over them after boiling, so they would be cool to the touch. "Help yourself," said Hatu. "Free to guests."

"Thanks," said the second man. Both took four eggs, putting two in each jacket pocket.

The man who had arrived first said, "I've been asking around and so far no one has seen them."

"Big town," said Hatu. "I run the busiest inn in Beran's Hill—"

"Saw that last night," said the second man.

"—and I doubt I see one person in a hundred who passes through. Who are you looking for?"

The men exchanged glances, and in that instant Hatu knew he was about to be lied to. Master Bodai's lessons on getting information were far subtler than Master Kugal's harsh interrogation methods: the trick Hatu had been taught was to know which of the approaches to use at the appropriate time when questioning captives. Bodai had talked about questioning two prisoners and what to look for in comparing stories. Without being aware of it, the two men had just revealed they had concocted a story, and each was checking with the other without even being aware that was what they were doing.

The first man said, "My cousin is married and they have two children—adults now, about your age I should think—a boy and girl, a year apart." He again glanced at his companion. "One thing about them both: they have red hair."

Hatu shrugged.

Hava chimed in as if on cue. "This far north there are lots of people with red hair. Lots of the Kes'tun people from the far north come down here all the time; some have settled. Half of them have red hair. I have reddish hair," she said, though it was more a dark chestnut.

"You'd notice," said the first man. "It's unusual, bright, almost copper colored, and turns gold in the sun."

"Haven't seen anyone like that," said Hatu. "Sunburned copper we see occasionally, but we spend most of our time inside, so if they didn't stop in here for a meal or drink, we'd likely have missed them."

Hava said, "You know, I might have . . . at least I think maybe . . ."

Both men looked at her intensely. "Yes?" asked the first man.

"Well, it was only this pair . . . a man, and he was bald,

and dressed like an islander from the east. That's where we come from. But he had a girl with him, and when the sun hit her hair . . . I only saw because she was adjusting this scarf she wore. I remember it was a very unusual color."

The men exchanged glances. "Where did you see her?" asked the second man.

"Down at the stabling yard . . . no, wait, not the stabling yard, but the caravanserai. They were looking for a ride to Port Colos, looking for a ship, I think." Hava nodded. "Yes, now that you mention the hair color, I remember. If you head down to the caravanserai, you might find out who gave them a ride."

The two men nodded and the first said, "Thanks," and they were out the door.

Hatu gave a wry chuckle. "You can be evil, anyone tell you?"

Hava gave a slight shrug. "You and Donte, regularly."

Hatu felt a cold jolt in his stomach. "I do miss him."

"Me as well," agreed Hava. "Back to matters at hand. Those two are not very subtle."

"I don't know. They may be playing dumb thinking we or someone else here may betray information."

"They were staring right at the man they seek."

"But either they don't know that baby long ago was a boy, or they're disguising . . ." He waved away further specula- tion. "Here's what I probably shouldn't be telling you, but that second man, I saw him in Sandura when I traveled there with Bodai. He works for the Church of the One."

Hava took a deep breath and said, "Should or shouldn't tell me?" She punched him in the arm. "If you knew he was with the Church, then of course he's attempting to gull us. And his looking for a girl your age may be part of the act." She crossed her arms and bit her lower lip, a gesture Hatu had rarely seen, but he knew it meant she was concerned and concentrating. He knew to leave her alone.

Finally Hava uncrossed her arms and said, "Yes, you need to travel to Marquenet tomorrow. If Declan is reporting to the baron and Ratigan unloading his wagon, you should have time to send a message"—she glanced around out of habit—"and pick up a few things to make it look as if all you did was shop."

"I'll need a list."

"You shall have one," she replied.

"I'll first go to the Sign of the Gulls and send that message." He shrugged. "If I am late returning to Declan and Ratigan, I can easily claim I haggled a lot, got turned around, and got lost. It is my first visit; all we did was pass through the last time."

"What about those two?" She hiked her thumb over her shoulder, indicating the two men who had left shortly before.

"We wait, and maybe in a couple of hours one of us needs to do a bit of shopping and see if they've made an impression on any of the local shopkeepers."

She gave a nod and said, "I'll go and make a list."

She went back to the kitchen, where they had a small table for doing ledgers and letter writing, which apparently Leon had rarely used. Hava had replaced the dried-out ink jar and purchased a metal-nib pen to replace a completely worn-out quill.

Hatu cleaned up a bit of imaginary dirt and returned to contemplating the mystery of these men and how they related to what he encountered in Sandura. One thing was clear to Hatu. It could be nothing good. And it was also clear to him that they were looking for him, the Firemane baby.

A sudden chill spread through the pit of his stomach as he reminded himself that most of his life he had been ignorant of his true identity. The anger in his childhood, the odd feelings that night in the Narrows when he'd sensed something of his unusual nature. That led him to reflect on the past, and he remembered Donte.

His memories of Donte showed no sign of departing. There were funny memories, like trying to steal sausages with a tree branch, and reassuring ones, like the many times when they were very young that Donte had chased off the bullies. But there were also the images of Donte hanging by chains in that crimson grotto. He desperately tried not to think of those, but he could not push them away. He took a deep breath, calming himself as he accepted that Donte's loss would always haunt him. The best he could do was accept that and keep living.

EARLY THE FOLLOWING MORNING, HATU found himself leaving Beran's Hill, with Declan driving the team of horses. When asked about this, Declan's answer had been: "I can drive a team and Ratigan is short of drivers."

Hatu was amused. "So he's not hauling your and my freight, he's renting you a wagon?"

That realization put Declan in a darker mood, for not only was Ratigan getting paid to deliver a load of weapons to the baron and bring back the wagon with whatever goods Hatu purchased, he didn't have to drive it himself or pay a driver. Declan snapped back, "You're paying the fee for the return trip."

Hatu struggled not to laugh at that moment and changed the topic. "So, what do you think about those two men Molly and Hava saw on the road three days ago?"

"I think I need to talk to the baron about it, or his man Balven. What do you think?"

Hatu shrugged. "I don't know what to make of it. I mean, I understand why you'd warn the baron about armed men from some army skulking around but . . . I have no idea who they could be."

"You've traveled, seen things. You must have some thoughts," suggested Declan.

Hatu had ensured the two men under suspicion were still abed, their horses—a sorrel gelding and an off-grey mare, according to Hava—still over at Jacob's barn, before leaving. Both men had returned in the evening after having spent a futile afternoon asking around the caravanserai about the redheaded children. Hatu had bid them both good night. Passing Jacob's barn, he saw that both their horses were there, so Hatu knew they couldn't reach Marquenet without passing Hatu and Declan's wagon. To do so unseen would require a large looping course beyond farms on both sides of the baron's road, so they could not reach the city before the wagon.

In reply, Hatu said, "They rode in from the east, and rumors claim Sandura is making trouble for everyone." He shrugged, then continued. "They were alone in a corner of the inn last night and barely spoke to either Hava or me yesterday, other than ordering food and ale." He elected not to share the questions about redheaded youngsters passing through Beran's Hill with fictitious parents. Declan apparently had enough cause to alert the baron to the strangers' arrival in town without Hatu even remotely suggesting he might be part of their reason for being there. Others might bring it up should Declan speak to them of it, for if those two travelers were as indiscreet with others as they had been with Hatu and Hava, word would spread. It was also likely someone would bring up the rumors of the Firemane child.

Declan was by nature a man of few words, and Hatu

had a tendency to guard *his* words, a trait drilled into him since childhood, so the two of them fell into a comfortable silence.

Hatu scanned the horizon as a matter of habit and was taken with the beauty of Marquensas, the rolling hills, distant orchards, and lush fields. The weather was kinder than any place he had visited before, warm and sunny with cooling breezes off the ocean in the late afternoon. If fate determined this would be his home from now on, he could embrace it with enthusiasm, he decided.

He glanced past Declan, then to the rear. Declan said, "Worried we're being followed?"

Hatu feigned a dismissive chuckle. "Old habits are hard to break, I guess. Moving horses from market to market is risky." He fixed his eyes on the road ahead. Still, he could not shake the feeling that they were being watched.

A SMALL HUT STOOD AT the edge of a tiny clearing in the woods east of Beran's Hill. It had once been occupied by charcoal burners but had long since been abandoned. Inside waited two figures crouching under heavy blankets, for they did not risk fires at night. A third figure had just dismounted a horse and entered the hut.

Catharian, wearing his disguise as a friar of the Order of Tathan, had once been worshipped as a god, but was now regarded as a "prophesying divine spirit" of the One. He looked at the young woman who sat across from her bodyguard and asked, "Anything?"

"Just flickers," answered Sabella. "Even without training he's managed to develop . . . a shielding of his presence. An instinct, perhaps." She sighed. "I only get a hint of him being in the town two, three times a day." With a shy smile, she added, "Mostly his guard lowers when he's having sex with that girl."

"His wife," amended Catharian. He knelt. "How are you holding up?"

"I'm all right," she answered.

Catharian glanced at the man—Denbe, a master of the martial order of the Flame Guard—then returned his gaze to Sabella for a moment and smiled. Despite the privation of this journey, Sabella looked better than she had at the Sanctuary. Getting out in the sunlight, breathing fresh air, and not sitting all day in a dark room using her gifts to search for the lost son of the line of Firemane seemed to be reviving her. For a passing moment he wondered how the other Far Seers were doing now that this hunt was over. He had little doubt that their leader, Elmish, had found plenty for them to do.

The Flame Guard had become complacent over generations with the rise of the Firemane line and had taken root in Ithra, the capital city of the kingdom of Ithrace. In so doing they had enabled their enemies to almost obliterate the order in one blow.

It was thought that all of those in the sacking of Ithra had perished where the former Hall of the Guardians had stood: what few knew was that some survivors had retreated to the original hall in the distant south, which had been abandoned centuries earlier, a hall within the ancient Sanctuary. Enough members of the Flame Guard had survived that the order had managed to endure. For nearly two decades they had hidden and slowly recruited adepts and willing soldiers, but people with the vision and capacity to serve a higher calling were rare. Now they were beginning to venture into the world again, despite being few in number, to ensure a balance was restored. Still a long way from the power they were twenty years ago, they were continuing to find recruits to their cause and were getting prepared for a battle they knew must eventually come.

Catharian sat down. They had spent almost a month identifying which young man in the town was the Firemane child. By process of elimination it had quickly become obvious that the lad from an unnamed eastern land who had purchased a burned-out inn and restored it, with his wife, was the missing heir. Many questions remained unanswered as to how he had survived until adulthood, how he'd come to somewhat conceal his powers without proper training, and whether he knew how much danger he was in, as well as the more mundane questions of how he had ended up an innkeeper in Marquensas. All this was piquing Catharian's curiosity.

The false monk had become a familiar face to Hatushaly because of his acquaintance with Declan and Ratigan. Catharian was known as a mendicant friar, so when he passed through the town on his way to Port Colos, Copper Hills, or Marquenet, it raised no suspicions when he appeared at the Inn of the Three Stars. Hatu and Hava had even taken to providing him with a meal or food for the road, for they found his stories amusing.

Catharian had hinted he might be given the duty to raise a shrine to Tathan in Beran's Hill. That had given him a reasonable excuse to be in town often, and should the need arise to have agents of the Flame Guard there constantly, they could start construction on the false shrine.

The earlier arrival of a newcomer had made him think that the latter option was now unlikely and that the three of them might have to act sooner rather than later, but the story that they were going to build a shrine gave him good reason to linger. He hoped it wasn't too soon, as he would prefer to act when more agents of the Flame Guard had arrived and Sabella and Denbe were better rested.

"I think I recognized a man who arrived the day before yesterday," said the false monk.

"Who?" asked Denbe, looking interested. The old soldier had no problem with taking rest when it came his way, but while weeks of traveling up to Beran's Hill had kept him alert, a week of sitting in this hut had made him restless. The hint of a possible upcoming fight made him sit up and take notice.

"If he's who I think he is, he's an agent of the Church."

Denbe nodded. No further clarification was needed: the Church of the One was now simply "the Church" to most people. "What's his name?"

"They call him Piccolo," said Catharian. "He's Episkopos Bernardo's man."

"I've heard of him," said Denbe. "He's a murderous swine. Very dangerous."

"Odd name," said Sabella. "He's a musician?"

Denbe shook his head solemnly. "When he was a boy he killed another boy with a piccolo."

"Oh," said Sabella, taken aback.

"His brother," added Denbe.

"Oh!" Sabella blinked rapidly for a moment, as if trying to erase an image from her mind.

Catharian motioned for Denbe to step outside the hut, and when they were out of earshot, he asked, "She seems to be doing well. Is she?"

"Surprisingly, yes," said the older fighter. His sun-darkened skin made his face look as if it were sculpted from darkly tanned leather, but the brilliance of his smile lit up his face in a stark contrast to his usually stern countenance. "I often fretted over what we put those poor girls through." Women were the only ones able to use the gift of long-distance seeing. Some men had the power, like the young man known as Hatushaly, and some were trained to hold that power, but the ability to channel and manipulate what was thought of as "magic" was the province of women alone.

Catharian put his hand on his friend's shoulder. "As have I. More than one poor girl has ended up . . ." He let the thought remain unfinished. Denbe knew as well as he that there had been brilliant youngsters who had ended up almost mindless, living under the Flame Guard's care, youngsters left with little coherent thought, skipping from moment to moment in their days with no more than the desires of a child. They had vacant eyes, intense reactions of fear or joy, but they just existed until the day they died. If they were lucky, they passed early, but a few lingered on for decades.

"Just keep watch for a day or two longer. I think it's time for me to announce we're going to build a small shrine to Tathan in Beran's Hill. When you arrive in the town, I can explain your presence easily then; you are going to be the protector of the shrine, and Sabella is my novice. So I'll expect you . . . the day after tomorrow. Should we need to act sooner, I'll ride back here."

"What if someone else from the Church arrives, someone in an official capacity, not an agent for the episkopos?"

"I know enough about the bureaucracy of the Church to have them scurrying to send messages back and forth across a continent and an ocean before they decide we are not who we seem to be—ample time to depart safely. Baron Daylon has a far more tolerant attitude toward faith than most others these days and refuses to let the Church establish any sort of control in his barony. There are no members of the Church Adamant in Marquensas, at least not officially, so the burning of heretics as theater has not become a habit here."

"Speaking of messages," said Denbe. "Should we notify the others?"

"Not yet. We may need them but sending messages is problematic. One of us would have to ride back to Marquenet, as we have no pigeons."

"Don't like pigeons," said the fighter. "Hawks eat them."

"That's why we send more than one," replied Catharian. "If all goes according to plan, a boat should put in soon and pigeons will be arriving that can fly to our enclave outside Ithra. From there, if need be, they can send messages quickly back to the Sanctuary." He paused as if considering something. "Let's see what tomorrow brings. If this situation remains unchanged it could benefit us doubly. Establishing a presence here in Marquensas before trouble arrives would be of benefit.

"If we have to depart in a hurry, so be it, but if we can deal with our enemies in a calm and considered fashion, I would prefer that. Until then, we can keep an eye on young Hatushaly and, when the time is right, ensure that he finds his destiny."

"Whether he wants it or not," Denbe said dryly.

"'Tis ever thus," returned Catharian. "Had his father lived and turned him over to us for his early training, as his brothers were, there would be no fear of him arising to full power without our guidance. By any reasonable measure, he should be dead a dozen times over, either from enemies or simply his inability to contain his fire."

Denbe shook his head. "Nothing easy about this."

"No . . ." Catharian said. "I think you've changed my mind."

"I have?" said Denbe with a look of honest surprise.

"I thought locating the lad would be easy. It wasn't. I thought scooping him up and carrying him off would be simple. It's not. We do need pigeons who will home-fly here, so we need to find a breeder and arrange to have at least a dozen eggs sent to our safe house in Marquenet and another dozen here for our shrine. Once the squabs have matured we can swap them so they can fly messages. Getting messages to the Sanctuary quickly is important, but if we do actually become ensconced here, our brethren will need to get messages to us quickly as well."

Denbe nodded his agreement.

"While I look for a pigeon breeder around Beran's Hill, and sniff around to see what the boy has been up to since I last saw him, you take a quick trip down to Marquenet to send word to Elmish that we will take things into our own hands after your soldiers arrive."

"Pigeons," said Denbe. "As I said, I hate sending word by birds. So many things can go wrong."

"And as I said, that's why you send more than one. How many do we have down in Marquenet that can fly to the Ithra enclave?"

"We're down to three."

"Well, then, send all three. Inform Elmish of the situation here, in as few words as possible."

Denbe scowled. "Another reason I don't like pigeons. You can't explain much on a tiny piece of paper."

Catharian chuckled. "True."

Denbe didn't look amused. "I'll leave now. You look for a pigeon breeder."

Catharian nodded. "You take the horse to Marquenet. I'll spend the night here, then Sabella and I will walk into town tomorrow morning, the poor friar and his apprentice." He shook his head. "Piccolo, here. At least he's never seen me, as I only saw him once from some distance in a large crowd when he was with Delnocio." He forced a smile. "All will be well. Now you'd best leave."

"Fare you well," said Denbe.

"You as well," replied Catharian.

They went back into the hut and Denbe gathered up his travel bag and took Catharian's horse.

The false monk of Tathan sat down opposite Sabella and asked, "What do you know about the Order of Tathan?"

"Nothing," said the young woman.

"Well," said the older man, laughing, "let's discuss theology over a meal. All right?"

She found that amusing.

Catharian realized that was the first time he had ever heard the young woman laugh aloud since she had come to the Sanctuary as a child.

HAVA LINGERED IN THE MARKET as the two men who were staying at her inn moved away. She had left the inn under the supervision of the girl Millie, unofficially Jusan's betrothed. Apparently everyone just took it for granted, including Millie and Jusan. She was a tiny bit of a thing, but she knew the inn, and she was under instruction if anything of consequence arose that she was to come straight to the market and find Hava.

Hava wandered over to the vendor who had just been speaking with the two men and looked at his wares, some heavy woolen shirts, trousers, scarves, and capes, some treated with extra lanolin to repel water, which were useful for work outdoors in foul weather and for travel.

"Hello," said the merchant, a stout man who wore a rust-orange shirt and a wide leather belt, which was attempting to prevent his stomach from completely drooping by means of a big brass buckle; it hardly looked comfortable to Hava, but he seemed oblivious to it digging into his gut. His hair was a grey-shot thatch of light brown that was in desperate need of a comb, and he sported a few days' beard stubble.

Hava smiled. "Hello. I'm Hava. My husband and I—"

The man laughed, his blue eyes sparkling in his sun-freckled face. "I know who you are. You and your man bought the Three Stars from Gwen." He smiled as he added, "Beran's Hill isn't such a big town that we haven't all seen you around the last few weeks. I'm Pavek. Now, what can I do for you?"

"My husband and I came from a place warmer than here in the winter, but even then we didn't get this much rain. So we need better clothing."

Pavek chuckled again. "Wait a few months until the real rainy season starts. The smart buyers get their gear now, so they're not scrambling at the last minute. It will be cold!"

Hava nodded, realizing the man had just confessed that business was slow. "My husband doesn't have a decent cloak. He works inside most of the time, but given that he's traveling to Marquenet to stock up on some things we can't secure here, he'll be out in the open on a wagon, getting drenched, if the rain comes suddenly."

"I have just the thing," said Pavek, holding up a large dark grey cloak with an attached hood. "Feel that!"

Hava ran her hand over the material and nodded. There was a slightly oily feeling to the wool, so it would repel water for some time. "I know from experience that wet wool is the worst thing to be wearing in the cold."

"I thought you said you came from a warmer land?"

She kept her smile. "My father was a horse trader and we traveled a lot."

"Ah," said the merchant with a nod of the head.

Hava spent a few minutes looking at other items but had already decided to buy the cloak. It gave her a reasonable excuse to be in the market, and besides it was true that Hatu had nothing to wear outside in foul weather.

The climate on their home island was fairly constant year-round, rarely getting cold enough to notice. Rains came regularly, but they were of short duration and warm. Occasionally a storm would come through, lasting a day or two, but they were not often extreme.

Here the weather from the coast came down from the Ice

Floes and the Westlands, and it could be very cold. Mostly the climate was temperate, but when it wasn't, fireplaces were ablaze and warm clothing and heavy boots were the order of the day, according to what Gwen had told her. Short-sleeved shirts, simple cotton trousers, and sandals, common in Coaltachin, were unheard of in Marquensas.

After settling on a price for the cloak, Hava asked Pavek, "The two men you were talking to who left as I arrived . . ."

"Yes?"

"They're staying at our inn, but truth to tell . . . well, they keep to themselves and I've barely spoken two words to them."

"That's odd," said Pavek. "All they did was chat. Didn't buy a damned thing."

"Odd," agreed Hava.

"They kept talking about travelers who might have passed through sometime recently. A man or a woman, a boy and a girl, they couldn't seem to make up their minds. They only mentioned one thing they agreed on: the man, woman, or child would have bright red hair, copper and gold in the sunlight."

Hava feigned indifference as she picked up a woolen scarf, which was actually quite nicely made. "Quite a few people with red hair around here, aren't there?"

"Aren't there?" agreed Pavek. "I think they're idiots looking for the legendary Firemane child."

Hava made an instant decision to pretend ignorance. "I'm sorry, the what?"

"You must come from a long way off. The legend of the Firemane . . . well, it's an eastern kingdom, or was," began the merchant. He then launched into a quick retelling of the legend of the fall of Ithrace and the rumor of the lost child. There was even something about a curse involved, he claimed.

Hava was relieved to hear a jumble of facts and fancy that bore little resemblance to what she and Hatu had learned from the baron.

Pavek finished by saying, "There's word that the King of Sandura will pay a man's weight in gold to learn of the child's whereabouts. Though, come to think of it, that battle was so long ago, he or she is hardly a child anymore, right?"

"If you say so," said Hava. "I'll take this scarf, too. How much?"

The haggling took the merchant's mind off the story of the Firemane, and as she walked back to the inn, Hava wondered what the two men were playing at. There was something Hatu hadn't shared with her yet, and she imagined it would help make a bit more sense of the story. This wandering about openly searching for the legendary heir must be a bid to draw attention. *But from whom?* wondered Hava.

Obviously Hatu was doing his level best not to be discovered, and the reason for his hair always being colored since childhood now made complete sense to both him and Hava. Now that they were clearly alerted, they would be doubly cautious in keeping Hatu's identity secret.

Agents connected to the Church could never be this artless, so their behavior must be by design. The men would surely know their outspoken questions would bring a reaction, so again the question: Whose attention were they seeking?

Hava was so lost in thought that she almost walked past the inn, and suddenly she realized that the answer was simple: there was another player in this game. Someone besides those already known: two men and their masters in the Church, Hava's masters in Coaltachin, and the baron and his brother. Before entering the inn she paused, holding her bundle of newly purchased clothing. The key question was: Who was the new player?

THE WAGON ROLLED UP TO the gate Declan had used before when delivering weapons to the baron. Hatu said, "How long to finish your business, Declan?" They had spent an uneventful night sleeping under the wagon, so they were arriving in the city just as it was coming alive with the morning's clamor.

Declan said, "The wagon will be unloaded in an hour at most, but I don't know how long the baron will keep me waiting to make my report."

Hatu nodded. "I'll be quick as I can. I don't have much to secure, just a few things Hava wants that can't be bought in Beran's Hill."

Declan nodded. "Leon prided himself on . . . delicacies, he called them. Some cheeses, strange fruit—at least I thought it tasted strange—exotic nuts, and of course—"

"His whisky," interjected Hatu with a smile. "I'll have some porters lug what I buy here, and if you're not out, we'll wait for you over there." He pointed to a space that stood empty almost opposite the gate.

Declan said, "If I finish first, I'll park the wagon there."

"I'm off," said Hatu with a wave, and started walking toward the old keep.

Declan waved after him, then drove his wagon to the gate. The soldiers on duty recognized him from previous deliveries and motioned him through, and he moved his cargo around to the stabling yard where he had first come to visit.

It took only a few minutes to get the unloading started, and he walked toward the central keep of the sprawling castle. As he had anticipated, the baron's body servant, Balven, exited before Declan got there. "Declan!"

"Sir," said Declan, still unsure exactly how to address the baron's illegitimate brother.

"Full order?" asked Balven, stopping before the smith.

"Yes, sir. Twenty-four new swords, and that shield you asked me to make."

"Ah," said Balven. "What did you think of it?"

"It's a bit heavy to lug around the battlefield, I think." The shield was one of the baron's notions, for men to stand against a cavalry charge. Baron Dumarch had called it a "leaf shield," though the resemblance to a leaf on any tree Declan had ever seen was vague. It stood to shoulder height, with long sides, a slightly curved top, and a pointed end that could be planted firmly in the soil. Trained men in line formed a virtual wall, and Declan imagined that men standing just behind with long spears or pikes would stop all but the most determined charge. But the shield was three or four times heavier than the smaller round or heater shields he had been taught to fashion.

"I'm sure it is, but it may prove useful in defending a position."

"Might I suggest a wooden frame instead of this metal one? It would lower costs and be quicker to fashion. Good hardwood would be as effective, even with the reduction in weight. Only your strongest men could lug one of these around all day and not be exhausted."

Balven considered this. "Make one and we'll test it against lances, side by side with this one."

Declan nodded. "If I might ask, sir, where did the baron come up with this idea?"

"From a book," said Balven with a laugh. "The baron is the best-read man I've ever known. He got that from his father."

Declan nodded. The one time he had visited the inside of the castle he'd seen it had shelves full of books, more than he had ever imagined existed in the world.

Balven quickly inspected the swords and nodded his approval. He handed a purse to Declan. "Is there anything else?"

"There is one thing, sir," said the young smith. He recounted Molly Bowman's description of the men who had arrived in Beran's Hill a few days earlier.

When he had finished, Balven looked slightly concerned. "You did well to bring us that news, Declan. Armed men, and . . . and castellans, from what you said, disguised as mercenaries . . ." He took a deep breath. "This is very troubling. Wait here while I bring this to the baron's attention."

"Very well, sir," said Declan, as Balven turned back toward the doorway into the keep. He hoped this didn't take too long, as he wanted to start back as soon as Hatu returned. If they pushed on with a lightened wagon, they could arrive home a few hours after sunset, and he'd much rather spend his night in bed with Gwen than under a wagon with Hatu.

After an hour had passed, without Balven's return or Hatushaly's, Declan felt a rising sense of resignation that he would be forced to stay the night and depart the following morning, but eventually, the baron's man appeared and said, "You're free to go, smith. My lord will investigate this matter."

Balven turned his back before Declan could ask even a single question and left the annoyed young man alone. Declan took a breath and decided it best to ask the closest soldier where he could stable his wagon and find lodgings.

WHEN HATU GOT CLOSE TO the river that cut through the eastern third of the city, he found the Sign of the Gulls. He entered and looked around for a moment, letting his eyes adjust to the gloom and doing a quick inventory of faces.

His first thought upon taking in these surroundings was that his inn was a palace compared with this one—a waterfront inn with dockworkers, rivermen, whores, and no doubt an abundant supply of criminals.

He took another moment and saw a man standing in the corner behind the bar. He waved away an approaching whore, a girl who looked younger than Hava had been before she was sent to the Powdered Women, and she quickly retreated. Hatu made his way to the barman and said, "I have a message for Grandfather."

"I'll give it to him," answered the barman. He was a lanky, blond-haired man of middle years, broad shouldered and with enough marks on his face and neck to label him a brawler.

"I have a message for Grandfather," repeated Hatu.

The man pulled a large cudgel out from under the bar and said, "He's not here. As I said, give me the message and I'll see he gets it."

"I have a message for Grandfather," Hatu repeated a third time.

Immediately the barman put the cudgel back under the bar and said, "Come with me."

He led Hatu through a door behind the bar, through a filthy kitchen, and down a flight of stairs. The cellar was below the level of the river, Hatu reckoned, seeing how the stones in the wall seeped. A miasma of mold, stale beer, and deceased rodents left unburied almost made him gag, but he fought back the reflex.

They worked their way through a chaos of empty pallets, stacks of barrels, abandoned crates, and half-filled sacks to reach an unblocked section of wall. It was a maze with a purpose, Hatu decided; you would have to know exactly where you were going down here in order to find this space.

They had reached the other side of the storage room, as

far from the stairs leading down from the inn above as possible, Hatu judged. The barman pushed on a stone, and a door revealed itself, swinging away easily, wood painted to look like the bricks that surrounded it.

They walked down a sloping, stone-walled tunnel with a ceiling reinforced with supports and beams like those one would find in a mine. Water dripped from the ceiling, so it must run under the edge of the river, Hatu calculated. At last they came to a well-lit room.

A man sat at a table looking at what appeared to be ledgers, which he covered with a cloth as soon as he saw the barman with Hatu.

No words were exchanged as the barman turned and began his way back. "Yes?" said the man at the table. He was well dressed, looking more like a merchant of some importance than a master criminal, which Hatu knew he must be to hold the position of this city's crew boss.

"Who is the message for?" asked the man behind the table.

Hatu said, "Master Bodai."

"Alone?"

"No other," said Hatu, "save Zusara."

The man stood and removed the covered book and cloth. "I am neither's man. Can you write?"

"Yes," said Hatu.

The man set the ledger down on a shelf, produced clean paper and a pen and a glass inkwell, then fetched a stick of sealing wax and a seal. "When you've finished your message, fold it twice and seal it with wax. Leave it here on the table; do not carry it up to the taproom. When you have left the inn, I shall return and send it off. I assume there's some urgency?"

Hatu nodded. "Great urgency."

The man said, "I'll have a man start downriver tonight.

We have a fast ship near the mouth of the Narrows and it will be safely aboard by the day after tomorrow. With favorable winds, it should be in the hands of one of the masters within the week." He paused, then added, "Should a reply come, where will I find you?"

"Beran's Hill, at the Inn of the Three Stars. I am the proprietor."

The man nodded once and turned and walked up the tunnel.

Hatu moved behind the table and sat down as the man departed. He paused for a moment to organize his thoughts, then dipped his pen in the inkwell and began to write.

4

REFLECTIONS AND BLOODSHED

D aylon Dumarch, Baron of Marquensas, listened to his half brother sum up Declan's report and sat back in his chair. When Balven concluded the baron asked, "What do you think?"

"Castellans? Escorting someone through miles of the barony, only to drop him off out of sight at the edge of the town?" Balven shrugged. "It can't be anything good."

"Agreed, but whose man is he?"

"There's a small chance it's not what we imagine," said Balven. He glanced out a north-facing window, as if he could somehow magically see Beran's Hill from where he stood, then said, "But there's a very good chance it's Lodavico."

"Or the Church," said the baron, taking a deep breath. "They are none too pleased with me lately, as their missives make clear."

"In the politest manner possible," added Balven.

"I've seen what they're doing across the rest of the twin continents, and it's clear they seek domination—with influence rather than armies, but given enough control over the likes of Lodavico, they don't need their own army."

"If you just let them burn the occasional heretic," said Balven dryly, "they'll stop complaining."

"Perhaps," replied the baron. "But it would cede control, and that I oppose. Their rising power concerns me. And I don't care which god anyone else worships." The last was said with a dismissive tone and a shrug.

"Because you do not believe in gods," said Balven. "I believe you've been inside a shrine or temple . . . three times . . . in what, the last five years?"

"There are rites that need observing: prayers for the dead, sanctifying a marriage, anointing an heir. I respect the rituals, and the need people have to observe them, but I stopped believing in the gods years ago. Too many people I loved have died needlessly."

Balven knew that his half brother was thinking of his first wife, who had died in their third year of marriage. That was when he believed Daylon had started to lose his faith.

"The rise of the Church is far more about the ambitions of men than any divine purpose I can perceive."

"Well, that may be," said Balven, "but whatever the cause, there are real consequences attached to your choices, and those choices are narrowing, and soon you'll be left with two: submission or opposition. But at the moment it's still possible to come to an accommodation."

"Accommodation?" Daylon said, seemingly on the verge of laughter. "You mean a long pause while the Church consolidates its power, builds churches, converts more of my people, then finally demands to be recognized as the only true faith?"

Balven said nothing.

"Or they'll decide on who the next baron is as soon as I'm burned at the stake?" added Daylon.

Balven tilted his head slightly in a gesture both men knew meant he conceded the point. As boys growing up together, they had developed a host of small signs and signals that stood in lieu of words.

"If the Church has agents poking around Beran's Hill," said the baron, "that means they're probing for the weakest point of attack."

"Where you want them to attack, at Beran's Hill," conceded Balven. "But it seems a premature reconnaissance given they still have some unfinished conflicts on the other side of Passage Town. Even Lodavico isn't rash enough to launch a separate offensive and split his forces."

Daylon nodded. "Perhaps he is hearing rumors of our Firemane ghost and wants to investigate their validity."

"That ghost looked rather hale last we saw him," replied Balven. "Though young Sefan may find himself a true ghost soon enough."

"One thing," interjected Daylon.

"What?"

"His name, Sefan. I never remembered to ask, how do you know that was his given name? No note was left with him."

Balven looked distracted for a moment. "Whoever brought him to your pavilion . . ." He shook his head slightly. "I still wish to know how he, or she if it was his nurse, got in and out without detection."

"The question?"

"I had a few agents tucked away in a couple of bands of mercenaries who went with Lodavico's forces, and not every single person in Ithrace was killed, just most of them. One of the bits of information one of our men returned with was that the queen's unexpected baby was a boy. Very few know that, so there's rampant speculation as to whether it's a boy or a girl. He also found out the baby was to be blessed after the battle, when the king came home, and given the name of Steveren's—"

"Great-Uncle Sefan," interrupted the baron. "That makes sense." He let out a long breath that was almost a sigh. "The eldest son had been named for Steveren's father, the second for the queen's father, the small boy for his grandfather. So as the queen had no uncles, that left the king's only . . ." He smiled at his half brother's clever mind. "Yes, Sefan." Then he laughed out loud. "Besides, who is there to contradict you?"

Balven also laughed. "Well, there is that."

Daylon was silent for a moment, then stood up and went to the north-facing window near his most trusted adviser and half brother. Putting his hand on Balven's shoulder, he gave him a look that Balven recognized instantly as the silent question: What should we do?

Balven said, "I'll send two men to Beran's Hill tomorrow."

Daylon nodded. He had no doubt they would be two agents in Balven's secret little corps of spies and assassins. Daylon knew roughly who those men were, but he had long ago stopped worrying about every detail of those tasks he entrusted to Balven.

Without another word, Balven left his half brother to ponder the fate of people and nations.

BERAN'S HILL WAS FULLY AWAKE as Catharian and Sabella entered the outer limits of the town. They wore nearly identical robes, his a bit more tattered than hers, bearing the crest of their order over the heart. Catharian's hood was tossed back, exposing his bald pate to the morning sun. Sabella wore a wide-brimmed straw hat, grey from road dust, but otherwise sturdy. Each held a staff in one hand—to aid in climbing and self-defense—and travel bags slung over their shoulders.

They wended their way through Beran's Hill. Sabella

tried not to gawk, but until recently she had never seen more than a handful of people in a single place. Despite her attempts at remaining calm, colors and sounds made her want to glance this way and that, glimpses of things unimagined in the quiet confines of the Sanctuary fascinating her.

As a child, her talents had been detected by one of the few surviving members of the order, and she had been secreted with that woman, and two or three others, along the way. She had flashes of memory of the greater world, but nothing more than a child's impression of sounds, smells, textures, voices. There had been a large man—though as a child probably all men looked large to her—who had carried her for what she recalled as a long time; he would hum to keep her calm, and she remembered when he occasionally whispered in her ear or kissed her cheek, his whiskers would scratch. She could call up the sensation of that rough scraping on her face and she found that memory reassuring.

She remembered being put aboard a small boat and spending a long time in the dark with everything around her swaying, almost certainly in the hold of a ship. She recalled flashes of other people calming her, and odd smells, but little else. A dusty ride on a creature she now knew was called a camel, but she had not seen one since. It had been very hot, and she remembered being thirsty, but little else.

Then the rest of her life had been in the Sanctuary, the original, ancient Hall of the Guardians, all but abandoned ages before as the Flame Guard spread and took root in Ithrace. Once those massive stone halls had been the seat of the Flame Guard, but in her lifetime it had become a refuge, a place of hiding, while those living there had but one task: to find the surviving Firemane child.

All she knew beyond that she had learned from history, stories, and what others had told her.

Until this journey, she hadn't fully realized how cloistered her existence had been, how little she truly understood of what she had been taught. She had been raised in a secret world, one unknown to every person she passed today, and this realization alternately filled her with delight and fear, for if anyone could guess who she and Catharian were under their disguises, that person could only be an enemy.

Catharian took notice of her taking in everything around them and said, "Are you all right?"

Eyes wide, Sabella spoke softly. "So many people!"

"Wait until you see a real city," he replied, smiling. At that moment he suddenly realized what this young woman had been subjected to in aid of the Flame Guard. He felt a stab of regret. It had been deemed necessary, but he had never considered the toll it had taken on Sabella and the others.

"I wish my sisters could see this!" she said in a half whisper.

For a moment Catharian was at a loss. She had been brought to the Sanctuary as a small child, perhaps no more than four or five years of age, a foundling. Then he realized she was speaking of the other Seekers. All he could manage to say was "Perhaps they will one day."

Sabella impulsively gripped Catharian's arm with her free hand, giving it a familiar squeeze, as if she was trying to convince herself everything she saw was real. "What am I to do here?"

"We watch. We listen. We wait."

She looked up at him and nodded.

"Mostly we spend time apparently looking for a suitable place for a shrine, one that might be given freely, as we have no coin with which to pay. Say nothing and watch as I negotiate with a false promise of divine blessings, possible rewards later, or some other payment in kind: you will learn much about how people are." He smiled. "Most will say no outright, or promise to consider our plea. That should keep us free to roam around and talk to people." He paused, opened his shoulder bag, and removed a bowl, handing it to her.

"What do I do with that?"

"You hold it. You are a Sister of the Order of Tathan, a novitiate. My apprentice. Instead of being my beggar boy, you are my beggar girl."

"What do I do?"

"Mostly say nothing, watch, and hold that bowl out. Occasionally kind people will drop coins into it."

She appeared amused by that. "I can do that."

"We'll speak more about this when we're sure we're alone, but there are a few things to watch for, things that could prove critical."

"The . . . young man?" she asked.

"He is the most important, but we know now who he is and where he is, so it will be easy to ensure we don't lose track of him again."

"How is it easy?"

"If possible, we will be staying at his inn."

He pointed down the street, and there, a short distance away, was the Inn of the Three Stars. He led her to the doorway and motioned for her to follow him.

Stepping inside, Catharian saw that the inn was empty, save for Hava standing behind the bar attacking the dust with a clean rag.

She smiled. "Welcome," she said.

Catharian nodded and adopted a serious expression and offered in a deep voice, "We are travelers, relying on the generosity of those we meet, sent by our order to seek land for a shrine."

Hava laughed at the false monk's theatricality.

"Hava, this is my acolyte, Sister Sabella." Sabella nodded in greeting, a gesture Hava returned. "I wondered if we might drink from your well?"

Hava chuckled and said, "Help yourself. You know where it is."

Catharian and Sabella passed through the kitchen and out the back door, paused to glance around the completely rebuilt stabling yard, then went over to the well. Catharian pulled up a bucket of cold water, and both drank their fill. "Let's see what we can find out," suggested the false monk. "There have been great changes here since I last passed through. Watch and listen."

Reentering the inn through the kitchen, Catharian smiled as he said to Hava, "This inn . . . it's been rejuvenated."

"We put in a lot of work here," said Hava.

"Some time back," Catharian said to Sabella, "I first passed through with a young man named Declan and his friend Ratigan."

Hava said to Sabella, "My husband and I bought this inn from Declan's fiancée." Hava paused for a moment, then asked Catharian, "You met her father, Leon?"

"I met him," said Catharian. "I spent a night out in the barn, then continued my journey south. His daughter sold you this inn?"

"Bandits murdered him, burned the inn, and abducted Gwen and another girl. Declan and the other men of the town, and a skilled archer named Molly, fetched the girls back safely after dealing with the bandits." She recounted the story as she had heard it, then said, "So, you're seeking land?"

"If possible," said the false monk. "We serve the Harbinger, and as members of the Church of the One we'd like to secure land for a shrine, perhaps one large enough for a poor monk and his assistant to shelter in while they attend to the needs of the faithful."

Hava laughed, and when Catharian's face betrayed confusion, she said, "Sorry, I wasn't laughing at your needs. It's just that I've traveled a bit and some of the faithful have larger needs than a small shrine."

The humor was lost on Catharian and Sabella. Hava realized that her memory of Church clergy frequenting brothels owned by the Powdered Women was leading her into a conversation she was better off avoiding, so she waved away the comment. "Never mind, brother."

"Eventually the Church will build a proper house of worship, but that will be left to an episkopos or his deputy to decide, not a lowly monk."

Hava addressed Sabella. "My husband and I first learned of this place from Declan . . . we were horse trading with my father . . ."

She launched into the tale of how they had come to purchase the inn, and finally when she finished, Catharian asked, "Would you know of someone who might be inclined to sell off a small piece of land, somewhere near the edge of town, at not too expensive a price? Perhaps even as a donation to the Church?"

Hava laughed. "Not personally, but I'll ask around."

"Then you have my thanks." He turned toward the door. "We'll return tomorrow."

Hava saw that Sabella was staring at the kitchen and realized that while making their way to the well, they had had to pass the food waiting to be prepared for the day. Taking in the young girl's frail appearance and travel-worn clothing, she asked, "Have you eaten?"

Sabella was caught off guard and glanced at Catharian

as if asking permission to speak. He nodded, and she shook her head. "We ate yesterday, some dried fruit and a bit of hard cheese."

Hava shook her head at the folly of people motivated by beliefs she could not understand. "We can't have you starving to death." She cast a disapproving glance at Catharian, then said to Sabella, "Sit and I'll bring you something." She waved at the empty table closest to the kitchen.

"Why, thank you," Catharian said. "You're most generous."

With a half smile, Hava said, "Usually he waits until my husband or Declan is here, then plies them with tall tales and they ply him with food and drink." She turned and disappeared into the kitchen.

As they sat down, Sabella whispered, "That's the one, isn't it?"

"What?"

"The woman he has sex with."

"Huh?" Catharian was taken aback.

"There's an . . . energy . . . a glow." Sabella shrugged. "I don't know what to call it. It's not like the energy I feel from him, but . . . perhaps because they're together, I sense her."

Catharian held up his hand and softly said, "We'll talk about this later." Wondering what he might have gotten himself into bringing along this totally unworldly girl into what could easily become a center of violent conflict, he began to doubt his choice, even though her ability to sense the Firemane youth's whereabouts was vital. Pondering this, the false monk sat in silence, waiting for Hava to bring food.

SUNRISE SAW TWO WEARY YOUNG men ushering a wagon out through the northern gate of Marquenet as the city awoke. The day before Declan had discovered that while there was a good choice of inns for him and Hatu, finding a safe spot for the wagon and Hatu's goods had proved impossible. Those with large stabling yards were full, and the rest provided no place to keep a wagon. Finally, the sergeant of the keep, who knew both young men from their previous visits, permitted them to put the horses and wagon in the baron's stabling yard, as long as they stayed with them.

So, not for the first time, they had slept under a wagon, but for the first time in a city. While it was quiet compared to the day's tumult, the city at night still produced unexpected noises, especially coming from within the baron's keep and the barracks, where men changed guard every four hours. Both Declan and Hatu awoke several times, only to recognize a sound a moment after waking, then attempt to return to sleep. Hatu had prided himself on being able to sleep aboard a ship at sea and in other noisy places, but he discovered it was new sounds that were disturbing his slumber.

Hatu cast a glance back at his cargo, a selection of fruit not readily available in Marquensas, guaranteed to stay fresh for a week or more in a good cold cellar—at least that was what the fruitmonger promised. Several looked interesting, being unknown to Hatu despite his relatively wide range of travel. He was dubious about a fuzzy green item the monger called a "gooseberry," but he was promised that once the skin was off it would prove delectable.

He also had several large rounds of hard cheese, again unlike the local varieties, and a few smaller sacks of nuts and some jars of spices listed by Hava, but still only occupying a small part of the wagon's capacity.

Declan proved quiet this morning, content to drive the

wagon. Hatu was left to his own thoughts and discovered himself again torn by his almost impossible situation.

He had been told that Coaltachin, the nation of spies, thieves, murderers, and other assorted criminals, no longer demanded his loyalty. Yet he still worried over the part he now played as a spy on behalf of that nation. Here he sat, aboard a wagon bumping along the road back to a town he barely knew, to a wife who was his in name only, to play the part of an innkeeper, but mostly he was concerned over the message he had sent yesterday, what it meant, and what his part would be. Master Bodai's last instructions had released him from his obligation to the Council of Masters, yet he was still enmeshed in whatever business they had in this far-off barony, and Hava's presence more than anything made it clear they were not done with him, or he with them. It was a nagging contradiction.

He might have no official duty left to those who raised him, but he felt an urgent need to send that report to Master Bodai—not to aid Hava, who couldn't leave town alone without arousing suspicion, but because he also felt obliged, and the only explanation he could find for this feeling was because he had endured a lifetime of obedience.

It was also clear from what he had discussed with Hava that someone would be taking over Master Facaria's crews, so he couldn't even be certain who Hava's new boss would be. If it was Master Kugal, Hatu was certain that an order for his death would eventually reach Hava, since Kugal blamed Hatu for his grandson Donte's death. If it was another master, he might also want to see the heir to Ithrace dead, or he might simply order Hava home, leaving Hatu without her for the rest of his life. All these thoughts rolled through his head as the wagon rolled through the countryside.

After traveling for almost half an hour Declan said, "What?"

Hatu turned his head. "What?"

"You've been silent for longer than I've ever known you to be. You look lost in thought, and not a good one from the look of you. You worried about something?"

Hatu realized he had somehow let his guard down with Declan. He shook his head slightly. "Just having a bit of a moment, wondering about whether I'm cut out to be an innkeeper."

"Really?" asked Declan. "You didn't seem to hesitate when the opportunity appeared."

Hatu gave a shrug. "Traveling with Hava's father . . . was difficult at times. At his age he . . ." He let the words trail off. "I was getting more work and less . . ."

"Thanks?"

Hatu gave an emphatic nod.

Declan kept the team of horses moving smartly down the road, while maintaining a pace that wouldn't exhaust them by noon. "How'd you meet?"

Hatu and Hava had concocted a story that maintained several key points of truth; they had decided any inconsistencies could be explained away as simple faulty memory. "I was an orphan, scraping along in a town called Bidwitty, in Materos. I saw Hava and Bodai at the market square and . . ." He laughed. "I think I was in love with Hava from childhood but just didn't know it. Somehow I convinced Bodai I could be useful and he let me come along with him as he traded.

"One thing led to another, and after a while Hava and I just . . ." He shrugged. "Truth to tell we're not even properly married."

Declan feigned surprise.

"I should have told you before."

Declan laughed. "Your secret's safe with me."

Hatu did not have to feign looking embarrassed. His

uncertainty about Hava did make him feel self-conscious. He was almost sure she loved him, but he was sure she didn't love him as much as he loved her, and he did not know if her love for him would outweigh her duty to their homeland.

"I just didn't know if that sort of thing was important around here," he said, trying to sound both amused and concerned.

"Really?" Declan said. "Well, Gwen and I will wed at the midsummer festival, and no one cares that she's been living with me since the inn burned down."

Hatu looked relieved. "That's good to know. I've been to some places where that sort of thing is important."

"Really?" repeated Declan. "I haven't traveled much, just from Oncon to here, and up to Copper Hills and back. Most of the people around here are like those in Oncon, pretty much not worrying about other people's business."

Hatu reflexively glanced around and realized the folly of it, as there was no one else on the road. "The Church seems to be."

"Seems to be what?"

"Worrying about other people's business."

"I suppose so," said Declan. "Still, if you and Hava are going to wed at the festival, you won't be the only couple living together to do so, and a couple of the gals will be with child." Declan shook his head in disbelief. "Why some people would care . . . it's beyond me."

They continued to ride in silence for a while, and Hatu tried to keep concern over Hava's loyalties out of his thoughts, but failed. He glanced over his shoulder out of habit and saw two distant riders.

"Riders behind us," he said to Declan in a casual tone.

The smith said, "It's a busy road."

Hatu tilted his head slightly as if considering that remark, then said, "I'm carrying cheese and foodstuff. You just got paid for a load of armor, so I assume you've a tidy bag of gold on you."

Declan let out a slow, long sigh. "True. Let me know if they start coming hard after us."

Hatu said, "I will."

He kept a surreptitious watch on the two riders: they were closing the gap between them but were not in any obvious hurry. Men on horseback should be faster than a pair of dray horses even with a largely empty wagon. Hatu decided they were probably not a threat and he saw no other sign of potential trouble.

His mind was occupied with thoughts of his early life, at school with Donte and the other students, when he realized that four riders had appeared over the crest of the hill and come to a halt before them, arrayed athwart the road, leaving no room to pass.

Declan said, "No sword?"

"Just my dagger."

"Know how to use one?"

Hatu said, "If I must." He rested his hand on the hilt of his dagger.

Declan reined in and shouted, "Move out of the way, man!"

The four were wearing a collection of dissimilar armor, mostly leather or quilted jacks. The two in the center had leather headgear, while the two who flanked them were bareheaded. None bore a shield. "We're collecting duty for those using the baron's road!" shouted the man facing Declan. That brought chuckles from the other three.

Declan spoke quietly. "This will be a fight. I'll take the two on my side."

Hatu slowly adjusted his position so he could leap off the wagon and land exactly where he chose. "Obviously," he whispered, as he studied the two men to his right.

He made his movements slightly more exaggerated, as if he were shifting his weight, then said loudly, "All we have are some cheeses and fruits for an inn in Beran's Hill. How much duty does the baron claim?"

The first man laughed.

"They know about the gold," Declan said quietly. "They know I was paid for a wagonload of swords."

"What are the odds," Hatu said, "that the two who are following us are with these pigs?"

"Let's not wait to find out," said Declan, as he sprang from the wagon, moving straight at the nearest rider. As he knew would happen, Declan saw the two horses closest to him shy back at the sudden lunge in their direction, the outermost one forcing its rider to turn it in a full circle. Declan stepped between the two mounts, bringing him within reach of the innermost rider. He brought his sword high, in what Edvalt had taught him was the proper position for receiving a blow from a mounted opponent, and felt the shock run down his arm as the rider delivered that blow an instant later. Declan kept moving and threw his weight into the right shoulder of the horse, just where it joined the neck, and the animal shied suddenly backward. Declan was relieved that these were not battle-trained war mounts. The horse started to wheel around so that it could kick Declan, and its rider had to fight to retain control.

Hatu seized on the distraction caused by Declan's sudden move, drawing his dagger and throwing it with force at the outermost rider on the right, who, rather than keeping his eye on Hatu, had turned reflexively to see if Declan's attack threatened him. Hatu was gratified to see his target tumble over the horse's croup. He was out of the wagon and moving at a run as the rider hit the ground.

Hatu covered the distance between himself and the fallen rider in three quick strides and unceremoniously kicked the man's head as hard as he could. It was a glancing blow, but enough to stun him. The dagger had hit with enough force to carve a nasty gash at the junction of his neck and shoulder, but it wasn't a killing wound unless the stupefied fighter bled out before someone could tend to the injury.

Hatu retrieved the fallen rider's sword as the rider next to him kicked his horse's flank and the animal leapt at Hatu. Hatu threw himself to his right, striking the ground and rolling back to his feet as the horse passed to his left.

Meanwhile, Declan was realizing that he'd made a critical mistake, as he found himself caught between two horsemen, so he took a chance and dodged to his left, ducking under the neck of the outermost horse, which brought him into striking range of the other rider, who had just gotten his mount under control.

This was a lesson Edvalt had never discussed, let alone taught him: to be on foot facing two riders. Declan felt a stab of fear, which triggered a hot flash of anger.

In that moment, he felt a burst of clarity, a calm and precise certainty of what he was doing, even more intense than what had overwhelmed him in Oncon, when he was facing the slavers. It was as if time slowed, and he had a perfect awareness of what was happening all around him. He knew that he needed to take one step forward, not back or to the side, then turn around.

As if nothing impeded him, he was suddenly behind both riders, and neither of them was able to turn his mount. He set his feet firmly, and in that instant he could see that Hatushaly had unseated one rider, had picked up his sword, and was using the riderless mount as a shield against the other rider.

He could see to the end of the road, where the two riders who had been following them were now coming fast. One bandit was down, so they might face five instead of three.

With that realization came more rage and in that rage more clarity.

Declan rushed between the wagon and the horse closest to it just as that mount's rider tried to turn. He jumped onto the wagon's wheel, then pushed off, throwing all his weight into the rider trapped between the wagon and his companion's horse.

Declan carried the rider off his mount, and both men fell close to the outside horse, causing it to rear, its rider fighting to control his skittish mount while Declan kept his arm tight around the waist of the spokesman for the riders until the two of them slammed into the ground. Declan landed on top of the other man, knocking the wind out of him, and Declan was immediately on his feet, driving his sword's point into the man's throat before he caught his breath.

Hatu was still using his first attacker's horse as a barrier and doing a good job of looking as frightened and uncertain as he could, hoping the man trying to kill him thought his dagger throw had been a lucky toss. Hatu had never had to face a mounted opponent while on foot, not even in training. Armed riders in Coaltachin were all members of the nocusara, and beyond the Kingdom of Night, open fighting was to be avoided at all costs.

The rider was showing frustration at the resistance, and from what Declan could see there were only two of the bandits left to steal the gold.

Hatu tensed as the horse he had been sheltering behind spooked and, seeing an opening, bolted to be free. For a brief instant Hatu realized he should have grabbed the animal's bridle.

Hatu couldn't see Declan and only one attacker remained on his side of the wagon, so he turned his full attention to that man. The rider set his heels to his horse's barrel and the animal lunged forward. Through sheer luck Hatu avoided being trampled or beheaded—just. He threw himself in the right direction, then rolled to his feet, turning as the rider wheeled his horse around to charge him.

Just then the two riders who had followed them on the road arrived, riding hard. Hatu froze for an instant, and as he did so, one of the newcomers passed him to attack the bandit Hatu had just fought. He glanced to his left to see the rider's companion likewise engaged with the swordsman Declan had faced.

Both bandits saw the wisdom of turning tail and tried to flee. The one Hatu faced made good on his escape, but Declan pulled the one he had fought out of his saddle the moment he began to turn away from the smith.

The newcomer who had helped Hatu turned his horse around, seeming content to let the rider escape. He looked down at Hatu and said, "How are you?"

"Fine," said Hatu. "Bruises, but otherwise none the worse. My thanks."

The rider was a broad-shouldered, dark-haired fellow with one of those instantly likable faces, a ready smile, and something cheerful about his striking blue eyes, all of which was in stark contrast to the brutal efficiency he had just demonstrated, which was a quality Hatu recognized from years of being around men like him. This cheerful man was a trained soldier, very well trained.

The rider and Hatu joined Declan and found the last remaining bandit, bloodied but alive, being held at sword's point by the blacksmith. Hatu saw that the other newly arrived rider was also possessed of the bearing of a trained fighting man, but there was nothing jovial in his countenance. His hair was shot through with flecks of iron grey, his eyes squinted from beneath dark brows, and he favored a close-cut beard.

The more jovial fellow looked down at the bleeding

bandit and said to Declan, "What do you want to do with this miscreant?"

The other rider said, "Let him bleed, I say."

Declan said, "Maybe." To the wounded bandit, who was obviously in pain, he said, "How did you know I was carrying gold?"

"Doesn't take a scholar to see you ride into town with a wagonload of swords for the baron to know you'd leave with a sack of gold."

"So you waited?" demanded Declan.

"We waited. All night. Figured you'd leave last night, but . . . you didn't." He winced and his color grew paler.

"He's going to die," said the dour rider. "If you have more questions, best ask them quick."

"I don't," said Declan. With a quick jab, he used the edge of his sword to sever the man's neck artery, then let go of his collar and stepped aside as blood fountained and the man fell over.

"If you don't have a shovel, we'll just have to leave him for the crows," said the more cheerful rider.

"I don't," said Declan.

"Then crows it is," said the older rider.

"I'm Tucker," said the younger man, "and my friend here is Billy."

Hatu nodded in greeting. "As I said, thanks."

Billy's mouth moved slightly, in what Hatu judged passed for a smile. "You looked to have things under control. Two down, the third about to be, and you"—he pointed at Hatu—"you're quite the dancer."

Hatu was about to say he'd never been trained to fight a mounted man but caught himself instantly. "Ah, I was trying to stay alive while I worked out how best to unseat him."

Declan said to Hatu, "I'm getting good at it. I'll show you sometime."

Hatu didn't know if he was joking or not. "Staying alive or unseating a rider?"

"Both," said Declan with a wry expression.

Hatu shook his head, then turned his attention to the two newcomers and said, "So you two jumped in. Thanks."

Declan nodded. "My thanks as well."

"Well," said Tucker, "we've traveled a fair bit together and don't have a lot of use for bandits."

"Put a few of them in the ground," added Billy.

"Beran's Hill?" asked Hatu.

"For a bit," replied Tucker. "Then somewhere else."

"Then if you ride with us," said Hatu, "I'll be pleased to feed you and give you a room at my inn."

Billy's eyebrows shot up and his eyes widened. "You're an innkeeper?"

"I am," replied Hatu.

"Bit young," said Billy.

"You're not the first to say that," replied Hatu. He motioned to Declan, and they pulled the man the smith had killed over to the side of the road. "If you fellows don't mind, those three horses would fetch a couple of pieces of silver from a horse trader we know. Be happy to split what Tenda gives us."

"Keep my share," said Declan, as he let go of the corpse and moved toward the second dead man, the one he had impaled after knocking him from the saddle. "You more than earned it."

The two riders nodded and went off to gather the horses, which were now grazing in a distant meadow.

As Hatu helped Declan carry the second body over to where the first rested, he said, "More well-trained soldiers."

"Yes," answered the young smith. "There seems to be a glut of them around these days, doesn't there?"

"So now we'll have four to watch," said Hatu.

"It's good to have an inn, I guess." Declan chuckled as he and Hatu deposited the second corpse on the ground.

As they moved to fetch the third dead bandit, Hatu began to wonder if that was remotely true, then thought that had Donte been with them they'd have needed no aid from the two newcomers. His mind turned to the lingering question of Donte and his tragic death in that dark, watery cave. His loss still hurt bitterly.

DONTE SWEATED UNDER A HOT, setting sun as he arranged the nets on the drying racks. The racks were all crudely constructed but had served the family for a generation or longer. The village was called Calimar, and it lay on the tip of a little jut of land extending from the westernmost peninsula in the Barony of Marquensas. From a hill behind the village it was possible to see the ocean to the north and to the south.

Donte knew the name of the village because a man named Macomb had told him where he was when Donte had climbed out of the surf. Macomb had been night fishing when Donte had stumbled out of the darkness, his clothing soaked, shivering from the cold, and completely confused.

Donte had no memory from before that night, not one thing prior to crawling out of the surf. Occasionally odd images appeared to him as he awoke in the morning, but they were fleeting and unhelpful. The occasional flash of a sound, an aroma, or a movement seen out of the corner of his eye, but with all of these sensations it was as if they were behind a wall of dark smoky glass, hinted at, glimpsed, but never fully grasped. In the instant at which they presented themselves to him, Donte would feel the slight tingle of an emotion; then both image and sensation would be gone.

What seemed to trouble Old Macomb, as he was known, and his family was Donte's apparent lack of curiosity about his past. Since coming to the village, he appeared content to fish with Old Macomb's sons, grandsons, and nephews and the other fishermen of the village. At times he showed a streak of humor and apparently enjoyed pranks, but other times he was quiet almost to the point of seeming mute.

It was clear to them all that Donte had some familiarity with hauling nets and boat care. Donte worked without complaint, smiling at other men's jokes, but hardly said a word.

Some of the villagers had said within his earshot that they suspected whatever had caused Donte to lose his memory—a blow to the head perhaps as he fell off a passing ship—had also made him simple.

In the time he had spent in the village he answered questions as best he could, but volunteered nothing, rarely asked questions of others, and ignored much of the daily life taken for granted by the villagers. If a joke was shared, or children played pranks on one of their own, he laughed, but he did not join in.

A couple of the village girls had tried to flirt with him at first, as he was a broad-shouldered young man with a nice smile and good looks once the bruises on his face had healed, but he seemed oblivious to their remarks and hints.

Inside he felt distant stirrings when the girls approached him, but these feelings were muted and more of a distant memory than any immediate urge. There was something that continued to nag at him, a sense more than a thought, that he should be somewhere else, doing something else, but this was also behind that wall of dark glass in his mind.

But a sense of need began to grow in him once he had regained his strength, and he felt the impulse to depart soon.

He just had no idea why.

When the last net was properly hung, Old Macomb came over and said, "Don't worry about the nets anymore. We're going to use them again tonight. After we eat, we're going to do some night fishing. A trader coming up the coast hove in while you were out netting, and he says there's a run of bottom-wallowers headed our way."

"What are bottom-wallowers?" Donte asked.

"Very tasty, is what they are," replied the old man. "They're night fish. They wallow on the seabed near the shore and cover themselves in silt so other fish can't see them during the day. After sunset they come up and start feeding. Then when the sun comes up, they go wallow again. Don't see them often—once or twice a year—so they fetch a handsome price if we can catch a netful or two. We don't have to go far, and they won't linger too long, so an hour or two we'll be back hanging these nets again. You understand?"

Donte shrugged. "I think so." He felt on the verge of saying something else, but the thought fled. Finally he nodded and turned toward the hut where he would eat with Old Macomb's family.

As was his habit, he took the offered food and sat just at the edge of the family circle near the fire, close enough not to seem apart, but distant enough that he rarely was spoken to, which suited everyone. He was accepted, but only to a point. His odd behavior communicated to the family there was something "wrong" with him, and he knew that. He also had no idea what that "wrong" might be. He just lived from moment to moment, experiencing the flashes of images and voices, odd sensations of distantly felt anger, amusement, lust, and hunger, as faint echoes of his past life.

Yet even those tantalizing bits of experience, lingering behind that smoky glass wall in his mind, held no interest for Donte. He marked their passage as he would a flight of birds overhead or a school of fish passing under the boat, just something to notice briefly, but not worthy of consideration.

Someone said something funny, probably Old Macomb, and Donte noticed that people were laughing. He realized for perhaps the first time since arriving that his ability to perceive more than one thing at a time was impaired and felt a faint stab of concern. That wasn't as it was supposed to be, he suddenly knew.

For a brief instant he attempted to seize that thought, not let it simply fade, and it lingered.

Then someone spoke, and his attention shifted. His sense of wrongness disappeared as people finished eating. He was suddenly empty again, as that momentary pang of something missing vanished into the nameless void within him. He stared into the distance, as if trying to recall something.

Moments fled and someone took his food bowl from him and the cup from which he drank well water, and someone said, "It's time to go."

He stood and followed them outside and began to help remove the nets from the rack and return them to the boats. For a brief instant he wondered why they had put them on the racks rather than just leaving them in the boats, then that question fled.

Donte readied his gear along with the other men; then they pushed the largest boat, holding a dozen men, into the surf. These villagers had spent their lifetimes fishing, and they did what was needed without hesitation, knowing exactly when to jump into the boat. Donte was only a moment behind them. He had quickly learned the skills of the fishermen and felt a distant stirring of something akin to pride at this accomplishment.

In short order their boat was outside the breakers, and a pair of villagers remained at the oars to keep the boat from drifting back toward the beach, while the rest readied the nets.

Old Macomb smiled as he looked at Donte. "This was quickly done. We'll wait until the waters churn, which means the shoal of bottom-wallowers are feeding just below the surface, then we'll cast the nets and haul in the catch." He nodded toward a large square box athwart the center of the boat, leaving room for only one man to pass on either side. "We'll dump the catch there and go home."

"Only one cast?"

"By the time we dump and cast again, they will be gone. It's why they are so hard to catch, but also why they fetch such a good price."

"Assuming they are actually there," said another man with a dry chuckle.

Macomb shrugged. "If they're not, we try again tomorrow."

Another man said, "And the night after."

Old Macomb gave a theatrical sigh. "Or until we hear from one of the villages north of us that they've already passed."

Donte wasn't quite sure why the men seemed amused, so he just nodded and waited. One of the others explained quickly that there was a special "scooping" technique they'd use, as the fish would start their feeding near the bottom and work their way up and then turn to migrate up the coast when they were close to the surface. Drop the nets correctly and scoop, and the fish would swim into the nets quickly. If the nets were filled, the profits from this one catch could equal a half year's earnings for the village.

The water lapped the sides of the boat as it sat relatively motionless, held in place by expert rowers. The gentle rocking of the boat was in counterpoint to the rise and fall of the combers as they moved toward the shore, forming breakers. It would have been almost soothing, had the boat not been crowded with men keeping a keen watch on the surface: the tension in the air was palpable.

A burst of bubbles on the seaward side of the boat was the first sign, and suddenly a massive creature erupted from beneath the waves. Wide shoulders and thick arms were attached to a very humanlike chest and abdomen, which turned into a fishy tail that swished from side to side as the creature kept itself above the surface. The face had gill-like slits where a nose should be. No hair grew on its head and its eyes were dark, with amber irises like those of a fish. Its skin was almost fish-belly white, and its expression was a mask of anger.

The men recoiled, two knocking those behind them into the water, and a shout arose.

Suddenly Donte heard a voice in his head. *Awake!*

Abruptly memories flooded into his mind, almost driving him to his knees with a pain unlike any he had felt before, as if lightning were exploding in his brain, ripping through his body down to his feet, vanishing into the water below the boat.

He cried out in agony, trying to focus on the creature, which he now recognized as a "swimmer," a magically changed man who had been transformed into a near-mindless servant of the Sisters of the Deep. Just the thought of those witches turned his stomach, and he swallowed hard to keep the bile in his throat from being vomited out.

Then the pain vanished almost as quickly as it had arrived, leaving not even an echo of torment.

In his head the voice shouted, *You must hunt! Find the other! Go!*

All around him, the men in the boat were begging gods they had not prayed to for years to spare them.

Donte felt control return.

Without hesitation, he pulled out his belt knife and leaned forward, slashing the swimmer across the throat. It was a move so swift that those in the boat with him didn't even register his act for long moments.

The creature's eyes widened and crimson blood fountained out of the wound, then its eyes rolled up into its head, the tail's swishing ceased, and it fell back into the dark sea, vanishing below the surface.

Donte shouted after it, "No one tells me what to do!"

For a brief moment, silence gripped everyone in the boat, then a babble erupted as the terrified fishermen all tried to speak at once. One of the men who had gone over the side attempted to haul himself back into the boat, and Donte glanced shoreward to see that the other man had swum past the breakers and was wading onto the shore.

"What was that?" shouted Old Macomb.

"Water demon!" said another man. "Haven't you heard the tales?"

Donte drank in his returning memories, feeling twinges of emotion at the thought of his grandfather, Hava, and Hatu. Hatu! He was supposed to find and kill Hatu!

Looking out to sea, Donte muttered, "Like hell I will."

Old Macomb reached out and tugged at Donte's arm. "Do you know what that thing you killed was?"

"It was once a man," said Donte, and instantly every man in the boat could sense the change that had come over him.

"You've got your memory back," said Macomb, a statement, not a question.

Donte nodded. "I must leave."

Macomb returned the nod. "Yes, you must."

Without further discussion, the men gathered up the nets and turned the boat toward the village.

ACROSS A VAST EXPANSE OF water, deep below the surface in a cave illuminated by glowing lichen, a small group of women gathered near one who sat as still as a rock, her eyes staring into the void. Then she blinked, shook her head, and said, "It is done."

The old woman named Madda asked, "He is awake?"

The other old woman, named Madonna, nodded once, then said, "He has his mind back . . ." Then slowly she smiled. "And he thinks he is free of us."

5

CELEBRATION AND MURDER

Hatu hurried to clear the mugs and plates, as four wagoners moved away from the table. The inn was doing steady business as the midsummer festival approached. A few relatives from smaller villages in the area were visiting family, and the usual business of travelers moving through the northern portion of the barony continued unabated.

Since returning from his journey to Marquenet with Declan, Hatu had begun to get into the rhythm of managing an inn, and not for the first time he thanked whatever deities cared to listen for giving Hava an instinct for organizing their day around the needs of the inn.

Hatu was no fool, but it took him a while to sense things that came almost immediately to Hava, from what to shop for and when, to the precise moment at which to vanish into the kitchen to wash, prepare more food, or whatever other task demanded attention. What he had to realize logically, she intuited.

He carried his load of dirty plates and mugs into the kitchen, where Hava was doing a fast inventory of what was there and what needed preparing. She gave him a quick nod and asked, "Are you all right out front? I need to watch the stove." Her tone was matter-of-fact.

"No problems," he said with a smile. He contrasted the so-
lidity of their lives in the town of Beran's Hill with the chaos
they'd lived before coming here and was certain he could
happily live out his days as an innkeeper with a wife and,
possibly someday, children.

He shook his head slightly, a gesture she didn't notice,
his own admission that sometimes he worried too much
about things he didn't understand. Eventually this question
would fade or finally be answered, but wasting time on it
would not make those waiting for drinks and food happy.
One thing he had learned in the short time he had been an
innkeeper was that keeping customers satisfied was paramount in this occupation.

The demands of the inn took Hatu through the afternoon
and into the evening without him being aware of the passing of time. Declan's entrance with Gwen made him realize
the day had passed, for the smith had closed his shop for the
evening.

Looking at Gwen, Hatu smiled and shook his head
slightly, an expression of open admiration on his face. "I
don't know how you did this every day. I honestly do not."

Gwen laughed. "It was rarely this busy. You've already
built a reputation my father only wished he had."

Seeing an open table near the bar, they moved to it and
sat down, and Declan said, "We decided to come here so
Jusan and Millie could have some privacy."

Hava came out from the kitchen, glanced around the
room, then came to stand next to Hatu. She nodded a
greeting to Declan and Gwen while Hatu smiled and said,
"Privacy?"

Declan looked annoyed while Gwen said, "The festival.
Jusan wants to wed Millie—"

"But she hasn't said yes," finished Hava.

Gwen nodded.

"It's making the boy crazy," said Declan with a slight scowl. "It's showing up in his work. He's not paying attention to details."

Gwen put her hand on Declan's arm, in a gesture suggesting it wasn't time for his complaints, and said, "She's uncertain."

Hatu started to say something, thought better of it, and glanced at Hava. She said with a shrug, "I thought it was taken for granted. Obviously I was wrong."

Declan said, "Everyone did."

"Except Millie," said Hatu.

"That's the problem," said Gwen. "Jusan was smitten the moment he set eyes on her, but she . . . she's been through a lot."

"So have you," Declan said softly.

Gwen glanced at him with an expression that mixed gratitude with a hint of annoyance. "I'm not Millie. She was always a timid girl, even before she came to work here. She was just beginning to . . ." She fought for words.

"She had stopped jumping at every loud noise," supplied Declan. "She was getting used to being around people. She was . . . likable."

Gwen shook her head at Declan's choice of words. "She was always likable."

Hava said, "She was getting over her shyness?"

"Yes," said Declan, as Gwen nodded. "That's what I was trying to say."

"Badly," Gwen added with a rueful smile.

Hava laughed. "Maybe Millie just wants to be asked properly, not taken for granted."

Gwen nodded, indicating Declan. "This lout asked my father's permission to pay court."

Hava stole a sidelong glance at Hatu, who said, "I did with Hava's father." Then he stopped speaking, since embellishing the lie of who they were and Bodai being Hava's father was risky.

Gwen said, "Millie's got no family to ask, and I just supposed he'd asked her . . ." She laughed. "Did he?" she asked Declan.

Declan said, "I thought he did."

"Men," said Gwen to Hava, who nodded emphatically.

"Well, at least these two were trained right," said Hava with a laugh.

Declan and Hatu exchanged looks that suggested they had had enough of this conversation. Hatu asked, "You two staying for the evening meal, or just something to drink?"

Declan looked to Gwen, who said, "Millie and Jusan may need a lot of time to sort this out, so we'll stay for supper."

"An ale?" asked Declan of Gwen.

"I'd rather that wine Hatu fetched up from the city, assuming you still have some left?" she asked him.

"Still a few bottles. I'll bring up more next time. I didn't think we'd sell so much."

"Better stock up even more," said Gwen. "Much bigger turnout for the festival this year. Not just outlying farmers, but a lot of strangers."

"I've noticed," said Hatu. He glanced around the room, to see if any of his customers needed attention or someone new had entered. "I may have to hire someone, at least to help out around here while I head down to Marquenet for more of that wine and other supplies before the festival."

Hava said to Gwen, "I keep forgetting to ask about this festival and the wedding. I've seen weddings in a few places, but is there a traditional garb, or . . ." She shrugged. "If you know what I mean?"

"I do," said Gwen. "We'll talk when it's not so busy. No special dress, but you'll be expected to wear a flower garland . . ." She stopped herself with a laugh. "Later when it's less busy."

Hava smiled and nodded. "I better see to the kitchen."

"And I need to clear some tables," said Hatu.

Declan rose and said, "Let me lend a hand. I have something to ask you."

Gwen nodded as Declan looked to see if she objected, and Hatu tried not to laugh as Gwen remained, sipping her wine and apparently content to have Declan clear the tables. They were already acting like many married couples he'd met in his travels. Since fighting off the bandits on the road, Hatu found himself viewing Declan as more of a friend than anyone else who wasn't from Coaltachin.

A group of six travelers had left a moment before, so Hatu appreciated the help clearing away mugs and plates. At the sink behind the bar, Declan said, "Have you had any word from anyone about those two men who were here before our last trip to Marquenet?"

"No," he replied. "I think I heard they may have headed out to Port Colos." He studied Declan's face for a moment, then asked, "Why?"

"Just that the baron's man was curious as to why they were here." Declan paused, collecting his thoughts. "He suspects something; I don't know what." He looked around the common room, to see if they would be overheard, then added, "He wasn't surprised, I guess is what I'm trying to say. I said, 'These men turned up,' and his reaction was 'Oh, so they finally did,' or something like that." Declan put the last of the mugs into the sink to soak and said, "There is something going on, and I have a bad feeling about it."

Hatu's mind raced. He couldn't share what he'd done, communicating with his masters in Coaltachin that agents of other powers were investigating Beran's Hill, or that he served masters in distant nations. So he said, "If the baron thinks something is important about those two, I guess that means there is, right?"

Declan nodded. "And those two"—he lowered his voice—"baron's men . . ."

"Billy and Tucker," supplied Hatu.

"They've been gone a bit, too, right?"

"Left the day after the other two." Hatu's expression was thoughtful. "I think they headed for Port Colos as well."

Declan gave a wry chuckle. "I think the baron judged what I told him to be worthy of further investigation, enough to send his own men in disguise."

Hatu quickly washed the mugs in a barrel of soapy water, then dunked them into cleaner water for a rinse, and set them upside down on a drying rack. He motioned with his head as he picked up the bucket of rinse-water for Declan to follow him.

He dumped the water into a runoff gully he had dug to take such wastewater down the hill behind his property, then quickly moved to the well. As he cranked the handle to haul up a bucketful of fresh water, he said, "Which means the baron doesn't want us to push this further, I guess—right?"

Declan picked up the larger rinsing bucket and placed it on the edge of the well. "I suppose so."

Hatu filled it with fresh water and Declan chuckled. "Leon only changed the rinse-water when the customers complained about the ale tasting like soap."

Hatu grinned in return. "How often was that?"

"Not often," replied Declan. He started walking toward the kitchen door. "I think because he never used much soap."

Hatu laughed aloud at that, and once inside at the sink, he quickly finished rinsing the mugs. He and Declan returned to the table as Hava moved past them into the kitchen.

Hatu raised an eyebrow and she said, "It will quiet down soon, I think." She was gone before he could reply.

Hatu and Declan returned to Gwen, and soon, as Hava had predicted, it began to quiet. She returned, and the four friends had a relatively leisurely supper, Hatu having to leave only twice to see to customers.

They spent two hours dining and chatting, discussing the small matters that seemed important to the residents of Beran's Hill. Gwen seemed genuinely intrigued by gossip and rumors surrounding various people Hatu and Hava barely knew. Declan appeared attentive, but Hatu suspected it was more a matter of satisfying Gwen's need to be heard than any genuine interest in the topics. Hatu and Hava both listened closely, their interest being more about picking up hints of more significant matters than who was stealing berries from a neighbor's yard, who had bought a new horse, or who might be cheating on a spouse.

As the evening wound down, Declan said, "Jusan and Millie must have sorted whatever it is they need to sort by now. But one way or another, work is building up and I need sleep." He and Gwen stood up.

Hava and Hatu rose as well, and Gwen said, "And we need to plan for the festival. It's only a week off."

Hatu said, "I was going to ask about that. Do I need to open the inn after?"

"Not right after. There will be food and drink brought by people from the whole town on the meadows, but afterward some people will want to continue their celebration, so the inns in the town open. My father was always the first to do so." A momentary sadness crossed her face, then she brightened. "Nothing gets done on festival day, and not a lot more the day after," she added with a slight laugh. "Between now and then I suggest you stock up on as much ale, wine, and whisky as you can fit in here. This festival is going to be twice the size of last year's, I think, and that was the biggest I'd ever seen."

Hatu nodded his thanks. "Another journey to Marquenet then." He bade Gwen and Declan goodbye, then looked at Hava. Her gaze was distant: she was deep in thought. He wondered for a moment if she was already compiling a list of things he needed to bring up from the nearby city or whether she was speculating on who might be coming to kill them.

THE MUSICIANS STRUCK UP A merry tune that was unfamiliar to Hatu and Hava, but obviously a favorite of the crowd, who shouted their approval as many couples began to dance. Onlookers formed a circle to watch, many clapping along in time, as the midsummer festival officially commenced at noon. Hatu had taken his quick journey to Marquenet, bringing up all the goods and ale he could fit into one of Ratigan's largest wagons, and he and several of the local townsmen had brought a generous amount of ale and wine to the festival site, a clearing near the center of the town. Despite the unusual midday heat, everyone seemed ready to celebrate.

Hava cast a sidelong glance at Hatu, who stood across the "wedding circle," as a cleared area near the tables was called. It wasn't a circle as much as an irregular patch of flat land with a few stones placed around the edge. For some odd reason, the men and women who were going through the ceremony were supposed to wait apart from each other until called into the circle for the wedding.

Hava wore a dark green dress that brushed the tops of her feet. It suited her skin tone, and the high bodice, sleeves, and hem were edged with an intricate pattern of yellow stitching. On her head was a garland of flowers, tiny white blooms seeming to peek out of green leafy cups alternating with larger pink blossoms with red centers. Hatu had no idea what those flowers were called, but he thought they looked perfect. He thought she looked perfect.

Hatu glanced away from Hava, struggling with an old feeling, one not felt for a while, a hot seed of frustration that could evolve into a full-blown rage if not stemmed. The sudden appearance of this hint of fury surprised him, as he had not had to deal with it for months, not since taking the ship through the Narrows with Hava. He had thought himself "cured," and the return of the feeling troubled him. He tried to employ those mental exercises he had developed to put the rising anger to one side.

Playing the part of husband and wife, even with the contrived story that they had never been through a ceremony until now, had seemed at first a convenient ruse that enabled him to stay with her and serve Bodai's mission—whatever that might be—but actually going through a ceremony made it feel like something entirely different. He knew he loved Hava down to his bones and also hoped she felt the same way, but . . .

Declan asked, "Hatu, are you all right?"

Hatu forced a smile. "Sorry, just . . ." He glanced around, pushing down the rising turmoil within. "It's a big day, isn't it?"

The men stood together in their best clothes, which for some meant recently washed, but they all appeared ready for the ceremony. A man named Donald nodded. "My Mary says so, so it must be," he said, before taking a long pull on his mug of ale. He smacked his lips, foam in his mustache and beard, then added, "Don't see much reason myself, but she's very taken with these rituals and prayers from the Church."

Other men nodded, and Hatu gave a small shrug that could be taken as agreement. He knew he had a vastly different view of the Church of the One from that of these men. They simply saw the Church as a rising faith, with tenets that appealed to some of them, like eternal rest after life with no threat of the various specters of hell and torment offered by other faiths: the cold isolation of life without life, the flames of perdition, or the nothingness of a nameless void. Hatu knew the Church of the One had an agenda in league with sicari-like men called Azhante.

That name, whispered in the dark to him by Master Bodai, with the warning he was never to repeat it aloud to anyone but himself or Master Zusara, terrified Hatu. Because it was the only time in his short life he'd seen the otherwise imperturbable Bodai genuinely troubled, perhaps even fearful. Hatu felt that if the Church was in league with men who could do that, then the Church was to be feared.

Hatu shook off the distracting thoughts and returned to mastering his rising anger. He looked at Hava, who returned his gaze and barely shook her head, but he knew what she was silently saying to him: "Stop it! You're doing it again!" Remembering the scolding tone of her admonishments about not getting himself into pointless rages over things long past made him smile and his face relaxed. She blinked, then her face also transformed, revealing an expression of simple happiness that he had rarely seen in her.

Again he wondered at how much he loved Hava.

Declan glanced from Hatu to where Hava stood near Gwen and said, "Easy. It's going to be a long day."

"I think I just realized that," Hatu said ruefully. He watched Declan's gaze return to Gwen, who wore her best dress like the other women, in a light shade of blue she seemed to favor and that suited her fair skin and dark brown hair. He could tell from Declan's expression that he was still besotted by her. "Looks as if you just realized it, too," he said to Declan with a laugh.

A man named Joseph Rowe, who was showing signs he might not make it through the day, wobbled toward them. "Never understood this marriage business. My ma and da weren't wed, and for the life of me I can't understand why Jenny is so . . ." He lifted his mug and gulped ale, then shook his head a little.

"Easy there," said another man. "You need to be standing upright when the vows are spoken."

The other men laughed as someone managed to pull the almost empty flagon from his hand.

"Well," said Rowe, "got to keep 'em happy, right?"

Hatu tried not to laugh and failed. Declan joined in as another man said, "Here comes the priest."

Hatu glanced over and Declan said, "Monk, not priest."

"Does it matter?" asked a man named Hamed.

"Seems to," answered Declan. "Catharian always corrects people when they call him a priest. Seems that the Church has rules about such things."

"Well, as long as my Meli is satisfied we're properly married," added a man named Moji Trasti, "he can call himself a barnyard goose for all I care." He nodded toward Sabella, who was following close behind Catharian. "What do they call his girl?"

More chuckles, and Declan said, "He calls her 'Sister.'"

"That's his sister?" slurred another man. "I thought she was his daughter."

"Lover?" said another. More laughter followed.

Declan looked caught between amusement and annoyance. "Sister is her title. He's 'Brother Catharian' and she's 'Sister Sabella.'"

"Oh?" said Moji, clearly uncertain what had just been explained to him.

Catharian reached the center of the circle. He motioned for those about to be wed to come to him.

Hatu, Declan, and the others moved toward the false monk, while the women came from the other side. With a few hand gestures, he motioned for them to pair up in a circle around him. Then he raised his hand and motioned the onlookers to come closer so they could hear him.

After a moment, as people settled in and stopped talking, he said, "Today is the festival of midsummer, the brightest day of the year." He looked from face to face for a moment, then continued. "I've traveled a great deal, from lands half-way around Garn, and one thing we see in all people, no matter what other beliefs they may have, is their need for others: friends, family, a partner in life."

Catharian paused as if weighing his words, and then he looked at those gathered before him. "You've come here to wed, to bind your lives together, and before you do, we must ask why. Why have you chosen to spend the rest of your days with this one person, to hold that person's needs equal to your own? Why pledge yourself? Many don't. I have been to nations where marriage is arranged by parents and those who wed have no choice. I have visited nations where marriage is merely living together without anyone's consent. So why here, today, do we do this?

"Because we are seeing each pair of you make a vow before the world—or that part of it gathered here today," he added with a slightly wry tone, and the crowd laughed lightly in approval. "It is our way of saying to witnesses, 'This is what I feel, what I must share with the world, how dear I hold this other person in my life. That my life is not full without this partner.'"

Hatu glanced at Hava and saw that apart from a slight smile her face was otherwise expressionless. He noticed by contrast that Gwen was fighting back tears and Declan had what could only be called a silly grin on his face.

Catharian said, "I serve the Harbinger, who announced

the coming of the One, and in the Church there is no canon or ritual specific to marriage. Some members of the clergy are wed, others are not, and the only rules and rituals that apply are those in the places where those who wed choose to be married. The one truth held true is this: I put my partner before all others and will vow fidelity and commit to a lifetime together. Nothing more, for that is everything." He paused, looking around at them all, then declared, "Therefore, it is my place to announce to the gathered witnesses that those gathered here today are now wed!"

There was a moment's silence, then the crowd cheered loudly.

Hatu looked around, confused. Hava cupped his face between her hands, pulled his head toward her, and kissed him, long and deep. As he caught his breath, she said, "There, now we're married."

He grinned, unable to help it. "Now what?"

"Drinking, dancing, I expect," said Hava, snaking her arm through his as she turned to stand next to him. Pulling him close for a second, she added, "Then open the inn and stay busy all night is a good guess."

Music began as those who played struck up a lively tune. It was repetitive, without any obviously recognizable melody, but all those playing seemed to know it and managed to produce something enjoyable. Hatu saw a few newcomers with small drums, tambourines, and other instruments coming to join in, and in moments a dancing throng was moving rhythmically to the increasing volume of music.

Hava tugged at Hatu's arm. "Let's dance!"

His eyes widened. "I don't know how!" Of the many abilities he had been taught as a student in Coaltachin, dancing had been noticeably absent.

She laughed and kept tugging on his arm. "You put your

right arm up and your left hand on your hip and you jump around."

He watched the dancers as she moved him slowly forward and realized she wasn't entirely wrong. There seemed to be steps, a combination of two steps forward and one back and then a turn, but mostly it seemed there was a lot of jumping in time to the music.

He gave up trying to resist and let her take him to the edge of the dancers. He noticed that she had quickly picked up the steps to go along with the hand-in-the-air position, then noticed also that some of the men apparently had no sense of rhythm or any idea of the steps. Giving himself over to the inevitability of the day's festivities, Hatu assumed the position and leapt into the air.

He quickly got into the pattern of the steps and found a relationship between the rhythm of the music and the moves he made. Hava kept up with him, and seeing her smile filled him with what could only be called joy.

The afternoon became a blur. Musicians arrived and departed, as men who were playing danced and dancers played, and women sang songs both new and lovely to Hatu's ear, and there was a pattern to how it all unfolded, and he didn't care that he didn't recognize the pattern, and didn't become frustrated by not grasping how it all evolved, but just gave himself up to the moment, enjoying the wonder of it all.

Finally he felt in need of a rest and enfolded Hava in his arms and kissed her. "This is wonderful," he said with a grin.

She returned the grin. "We should get married more often."

Laughing, he nodded. "Or at least make sure we attend more weddings!"

After another blur of dancing, drinking, and conversations

quickly forgotten, Hava grabbed his arm. "You're having too much fun. We need to get back to the inn and get ready for a crowd."

Hatu's joy faded a little as he realized she was right. He took a deep breath and looked around, savoring the moment, as he understood he'd never feel its like again. As someone had once said, "You only get a first time once."

One of the town's boys ran up to Declan, his frantic appearance catching Hatu's eye. He motioned with his chin to Hava, who turned to see the boy gesturing to the east. Hatu looked at Declan, who spoke loud enough for those nearby to hear: "Riders!"

Hatu looked where the boy indicated, and while his view of the eastern road was blocked, he could make out enough dust to see they were only minutes from the festivities. He hurried to Declan, Hava a half step behind him.

As Hatu got nearer, he heard the boy say, "—not fast, but at a canter. They ride easy but there are a lot of them."

"How many?"

"I didn't count," said the boy. "Twenty, I think."

Declan noticed heads turning to see what was occurring and the music began to fall away. He waved his hand in the air, indicating the festivities should continue, then said to Hatu and the others nearby, "Quickly, but quietly, go home and fetch weapons. They may be peaceful, but a company that large is a threat. By ones and twos, no fuss. Keep the celebration going."

Hatu nodded and turned to Hava. "Do you know where Molly is?"

"With her dad. Festival makes him even sadder, so—"

"He's drunk again," finished Hatu. He had met Molly's father only once since coming to Beran's Hill and had the strong impression he'd met a man determined to drink himself to death. "Go get her and two bows. You're the two best archers we have."

Hava ran off and Hatu looked at Declan. "Let's welcome our visitors," said the young smith.

By the time Declan and Hatu reached the eastern edge of the crowd, the riders could be seen coming up the eastern road. As the boy had observed, they were coming at a leisurely canter, and as they came closer, their leader held up his hand in a casual signal and the company slowed to a trot.

Hatu counted seventeen riders. A quick evaluation of their gear indicated this was indeed a company of mercenaries, not soldiers in disguise. They reined in before Declan, and their leader said, "We too late for the festivities?" The men closest to him laughed.

Declan said, "It's midsummer. Everyone's welcome."

The leader dismounted and said, "I'm Bogartis." He pulled his right gauntlet off and offered his bare hand to Declan.

"Declan," came the response, and they shook. Hatu followed, and Bogartis glanced at the gathered townsfolk. He was a sturdy man with long brown hair that hung past his shoulders. His face was sunburned and he sported a pale scar on his left cheek. Dark eyes regarded the two young men and he asked, "I didn't see any posts nearby."

Declan glanced at Hatu and said, "No garrison here, just a militia."

"Pretty big town not to be garrisoned." Bogartis broke into a wide grin. "Well, we're not here for trouble, in any event, so it doesn't matter to us. I was looking out for my boys; sometimes garrison lads tend to start trouble with sellswords." He grinned again. "Tell me, Declan," he said, putting his hand on the young smith's shoulder, "there wouldn't be a nearby stable to put up weary horses before my men make free with your generous hospitality?"

Declan pointed him down the road and indicated the three places where he could stable his animals. Hatu noticed that the men who made up the core of the local militia had all returned with their weapons in hand but not displayed in a threatening manner. He was also sure Bogartis had noticed.

As the crowd returned to the festivities, Declan leaned over and said quietly to Hatu, "We need to keep a watch on these lads."

"Agreed," said Hatu. "They may have no ill intent, but they did look to see how well we can defend ourselves."

Hava appeared with a bow slung over her shoulder, with Molly Bowman a step behind. Next to her walked a heavyset man, Tomas Bowman, his bow over his shoulder. Hatu and Declan nodded greetings.

Tomas seemed sober—a rare condition, from what Hatu had heard—but his face revealed the damage drinking had caused since his wife's death. Hollow cheeks and deep bags under the eyes gave him a shrunken appearance, even though he was large of frame. His skin was pale from days away from the sun, and his clothing was disheveled.

"Couldn't have Da miss the celebrating," Molly said curtly.

"Do me some good to get out, I suppose," said Tomas, as he passed Declan and Hatu on his way to where the food and drink tables awaited.

Declan watched and saw Gwen waiting at the tables and said, "Best get back to my gal, else I'm courting trouble."

"I'll stay alert," said Hatu, glancing at Hava, who nodded in agreement.

"You two best tend to your inn soon," said Declan, turning and walking backward for a few steps. "Those mercenaries will be seeking more food and drink after today's tables are empty. And that's likely to be soon!" Then he pivoted and picked up his pace to run toward Gwen. He swept her up in his arms and spun her about as she laughed, pleased to have him back with her and no trouble in sight.

Hatu watched but his expression was somber.

Hava gripped his arm. "Calm before the storm?"

"My thoughts as well," replied her new husband.

She chuckled lightly and with a slight shake of her head observed, "Lovely day."

"So far," said Hatu. "Come, let's get home and make ready."

"Home," she echoed, as if the sound of it was both strange and reassuring.

As Gwen had predicted, many townspeople and visitors arrived at the Inn of the Three Stars after the food and drink were exhausted at the festival site. Enough of the townsfolk had gone home that the inn wasn't packed, but it was a lively crowd, mostly Bogartis's men, some cloth merchants up from Ilcomen, and a few young local lads who looked as if they would be feeling the full brunt of nasty hangovers the next day.

As Hava and Hatu saw to their customers, Declan and Gwen entered and came over to the bar. "We decided to stay out for a little while."

Hatu raised his eyebrows and asked, "Jusan and Millie?"

Gwen's expression was one of exasperation. "I'm at my wits' end. Millie said she didn't want to get married, and now that the ceremony's over, she's in tears because they didn't get married."

Hatu tried hard not to laugh. "Is it me, or is Millie a bit confused over what she wants?"

Declan made a sound halfway between exasperation and

resignation. "If this keeps affecting his work, I will have words with the lad."

Hava said, "Either way, ask Millie if she is ready to come back to work."

"Ask her yourself," said Hatu. "She just walked in."

The slender girl marched through the door and stopped in front of them. "I would like to go back to work," she said with as determined an expression as either had ever seen.

Hatu looked at Hava, who nodded. "Glad to have you back," she said. Glancing around the room, she added, "Get some more sausage and cheese from the cold cellar, please, and we'll keep this lot happy." To Hatu she said, "Better see what else we need." She hurried off to make the rounds of the tables.

"Well, that was unexpected," Hatu said to Declan. "Let me know what Jusan says when you find him."

Declan pushed up from the table and stood. "I will." Looking at his brand-new wife, he said, "I think we need to go home."

Gwen nodded, and the two of them started toward the door.

A scream from the kitchen froze everyone for a moment and the clamor in the inn fell away instantly. Both Hatu and Hava were at the kitchen door in seconds, Declan a step behind.

Entering, they saw Millie and one of the mercenaries from Bogartis's company holding up the man named Tucker, his face a mass of swollen lumps and cuts, his body drenched in blood. They lowered him to the floor, and Declan pushed past Hatu to kneel before the wounded man. Hava said, "Millie, there's a basket beneath the bar, next to—"

"I know where it is," she said, shaking visibly but somehow able to ignore her terror. She moved past a clutch of onlookers gathered at the door, saying, "Make way!" and pushed on through.

The mercenary asked, "Is my captain here?"

"No," said Hatu. "He's probably at one of the other inns nearby."

"I'm going to find him." The young fighter hurried out the kitchen door.

Catharian used the opening to dart past the others. "Can I help?"

Declan looked at him. "Can you?"

"I've treated more than my share of injuries," Catharian replied, kneeling down by Tucker.

As Declan made to move away, Tucker reached out and gripped his arm, pulling him down so that their faces were inches apart. Mustering what strength he could, the wounded soldier said, "Send word to the baron. They're coming."

"Who?" asked Declan.

"You know," said Tucker. "A hundred, maybe more. He—" His eyes rolled up and he lost consciousness.

Catharian looked at Declan and shook his head. Millie appeared with a large basket full of bandages, silk thread to stitch wounds, and some creams to prevent festering, but Catharian said, "He's not going to need them."

Declan paused for a moment, weighing his choices. Then he stood up, pushed his way through the door into the common room, Hatu and Millie a step behind him, and found a circle of faces staring at him. "Jason Green," he said to one. "Where's Peri?"

"Home, I guess," said the man.

"Peri Green's the fastest rider in town. Get word to the garrison at Esterly as quickly as you can. We're under attack."

The half-drunk man said, "We are?"

"We will be soon," said Declan, shoving him toward the door.

Hatu said, "Half the militia is drunk by now, and the other half is half drunk."

"That's why they're hitting us today. They knew it was the midsummer festival."

"Who?" said Hatu, as everyone began muttering.

"I can only guess. But the baron is sure to know."

"Those men?"

Declan nodded. "The two strangers who were asking all those questions before they went to Port Colos? I'm certain they had something to do with this."

"Who's going to Marquenet?"

"We need another fast rider, and two horses."

Hava appeared. "I'm fast," she said. "I can change mounts at a gallop."

Declan's eyebrows rose.

"My father was a horse trader," she reminded him.

"The baron might not listen to you," said Declan. "I should go. He knows me."

"You need to stay and organize the defense," said Hava. "The baron knows me as well."

"He does?"

"I'll explain later," said Hatu. Turning to his wife, he said, "Ride, and be careful."

"I need to borrow some horses." Without another word she hurried from the inn.

Declan pushed past a pair of men to where Gwen waited. "What's happened?" she asked.

"That fellow, Tucker, who helped a while back with the bandits." With a tilt of his head he indicated the kitchen.

Millie said, "He's dead."

Declan gripped Gwen's arm and said quietly, so as not to frighten her, "Go home, gather what you can easily carry, then flee south. Jusan should hitch the horse to the two-wheeled cart, and you and Millie should ride—you weigh less—and he should saddle my horse. Get on the road south as fast as you can."

His calm, even tone implied that this was not a subject for any debate and Gwen nodded. "You're coming?"

"I will find you as soon as I can," he said. He kissed her and then said, "Go."

After she was out the door, Declan stood on a chair so he could see everyone in the room. "Go home!" he shouted. "Get weapons. Anyone who can't fight should head south as soon as possible. Take with you as little as you can. Anyone who can't flee should hide, away from the town. We're going to be raided."

"What?" said a very drunk man in the back.

"We're about to be raided!" shouted Declan, fully appreciating why the attack was coming near sundown on midsummer's day. Even when organized the local militia would be overwhelmed by trained soldiers, but when drunk they'd hardly offer any resistance.

The room erupted into a babble of questions. Declan motioned for them to settle down, and when his palms-down gestures were ignored, he finally shouted, "Quiet!"

The chatter diminished but didn't entirely go away. Some of the men who'd fetched weapons when the mercenaries had arrived still had them at their belts. "Those of you who are armed, get outside and stay alert. Those of you who are unarmed, go home, get your weapons, and get back as soon as you can."

"Who are we fighting?" shouted one man.

"Whoever shows up!" replied Hatu, short-tempered because of the dithering and because he knew Hava was riding into harm's way, even though of any woman in Beran's Hill she was the most capable of defending herself.

"Where are they coming from?"

Up to this moment Declan and Hatu had assumed that any attack would come from the east, but they realized that both the two mysterious men who had been asking questions around town and the two who followed them, Tucker and Billy, had traveled west.

Declan said, "Almost certainly from the west, from Port Colos!"

A voice from Declan's left shouted, "You have the right of it, lad!"

The mercenary leader, Bogartis, was standing in the doorway with his sword drawn. "The raiders are already here!"

6

DESTRUCTION,

ABDUCTION, AND RAGE

Declan's sword was in his hand instantly, and Hatu produced a dagger seemingly out of nowhere. Bogartis held up his left hand, palm out, and let his sword point drop down. "Hold a minute, lads. They're not behind me just yet."

"Say on," Declan said.

"I never stay in a town without a local garrison or sheriff without putting a lad on guard. That fellow over there"—he pointed to the kitchen—"came down the road barely hanging on to his horse's mane, and the horse was in a lather. My lad saw him fall from the saddle, but before he staggered here he said there's a small army heading this way."

"From the west?" asked Declan.

"Yes," said Bogartis. "The eastern road was quiet as a mouse in hiding as we rode all the way from the middle of the Wild Lands. Don't need any sentries to the south, because your baron keeps things in order. So I rotated a few lads to watch to the west and north, in case. This bunch is coming from the west."

"From Port Colos?" asked Hatu.

"Almost a certainty," said Bogartis. "We were heading

that way. Word was passed a few months ago someone was assembling an army there. Good pay was the rumor, and things are either crazy in the east or too quiet for a mercenary company, so we thought we'd see about this army building in Port Colos."

Declan and Hatu exchanged glances, and Hatu said, "We can speculate about what happened later." Looking at Bogartis, he said, "Are you staying?"

"I fight for money, lad, and we'll be on our way in a bit, heading south to the baron's shelter."

"We have money," said Declan.

"Oh. And what do you propose?"

"I can pay you a gold weight per man if you stay and fight."

"Now that's not a bad offer," said Bogartis, rubbing his chin. "One fight should do it, give your folks time to flee . . ."

"I'll make it two," said Hatu, "if you stay until we drive them off."

"You have a bargain," said the mercenary captain. "Glad to help, as I wasn't looking forward to a night ride anyway, and you folks have been lovely hosts." He grinned. "Besides, my lads would be drunk and picking fights in a few hours anyway."

Declan asked, "Did your lookout see how many were coming?"

"No, he was smart enough to run away when he heard them. A force that big on the march makes a lot of noise."

Declan looked at Hatushaly and then at Bogartis, his face revealing confusion. "That man, Tucker, said maybe a hundred. What do we do?" he asked.

Hatushaly looked at the old fighter.

"Well, here's what will certainly happen. If it's as big a force as that fellow thought, they're not here for a fast raid. They'll not go past to Esterly, north to Copper Hills, or south into the barony. They're coming here." His expression showed no uncertainty. "The buildings will be ransacked, a few even burned out of spite. They'll grab everything they can of value and turn back to Port Colos, is my thinking.

"By the time the baron's men get here, they'll be back under whatever protection the governor of Port Colos has sold them, or on ships sailing off to somewhere distant." He glanced at both younger men. "You've already sent the children and those who can't fight out of here, right?"

Declan nodded.

"Then know this: it's better to survive and rebuild than to die trying to protect something you can't save. Now there's two ways to do that. What's the best building to defend in town?"

Without hesitation, Declan said, "My smithy. One large door we can jam, leaving only a small one they would have to come through one or two at a time."

"Fire?"

"The wood is treated, because forges get hot," Hatu said. He had helped Declan paint an entire wall with some foul concoction that would ensure the wood smoldered but didn't burst into flame. He'd used the same mixture on the roof of the inn afterward.

"If they're just looking for loot, making it painful to root you out might make them just take what they can carry and leave. They'll burn some buildings if you annoy them enough. And that would give those fleeing south more time to get clear."

"You said two ways." Declan looked into Bogartis's eyes. "What else?"

"Well, this whole thing troubles me. You don't need an army to raid this town, lad. Yes, you've got a militia, and from what little I've seen some of your lads might put up a good fight, which suggests they'd be better leaving you alone. But a hundred men or more isn't just raiding. I think they mean to take this town and hold it." He paused again, then said, "Someone is trying to send your baron a message, and a brutal one at that. It's an invitation for him to ride out here to retake this town."

Hatu and Declan exchanged glances again, then Hatu said, "Whatever happens between our baron and any foe isn't what concerns us right now. What does concern me right now is our best chance to survive."

"There's an old saying," replied Bogartis. "When elephants fight, mice do best by hiding."

Declan said, "No." He weighed his words. Finally, he said, "If someone wants to insult our baron, they wouldn't take this town and invite attacks from the south and east and maybe from the north if Baron Dumarch gets word to Copper Hills." He shook his head. "They don't mean to take this town. I think they mean to raze it. They'll burn every building and kill as many as possible, then invite the baron to chase them to Port Colos. They know something we don't, and I think they have something waiting there."

Bogartis considered this for a moment, then said, "Interesting."

Hatu said, "Can we . . . return insult for insult?"

Bogartis's face revealed a wry smile and he gave a bitter chuckle. "I like your stance, youngster, but there's only one way to defeat a larger force."

"How?" asked Declan.

"You've got to surround them, so those in the middle can't fight, and you whittle them down from the edges, like a blade on a twig."

"And there are too many of them," said Declan.

"What if we box them in?" asked Hatu.

"How do you mean?" said Bogartis. "Quickly, time is short."

"If we can tempt them past the edge of the town, get them to turn south and then again east on the old—" began Hatu.

"They'll be boxed in!" Declan almost shouted.

"There's three warehouses," added Hatu, "with no doors, just high windows and—"

"Archers on the roofs keeping them far enough away from setting fire to the building!" Declan said. "Molly!" he shouted, knowing she'd be nearby.

Molly Bowman pushed her way through the onlookers, her father a step behind her.

Declan said to Bogartis, "How many archers do you have?"

"I've four lads who are serious with a bow and two who will do some damage in a crowd."

"Molly," said Declan, "get down to Crawford's and take his men with you and your da. Get up on the roofs, and make sure the doors from the street at Alice Hardy's store are barricaded."

"Eight decent archers can do a lot of damage," said Bogartis, nodding his approval. "Now, how do we get them into the snare?"

Hatu didn't look happy, but he said, "I'll be bait. I'll lead a half dozen of the fastest runners to the intersection to the north, where the western road to Port Colos meets Three Stars Road. We sting them, run like hell, and when we get to the dead end . . ."

Catharian elbowed his way through the press around those planning the defense and said, "I'll pull you up with a rope!" He looked from face to face and said, "My order forbids me from fighting, but I can't abandon those I am charged to care for, so I can aid in your escape."

"Rig up enough ropes to pull up four at a time, and secure one at the trapdoor in the roof if we have to get out in a hurry.

There's a door that leads out to open pasture and woods. You'll find plenty of ropes and spikes in the warehouse."

Catharian nodded and hurried off with a pair of men.

Hatu singled out two young men, barely old enough not to be considered boys, and said, "Start passing the word throughout town: everyone who's not staying to fight heads south, fast. They only have minutes. Those who can't travel far, head for the farms to the east. Those who can't move, carry them!"

Declan looked at the boys Hatu had picked, who were pale with worry but trying to look determined as they held weapons they barely knew how to use.

"Once you've spread the word, go to the south edge of town, and when everyone has passed, follow them."

When one of the lads seemed on the verge of objecting, Declan said, "You're their last defense. Keep them safe until you run into the baron's soldiers. Then you can turn around and get back here with them as fast as you can."

The two lads glanced at each other, nodded, and hurried off to do as instructed.

Declan looked around and saw Molly Bowman. "You're not heading for the roofs?"

She said, "You'll need me if you're going to get their attention. My da is still pretty sober: he'll do some serious harm until I get there." Hatu knew Molly well enough to not argue with her even if he was so inclined. She was the best archer in the town and probably as tough as anyone else. He suspected that only Hava could have held her own against her among the women of Beran's Hill.

Declan nodded and said, "Hatu, get to where you need to be."

Hatu studied the face of each of them in turn, those who remained to act as bait for the raiders. "Ready to run?"

"As if a wounded bear were chasing us," Molly replied.

Declan and the other men in the inn put together a hastily concocted order of battle: who would charge, who would stand back, and who would stand in reserve to plug holes should they appear. At last the young smith looked to Bogartis. "Ready as we'll ever be."

"When you come out, hit them hard," said the older mercenary. "You want to keep them bunched up as long as you can so the ones in the middle of the group can't fight, but if they push back hard enough and you break, then run like hell. Don't just try for the south; head anywhere there's open space in front of you."

"Understood," said Declan as he led the men out of the inn.

Hatu organized his small group and went outside, turning north on Three Stars Road as a large dark-skinned man rode past him. For a moment he thought it was one of Bogartis's men, given that he was obviously a fighter from his chain hauberk and sword. Then he noticed he wore a tabard in the same design as Catharian's and Sabella's. For a brief instant he was troubled by something, then he pushed that thought aside and waved for his band to follow. They hurried up the street to the intersection of what was becoming known as Three Stars Road, now that the inn had turned into a center of activity, and the western road leading to Port Colos.

With Hava gone, Hatu was perhaps one of the top archers in the town, after Molly and her father, so he looked at the other four young men. "Molly and I will shoot, so they'll be a good bowshot's distance away when they come after us. If they're on foot, make a brief show, wait a moment, then run south past the inn. Get out of sight as fast as you can. You know where to gather?"

The four nodded, their faces showing their fear despite their attempts to look stalwart.

"Hold fast for a moment, then run like devils were behind you," Hatu repeated, "because they will be."

To Molly he said, "Two shots."

"I can do three while you do two," she said with confidence.

He couldn't help smiling. "A contest?"

"Some other time."

Hatu turned to the others. "If they're mounted, don't wait. The moment you see horses, run."

Less than five minutes went by before Hatu heard the approaching band of soldiers. At first it was a faint sound of horses over a steady thud of boots. With surprising speed, that sound grew louder by the moment—the creaking of leather, the clink of metal, and the steady tread of boots on hard ground in counterpoint to the staccato hoofbeats.

In the dark of night the torchlight coming through shop windows and doorways gave Hatu and his companions some illumination, yet the sound seemed to come from different directions. Hatu knew it was a confusion of echoes as the sound from the approaching raiders grew louder.

Then torchlight appeared in the distance, coming out of the gloom. For a moment that seemed suspended in time it felt as if the universe held its breath.

Then a wall of armed men was heading straight at them. They marched at a quick pace, but the moment they caught sight of the defenders the front rank broke into a run. Hatu's mind wrestled for clarity amid the muddle of sound and images in front of him; then he heard Molly loose her first arrow.

Training took over and Hatu raised his own bow and also let fly. The oncoming men were packed so close together in a marching column, flanked on either side by riders, that he was certain his shaft would strike true. A horse gave a roar, a sound Hatu had heard only once before, almost a human cry of pain as it collapsed. Again, Hatu nocked a shaft and shot, but he didn't wait to see if his target fell.

He was the last to turn, as Molly had loosed her third

shaft and was now one step ahead of him, the other four lads a half dozen paces beyond. As they had been told, the four younger fighters raced to the next street, past the Inn of the Three Stars, and instead of turning left, they turned right and to the west.

Hatu and Molly reached the intersection, and Molly ducked to the left while Hatu stopped and turned, ensuring that the first of those behind could clearly see him as he fled. He waited as four riders came hurtling toward him, blindly shot an arrow in their general direction, then darted toward the waiting ambush.

If all was going according to plan, the one door to his left, facing the street, leading into the back of Alice Hardy's storeroom, would now be blocked off from the inside. Hatu saw that Molly had already reached one rope and was being hauled up to the roof while she pulled herself hand over hand, her bow slung across her back.

Hatu slung his bow and leapt, propelling himself upward with a boot on the wall as he grabbed the remaining rope. And then he was being pulled up and he made a concerted effort to hang on. Glancing down, he realized it was a good thing he was being pulled up, as a rider had just wheeled his mount to the left and was trying to reach up and grab his boot. Missing that, he grabbed at the rope, and Hatu felt a sudden jerk that almost caused him to lose his grip. Hatu avoided the man's wild sword blow and kicked out, grazing the top of the man's bare head.

An arrow sped past, missing Hatu by a scant enough margin that he felt the wind of it, and it took the rider between his neck and shoulder, knocking him backward out of the saddle. Hatu barely had time to turn his attention upward when he was yanked across the eaves of the roof.

The reason for his rapid ascent was made clear when he saw that four people had been hauling his rope. By the time he stood and unshouldered his bow, the archers were shooting almost blindly down into the blocked street. The attackers were packed together so tightly it was impossible not to hit someone.

Hatu saw that those who were only just arriving at the intersection were being held up by warnings from those within the U-shaped trap. He was trying to take down the remaining half dozen riders that he could make out in the faint and flickering torchlight when a shout erupted from the other side of the street.

The remaining mercenaries from Bogartis's company charged from where they had hidden in the dark, the captain on his horse so he could see over their heads and give orders. Behind the fighters came the men of Beran's Hill, armed with everything from swords to scythes and pitchforks. In an open field, they would have been slaughtered, but the advantage of surprise and close quarters made for an even fight.

Hatu heard Molly say, "I'm out of arrows!"

He took off his half-full quiver and tossed it to her. "Here!"

She caught it as Hatu looked for a way down without trying to climb down the rope into the fray. He noticed the monk, Catharian, motioning him over. Hatu found him standing over a trapdoor in the roof. "Into this warehouse and around to the end door!" Catharian shouted. "You can circle around and join Bogartis from behind."

Hatu saw that ropes had been affixed to the roof by a spike, and he lowered himself down. At the bottom, a dim figure waited, and it wasn't until Hatu was standing next to him that he recognized the big dark-skinned man he had seen riding past earlier, wearing the same tabard as Catharian.

Hatu realized what had bothered him before: Catharian had said that his order forbade armed conflict, but this fellow sported a hauberk and a sword. Then the man said, "Sorry," and Hatu barely saw the man's fist as it struck him hard.

For a second, lights exploded in Hatu's vision, then he fell unconscious.

DECLAN STOOD FAST BETWEEN TWO of Bogartis's men, and for the third time in his life everything seemed to slow down. He took in the men opposite him, ragged mercenaries of all stripes, and by their look from many distant lands. Despite the struggle for survival, he noticed a dark-skinned man with a gem piercing the side of his nose, a tall blond man, and a bearded soldier with a two-handed sword—hampered by those pressing close around—who shouted in a language Declan did not recognize.

He saw an attack aimed at the man on his right out of the corner of his eye and raised his sword and blocked it, while the intended target was busy with a man directly opposite him. Declan's moves seemed normal to him, yet those around him seemed to be getting slower by the moment, and he did awful damage to those he could reach. A cut to a shoulder, followed by a jab to the ribs where a quilted jack had ridden up, and one man's leg cut from below the knee, forcing him to the ground, and a swift killing blow.

Time lost meaning, as it had before for Declan when he was in the grip of battle clarity. He sensed what was around him more than he saw shapes or heard sounds, and he felt focused rage, as if his mind had become a weapon as well as the sword he held in his hand. He seemed to know where to turn, how to hold his blade, when to lash out, and when to guard, not only himself but those companions standing close to him.

The struggle waged on for what seemed like hours, though Declan knew in truth it was mere minutes. A balance between the defenders and the invaders held, as those trapped in the street between the warehouses were unable to use their superior numbers against the less-well-trained townsmen. Still, the defenders were fighting for their homes, which gave them a fury the invaders lacked. The attackers had apparently expected little or no significant resistance as their comrades fell around them; a sense of desperation was on the rise.

Then Declan became conscious that something was wrong. Just as he stepped back and looked toward the north end of Three Stars Road, he heard Bogartis shout, "Beware your left!"

An instant later, Declan saw more riders charging down the street. "Everyone leave now!" Declan shouted.

Bogartis echoed the order. "Flee! Scatter!"

It took little to convince the townsmen to turn and run, with the mercenaries and Declan acting as a rearguard for a few moments to allow them to escape. Declan felt no panic. He heard the riders approaching and switched from aggression to defense, then without anticipating it he lashed out at a man opposite him in what looked to be a predictable attack, causing the man to leap back, and before the man had regained his balance, Declan turned and ran.

He knew he had only seconds to get off the street, or riders would be running him down from behind, so he bore to his left, knowing the bulk of those trapped in the alley who still survived would be spilling out into the street, giving him seconds more to avoid the horses, as they would have to slow down and circle around their comrades. He was going to need every instant he could squeeze from this fight if he was going to survive.

Declan knew he couldn't outrun a horse, but he could dodge where it couldn't follow, and he leapt over a stack of crates at the corner of the last alley in Beran's Hill. He chanced a glance behind him and saw that the riders were slowing as they dealt death to any citizen of the town they could find. The sky was lightening with a yellow glow, and he realized the raiders were putting the town to the torch.

For a brief moment, hot anger flashed through him, and he felt a rising bitterness in his mouth, as if he was going to vomit, but he choked it down. This was the baron's fault. He'd been told the town was at risk, but his concern over costs in gold had resulted in a horrific cost in blood.

Declan pushed aside his sudden anger at Daylon Dumarch and took a breath, pausing for a moment to gather his wits. This tiny respite allowed him to see a path beyond the end of the alley, where a building built on the south side of the alley narrowed the passage. He could run through it, but no horse could. Beyond were farms and orchards, places he might shelter until his next choice presented itself.

He hurried toward his goal, the chance of escape giving him new energy. He was less than two strides from his objective when a searing pain erupted in his right shoulder, as an arrow struck with enough force to spin him completely around. He fell facedown into damp soil, his body in agony and the wind knocked out of his lungs. He forced himself to breathe and found the effort caused more pain, and then his vision went foggy.

In a half-numb state, he barely understood what was happening when hands grabbed him, the movement causing more pain in his shoulder and back. He heard the twang of a bowstring's release, and agony erupted as someone fell on top of him, and then there was nothing but darkness.

DECLAN LAY IN A WORLD of hurt. When he concentrated on it, he could feel it in his right shoulder, running down the right side of his body to his hip. He could barely breathe for it, and for a time—seconds, minutes perhaps—he lay motionless, forcing his wits to work out what was happening.

He forced his eyes to open, despite a demand coming from somewhere inside urging him to stay motionless. Above him he saw open sky and the faint grey of a coming dawn, perhaps a half hour before sunrise. But something about it didn't look right.

"So, back with us?" came the deep rumble of Bogartis's voice.

"Where am I?" asked Declan, his voice a faint, dry croak.

Hands gripped Declan and helped him sit up. Pain shot through him, and his vision swam as he fought off losing consciousness. Someone held a waterskin to his mouth and he took a drink.

"Slowly," urged Bogartis. "It won't do you any good to spit it back up."

Declan sipped and, after a few swallows, grunted that he had had enough.

"Where—" he began, but the pain came again.

"You're a mess, lad, and lucky to be alive."

Declan nodded and even that hurt.

"We're hiding behind a wall a short walk from the town, waiting for those bastards to leave. They won't linger much longer, as they know the garrison from Esterly and the baron's army from the south will show up around midday, I should think."

"When's the sun rising?" Declan croaked.

Bogartis's face came into his field of vision as the mercenary captain shifted his position and looked into Declan's eyes. "Can you see?"

"It's hazy," said Declan. "Sunrise soon?"

"Sun's been up for a few hours, lad," said Bogartis. "It's dark from the smoke."

"Smoke . . ." Declan sighed, ignoring the pain in his back.

Bogartis moved out of Declan's field of vision so that the young smith could see the smoking ruins of a small farmhouse. "You had the right of it, son. This was no raid; this was a declaration of war. They've burned everything."

"Everything?" Declan croaked.

"If it wouldn't burn, they pulled it down. Never seen anything like it. Your smithy resisted the fire, but even that is nothing more than a charred husk now."

"The people?"

"Those bastards chased down a lot of them, sorry to tell you," said Bogartis, waving one of his men over. "Two of my boys fell, and three—" He held out his hand, palm down, and made a rocking motion. "Might be down to twelve of us by the time the baron gets here."

Declan let the news sink in. Everything he had worked for since arriving in Beran's Hill was gone. The gold hidden in the forge was almost certain to have been found, and only the anvil, some of the tools, and fittings for the bellows were likely to have survived the fire, unless the heat of the flames robbed them of their temper. "Gwen?" he asked.

"Your girl?"

"My wife," said Declan.

"Don't know, lad. Some of those heading south might have made it before the bastards took after them. I doubt they ventured too far to the south, fearing the baron's patrols." He tried to sound reassuring but failed.

"What about Hatu? Last I saw he was climbing to the roof."

One of the mercenaries said, "A wounded boy, don't know his name, said the lad who played fox to the raiders' hounds was carried off."

"Carried?" said Declan, trying not to cough. He accepted another sip of water. "He was wounded?"

"Maybe. The boy told me he was slung over the shoulder of a big black man wearing the same tabard as those robes the priest and his girl wore."

Declan didn't know if he could make sense of that. "The priest . . . You mean monk. Brother Catharian and his beggar girl."

"And a big fellow wearing armor. Looked like a soldier, the boy said. Then he died."

"Hatu?"

"No, the boy who told me," said the mercenary.

"When the baron's men turn up, we can sort all this out," said Bogartis. "Hope he has a healer with him. We stopped your bleeding and put a rough patch on the wound, but you need proper tending."

Declan had no argument with that. As desperate as he was to know that Gwen was safe, and almost as concerned about Jusan, Millie, Hatu, and Hava, he was as weak as a newborn kitten. Fatigue was causing his eyes to go unfocused and his lids were getting heavy.

Soon he was asleep.

7

LOSS AND DETERMINATION

Hava tried to rein in her impatience along with her horse; the horse responded, but the desperate anxiety within did not. The baron's man Balven had recognized her at once and heeded her warning. It had been barely more than an hour before she rode out of the city on a fresh horse with a vanguard of soldiers, a single squad of only thirty men, but they were castellans, the baron's very best personal company. A full company of garrison soldiers with two recruited squads of mercenaries would follow within half a day.

Her body ached from exhaustion and stress, for she had ridden two horses into the ground and had eaten only a few bites fetched from the kitchen for her while the cavalry mustered to ride to Beran's Hill. While it usually took more than a full day by slow wagon, she had made the journey in less than half that time, leaving at sunset and arriving before dawn the next morning.

As they crested a hill in the late afternoon, they saw the first signs of the conflict. Birds circled above the town. Bodies lay in the road some distance ahead. Even before Hava could react, the two point riders had urged their horses to a gallop, and by the time Hava caught up they were already circling among the dead, their approach driving off the carrion eaters.

One of the riders told the other, "Let the captain know," and to Hava he said, "Looks like they were cut down while fleeing."

Hava's stomach tightened and for an instant her head swam. Bodies lay sprawled in the dirt, most facedown with wounds to the head, shoulders, or neck, having been struck from behind by riders wielding swords or maces. A few had turned to face their attackers, perhaps begging for mercy at the last moment; now their eyes stared blankly up at the afternoon sky, if they still had eyes. She recognized some of the closest, not by name, but she was sure she'd seen them around town.

Hava forced down a fear that had been inside her ever since she had started her race to Marquenet, but something else lingered: a revulsion that was new to her. She'd seen death before, had even killed an attacker with her own hands, but this was a slaughter of people who had done no harm, who were merely living in the wrong place. She started to look for Hatu among the bodies, then immediately scolded herself, for she was sure he would not have run away but would have remained to the last. She wondered if anyone had survived this attack. Who had pursued these poor souls so far from the battle?

The captain of the company, whose name she had yet to ask, came to where Hava waited with the remaining scout and asked, "From Beran's Hill?"

Hava could barely speak for a moment, her gorge rising as it had after killing the spy whom she had confronted at the School of the Powdered Women. She swallowed hard, refusing to vomit, and said, "I recognize some of them. Yes, they are from the town."

"How far?" he asked the scout.

Before the soldier could respond, Hava said, "Less than half an hour if we push hard."

The captain was a man of middle years, an experienced soldier who was at ease with being in charge. He gave Hava a brief nod and said, "Then we'll push hard." He looked over his shoulder and with a wave of his arm shouted, "Forward at the gallop!"

Hava didn't wait but pulled her mount around and heeled its flanks hard, and in three strides the animal was racing down the road. She heard the squad of riders behind her and knew they were doing the same, but she didn't spare an instant for a look back. All she cared about was what lay ahead.

Sparing the horse took all her self-control. The horse's breathing had become labored, and she knew by the sound of him that he was going to need days to recover. To overtax his stamina put him at risk of permanent injury, so after a few minutes at a gallop she reined him down to a canter. Every moment was agony, but Hava focused on her need to reach Hatu.

She pushed aside her fears and reviewed her duties to her masters. Whatever happened in Beran's Hill, she would need to return to Marquenet quickly to send a message. No matter what she felt for Hatushaly, the masters of Coaltachin would want to know as much as she could relay about this attack: who was behind it, how it had happened, and—probably most important of all—what Baron Dumarch's response would be. Every fiber of her being told her that some larger scheme was in place, and this was just the prelude to war on a wider scale.

Smoke covered the sky to the north like a massive canopy, transforming a bright afternoon into a gloomy overcast one. Every breath she took tasted of char. As she topped the last hill before the long rolling meadows that led to the town, she saw more bodies, and the identities of those who had stayed too long before attempting to escape struck her hard. Old and young women, elderly men, children, many who appeared to have been trampled by horses, lying in contorted positions. Blood stained the ground in every direction, so that even the greenest grass bore a reddish-brown tinge. Hava didn't even try to count the corpses; there were simply too many.

Despite her young age, she had seen more blood and death than most, yet this was different. She had come to know these people. She was unsettled by her feelings, which were strange to her, as she had seen death since her child-hood, but the people she had seen dead before had been en-emies. None of these people were her enemy.

Hava took a deep breath and collected herself. She was certain of one thing: this hadn't been a simple raid for what could quickly be carried off, but a deliberate wholesale slaughter.

She urged her exhausted horse to move as quickly as possible, passing the smaller farms that surrounded Beran's Hill.

The view on all sides refused to resolve itself, confus-ing Hava as she sought familiar landmarks and found none. What should have been a tidy shepherd's cottage on the other side of a small rill, which became a swollen stream in heavy rain, was missing. A square of charred soil topped by a pile of still-smoking ash and embers had taken its place.

Gone were the colorful roofs of tile, thatch, and painted wood, so what had once been little bright boxes in the dis-tance were now black dots and burned-out patches of land. She could mark their locations from the rising smoke that dotted the hills and meadows on both sides of the road.

As she reached what should have been the edge of the town, Hava pulled up. It took a few moments for her to get her bearings; there were no familiar landmarks left, just smoking rubble in every direction. Beran's Hill was no more.

She had imagined all manner of things on her ride for help: returning to find a battle-scarred town, perhaps one still besieged. But while she had considered many possibilities, this complete and utter destruction had not been one of them. A scream of protest lurked, barely in check, a reaction to the sheer savagery of the attack.

She had seen evil, had even contributed to it, according to the requirements of her masters, but this was something far more vile. This was the obliteration of an entire population . . .

"Hatu!" she shouted without thought, a frantic panic rising so rapidly she could barely draw a deep enough breath to shout his name a second time. "Hatu!" she repeated, but only a breeze carrying the stench of burned flesh and charred wood answered.

The advance riders from the city were overtaking her, so she put heels to her horse's flanks and moved deeper into the destruction, thinking she heard voices ahead. But as she urged her mount forward she realized that the exhausted animal was almost staggering. When she paid attention she heard the wheezing when he breathed and realized he might be ruined, for if his lungs were damaged, he would be useless. At best she would have counted it a waste of a valuable horse, but at this moment she just didn't care.

She dismounted, leaving the drained animal to his own devices, and hurried on foot toward the faint sounds. She saw movement through the haze and pushed on, only holding back slightly because an inner voice was warning her to be cautious.

A few baronial soldiers were already here, from the garrison at Esterly, Hava assumed. She walked quickly through a dense cloud of choking smoke from a wall of smoldering wood nearby, her eyes tearing up from the acrid sting. She ignored the stench of burned human flesh and focused her attention on what was ahead, forcing her now-numbed mind to reject understanding what lay around her. She walked past Three Stars Road before realizing she had done so, paused for a confused moment, then turned back, fighting tears that threatened to blind her even more than the smoke had.

The charred corpses of those seeking to flee the flames were scattered all around. Hava turned in a full circle, uncertain of which way to go, then for a painful moment stood motionless and screamed, "Hatu!" Fear rippled through her body.

A few of the soldiers near enough to hear her turned to see what that shout was. A couple called out but she didn't understand what they said. Tears welled and spilled, and she cried, "Hatu!" again and again.

She tried to get her bearings, but the rubble on all sides and the few surviving smoking walls gave her no sense of place. Overwhelmed by grief and rising panic, she almost collapsed, barely keeping herself upright. Every lesson learned on how to distance her feelings and retain her wits had fled. She was at sea and rudderless, confused and lost. She sobbed and fought to catch her breath.

After a while her training finally took over. She stared at a single point on the ground, a charred rock, and forced herself to center that rock in her mind and shut out the cascade of sorrowful images on every side. She took control of her breathing, slowing it down, and stood motionless for long seconds. Then she lifted her chin and looked slowly around, allowing the full horror to wash over her, but letting it "go through her," as she had been taught, not permitting herself to grapple with it, hold on to it, or let it linger and rob her of her abilities.

Slowly the panic and horror faded, and she pushed down her feelings. In less than two minutes she felt somewhat back in control.

A man with a sword, not a soldier, appeared in front of her. "You the innkeeper's wife?"

It took a moment for the question to register, and Hava nodded.

"I thought it was you. Come with me," he said, turning without another word.

Hava followed him. She thought she recognized him as one of the company that had arrived during the festival . . . Had that only been yesterday? It felt like a week ago. She knew the captain's name, but for the moment couldn't recall it.

Hava followed the fighter to a hastily erected shelter near a low wall, four poles providing support for a large canopy of heavy cloth, rigged up as a field infirmary. A healer had ridden with the company from Esterly and he was already tending to a dozen men resting on makeshift pallets of blankets and straw.

The one uninjured man other than the healer was the mercenary leader. He was standing over Declan, who was apparently sleeping. He motioned for Hava to come with him, while the soldier who escorted her left to return to his post.

She approached and said, "Captain . . ."

"Bogartis," he reminded her.

"Yes, Bogartis," she repeated weakly.

"You look like you could use the medic's attention yourself," he said when she came up close.

She shook her head. "I thought . . ." Her eyes betrayed her confusion, the inability to organize what she saw into a coherent whole that could be understood. She could only whisper, "What happened?"

"Someone turned an army loose here, girl."

"Who?"

"Hard to judge. I just go where there's money for fighters and don't pay much attention beyond that. There are a few truly evil bastards I won't serve, but I have worked for my share of mean ones in my day. I've fought for and against the same rulers over the years. But this . . ." He glanced around the ruins of the town. "Whoever did this is someone who wanted Baron Dumarch to know something."

"What?"

"That his trap wouldn't work."

"Trap?"

"Your baron wanted someone to attack Beran's Hill, almost for certain, but on the baron's terms when the baron was ready. By everything I've seen—and I've seen a lot—the baron expected the attack from the east. And he expected to know it was coming." Bogartis lifted his hand to his chin and scratched. He looked back at the unconscious smith, slowly shook his head, and said, "That lad put up a hell of a fight. Whoever trained him knew his craft. He wouldn't back down a step and made the bastards pay." He looked at Hava and saw she was waiting for some sense of what all this madness was about. "Someone anticipated the baron's plans or has a spy in his court, but while the baron was preparing his enemy acted. Find out who truly hates your baron and it's a good bet that's who destroyed your town."

Hava felt something go cold inside her. Hatu might be dead . . . Her wits cascaded and again she could barely hold on to any passing thought. Yet through the torrent of feelings years of training began to assert themselves once more and she realized she should return to Marquenet and send a message . . . Unexpected anger at the thought of what her duty required of her rose up, but she forced it aside. She would deal with everything later. At this moment she turned her attention to something immediate, something right in front of her.

She looked at the sleeping blacksmith. "What about Declan?"

"He'll pull through. He's as tough as anyone I've seen, and I've seen a lot of men fight." He looked as if he was going to say something, then apparently changed his mind.

"My . . . husband. Has anyone seen . . . ?" Hava couldn't bring herself to ask if he was still alive.

Bogartis put his hand on her shoulder. "Last anyone saw of him, he was alive."

"When was that?" she asked, instantly finding the painful cold within begin to dissipate.

"Just before things fell apart, according to one of my lads. That priest and his girl and another man of their order were seen riding away with your husband slung across the neck of the other man's horse."

"He was hurt?"

Bogartis shrugged. "Maybe. If he was injured, perhaps they saw the end coming before the rest of us and fled with your lad to care for him."

"Perhaps," she said, her mind calming as she turned her thoughts to Hatu being alive.

"Excuse me now: I've got to see to a couple of my lads who may not make it," said the mercenary captain. He moved back toward the makeshift pavilion.

Hava stood silently. She had thought she was the only person in town who knew of Hatu's unique situation. Conceivably, she had been wrong and those who had ridden off with him also knew he was the heir to the throne of Ithrace. She was on the edge of collapse, but her mind saw bits of a puzzle that she couldn't quite put together to create a coherent whole.

There was a reason Hatu's identity had been hidden for

his entire life and a reason the masters of Coaltachin had participated in hiding that identity. What was the baron's part in this, beyond saying he was indebted to Hatu's true father, or whatever it was Hatu had said the baron had said? She took a deep breath and gave herself permission to stop wrestling with her thoughts. She was beyond exhausted.

A mercenary approached and said, "We don't have much, but if you're hungry, my captain says you're welcome to share our meal."

Hava's appetite had returned with the news that Hatu was likely to still be alive. "You don't have much?" she echoed.

"Just what we had when we got here. We were going to reprovision . . . today." He looked at Hava and his expression mirrored what she'd been thinking since arriving: *It's only been one day.*

"Maybe I can help," Hava said. "Come with me." Quickly she led the fighter through the rubble of buildings until she reached what was left of the inn.

She was greeted by a sight so incongruous that she barked out an unexpected laugh. The concoction Hatu and Declan had smeared all over the roof had indeed been fire resistant. The timbers inside the building hadn't been, so when she reached what was the stabling yard, the roof sat intact on the ground, at a slightly canted angle due to the timbers from the stairs on one side propping it up. It was blackened and scorched, but still there.

"What?" asked the warrior.

"Come with me," said Hava, picking her way through the rubble. Finally she reached her destination: the entrance to the cold cellar. She tugged on a door. Despite being heavily charred, it resisted her efforts.

"Let me," said the young fighter.

When she gave him a narrow gaze, he added quickly, "You're about to fall over with exhaustion."

She grudgingly admitted as much and stepped aside.

The soldier heaved at the door and it slowly opened until it was wide enough that he could step inside and push from within. Suddenly it burst free with a loud scrape and the soldier barely kept his balance, avoiding falling on his face with a quick step.

"Thank you . . ."

"Bernard," he supplied.

Hava paused for a moment to really look at the fighter. He was close to her age, she judged, maybe a little older, but there was a battle-hardened toughness about him that put her in mind of the crew bosses back home. By twenty-five they were either tested and worthy or dead. This young man had a simple look to him, but she decided that was deceptive. He had a calm manner and seemed as if he might be the sort that listened and paid attention to what he heard.

"Thank you, Bernard," she said as she passed him. By the light coming through the door she saw that the entire larder was intact. "I thought the raiders might not take the time to look for a cold cellar before setting this place ablaze." She turned to the young warrior. "Get some of your fellows and bring a torch. We're well stocked and there will be a need for food. Whoever survived the attack will soon be hungry."

"Right back," said Bernard as he hurried off.

When she was alone, Hava hurried to the far corner of the cellar. She moved a small barrel of salted meat, which was only for use should they run out of fresh, and dug at the earth underneath with her belt knife. As she had expected, the point hit the top of a box, and she quickly dug it out.

Relief rose up as she opened the top and saw its contents: a few coins for quick spending rested next to a half dozen precious stones. Taking what the baron had given and turning it into a profitable inn had produced enough wealth for her and Hatu to hide what was left of the baron's gift as well

as some of the profits. It was a Coaltachin habit to convert
gold to precious gems when possible, as they were far lighter
and easier to carry than metal coins. A gem trader had come
through the town on one of Ratigan's wagons just a week
before, and Hatu had purchased a handful of stones. It was
not enough to operate an inn for more than a few months
or so, but it was more than enough to finance a search for a
missing husband.

Hearing Bernard come back with the others, she returned the box to its hiding place. Within minutes, half a
dozen able-bodied men were stripping the Inn of the Three
Stars of the last of its resources.

HAVA HAD HELPED DOLE OUT the food as the afternoon
faded, and near sunset she had taken a moment to eat. She
felt no pleasure in it, but swallowed every bite, knowing she
needed the nourishment, as she sat with her back against
a section of stone wall facing the pavilion erected for the
wounded, ignoring the soot that now covered her back and
shoulders. She would need to wash soon to get rid of all
the grime she had acquired since arriving in town, but she
pushed aside the question of where she would bathe.

A familiar figure appeared a short distance away, half
hidden by the fading light and growing shadows and the
still-masking smoke, though that had begun to fade as the
winds carried it away and the last dying embers cooled.

Molly Bowman came to stand before her. "Good to see
you."

Hava felt tears rising again and understood in that moment she had come to care for Molly more than she had
realized. Reaching out, she took the young woman's hand
and said, "Good to see you, too."

She allowed herself to be helped to her feet. They hugged
and Hava asked, "Your da?"

Molly gave the slightest shake of her head and a hint of moisture gave a sheen to her eyes. "He went down fighting" was all she said in a whisper.

Hava let out a long sigh. "So many . . ."

"Friends," added Molly.

Hava recognized that as painful as this was to her, Molly had lived in Beran's Hill her entire life and knew most of the murdered townsfolk. Hava had run out of words, so she squeezed Molly's arm.

Molly studied Hava's face. "Hatu?"

"Alive the last anyone saw him," said Hava softly. "Or at least, I think so."

Then Molly looked over to where Declan lay.

Hava said, "Bogartis says he'll live, but from what I saw he's going to be recovering for a while." Molly's gaze returned to Hava, and Hava felt a stab of fear as she asked, "Gwen?"

Molly shook her head, barely able to speak. "No."

Gwen had been the first woman to welcome her and Hatu to Beran's Hill, and as Gwen had helped rebuild the inn she had grown fond of the young woman. The pain that visited her revealed to Hava that she cared more deeply than she had ever expected to for the people who lived here. Feeling the dread rising again, she asked, "Millie? Jusan?"

In a hoarse whisper, Molly said, "They were all trapped in the house behind the smithy. I saw . . . three . . . burned bodies in the rubble." Suddenly she broke down and the two women held each other tight. At last Molly whispered, "Declan can't know . . . what happened before they died."

Hava didn't need to be told what ravaging armies were capable of. "I know." Hava sat down and Molly knelt beside her. "What do you plan on doing?" she asked the young hunter.

"I don't know," Molly answered, sounding emptied out. "Go to Esterly, maybe. Lots of villages nearby and they can always use game. I also know I'm not going to starve as long as I have a few arrows." She regarded Hava in silence for a moment, then asked, "What about you?"

Hava let out a long, audible sigh. "Two things: find my husband; then find whoever was behind this and kill him."

8

RECOVERY AND RESOLVE

Hatu swam in a sea of numb sensations and distant sounds. He fought to stretch for a thought and hold on to it, but it slipped through his grasp like a feather dancing on gusts of air. He could barely comprehend the bounds of his existence in this moment, let alone find any purpose in it, yet passing glimpses of images and barely audible sounds beckoned. Finally he relented and slipped back into darkness.

DENBE ENTERED THE HUT AS rain lightly fell and he removed his helm, lowering himself into a cross-legged position to sit opposite Catharian. "It's over," he said softly.

Sabella sat in the corner, Hatu's head in her lap. She stared at him in a way that told Denbe she was using her arts to prevent his consciousness from awaking. With a slight twitch of his head toward the young girl and boy, Denbe asked, "Is all well?"

Catharian barely suppressed a bitter laugh, keeping it to a muted chuckle. "That depends on what you mean by 'well.' We're alive and hidden, so to that, yes, all is well." He looked at his old companion and asked, "The town?"

"Obliterated," the soldier replied. "Those bastards killed

everyone they could find. A few lucky ones got away or died swiftly. What they did to the others . . ."

Catharian said, "I've seen brutality before. No need to elaborate."

"This was like nothing I've seen before. Even when Sandura led the assault on Ithrace . . ." Denbe took a deep breath. "They raped and dismembered . . . they tortured without purpose, for the sport of it."

"A terror raid?"

"They left in a hurry, carrying off all they could. This was no military offensive designed simply to secure a base. They destroyed everything they could, then returned the way they came." He looked pointedly at Catharian. "They also made a point of carrying off their dead. As I attempted to lend aid, I made sure I examined as many bodies as I could. Not one attacker lay among the slain."

"Odd," said Catharian, sparing a second to glance over at Sabella and Hatu. "Usually they bury their dead where they fall or leave the bodies behind if retreating in haste."

Denbe looked deeply troubled. "They didn't want Baron Dumarch to know who they were."

"So, not Sandura?"

"Or the Church, I think," said Denbe with a quick affirmative nod. "We suspected another player, and now we have ample proof."

"But who?"

"When we fled I heard shouts, orders, in languages I didn't recognize."

"And you're one of the few men I know who's traveled as much as I have," said Catharian. He motioned to a small kettle of soup simmering next to a dying fire.

"Thanks, but I stole a bit of food from the garrison boys from Esterly when they weren't paying attention. I took off my tabard and wandered over with some mercenaries. Companies have been showing up from the south."

"Too little, too late, apparently." Catharian sat back against the wall of the hut they had been using as their staging point for forays into Beran's Hill since arriving in the area. "Damn," he said softly. "We can't stay here forever." He waved dismissively at the small pot. "I just boiled up what we had left and tomorrow we go hungry."

"Tricky getting our lad out of here," said Denbe, nodding toward Hatu.

"Steal a cart and be a family fleeing? With our wounded brother?"

"You two, perhaps," said Denbe, touching his dark cheek. "I don't look the part."

"Retainer?"

"Not a lot of people with personal guards left hereabouts," said the old fighter. "At least those who might be would be known well enough . . ." He shook his head, obviously frustrated. "No, we're going to have to rely on our wits and sneak out of Marquensas."

"How?"

Denbe was silent for a moment, then said, "We've got to get out through one of the smugglers' routes."

For a moment Catharian gaped, his eyes wide. "Are you mad?" he asked at last.

"There's little chance we can go south unnoticed, given Baron Dumarch is marching an army this way. Whoever raided here will have to know he'll be coming after them, right up to the gates of Port Colos."

"You still haven't told me how we're going to get to a boat and sail to the Sanctuary."

Denbe said, "We wait one more day." He indicated Hatu. "We can only keep him drugged for so long before we do some serious damage to his mind. Even with Sabella's help protecting him from the drug's effects, there are limits. And we're going to run out of that drug soon."

"What's the plan?"

Denbe leaned forward. "We cut a bit north of the road to Port Colos, staying out of sight, and if we're lucky, we slip along after the raiders but ahead of Dumarch, and once we get close to the city, we cut north a bit more. There are some villages where the fishermen also do a bit of smuggling on their own; the governor makes so much profit from the smuggling through his city that he ignores them. We take a boat and hug the coast at night, heave to behind an island or just over the horizon during the day."

"Slow going," said Catharian.

"True, but in less than a week we're south of all the fuss and bother."

"Fuss and bother?" Catharian barked out a laugh. "That's like calling a hurricane 'a spot of wet weather,' my friend." He was silent for a moment, then said, "But I can't think of a better plan. If we ride east we've got to get through the Wild Lands, and at the end of that we're on the wrong side of the continent. Besides, I've been to Sandura and don't like it much."

Denbe nodded. "Me, too." Looking at Sabella, he asked, "How are you?"

She smiled. "Well enough, but I need sleep."

Denbe looked to Catharian. "Which means he will need to be drugged again before morning."

"We don't have much left," said the false monk, reaching into his belt pouch and pulling out a small flask. He held it up, showing Denbe that it was about one-third full. "Three more doses."

"Five," said Denbe, "if we just keep him stupid while we travel, rather than unconscious."

Catharian shrugged as if to say that might be difficult. "He's going to be a handful when he's fully recovered. I hope I can find something else to use before we cross the ocean. When he recovers I'd like him to be in the Sanctuary. Dealing with him there may prove difficult enough."

Denbe allowed himself an audible sigh. "If it was a perfect world, we could snap our fingers, open some sort of magic door, step through, and find ourselves in the Sanctuary."

"If only magic worked like that," agreed Catharian. "Get some rest and we'll move out at sunset."

Saying nothing more, the old warrior made himself as comfortable as possible on the dirt floor of the old charcoal burner's hut and closed his eyes.

HAVA STIRRED SLOWLY WHEN MOLLY gently shook her shoulder, then came wide-awake. "What?"

"You've slept for a while, so I thought you might want something to eat."

Sitting up and taking stock of her surroundings, Hava saw that more people had found their way to what had turned into a makeshift headquarters. She had fallen asleep under what was left of a building's overhang and saw that outside, rain was gently falling. Whatever embers were still burning would quickly be extinguished, and the air was now steeped with a steamy smoke that still carried the reek of burned wood and bodies. Thankfully all that would soon be washed away. But as she came to full consciousness and took the bowl of broth Molly offered, she knew that once the rain stopped and the sun returned, the stench would as well.

Hava took a sip from a large wooden spoon and was pleasantly surprised to discover someone had put the spices from her inn to good use. She observed the activity around her.

The soldiers from both Esterly and Marquenet had established a base next to the field hospital, and as the sun touched the western horizon, a hundred or more soldiers, all covered in soot and filth, were making their way to a dozen campfires to the east, in what had been a rolling meadow.

Hava stood and looked around. Finally, she said, "Any more?"

Molly knew she meant any more survivors. "A few have wandered in. Mostly those who got to the woods first and just kept running uphill. There are places on the other side of the north creek that are trouble for a horse with a lazy rider."

Then Hava asked, "Declan?"

"Still asleep, but he seems to be resting well enough."

"The rest?"

Molly motioned with her chin, and Hava saw that the supplies she had turned over to the soldiers were indeed being put to good use. Everything seemed to be in as much order as circumstances allowed.

Hava quickly finished the broth and said, "Anything more substantial?"

Molly nodded and said, "Let's go and find out. It's your food, after all." She tried to keep her tone light, but Hava heard the hidden pain and knew she was mourning her father.

In the field kitchen she saw that the men were simply gathering up enough to sustain them but leaving plenty for others. She hadn't been as attentive a student as some others in school, but she knew that meant they were a highly disciplined force. Often hungry men would grab more than they could finish and food got thrown out. This was a command of soldiers who had been trained to eat what they took, or else have an unpleasant conversation with the company sergeant.

Hava left her bowl and spoon on a pile of dirty dishes, and then she and Molly helped themselves to plates and grabbed some dried beef, hard cheese, and a summer apple. Hava's head was still "fuzzy," as she thought of it, so she waved off a mug of ale.

Molly took some ale, and the two returned to the small patch of ground they had occupied before, out of the rain. They ate in silence, for which Hava was thankful. She enjoyed Molly's company and appreciated that of all the women Hava had met in Beran's Hill, Molly was the most comfortable with silence. Thinking of the other women, Hava felt an unexpected pang over what had happened to Gwen and Millie. She dreaded the moment Declan revived enough to be told his wife of less than a day was dead.

After finishing their food, Molly motioned for Hava to hand her the plate and without a word took her own and Hava's back to where the soldiers on kitchen duty were washing them and putting them out for the next hungry visitor. Hava's mind was still fatigued, and every time she considered what to do next her thoughts would slip away.

Molly returned and knelt next to her. "So, have you decided what you're going to do?"

"Haven't I already answered that?"

Molly smiled for the first time since Hava's arrival that afternoon. "I know you will go and look for Hatu. I mean how do you plan on finding him?"

"I have no idea," Hava admitted. "Someone said he'd been seen carried off across the withers of a horse belonging to . . . a soldier? Someone wearing a tabard bearing the same sigil as Catharian's?"

"You rest," said Molly, standing up. "I'll go poke around and see if I can get better information."

Hava was not up to arguing, as every one of her bones

seemed to ache with fatigue. Before she could form another coherent thought, she was asleep again.

HAVA AWOKE AND INSTANTLY REALIZED she'd slept through the night. In the distance a rooster that had somehow survived the slaughter a day and a half ago commanded the sun to rise. She saw the lightening sky in the east and realized the false dawn was upon them and the sun would be clearing the horizon in another half hour or less. Molly was asleep next to her, and Hava took a brief personal inventory.

She still ached, but it was now mild, the sort of feeling she had known the morning after a vigorous day of exercise back at school. The fatigue she had endured yesterday had been caused by a dose of stress and worry unlike anything she had experienced before. Just knowing that Hatu was probably alive and possibly nearby had rid her of that and replaced that bodily ache of despair with a spark of hope, even though he might still be in harm's way.

It was good to feel a sense of purpose again. She glanced at the sleeping Molly and wondered how the young woman was dealing with her father's death. Never one to outwardly show emotion, Hava knew that Molly's feelings were in there somewhere, and for the first time in many years, Hava found herself worrying about someone besides Hatu and Donte.

She let Molly sleep a bit longer, then gently woke her. "What?" asked Molly groggily. Hava wondered if she had had more than one cup of ale after Hava had fallen asleep.

"You asked what my plan was?"

Molly came alert. "What?"

"If I am going to find Hatu, what I need to know is: If you were trying to get away from the battle, but fearful of being out in the open, where would you lie low for a day or two?"

It only took a moment for Molly to say, "I know a place."

"Where?"

"I'll show you." Molly rose and began to gather her things.

"You don't have to show me. Just tell me where," said Hava.

Molly looked around and calmly said, "There's nothing left for me here. I might as well look for Hatu with you."

Hava realized that the pain Molly felt over the loss of her father and home and everyone she knew in Beran's Hill would probably stay bottled up inside the young archer. Hava had known others like that and knew that the day might come when Molly would pay dearly for her stoicism.

"We need provisions," said Molly. "We can forage if needed, but the less time we spend doing that, the faster we can travel."

With a wry smile, Hava said, "Well, it is my food."

"What's left of it, if any," said Molly.

They moved to the field kitchen, where two boys were tending the banked fires, so they could cook for the soon-to-be-rising troops. The baron's main force would arrive by midday from Marquenet and would be followed by its own luggage train, with ample provisions if the baron was anticipating a full-scale battle somewhere between here and Port Colos. Without speaking to the boys, Hava and Molly grabbed the most easily transportable food—some apples and a half wheel of hard cheese that would be edible for another few days—and then Hava led Molly to the cold cellar, where she dug out the little coffer of gems and coins she had reburied there. She quickly pried the lid off with her belt knife and poured the contents onto a cloth, divided these in two, and gave Molly an equal share. Each woman tucked the valuables away in their belt pouches, then left swiftly through the field kitchen.

If the boys were curious as to what the two oddly dressed women were up to, they said nothing: they were in a strange place, surrounded by lots of dead people and destruction. Given how long Marquensas had been at peace, for there had been no major conflicts since the Betrayal against Ithrace, this was the first exposure they had had to mayhem, and they needed no excuse to avoid additional confrontations.

When they had gathered all they could manage, including some empty waterskins they could fill upriver, Hava said, "Horses."

Molly nodded. "Ideas?"

"Many, but let's go for the simple one. We steal them. The one I had yesterday will take a week or more to recover, so let's go find where the remounts are picketed. Can you ride bareback?"

"If I must—why?"

"Stealing saddles may prove a bit more problematic."

AN HOUR LATER THE TWO young women rode across a meadow at the edge of which stood a row of pickets. Nearing one, they gave a friendly wave, and when the half-sleeping soldier started to say something, Hava said, "Hunting! Need more meat."

The soldier noted the bows across their backs, but he was still searching for a response by the time they were past him, and whatever he decided, it did not include hindering their progress.

Hava waited until they were at the edge of the forest before asking, "Where do you think they may have gone to ground?"

"There's an abandoned charcoal burner's hut on the road a few miles on. Deep enough in the woods and small enough you'd likely miss it if you didn't know it was there."

"How would they know it was there?"

"That Catharian . . . more to him than meets the eye" was all Molly said.

When Molly turned her horse's head toward the road north of where they entered the woods, Hava followed, hoping the young archer was correct and they might find Hatu there.

DONTE SAT IN THE BACK of a wagon, bouncing a bit as the road turned uneven, but glad not to be walking. He had had to bribe one sergeant and bully two younger fighters into letting him "guard" the contents of the wagon, food-stuff and resupplies for a company in the field. He had no idea where he was bound, save that it was to the north, and somehow he knew that was where he must travel.

The war seemed to be unfolding up there. A large army had left before he had arrived in Marquenet, and he had been able to secure a place with a ragtag company of mer-cenaries, overseen by a "captain" who went by the name Quinn. He had no intent of serving with the company, but this temporary enlistment gave him a relatively easy pas-sage, compared with walking to wherever this Beran's Hill was, or risking stealing a horse, which normally would have been no issue, save that the entire road between here and his destination appeared to be choked with the baron's soldiers. As he was traveling behind with the baggage and lesser swords for hire, he was spared scrutiny, but even so he would have rather avoided unnecessary delay.

His only regret was that he had spent so little time in Marquenet, as he was impressed with what little he had managed to see in the city. Since recovering his memories— all but a blurred jumble of impressions from the time he had been captured until walking out of the surf—he had found all the changes from the village where he had first found shelter refreshing. After the relative quiet and simple pleasures of that village, he now saw the world was a far bigger and more complicated place than he had thought, and he found he liked that fact.

Donte didn't deal in complex thinking as a rule, but he was by no means a stupid man. He thought he might have traveled with his masters and bosses as a youngster, but he had no clear memories of doing so, which was annoying. Indeed, the further he moved on from his imprisonment by the Sisters of the Deep, the more infuriated he became over his missing memories of that time. All he had been left with were impressions: a barely remembered chill, fleeting pain, and a stench of decay—things that came to the very edge of his understanding, then fled. He was left with conflicted feelings of anger and . . . some compulsion about Hatushaly. It was a constant frustration to him, one that would eventually blossom into full-blown anger. He pushed away his rising annoyance and considered his brief visit to the city he had just left.

Even the most prosaic fixtures there—the stalls of food-stuffs, a baker's cart, a clothier's shop—seemed fascinating to him and hinted of wealth beyond anything he'd seen before. Even the most commonplace clothing was of finer weave than anything he was used to, and the people looked happier. Also, it was the cleanest place Donte had ever seen!

He sensed that Marquenet would be a wonderful place to explore, and what little he had seen suggested it was rich with luxury items to steal and beautiful women to bed. He wondered if any masters had a crew there, and if so, who they were, and if not, perhaps he could persuade his grand-father to let him set one up. But as much as he had wished to linger in Marquenet, he could not escape the almost painful need he felt to find Hatushaly, and it lessened only when he was moving in what he assumed was the correct direction.

He felt a strange enjoyment at finding himself traveling with this army. His training had given him a keen ability to assess these mercenaries as if he had some enchanted lens through which to examine each man.

In every company there were some hired swords who were quite simply bullies, but who were easily avoided or put in their place as needed, but there were fewer of that type among the main army than he would have expected. Most of these men were truly hard-bitten veterans of combat, battles won or lost, bloody and unsparing; men who wouldn't waste time and blood over trivial issues. These men put Donte in mind of the more experienced crew bosses and younger masters at home, while the rest were like the familiar street thugs back there. Then there were those who were neither veteran fighters nor thugs: those who remained were thieves, confidence tricksters, pickpockets, and wily types, the last being the cleverest—they needed to be to avoid being killed by their fellow soldiers. But there were also ample camp followers, a sea of people from whores to tailors and armorers, to fortune tellers and sellers of trinkets and charms, to providers of drugs and drink—every manner of purveyor one could imagine following an army.

Donte looked at the company to which he had falsely pledged allegiance, trudging along on foot with a sad little donkey cart carrying their baggage, with only Captain Quinn riding as poor a horse as the donkey, and tried not to laugh. They were one step above scavengers, battlefield ghouls, and he expected they'd contrive to be at the rear once real fighting started. There wasn't one man he'd met in this small company who impressed him. Donte was openly boastful with his friends and always put on a show of bravado even when he didn't feel it inside, but with these men, he knew he could take away the sword any one of them held and hit them with it.

His perception of the bountiful serenity of this barony had begun to change earlier when the wagon trundled past the first graves. Enough slaughter had been inflicted on those fleeing south that individual graves had been counted a luxury beyond the capacity of those burying the dead. Graves for a half dozen bodies at a time had been dug and covered over, so freshly dug burial mounds arose on both sides of the road, easily identified by the large, bare patches of earth amid all the Marquensas lushness.

By midafternoon they had reached the burial details, who were hard at work, and even larger mass graves were being dug. Donte was impressed. He'd heard stories of war, like all students of Coaltachin, and was always caught halfway between wonder at the level of bloodshed and bravery claimed by those telling the stories and the conviction that those stories were exaggerations. But there was nothing exaggerated about the amount of blood spilled here. He couldn't begin to count how many had been slain, but it was at least in the hundreds.

"We're here," said a voice up ahead, and Donte jumped off the back of the wagon, took a deep breath, and reeled at the stench of burned flesh and the acrid sting of water-soaked charred wood.

Donte glanced to where Captain Quinn sat on his tired horse, waiting for someone from the baron's retinue to tell him what to do. Without a word, Donte walked off, looking for the most likely place for information, which was probably the soldiers' mess tent. As he moved away from the wagon, the captain's second-in-command, a bully named Beslan, shouted, "Where are you going?"

Without looking at the jumped-up "sergeant," Donte shouted, "I'm going to take a shit!"

He had discovered over the years that few people wanted to follow him once he shared that information. He doubted he'd ever see Beslan again, but if he did, he'd happily gut the man.

He followed his nose. The faint aroma of cooked food

cut through the stench. The morning mess was over, and the kitchen staff was busy preparing a massive evening meal for the baron's army. Donte saw a young kitchen boy. "I'm looking for someone," he said with as much faux authority as he could muster.

The boy's face drained of color, making an exaggerated contrast between his brown hair and eyes and his now nearly ashen complexion. "Sir?"

"I'm looking for a man, a friend."

The boy seemed void of answers and merely nodded.

"His name is Hatushaly."

The boy said nothing, but from behind Donte a voice asked, "Hatu?"

Donte turned around to see a young man, bloodied and bandaged, who was doing the best he could to help around the tent by attempting to pull a large sack along to the washtubs. Donte crossed to meet him and took the bag from him. "You know Hatu?"

"Not well, but I've drunk at his inn . . . or what was his inn before they burned it down."

Donte was surprised to hear Hatu had been an innkeeper and wondered, not for the first time, how long he had been a prisoner of the Sisters of the Deep, but he pushed all that aside and said, "Do you know if he survived"—Donte made a waving gesture with his left hand toward the rubble—"all this?"

"I heard one of the soldiers tell his wife—"

"Wife?" interrupted Donte.

"Yes, Hava."

Donte's eyebrows rose, but he said nothing.

"Someone said this monk—I forget his name—saved Hatu during the battle and carried him off. I saw Hava last night . . ." He glanced around to where Hava and Molly had been under the overhang. ". . . over there." He pointed. With a fatigued sigh he added, "I don't know where they are now."

"Thanks," said Donte, returning the heavy bag to the injured man. He moved to a soldier standing guard at the edge of the infirmary and asked, "A man named Hatu or a woman named Hava, do you know them?"

The soldier shook his head, and Donte moved on to ask the next soldier he saw. After a few more were questioned, a mercenary said, "Saw the gal—innkeeper's wife, right? Anyway, saw her and that archer friend of hers riding off across the field to the east, looking like they were going to get some hunting in." The mercenary, a greying veteran, scratched his neck as he continued. "But what sort of game they'll find this close to a battle is beyond me. Might be why they were packing gear. They may be out hunting for a few days."

Donte nodded. "Thanks." He knew without question Hava wasn't out hunting but looking for Hatu. He felt it in his bones.

He walked a short distance, glancing to the east. Pickets had been established just far enough apart to keep the men on guard down to a reasonable number, but close enough that slipping past would prove problematic, even if he hit the perimeter at a gallop. He made a quick survey up and down the line as far as he could see and spotted the most likely place to dash past the pickets into the sheltering woods. He paused for a moment in his observation and then turned to go and find himself a horse.

"What are you doing, lad?"

Donte turned to see a grizzled old soldier wearing the baronial tabard, his weather-beaten face set in an expression of suspicion. Donte knew instantly that the man knew he was thinking about leaving this destroyed town. Donte turned his back on the horse he had just been inspecting. The remounts were not guarded but attended to by stable boys who had arrived earlier with the baron's baggage wagons.

"Looking for a horse, Sergeant," he said, guessing the man's rank although he wore no clear insignia.

"Well, that's a horse," said the old fighter, "but what gives you the idea you're free to simply pick out one of the baron's own?"

Donte tried to look slightly confused and a little bit stupid as he said, "My captain just said get a horse. Mine went lame and he said something about a patrol or something."

"Who's your captain?"

"Captain Quinn," answered Donte without hesitation.

"Quinn?" echoed the soldier, his tone one of outright mockery. "That ragpicker?" He shook his head. "Well, he failed to mention that you had to find one that doesn't belong to my baron, didn't he?"

Donte shrugged. "I suppose so."

"Maybe we should go have a chat with your captain," suggested the sergeant, taking a grip of Donte's arm.

Donte sighed. "Oh, hell." He drew back his right fist and hit the old soldier as hard as he could.

The old man staggered three steps back, shook his head, and said softly, "Oooh." Then he fixed Donte with what the young man could only think of as a murderous gaze.

Donte didn't hesitate. He launched himself forward, drawing back his arm and hitting the old soldier as hard as he could.

Again the old man staggered backward, stopped, shook his head, and once more said, "Oooh!" rather more angrily.

"Oh, shit," said Donte, and for one last time he came at the sergeant. This time, before he could even draw back his fist, Donte saw the old man move with a speed he couldn't have imagined, taking a large stride forward to unload a blow that he barely avoided. The man's fist still grazed the side of Donte's face, and he felt something crack in his left cheek and a burning pain as his vision swam.

Donte's legs went wobbly and he staggered backward a step. He shook his head, trying to clear it.

The old soldier said, "If you want to play stand-down, youngster, you're going to have to put on a mite more weight and experience, though I'll grant you've got ample sand in your craw."

Donte thought he should probably say something, but nothing came to mind as he tried to focus his attention as another blow came his way. Again he ducked at the last second, and this time the blow glanced off his neck and shoulder, and pain shot through the left side of his upper body.

Abruptly two other soldiers appeared and one said, "Need help, Deakin?"

"I think I'm just about done here. Thank you anyway."

A third blow lifted Donte off his feet, and he never felt himself strike the ground.

DAYLON DUMARCH, BARON OF MARQUENSAS, with his half brother, Balven, at his side, rode into the destruction that had once been the pride of his northern border. As they approached the east side of the destroyed town, the baron said at almost a whisper, "Words fail me."

Balven said, "We couldn't have expected this."

"I thought the governor at Port Colos was firmly with us," Daylon said as they reached what appeared to be a field kitchen next to a field infirmary. Dismounting, the baron waited as Balven instructed the servants where to erect the pavilion.

Then Balven stepped close to his brother and said quietly, "We should speak in private, but I will say, between fear of your army and ample gold, the governor *should* have been firmly with us. Something impossible to anticipate must have changed his mind."

Daylon nodded. "I'll start taking reports now. You see what this is all about"—he waved at the field tents—"and who's arranged this camp, then catch up with me."

"Understood, my lord."

Daylon motioned for one of his personal guards to accompany him, then did a quick walk through the infirmary, speaking briefly with a few of the men he knew by sight. At the makeshift field kitchen he stopped, surprised at how well provisioned it was. "Where did the food come from?" he asked.

A kitchen boy said, "The woman, sir."

"What woman?" asked Daylon.

At that moment one of the cooks came over and shooed the boy away.

"Who provided all this food?" asked the baron.

"Some woman who ran an inn, my lord. It seems she'd just provisioned her cold cellar for the festival. But it's a good thing you're here, as we were going to run out in another day or so."

Daylon said, "I should thank her."

"Last I saw," said the cook, "she and a friend went walking off that way." He pointed toward what had been the center of town before it was razed.

Daylon and his bodyguard picked their way through the rubble and found themselves standing in what had been a major street. The baron stopped and took a long look around. "Nothing left . . ." Daylon whispered.

"My lord?" asked the guard.

"Nothing." He looked at a knot of men near a makeshift corral in which a good number of remounts were kept and saw something that struck him as odd. Three of his soldiers were pounding a stake post into the ground. He couldn't quite make out what this was, so he walked in that direction.

As he approached, one soldier saw him and said, "My lord!"

Instantly the others turned and bowed in his direction. The center of their activity seemed to have something to do with a young man who had obviously been beaten almost insensible.

"What's this, then?" he asked.

An old veteran Daylon recognized, a former sergeant who had been reduced in rank for brawling several times, said, "Sir?"

"Deakin, isn't it?"

"Sir," he said, nodding. "We caught this lad trying to steal a horse, but there's nothing around high enough to hang him from, unless we drag him out to the forest, and we thought it would be quicker to just set up a post and garrote him."

Daylon's eyes widened slightly. "Who gave the order for that?"

"Ah, well, truth to tell, my lord, no one officially. Sergeant Mackie's hands are full with everything else, and we have no proper provost, so I just assumed . . ."

Seeing the swelling around both Deakin's eyes, Daylon said, "Assumed, yes. So the lad hit you, and you thought you'd settle things by crushing his throat."

"Well, he did try to steal a mount, my lord. One of your own horses."

Daylon was tempted to say several intemperate things at that moment, but realized he was on the verge of taking out every shred of anger, pain, and guilt he felt over losing Beran's Hill on this soldier, even though Deakin was a known malingerer and troublemaker.

Looking at Donte, who required two soldiers—one on

each side—to keep him upright, he asked, "Did you try to steal a horse?"

Through swollen lips, Donte answered, "Tried to borrow one."

Deakin backhanded Donte and said, "Show some manners to the baron!"

"Enough!" shouted Daylon. "Deakin, get out of my sight!"

"Yes, sir," said the old soldier, obviously familiar enough with his lord and master not to hesitate in obeying for more than a second.

To Donte, the baron asked, "Why were you trying to borrow a horse?"

"I was going to look for a friend."

"Friend? You from around here?"

"No . . . my lord," said Donte, then spat out a small clot of blood. "But she was here this morning. Told she went hunting."

"Hunting?" Daylon motioned for the two men to haul Donte over to a blackened stump that had once served as a shade tree before someone had toppled it. Donte sat and nodded. "So, after a girl then?" said the baron.

"Not like that, my lord," said Donte. "We grew up together before she moved here."

Daylon asked, "Where was that?"

"A little island far away. You'd never have heard of it."

Daylon instantly felt a chill run up his back and knew at once this was far more than what it appeared to be. "Her name?"

"She's called Hava, sir."

To the two men who had held Donte, Daylon said, "Take him over there"—he pointed back the way he had come—"and find my man Balven. As soon as my pavilion is up, take this man inside. Tell Balven I'll be there presently. No one else is to talk to him, understood?"

The two men nodded and helped Donte to his feet. To the remaining soldiers, Daylon said, "Take down that ridiculous garroting post."

They hurried to obey. The baron felt sure that while Sandura had no hand in this, someone else seeking the Firemane child might have, or it was the most unlikely coincidence he could imagine. He was determined to make a quick survey of what was left of the town, then return and question this fellow closely.

Glancing at the stump where Donte had sat, he thanked whatever god might be listening that Deakin had been too stupid to think of beheading the lad.

9

DISASTERS AND QUESTIONS

———†———

Declan awakened with a sharp pain in his right shoulder and gasped. A young woman turned from her position between him and the man she was tending to on his left. "Hold still," she said in a firm but not scolding tone. "You'll pull the stitches if you move suddenly." She moved away from the unconscious man whose forehead she had been bathing with a cool cloth and said, "Let me help."

As the young woman helped him to sit up, he ignored the sharp twinge in his shoulder. "Thanks," he said. "How long have I . . . ?" His voice was hoarse.

"Here." The woman held up a waterskin so that Declan could drink. "Slowly, or you might retch."

He did as instructed and sipped the water, feeling the cool of it soothing his throat; then, when he could, he took a good strong pull. "How long?" he repeated, handing the skin back to her.

"You were here when I arrived yesterday." She motioned to the oiled canvas ground cloth beneath him. "So, since the fight the day before?" She was a woman not much older than Gwen, thought Declan: sunburn, hard labor, and not enough food had taken their toll.

He looked around as much as he was able and asked, "Is this as bad as it looks?"

She studied his face. "You live here?"

"I'm the town smith," he replied.

"Let me get you some more water," she said without answering his question. She stood up, and he could see the view she had blocked. He felt a stab of fear. A misting drizzle fell, and he knew it must have been heavier before he regained consciousness, as there were puddles and mud everywhere.

His heart went cold: ruin was all he could see on every side. Even without standing and looking over the remaining section of wall to his left that served as one corner of the infirmary, he knew that all he would see would be more char and blood. Had any building been left standing, the wounded would be housed inside, and that included his smithy. From the icy center in his chest he felt a numbing chill spread throughout his entire body, muting any feelings for places and people, those emotions that just moments before he had counted as essential to who he was.

He recognized this new state as something akin to the remote awareness coupled with keen perception he experienced during a fight: a focus on something vital, with his life hanging in the balance. It was as if without volition he became someone else, someone he needed to be.

Without being told he knew Gwen was gone. Had she been alive she would have been the one kneeling at his side.

Pain faded from his chest. The numbness seemed to run up his neck to the sides of his face, a faint, tingling sensation unlike anything he had felt before, but one that seemed to be offering a sort of armor against pain. He felt moisture gathering in his eyes and blinked hard, as if denying the pain would drive it away. Even the agony in his shoulder began to fade a bit. He willed it away, and in one corner of his mind he felt that pain contract, shrivel, folding in on itself, as if he were folding steel, each fold creating strength.

The woman returned, the mercenary captain Bogartis a step behind her. Declan allowed her to help him take another drink, then she went about seeing to the needs of the other wounded.

Bogartis knelt and said, "Glad to see you're pulling through, lad. You took a nasty shaft to the shoulder. A little lower and you'd have been over in the field, in one of those big holes they've been digging. Can you move your arm, even a bit?"

Gently Declan tried, and while the pain was sharp, he could bear it. "A little."

"That's a good thing. When the stitches come out you're going to need to move it around so the muscles stay loose and strong. You might have some scars inside, or at least that's what the healers say, and if they tear loose it'll hurt, but you should get your strength and motion back."

Looking at the old fighter, Declan asked, "How are your men?"

"Two gone, three will recover, but one of them is going to have to find a new trade: his fighting days are over." He paused for a moment, his eyes searching Declan's face. "I don't want to be the man to . . ." The old fighter let out a long sigh. "There's no easy way, so I'll just say it, lad. Your girl is gone."

"My wife," Declan corrected gently.

"Ah, on your wedding day." Anger flashed across Bogartis's face. "I've seen ugly deeds, but attacking on midsummer's day to destroy an entire town, murder all the people . . ." He shook his head as if trying to cast off a memory. "I've seen more blood and death than a dozen men in their lifetimes, but this . . . I have no words."

"What about the others?"

"Which others?" replied Bogartis.

"My apprentice . . ." Declan found himself stopping. Jusan was a journeyman . . . or had been.

"We found two other bodies with . . . your wife. A man and woman."

"Jusan and Millie," Declan said softly. The small ball of pain inside him contracted even more. "Help me get to my feet."

Bogartis helped Declan to stand. He leaned on the mercenary as he took stock of what was left of Beran's Hill.

"I wish . . ." The old fighter shrugged. "What are you going to do? Rebuild?"

Declan's tone was flat. "Rebuild what?" He motioned with his left arm. He gazed and gazed for a long moment, then whispered, "Nothing."

"Nothing indeed, lad," Bogartis said sadly. "There looks to be as big a war coming as I've seen since the Betrayal, and Lord Dumarch is going to need a lot of weapons. When your arm recovers, you'll be working nonstop. I make no claim to know how any other man should feel, but work can be a balm." He hesitated. "Declan—I got that right?"

"Yes," said Declan, indicating that he'd like to sit down again. Bogartis helped him. "Thank you."

"I saw you fight and you're a man I'd go over any wall with, and there are only a few I'd say that to, in fact. I've seen veterans turn and flee facing less than you did." Bogartis surveyed the destruction on all sides. "I've traveled and fought most of my life. I started as a boy with the baggage for Baron Montalo, until he lost a war to King Lodavico's father, so I became a sword for hire, just another mercenary, until I took over this little band when my captain was killed. I've been fighting for my supper for nearly forty years now.

"I've been thinking lately that the day may come—if I

live through the next few fights—when I should take what I've hidden away and start a new life somewhere quiet. Beran's Hill seemed as nice and friendly a town as I'd ever seen. I thought it might have been a place for an old swordsman to settle down." He shrugged. "It's strange, Declan. It feels like I've just lost something."

Declan's voice was calm and emotionless. "And I've lost everything."

Bogartis said nothing for a long while. At last he said, "Rest, and I'll come by tomorrow before we leave."

"Where will you go?"

"Probably where the baron tells me. I'm certain he's about to be hip-deep in more war than he expected and will be hiring companies." He paused, then continued. "He's a decent enough noble, by accounts, and while I'm usually not too fussy about whose gold I take, if he's fighting the bastards that did this, I'll happily serve him."

Declan said nothing as Bogartis departed, then lay back on the oiled canvas. He felt numb and disconnected from coherent thought, and so tired his very bones seemed to ache. The last thing he saw before he lapsed back into sleep was a fitful image of Gwen smiling at him.

HAVA DISMOUNTED A MOMENT AFTER Molly, who stuck her head inside an abandoned hut, one the archer had said had once been the home to a family of charcoal burners who had left when she was still a little girl.

"Someone's been here," said Molly over her shoulder.

Hava knew better than to ask if she was certain, as Molly wasn't the sort to be uncertain about anything. Stepping into the small hut, Molly knelt by the remnants of a small firepit, barely big enough to heat one pot.

"How long ago?" Hava asked.

"A day or so, perhaps before dawn today. The pit is cold,

but it's dry, so no water from the rain has seeped in, and a lot of dust was moved around, probably from picking up ground covers and gear." Molly stood up. "Let's see if we can tell which direction they took."

Outside the hut, Molly walked around, motioning for Hava to stay where she was, presumably because she didn't want her making new tracks.

Hava watched Molly scout around for a good ten minutes, into the trees out of sight, then back toward the road, and up a small hill to the west. Finally, she returned. "Usually rain would be bad, but this was a light one, making the ground wet enough to hold tracks for a while without washing them away. Four horses headed out of here that way." She pointed.

Hava looked surprised. "West? You're sure? In the same direction as the raiders?"

"They might be blending in with whoever is following that bunch or—"

"Hatu wouldn't go peacefully."

"He might not have a choice," Molly replied. "Someone's got a knife to your ribs . . ." She shrugged. "Or maybe he's tied up?"

"So why would they follow an army of murderers?"

"That we will have to ask when we catch up," said Molly. Without another word, she crossed to her horse and mounted, Hava gaining her saddle a moment later.

DONTE SAT QUIETLY IN A corner of the baron's pavilion on a padded stool that was probably used by the baron when he changed his boots. The baron and Balven were quietly conferring in the far corner.

Donte had been given a cold, wet cloth to deal with his swollen face. He thought his left cheek might be cracked, as it throbbed more than the rest of him, which was quite a lot. But he had stopped spitting up blood, which he assumed meant he would keep his teeth, and the rest of him felt passable, so he counted himself lucky that the baron had turned up when he did.

Since coming to the pavilion, Donte had seen the baron and Balven talk with a half dozen men who had reported to them over the last hour. Each time the baron had turned to say something to Donte, a messenger arrived, and whatever conversation Daylon Dumarch, Baron of Marquensas, had planned on having with him had been postponed. Donte was fine with that, as he assumed whatever was coming after they finished talking would hardly be welcome.

The fact that the baron knew Donte was from Coaltachin meant that any story he might fabricate was pointless. Having to tell the truth seemed a more difficult prospect than he had imagined. He put the blame on his teachers, who had taught him only to be an adept liar. He found that idea amusing, but the circumstances seemed dire and he hurt too much to laugh.

Finally the baron turned to Donte and said, "Now let me be brief. It was my understanding that Hatu was no longer of any concern to the Kingdom of Night. Why are you here?"

Donte paused for a moment, then said, "I'm his friend, and Hava's. We got separated months ago, and . . . I washed up on the shore in Marquensas, Baron." He dabbed at his swollen cheek, but that only seemed to make it throb more, so he tossed the cloth aside. "I just wandered a bit . . ." As he began, part of his old nature and training to dissemble manifested itself, and he embellished his tale. "I heard from a traveler in a village I was in that a couple who matched their description had an inn up here." That was the one fabrication he thought he could get away with. Then he added, "Not a lot of couples look like them: Hava is darker than most around here, skinny, but . . . well, she's a nice-looking woman, and Hatu with his ridiculous sunburned pale skin and that . . . stupid hair of his."

Balven said, "Stupid hair?"

"He always put color in it, to make it darker, so it never looked completely right if you were close. Good enough for street work and running from guards, but if you spent enough time with him you knew he colored it now and again. We grew up together . . ." Donte stopped, remembering the first rule was not to embellish a lie too much, as it was easy to forget details, and too many details were a sign someone was lying.

Both the baron and Balven remained silent, so Donte said, "So anyway, I decided to come here, got to Marquenet, and heard of the army moving, so I signed on to a company and hitched a ride with the baggage. I wasn't trying to desert, just looking for my friends. Truth is, I never really swore to Captain Quinn or any other company, so I really couldn't desert, now could I?"

Daylon was silent for a moment, then said, "I'm assuming at best you're a thief and a thug, and at worst an assassin and a spy. But you might prove useful, as I may have to reach out to your masters again." Turning to Balven, he said, "I want him kept apart from the company, but under guard."

"I'll put him in a tent," said Balven. The baron's body man motioned for Donte to follow him. Donte stood up and trailed Balven out of the pavilion. They walked a short way to another tent. A pair of the baron's senior castellans were lounging on sleeping mats, and they both stood when Balven stopped in front of the open tent flap.

Balven said to one of the soldiers, "Find another tent." He made a waving motion with his hand. "Leave a mat but take everything else. Come back and tell him"—he pointed to the other soldier—"where you're bedding down for the

night. Then go find a medic and return to tend to this man."
The first soldier ran off, and Balven told the second, "Stand
guard, and if he tries to escape don't kill him; just beat him
up a little more."

He gave Donte a long warning look, then left without
another word.

The newly appointed guard gave Donte a black look.
Donte tried to smile, but his face hurt too much, so he just
nodded once and moved to the remaining mat, where he lay
down. He had learned in childhood that if you had nothing
else to do you should sleep. His future was out of his hands:
there was nothing else to do.

BALVEN RETURNED TO HIS BROTHER'S pavilion. As
soon as he entered the door he saw that Daylon was reading
another report. "How bad is it?" he asked.

"Everything to the west, from here to the coast . . ."
Daylon tossed aside the report and let it flutter to the floor.
"That's the third message reporting that the entire coast, to
the north and south, has been raided. Small boats, a dozen
men each, hit every village. More of the same, killing and
burning, but leaving with little by way of booty."

"Those villages don't have much, so there's a different
point, isn't there?"

Daylon nodded. "Page!" he shouted.

A young man, barely more than a boy, appeared a moment later from outside the tent. "My lord?"

"Wine and two goblets."

The youth bowed and departed.

Balven said, "It must be worse than I imagine, if you're
drinking this early."

"I have nowhere to go at the moment and some things to
discuss with you, so why not?"

Balven pulled over the stool Donte had used and sat

down on his brother's left side. It was a bit lower than Daylon's chair, but high enough that eating or drinking from the table wasn't awkward. And it wasn't the first time Balven had been in such a position. "What are your thoughts?" he asked.

"Let me hear yours first."

"The raids along the coast . . ." The baron's half brother shrugged. "I think they're to create terror, disrupt the usual commerce, create refugees who will flee to the city and put a strain on resources. Food will become scarce; the newcomers will have to steal to eat or die in the gutters. It's going to turn very nasty for a while before it starts to return to normal. If it ever does."

With a wry laugh, Daylon said, "You have been reading some of the military history books in Father's library."

"Your library," corrected Balven. "I lack your insatiability when it comes to reading, but I'm hardly an illiterate fool. Some of those dusty old tomes you adore so much are quite useful when it comes to understanding the requirements of governance. Since childhood my choice has been to wither inside, spending a useless life in envy, or to help my brother who is the only person on Garn I've grown to love. I chose the latter." When Daylon's eyebrows rose, Balven continued. "You're a rare and good man, brother, and I've felt that since we were boys, though it's not my nature to be overly . . . praising."

With a soft chuckle, Daylon said, "Well, I know that."

"Too many of your friends and enemies think they rule by some inherent superiority and therefore anything they do will be 'right,' and woe awaits the person who says otherwise. They will be overrun, ground under massive bootheels."

"As those ground under . . ." Daylon stopped.

"You're thinking of Steveren, aren't you?"

Daylon stayed silent, then nodded. "That lad from Coaltachin. That brought the memory of the Betrayal back as if it were yesterday." His chest heaved in a silent exhalation. "Steveren was nobody's fool, but he believed too much in people acting in good faith. He lacked the talent for treachery."

"That he did." Balven studied his brother for a long moment, then said, "What really troubles you?"

"You have to ask?"

"I think you need to put your thoughts out, not listen to mine, because I know you well, brother, and if I let you sit silently and brood, no good will come from it."

With a flash of annoyance, Daylon said, "Sometimes you are too vexing, despite your intent."

The page returned with a tray, put down a carafe of wine and two goblets, quickly served the two men, then departed.

Balven took a sip and nodded in approval. "I believe vexing you is part of my duties."

Daylon took a deep breath and nodded. "Perhaps. My thoughts are that we prepared for years for Lodavico to move westward. I've spent a fair bit of gold on your agents to track Lodavico's every move, listening to every rumor, and despite all that, our best assumption was that he wouldn't move west for another two years, one at the least. Now this." He swallowed a long draft of wine. "Some of the information we've seen for the last few years suggested that there might be another player in this murderous game we play, but it came to no more than hints and suggestions."

Balven nodded. "And some we dismissed as ill founded, even misdirections, from Sandura and its allies."

"So, what are our choices?" asked Daylon. Balven knew it to be a rhetorical question and stayed silent. "We retreat to our northernmost fortress at Barrier Rock—which we haven't reinforced in my lifetime—or all the way back to Marquenet."

"Or?"

"Or we move in force to Port Colos and sort out this betrayal with the governor and get ready to hand out some harsh retribution to whoever is behind this."

Balven said, "And either choice could be the wrong one."

"Do you think all this is to lure us to Colos, while someone else attacks Marquenet?"

Balven gave a slight shrug. "I've considered it, but you've left a strong enough garrison to hold the city until we return. And if someone were attacking, they would be faced with this force at their rear." He shook his head. "I'd choose some other plan, unless our unnamed enemy has a larger army than I can imagine, and I can imagine a very big one."

"To breach the city's defenses . . ." Daylon shrugged. "It would take both Zindaros's and Helosea's navies combined to transport that big a force if they come by sea."

"And by land we wouldn't be talking like this but fighting for our lives." Balven looked into his brother's eyes. "So, we go to Port Colos?"

"Let the captains and sergeants know we break camp at first light, and I want our screeners out at dawn, the army to follow an hour later."

Balven stood and bowed, a formality he had observed since joining his half brother's household as a child. It was his way of reminding Daylon that no matter how close they might be as brothers, he was still a bastard commoner, and Daylon, ruler of the richest known barony.

At the door, he turned and asked, "What about that lad, Donte?"

"We take him with us. He may prove useful. If he doesn't, maybe I'll hand him back over to Deakin."

"For his sake I hope he proves useful," said Balven with a rueful smile.

HAVA AND MOLLY RODE CAUTIOUSLY at the wood's edge, picking their way around deadfalls, all the time checking the road they could glimpse to the southwest. There were ample signs of heavy use recently, as rubbish had been dumped at various places, but Molly estimated the troops they followed were a good half day ahead, so unless they had mounted a rearguard, the two women were probably safe from observation until the following afternoon.

"At this rate, we won't reach the city until after sundown tomorrow," said Molly.

"That may be a good thing," replied Hava. "Let's walk the horses."

Both riders dismounted and led their mounts in single file. Doing this kept the horses fresh enough that they wouldn't be useless after a long journey. "We should camp at sundown," said Molly.

"The horses could use it, and so could I," said Hava, her impatience to find Hatu tempered by fatigue and sore muscles.

Since leaving the charcoal burner's hut, they had pushed themselves and the horses, and from Molly's assessment they'd made up significant distance between themselves and the raiding army. Hava knew that any large body of people moved as fast as the slowest member not left behind, which meant they might come upon the raiders at any moment. She knew it likely they'd hear them before they saw them, but that still didn't mean caution was unwarranted.

"How close to the road do you want to camp? This is as far as I've ever wandered from home . . ." Molly's voice betrayed a hint of emotion when she said that last word. "I know that from here we've got foothills rising on this side of the road and farms somewhere ahead on the other side. So, where do we camp?"

"Let's see where we are at sundown, then decide," Hava said.

Molly gave a single nod and they continued their journey.

As they rode on, the woods darkened to the point at which future travel would be difficult, if not impossible. After a few minutes, Hava halted and asked, "Do you hear that?"

Molly said, "People on the road." She kept her voice low even though they were still a good distance away and sheltered by thick tree trunks and dense shadow.

Hava handed the reins of her mount to Molly and moved toward the sound. The sun was touching the western horizon, and she and Molly were on the northern side of the high road leading northwest to Port Colos. They were still the best part of a day's quick ride from the city and were not expecting to see many travelers, but as Hava reached the thinning woods nearest the road it appeared they were in error.

The sky to the west was still illuminated in iridescent orange and vibrant pinks, throwing the figures before Hava into stark relief, but she saw enough.

She slipped back into the woods and said to Molly, "Slow wagons, the last of the raiding army."

"Baggage? Followers?"

"No . . . or maybe some baggage wagons, but not the usual followers. In the fading light it was hard to tell, but I did see prisoners."

"So they didn't kill everyone?" Molly sighed heavily. "How many do you think?"

"A couple dozen, at least."

"Make out any faces?"

"No," said Hava. "Too far away and too dark."

"What do you want to do?" asked Molly.

Hava was silent for a bit as she considered her choices. "If Hatu is among the prisoners . . ."

Molly nodded. "You have to get close to the prisoners to know."

"Let's follow and see if they camp."

Molly put her hand on Hava's arm. "Wait. If they were going to camp, they would have stopped by now and made fires."

"Unless they don't want to be seen. Perhaps a cold camp?"

"All right. We get close, and if they stop, maybe we can get a look at who's in those wagons."

"I can get close," said Hava.

"What if they don't stop?" asked Molly. "What if they get to Port Colos and enter the city?"

"I can still get close," said Hava.

Molly's face was barely visible in the gloom of evening, but Hava could read the dubious expression that crossed her features.

"What you can do in these woods, moving without startling your prey, I can do in a city. Cities are my hunting ground."

Molly still looked skeptical but didn't seem inclined to argue.

They led the horses along the edge of the tree line.

Hava could hear the wheels grinding along on the hard-packed road and the rare distant voice. Occasionally the breeze carried the sound of a whimper or crying.

HATUSHALY FELT NAUSEATED, A DULL anticipation of the need to vomit, yet no spasm came and no bitter saliva gathered in his mouth. He tried to open his eyes, but his lids seemed heavy. It required a focused act of will to open them.

He smelled . . . old salt . . . and fish. He felt rocking. He knew that meant something, but he couldn't quite piece together the puzzle. Sounds tickled the edge of his awareness . . . a lapping sound of . . . water?

For a lingering instant he remembered the cave in which he had been held by . . . The images faded: he felt unable to hold on to any thought.

A distant voice said, "He's stirring." He thought it might be Hava. It was a woman . . . It wasn't Hava. Hava . . . ? He fought to open his eyes and failed. Thoughts brushed against his awareness but fled as though a feather floating on a gust. Then he slipped back into unconsciousness.

10

CAPTIVES AND MYSTERIES

Hava watched as the last wagons rolled through the city gates of Port Colos. It was midafternoon, and both she and Molly were watching just behind the first line of trees.

The soil beneath their boots was rocky, and a ridge covered with enough trees to screen movement rose to the northwest. Hava said, "Let's follow that ridge and see if we can get a better view, though from this distance it's going to look like an anthill, at best."

They climbed and the trees gave way to low scrub and, finally, to bare rocks. To the north there was a dip down to a wide bowl where grass grew and a small pond offered welcome refreshment for the horses. Leading the fatigued mounts, Hava showed Molly how to stake them out so they could graze and drink, but not wander off. When they had finished, Molly said, "I hope we don't need rope any time soon. That was all of it."

The sky was darkening and shadows lengthening by the time they moved up the spine of the rock to a small promontory. Two massive ridges extended from below where they stood. One ridge ran to the north, into a bluff overlooking rocks preventing any boats from landing close to the city; the other dropped steeply down to the southwest, ending at the edge of the city wall. Hava eyed the one that led down to the city and said, "If I could get down to that spine of rock . . ."

"You'd have to be half mountain goat or bighorn sheep, if you could survive the drop from here to the top of that ridge," Molly said. "And we used all the rope. Besides, should you have to get out of there in a hurry, climbing back up that way looks like a problem."

Hava let out an exasperated sound, half sigh, half throaty growl. "I hate to agree."

They studied the scene below. As the sun sank below the horizon, Molly asked, "What's that?" She pointed to the sea just beyond the city, where a haze of white obscured the water.

"Haze. Not quite fog," said Hava. "I've seen it all my life. Some places it rolls in with the morning tide and hangs along the coastline. Sometimes it burns off with the heat of the day, sometimes not. I've ridden into a port city where it's bright and sunny all day and then a mile or so from the city, gloom." She shrugged. "I take it for granted."

Molly said, "I've never seen its like before."

"You're noticing now because of the sun shining through it." Hava looked at Molly. "You haven't got around much, have you?"

"Da took me down to Marquenet once."

After a few moments of silence, they heard a sound from below in the city, a low jumble of noise that at first was unrecognizable. Then, abruptly, Hava knew what it was. "There's fighting in the city!"

The cacophony resolved itself into a clang of weapons, screams, shouts, dogs barking, and hoofbeats. "Who's fighting?" Molly asked.

"I don't know," replied Hava. "Mercenaries and . . . who-ever they were working for?"

The tempo of the battle and the volume of sound in-creased, and after a few minutes, Hava said, "This isn't some falling out between companies. It's much bigger: someone is fighting the locals! The governor's army or whatever they're called!"

A fire had broken out in the southernmost quarter of the city, and as evening descended it provided a brilliant illu-mination. The air was replete with shrieks and cries, men shouting in concern, women and children screaming.

"They're sacking the city!" Hava said. She gripped Mol-ly's arm, digging her fingers in as if clinging to her compan-ion for support.

Molly looked at her friend's face, outlined against the fading sunset and the flickering distant fire. Hava's eyes welled with tears, though she remained silent. Her stoic na-ture was being tested, Molly knew. She didn't need to read minds to know that Hava was terrified of what might hap-pen to Hatu if he were indeed among the prisoners taken into the city.

HATU FELT A STRANGE RETURN to coherent thought, as if he were awakening from a fevered illness. His body ached and his chest hurt. He was thirsty and his throat was so dry he could barely swallow. He tried to open his eyes and found them crusted with dried tears and mucus.

He was lying in some type of hammock. It swayed gently and he realized he must be aboard a vessel.

A woman's voice said, "Don't move or you'll hurt your-self."

A wet cloth was applied to his face, cleaning away the crystallized mess on his eyes, and at last he could open them.

A young woman stood next to him, but when he tried to move he discovered he was tied to the hammock, a rope wrapped around him half a dozen times, confining his arms and legs. He tested the bonds slightly, and she said, "We had rough weather and didn't want you to fall out." She began to untie the rope.

"I know you," Hatu said, his voice a scratchy whisper.

"Wait." She stopped untying the rope for a moment, held a waterskin to his mouth, and let him drink. Then she returned to freeing him and, when the rope was removed, helped him get into a sitting position in the middle of the hammock, his legs dangling a few feet above the floor. "Don't try to stand yet. You're very weak."

Sitting up made his head swim, and Hatu found himself blinking to force his eyes to focus. "You're that . . . girl with Catharian."

"Sabella," she said, nodding. "We've been caring for you . . . for quite a while."

Still groggy, Hatu said, "My head . . . it's . . . it really hurts."

"We had to drug you for longer than I would have liked," said the young woman. She regarded Hatu in a way he found unsettling, though he couldn't say why.

"Drug me?"

"Catharian will explain. He's up on deck. I'll go and get him."

"No," said Hatu. "I need to move. Everything hurts, but I know my own body well enough to know lying around any longer will not help."

"Very well," she said, and put out her arm to provide support.

Hatu's legs were wobbly and he could barely navigate his way through the small forecastle and into the cargo hold, which smelled strongly of fish.

"Can you get up this?" asked Sabella, pointing to a ladder leading to a hatch above them.

"I'll try," he said, and he planted himself on it with slow, purposeful movements, reached up and grabbed the highest rung he could reach, then slowly pulled and pushed with his feet at the same time. His leg trembled a little but his arms felt adequate, and after pausing for a moment he repeated the movement and made it up another rung. It took a full minute to negotiate a ladder that should have taken mere seconds, but he finally stuck his head through the hatch.

Strong hands grabbed him under the armpits and he was half lifted over the edge of the hatch and sat on the deck.

Hatu looked up at a dark face set in a half smile. After studying that face for a second, he said, "I know you! You hit me!" Whatever flash of anger that woke in him was muted and distant.

"Sorry, but we didn't have time to argue. I knew you wouldn't leave your friends and that seemed the logical choice." The man smiled fully, but in a way that made it seem as if it hurt his face to do so. "I'm Denbe."

"I should hate you," said Hatu, "for making me leave my wife and friends . . ." He paused. "Why don't I?"

From behind him a voice said, "It's the drugs, I wager. The effects will linger for a while, and given the nature of your temper, that is probably a good thing."

Hatu looked over his shoulder to see Catharian standing near the mainmast. The false monk motioned for Denbe to help Hatu to his feet.

He looked around. They were on a boat, a decent-sized fishing boat, a lugger. It was a two-masted ketch with twin lugsails and a bowsprit to which a headsail was lashed and not in use.

Hatu felt strength slowly returning to his legs. "Hava?" he asked.

"Alive to the best of our knowledge," said Catharian. "All of Beran's Hill was razed, but she was with the baron, so she may be one of the only survivors of that battle."

"Not properly a battle," said Denbe. "*Slaughter* would be the right word."

Hatu's expression was a mix of disbelief and outrage. "Slaughter?"

"Too many to count," said Denbe.

Hatu wondered about Declan, Gwen, and the others he'd left behind, then gave silent thanks to any deity listening that Hava had been out of the town when this happened. He lowered his head a moment and just breathed.

Catharian asked, "Are you hungry? Thirsty?"

Hatu shook his head. "My stomach is . . . numb."

"Drugs," said the false monk.

"All of them are dead?"

"Not all," said Catharian. "The morning after we dragged you off, I scouted and saw a few people moving in the rubble. Some soldiers had put up a shelter of sorts with a kitchen. I knew the baron's men from Esterly would be there shortly, so I headed back to the hut we had you in. We waited until sundown and then took you away."

"Why?"

"That's a long tale. First, we need to get your strength back, so again I'll ask, can you eat?"

"If I must," said Hatu.

Catharian motioned for Hatu to follow him into a tiny rear cabin that barely held the two of them. "The captain slept here," said the false monk. There were three large sacks sitting on a bunk: he opened one and took out an apple, some hard cheese, and a slice of salt pork. "There's nothing like a proper galley on this lugger. It never sailed out of sight of land, as best I can judge."

Hatu recalled looking around the deck and said, "We're

out of sight of land now." He nibbled at the cheese. Finding the flavor less muted as he chewed, he swallowed and then accepted a skin handed to him by Catharian, took a drink, and almost choked. He had been expecting water but was greeted by the pungent bite of a stout red wine, though once he made the adjustment in his mind, the fruity liquid tasted acceptable.

"Not too much," said Catharian. "It helps nourish your recovery in moderation, but too much and I might as well drug you again." He held out a second skin. "Water."

Hatu accepted the second skin, discovering as he drank just how thirsty he was. After a long pull, he put the skin on the small table and asked, "Why did you abduct me?" As the food started to refresh him and the drugs slowly wore off, he found his old nature starting to assert itself. A hot spark of anger within him was slowly building in intensity, and he knew if he didn't put it out he would attack the false monk. Given that Denbe was standing only a few feet away outside, this was a very stupid idea, but part of him didn't care.

Catharian said, "How much have they told you of your past?"

"Depends on which 'they' you mean. My masters in Coaltachin always skirted any questions about my birth, simply letting it be known I was to be treated like any other student, except I wasn't. That was a cause of much anger in my life, the chafing at not knowing the truth about who I was.

"If by 'they' you mean Baron Dumarch and his man Balven, they told me that I'm the son of a dead king, of a kingdom reduced to ashes in a land I've never visited since my birth. My wife, Hava, and I joked about it: I'm the King of Ashes."

Catharian sighed. "That was, I suppose, necessary. But there's a great deal more to it, and that will take some time.

"First, be certain that no one here or where we're going means you harm. In fact, the opposite. We abducted you from Beran's Hill because we couldn't risk you dying there. For that I apologize, but after I've finished here, I hope you'll understand the need."

"I doubt it," said Hatu, for his anger was still rising, albeit more slowly. "Go on."

"Had your father, the King of Ithrace, lived, there were . . . secrets, you could say, about your lineage and who you were destined to be that you would have been told. Your eldest brother would have been king, but you and your brothers and sisters would have all been important members of his court, as your children and his also would have played a vital role in the future of Garn. A great deal of what you would have learned is unknown to me, as my role is relatively minor, but others can give you all that you should have learned as a youngster. It's vital that you, the last scion of Ithrace, survive. The future of Garn depends on it."

"I don't understand," said Hatu. "How can one kingdom be vital to the future of the world? And anyway . . . it's gone, right? Ithrace and my family are all gone."

"But you're not," said Catharian. "There's an old legend that a curse attends the death of the last Firemane." He tapped Hatu lightly on the chest. "That's wrong . . . or at least partially wrong."

"I don't understand."

"You will, in time. Do you know how to sail?" asked Catharian.

Hatu hesitated at the change of topic, then said, "I've crewed ships before."

"Good," said the false monk. He stood up. "If you're up to it after your long rest, we could use a hand." He led Hatu out of the small cabin.

The sun was setting and to the east, stars were appearing. Hatu gripped the railing of the boat as he attempted to get his sea legs back. He took a deep breath and accepted another draft of water from the skin Catharian had brought with him.

"I won't expect you up in the rigging, but if you could watch the lads—they're earnest, but inexperienced with anything bigger than a dinghy."

The lugger was being manned by Denbe and three boys who were maybe twelve or thirteen years of age from the look of them. Catharian pointed to one. "That fellow with the dark skin is William. The dark-haired lad who's not Williem is called Bowen. And the gangly chap with dirty-blond hair is Jenson."

The questioning look on Hatu's face was answered by Catharian. "Their village was destroyed. They were the only ones who survived—they hid deep in the woods. Everyone they know is gone. We couldn't leave them, and we needed help sailing this boat. So we scavenged what food we could, found this lugger anchored a short way up the coast—it's one of the few the raiders didn't burn to the waterline—and here we are."

"Where is here?"

"We're taking you to the safest place on Garn, Sefan." Catharian saw a reaction to that name. "Or do you still prefer to be called Hatushaly?"

"It's the name I've grown up with," Hatu answered.

"Then Hatushaly it will be."

"Hatu. Most people call me Hatu."

"Then so shall I."

"Where are we bound?"

"To a land very far from the twin continents. As distant a land as exists on Garn."

Knowing a little of geography, courtesy of Master Bodai, who seemed to know something about everything,

Hatu said, "We're heading west by south. Are we traveling to Alastor?"

Catharian seemed impressed by the question. "I forget you were raised by people who travel widely. No, Alastor is the most distant continent to the west, north of the midpoint of this world, an imaginary line called the equator. We travel even farther and south, to a continent as large as both Tembrias combined. It's a land called Nytanny."

Hatu's face showed no recognition.

"It simply means 'our land' in the language of the most dominant nation there, Aurenton Sothu, which means 'Empire of the Sun.' Oh, and they're very distant kin of yours. Anyway, we'll be at sea for a few weeks."

"In this?" said Hatu, looking at the boys scampering about their duties. "With them?"

"No," said Catharian. "There's an island on the way where we will leave this boat for a proper ship, one with a full crew and provisions."

"Who is 'we'?"

Catharian had discarded the robe of the Order of Tathan and was wearing a loose-fitting dark green tunic and heavy canvas trousers. "We are the Flame Guard. We have been tasked for a very long time to protect the line of the Firemane."

"From what?"

"From your extinction. Should you die, what we think of as 'magic' in Garn will die with you."

Hatu stood motionless, blinking in confusion.

HAVA AND MOLLY SAT ON the promontory looking down into the city as the sounds of slaughter carried to their distant observation post. Their vantage was close enough to the main gate of Port Colos that they could see people attempting to flee the city being chased down by horsemen. Some were cut down, but others were netted and dragged back. "Slavers," said Hava softly.

Molly's expression was one of confusion. "Slavers? Here?"

"Why not? The attack from inside the city was completely unexpected and those attempting to defend it were taken unawares."

"How . . . ?" asked Molly in hushed tones. The terror she was witnessing was reinforcing the horror of the slaughter she had survived.

"I don't know," said Hava. "The governor welcomed them as allies, and they betrayed him?"

Molly nodded. "When I fled the battle at Beran's Hill, some of us made it to a farm at the wood's edge—myself with that captain, Bogartis, and some of his men, and a few others. Those that came after us didn't expect the fight we gave them, and none got back to town for reinforcements. Hava, I know well what happened there, but I swear there weren't enough raiders to take a city of this size."

"Look," said Hava, pointing to the horizon.

As the evening mist thinned, dots of light began appearing on the water beyond the city. While Hava and Molly watched, the scattered pinpoints of light, like stars in the sea, increased in amount and intensity as night descended.

"Ships. There must be . . . hundreds," said Molly. Then she said, "A thousand?"

"Is there a fleet this big anywhere?" whispered Hava.

"They only sent a small part of their numbers to Beran's Hill. The rest . . . ?"

"Sitting here waiting," said Hava. "Or raiding up and down the coast."

"Why?"

"I have no idea. All I know of military matters is avoiding drunken soldiers." She stood up.

"Where are you going?" asked Molly.

"Down there," said Hava. "If Hatu is in that city, he'll need my help."

"You'll both end up dead!" Molly stood and gripped Hava's wrist. "He's either dead already or somewhere else."

Hava disengaged her arm from Molly's grasp. "I have to know."

"Then wait until it's over. People are being slaughtered from the sound of it, and as skilled with a knife as you might be, that's an *army* down there!"

Indecision rooted Hava to the ground. What Molly said was obviously true, but she needed to know about Hatu. At last, she said, "I have to know. If I'm not back by dawn, get as far from here as fast as you can."

Molly watched silently as Hava vanished down the ridge and into the darkness.

HAVA KEPT LOW AS SHE scurried along the rock face of the ridge that ran down from the overlook where she and Molly had watched, toward the northernmost wall of the city. She knew she was masked by the darkness, despite a lack of any sheltering trees or brush in this cleared area before the wall. And, from the sounds coming from the city, it was unlikely that someone would be looking out for anyone approaching the city.

Hurrying as fast as possible, she reached the intersection of the rocks and the wall. The fighting was starting to abate, or at least the sounds of battle were.

Port Colos had a wide bay backed by enough solid ground that there had never been a need to build a wharf. The city had erected the quay from this northernmost section and had continued adding to it to the south.

Hava had chosen this edge of the city because it had seemed to be the quietest section she and Molly could see before the fighting broke out. It still seemed relatively quiet, though no doubt anywhere inside the walls was fraught with risks. She reached the wall and looked up, and as she expected, there was a buttressed ledge supporting a defensive position for archers above her head. Without a grapple and rope, getting up there looked as if it would prove problematic.

Hava moved to where the ridge and wall met and found what she hoped: years before, the end of this wall had been nestled hard against the side of the ridge. Over the years, erosion and neglect had caused stones to crumble and earth to wash away, so there was a narrow passage between the wall and the rising ground.

She could see faint light ahead and reckoned it looked wide enough to scrape a way through, into the city. Turning sideways and making sure her large belt knife was on her left hip, so that she wouldn't impale herself trying to sidle through, she started. As she had expected, it was a tight fit—a large man would not be able to try this, or a large woman for that matter.

Slowly she inched along sideways, hoping nothing collapsed or moved, as this would be a terrible place to be trapped or killed. The rock scraped against her cheek three times, and her backside felt as if it was being rubbed raw, but she continued at a steady pace.

She had a jaw-clenching moment as she came to the end of the gap, for she would be helplessly exposed to anyone who might look her way as she emerged. But her luck held and at last she could see clearly around the wall: she was alone. Some lights farther down the quay indicated that someone was down there, but no one was moving this far to the north.

A noise to her right caused Hava to spin into a crouch, ready to fight. Although the ridge of stone sloping down to the ground had created a natural barrier, some old stone-

work had been added to the top of it, providing a defense of
sorts should an attack come from the north along the rocky
beach. Stacks of abandoned crates and rubbish had been
shoved into the corner.

From within that pile came movement, and Hava waited
silently, not wishing to investigate but knowing she couldn't
afford to leave a potential enemy at her back. She circled
slowly to her left and reached the end of the makeshift defense. Glancing to her left, she saw a steep drop-off to the
rocks and sands below and realized that defending this part
of the city had always been of minor concern.

Creeping over to the pile, she reached out and grabbed a
flat piece of wood. Yanking it aside, she peered in and saw
three small figures crouched in the dark, their large eyes
barely illuminated by the distant light.

Her stomach knotted and she felt her heart sink as she
recognized what she had found. "Damn," she muttered, as
three terrified children gazed up at her. Kneeling, she said,
"I won't hurt you."

Too terrified to speak, they crouched even lower, unable
to move. Half a dozen questions popped into Hava's head
only to be instantly dismissed. She knew their parents were
probably dead, their home either ablaze or being sacked,
and that these murderous pigs would either slaughter these
children or sell them into slavery.

Softly she asked, "Who is the oldest?"

No one moved or replied, and she repeated the question.
Finally a young girl whispered, "I am."

"You're the big sister?"

The girl nodded, the movement barely perceptible in the
gloom.

Hava did not know how to deal with children who had
not been raised as she had. The older girl looked as if she
might be nine or ten years of age, perhaps a bit more, but by

that time in her life Hava had already been trained to fight and survive. These children had not.

"Listen," she said as calmly as she could. "I need you to leave here."

The older girl immediately started shaking her head, while the two smaller children clung to each other with terror etched across their tiny faces.

Trying to think how she'd heard parents talk to children who weren't from the school, she kept her tone soft, despite the distant clamor, which sounded as if it might be getting closer. "Listen, I need you to be brave. Those men who are hurting people are getting closer. You need to go through that space." She pointed to the crack through which she had entered the city. "You'll be next to a big wall of rock. Follow the rock till you're outside the city. Can you do that?"

"I'm scared," the older girl whispered.

"I know you are. Being scared is . . . all right." Without thought she added, "I'm scared, too," and she realized at the moment of saying it that she was terrified. She was frightened at the prospect of not finding Hatu, at being captured or killed, of abandoning Molly. Swallowing hard, she said, "But you just have to do things even when you're scared, all right?"

"I suppose so," came the quiet reply.

"These your brother and sister?"

"Yes."

"You have to be . . . a big girl. In charge. Do you understand?"

"No."

"You have to look out for them, because you're all they have left."

"I can't."

"You must." She reached out and took hold of the smallest child, the boy, and pulled him away from his sisters.

Deprived of his siblings, the boy suddenly clung to her hard, trembling uncontrollably, and Hava found herself momentarily overcome by a need to do something, but having no idea what. Nothing she'd ever experienced seemed remotely helpful in dealing with this situation.

From the strong odor that reached her nostrils, it was clear that the boy had soiled himself, but there was nothing she could do about that. She moved slightly, freeing up her left arm, and motioned for the two girls to come closer. When they were cradled in her other arm, Hava said, "Some men are coming."

The older girl whimpered, and Hava quickly said, "No, some good men who will protect you. If you go through that crack and follow the big stone cliff away from the city, you'll see them coming along the road in the morning." She desperately hoped that would be true. "They will take care of you, but if you stay here the bad men will find you like I did, and you don't want that, do you?"

The older girl shook her head.

"What is your name?"

"Merrylee."

"Take your brother and sister. Can you do it, please?"

The older girl said, "I'll try."

"Be brave," Hava said as she opened her arms. The older girl took the two younger children by the hand and led them into the crack between the wall and the ridge. Hava felt a sudden stab of fear for them and tears stung her eyes. But there was nothing more she could do for them, and there were already hundreds of other children lying dead or captured.

She forced herself to remain calm as the children vanished from view and moved toward what looked to be a collection of abandoned stalls, perhaps the merchant stalls that had lined the city wall for about a hundred years or so.

These would provide a bit of cover as she moved toward the center of the city.

As she moved purposefully and cautiously along from stall to stall, darting in and out, a passing thought struck her. She'd never asked the names of the two other children.

11

INVESTIGATIONS, DISCOVERIES,
AND THE UNEXPECTED

D eclan waved away an attempt of help from a baggage
boy as he made his way through the almost abandoned
kitchen tent: the bulk of the baron's army had departed at
first light. He elected to grab a bowl and had it filled with
stew. He did accept a boy's offer to put a big wooden spoon
in it, as he was limited to the use of his left hand only.

He walked slowly, not just because his legs were weak,
but because he didn't want to lose control of the brimful
bowl: he was not in the mood to embarrass himself.

It took slow and careful control for him to lower himself
to the ground and position the bowl in the space between his
knees and crossed ankles. His shoulder still throbbed, but
less than the day before, he thought.

A soldier he recognized, one of Bogartis's company,
came over holding two mugs. He squatted and put one down
next to Declan's left side. "Thought you might need this."

"Thank you," replied Declan.

"Name's Bernard," said the soldier. He was perhaps only
a few years older than Declan. He glanced around. "Without
the lights . . ."

"I know. It's like camping along the highway at night."

"At least the rain's gone."

Declan nodded. After a couple of mouthfuls of the stew he asked, "What is your captain planning?"

"We just got word to hunker down for a while. The baron took his entire force, leaving a company of boys and the baggage, and we're to follow tomorrow as guards." He sighed. "I think we'll be taking his gold for a while to come."

Declan said nothing as he continued to eat.

After a few minutes of quiet, Bernard said, "If he force marches all night, he'll be at Port Colos at dawn. What do you think he'll find?"

"I have no idea."

"I've been fighting for about four years now, but I've never seen anything like this. Some of the older lads say they've never even heard of the like."

Declan continued eating in silence. He put the bowl aside and reached for the mug of ale. He drank, taking a momentary pleasure in the bitter tang of the flavor before falling back into the dark numbness he had been in since regaining consciousness.

Seeing that Declan wasn't inclined toward conversation, Bernard stood up. "Well, rest if you can."

As the soldier began to leave, Declan said, "Before you go, can you ask Bogartis to see me if he has a moment?"

Bernard raised a finger to his forelock as if saluting. "I will."

The void inside Declan was like nothing he had experienced before. He knew there were tears, rage, and pain buried deeply inside, but for some reason it was as if they belonged to another man.

Just as he finished eating, Bogartis appeared. "One of the lads said you wanted a word?"

"You're following the baron with the baggage tomorrow?"

Bogartis nodded. "He was in a fit to get started at dawn and didn't wait until things got organized. So he hired me and a couple of other companies to escort the baggage to Colos. I think he expects to be unwelcome and plans on besieging the city until the governor comes out for a chat. Why?"

"There's nothing for me here," said Declan, attempting to stand and arriving at his feet just as Bogartis steadied him.

"You're still pretty wobbly, lad."

"I'll be ready to ride in the morning—if you'll have me."

"Pleasure," said the old captain. "But you'll hardly be in any shape for a fight once we catch up."

"Even if I can't fight I want to be there to see justice done to whoever killed my wife."

"That I understand. Well, as it happens two of my lads are no longer with us, so I have extra horses. You're welcome to tag along, and after all this is said and done—and you have the use of both arms—perhaps we can get some smithing done."

"We can," said Declan.

Bogartis patted his shoulder. "Rest now, or we might be digging your grave along the way. You need another week before we can stop worrying about those stitches."

"I'll take it easy," said Declan.

Bogartis left, and Declan made himself as comfortable as he could on his ground cloth. He closed his eyes, but as tired as he felt, sleep took its time in claiming him.

HAVA CROUCHED BEHIND A HUGE pile of refuse. As the city was looted, raiders had piled up discarded goods, household items of all kinds, clothing, and dozens of bodies. She could feel waves of heat coming down the street and heard shouts and screams. She knew her time here was running out: the raiders were systematically working their way through the city and eventually would return this way. Besides the children, it appeared that no one had gotten past where she hid. A few wounded souls had fallen and died within sight of her, but as of now she thought she was probably the last person in this part of the city. She weighed her options. She could attempt to work her way back to the north and escape via the gap through which she had gained entrance, but the need to locate Hatu gnawed at her heart. She was desperate to find him.

The sight of slain children reinforced her sense that in sending Merrylee and the others off to safety she had done the only thing that might possibly save them. In fact, everyone who lay dead on the ground appeared either very old or very young: there were no older children or young men and women in sight. For the most part the people were grey-haired, and no doubt had been weak and slow, in poor health before death. But the lack of the able-bodied probably meant there were slavers with the army: such captives would bring a decent price on the auction block. Slavery was not commonplace in the twin continents, but it was in the islands and in some baronies. Hava hadn't encountered it much on her travels, but the masters took great pains explaining the risks involved in working a crew in a city that permitted slavery. The presence of slavers meant a fit young man like Hatu stood a better chance of still being alive—if he hadn't fought like a maniac.

Thinking of Hatu fighting rather than letting himself be captured brought tears to Hava's eyes, and she wiped them away and chided herself for losing focus. She was drained from lack of sleep, stress, and exertion, yet her heart was pounding and she felt more alive than she remembered in years. She knew from her training this was a false burst of energy, one that could leave her defenseless if she pushed herself too hard for much longer. It was hard to choose a course of action. She kept searching for her next objective, but the choices she imagined would not resolve themselves into a coherent shape.

She watched as a man running while holding some bundle that meant enough to him to risk his life for was struck down from behind by a horseman. He died as his precious belongings were scattered across the blood-soaked ground.

Hava moved back inside the last stall. Just south of her a street running from the harbor into the city limited her ability to hide, and across the street there were no stalls, just shops and businesses, or that's what they appeared to be from the numerous signs hanging above their doors. The wind was shifting now, so that the rising hot air was being forced down to the ground by incoming cooler night air, and that seemed to act on the flames like a bellows, as they rose up high for a few moments and then seemed to contract and expand outward, only to leap high again. Not only did this cause a strange pulsing light, but it also seemed to pump smoke along the ground for some distance before it started to rise, like a seabird running over the sand before launching itself into flight. The air was turning more acrid by the minute and her eyes began to smart and sting.

Hava stood motionless in a semi-crouch, peering around the corner, her belt knife clutched in her hand. She could see no further progress to be made: retreat appeared to be her only option. Then she heard voices, men on horseback, approaching. Her only advantage was that they were coming out of a brightly lit area with fires on all sides into the relative darkness behind her.

She slipped back into the next stall and risked a moment of standing to look for the source of the voices. Out of the smoke rolling up from the south, a group of four riders emerged, and Hava barely had time to duck behind an overturned sack of grain. Knowing that movement would betray her presence, she froze and waited.

The sound of hooves on the stones was leisurely. Hava suspected these riders assumed that no one was left in this part of the city and they were simply being thorough.

Their language was strange but oddly familiar. The sounds of movement slowed, and Hava resisted the temptation to peer over the top of the large sack. Then the riders stopped and she heard some of them dismount. Hava silently cursed fate and held her breath. She readied herself. If she had the element of surprise, she might be able to outrun them and get to the gap in the wall before they remounted and overtook her. If any of them were still on horseback, she was done for. One or even two she might elude, especially if she could inflict some damage with her blade before making her break, but four? That was out of the question.

The men were in a discussion of some urgency, judging by their tone. Two did most of the speaking and had distinctive voices, but the other two voiced agreement or made an occasional comment. Hava listened for what seemed like an hour, though she knew in reality only a few minutes had passed. She controlled her breathing and gently flexed the muscles in her arms, legs, and shoulders as much as she could without noticeably moving.

Trying to stay focused, she almost missed a shift in her own perceptions, as suddenly what the men were saying made sense in a way. They used words that she didn't recognize, but she heard enough in her own native tongue, though with a strange accent, with changed vowel sounds and different emphases. She'd experienced a little of that when first coming to school, as the accent on the home island of Coaltachin was a bit different from what was spoken on the island where she had been born. She concentrated.

". . . gone . . ." said one man, and then a curse she didn't quite understand.

Another man said, ". . . killed too many. Asjafa is not happy."

"Keep looking. There may be . . ."—more that she didn't understand—". . . hiding," said a third man, and she heard the shuffling of feet and the jangle of harness, and then they rode off. She looked up as the sound of their horses faded and saw they were riding to the north. She looked around, feeling the urgent need to find a better spot to hide. Despite her youth, she'd been a girl thief in the city several times and knew that if you couldn't go to ground you went to the rooftops.

Hava waited until she saw them reach the end of the street, just before the last stall next to the crack between the wall and the ridge she had wiggled through. She slipped around the corner post supporting the roof over the stall and with a leap, pushed with one foot off the low screening wall, turning as she reached up and gripped the brace. She said a tiny prayer that it would hold her weight. Hava pulled herself up till she was lying on her stomach across a fairly sturdy wooden shed roof and silently thanked the builder of these stalls.

As the men started inspecting the stalls, Hava rolled over on her back and looked up. The parapet of the wall was a good ten feet above her head, and without a rope and grapple, she wouldn't attempt it at night, even with the light coming from the fire to the south, which seemed to be getting brighter as the sounds of battle were fading. With a sinking feeling she realized that meant the butchering of Port Colos was almost over and Molly had been right. Actually, she grudgingly admitted she had known Molly was right from the start, but she had refused to admit it. Trying to find Hatu in the midst of this carnage had been the height of stupidity. It was the sort of blunder, while on a mission, that would have had her masters debating whether to kill her, as she was no longer fit to serve as a member of the Quelli Nascosti, or just to banish her to a distant village to bear children for a farmer. For a brief instant she felt her mind turning inward as she felt a conflict between her need to obey her training and her need to find Hatu.

In a moment of bitter anger at herself, she pushed it all aside. There would be time for self-recrimination in the future, if she salvaged a future. Now, her only requirement was escape . . .

HAVA HAD REMAINED HIDDEN IN the shadow of the wall for nearly an hour, and the men who had ridden in had finished their examination of the stalls, concluding that no one was nearby.

The fire was burning its way north as the entire city was being put to the torch. She knew in short order these stalls would be aflame as the rubbish below her was lit. She had only a little time to escape, and her quickest route would be back the way she came.

She began slowly crawling along the tops of the stalls, keeping close to the wall, in deep shadow, and pausing for a moment at each support joint, then snaking over it on her stomach, checking to make certain the next stall roof was as sturdy as the last.

It took painful minutes, but at last she reached the final stall. She jumped down, staying in a crouch as she looked around for any sign that she had been observed. To the south the level of noise had diminished: there were some shouted orders, men and horses moving, punctuated by the popping and crackling sounds of timbers burning and pockets of flammable goods igniting. It took a moment for her to realize there was no more screaming. That realization chilled her.

The smoke was now rolling continuously inland: she hoped it would mask her departure.

She wiggled through the crack between the wall and the ridge and again experienced the terrifying moment of being unable to peer ahead. Moreover, the now-burning city gave her no cover as she exited. She decided her best course was to start running as soon as she left the gap to reach the closest shelter, a stand of brush on the low hillside a quarter of a mile or so away. At her best speed she knew she'd be visible for more than a minute, so she calmed herself, focused, and, with one last deep breath, left the gap and began sprinting away from the burning city.

Halfway to her destination, Hava heard a shout from behind her. Rather than risk losing any momentum by looking over her shoulder, she tried to dredge up every bit of speed she could to reach the scrub brush, where she knew she could move uphill into cover.

Then she heard horses and knew she would come up short. She refused to turn, knowing if she had any chance of surviving the coming confrontation, she needed to find the most defensible terrain within the next fifty feet. A small outcropping dead ahead, one she would normally have to navigate around to continue toward the rocky ridge where she and Molly had looked out at the city, would afford her the best place to face multiple attackers.

She leapt for the outcrop as two riders were nearly on top of her, and as she had expected, they were forced to rein in. As she turned, she felt a tiny breeze in her left ear an instant before she saw an arrow take one of the two riders out of his seat. As she crouched to face the remaining rider, a second arrow took him square in the chest before he could react to his companion's fall.

"Horses!" shouted Molly.

Hava turned around so quickly she almost went down on

her face, tripping over her own feet. She recovered her balance enough to move aside as two riderless mounts ran past.

Molly half slid on her feet down from her firing position to where Hava stood. "I thought you were going to wait up there," Hava said, pointing to where they had watched the start of the battle.

"Never said that," replied Molly. "You said if you weren't back by dawn, I was to get away. So I fetched the horses from where they grazed—they're tied a bit that way"—she pointed north—"and I filled the waterskins."

Hava looked back toward the flaming city, then said, "Did you see three children?"

Molly looked confused at the sudden change of topic. "No, why?"

Hava pushed aside her concern for Merrylee and the others. "Never mind."

"What now? Wait for the baron? He's sure to be on his way here."

"No," said Hava.

"What then?"

"I don't know." She took a deep breath and then exhaled loudly as relief washed through her. "Thought I wasn't going to get back." She looked at Molly and added, "Thanks for coming down to cover me. I think I was a little overmatched."

"Just a little." Molly's expression showed her disapproval of the rashness of Hava's actions. "Let's go," she said, turning to trudge uphill. Hava followed, and soon they reached the horses. They'd had a few hours' rest, but she thought it unlikely they were going to be good for a long ride.

Mounting up, Hava led Molly down the narrow trail to the point at which it would intersect the road. In the distance they heard approaching riders. Hava turned and said, "The baron?"

"If he pushed all night," replied Molly.

Looking around, Hava said, "We've no cover if it's not the baron."

Molly pointed toward the north, barely visible in the distant light from the still-flaming Port Colos. "That way."

Hava let her take the lead and followed her into a stand of trees on an uphill slope. They dismounted and placed their hands on the horses' muzzles, lessening the possibility the horses might nicker a greeting to the other mounts.

As the riders approached, Hava whispered, "I don't think it's the baron."

"Not enough horses, and in too much of a hurry."

Within a minute, a dozen riders in black suddenly appeared out of the dark, well camouflaged for night raiding. When they passed directly before her, she felt the hair on her arms and neck stand up: they looked like sicari, though not quite. Their head covers were different; back home the head covering was a small cap, usually made of leather, but inside was a cloth face covering that could be pulled down so only the eyes showed. These men wore something more akin to a flat-topped turban, with a hanging cloth that could be pulled up and tucked in on the other side, leaving only the eyes uncovered. But most of their manner and dress made her certain these were "dagger men," sicari!

Once they were gone she felt no relief. She put her hand out, touched Molly's arm, and whispered, "Wait."

The riders veered toward the city gate.

"They're doing a sweep of the area, looking for . . . us and anyone else who got out of the city."

"What do we do?"

"Wait for a while." Hava tried to recall something Master Bodai had said about eluding an enemy when escaping a battle. It was hard to remember because there had been many conflicting details, and because she occasionally just stopped listening to him during those talks. The instruction was designed for those who infiltrated warring armies, under false colors, carrying forged orders, conflicting commands, and committing other acts of subversion to throw one side into confusion, or for assassins marking specific nobles and commanders, to "behead the snake," as Bodai had put it.

Now she wished more than ever Hatu were here, for he would remember those details, and almost as much as she missed him, she also wished she'd paid closer attention. She took a breath and calmed herself; such regrets were a waste of time.

"We still wait?" asked Molly softly after a few minutes had passed.

"If they think people got out of the city, they'll be around for a while, at least until the baron's army gets close."

"So, we just sit?"

"Unless they find us."

"Then what?" asked Molly.

"If we don't get boxed in, it's a race. If we can get ahead of them, we head east as quickly as possible. If we can reach the road where it turns south, we stand a good chance of running into the baron's vanguard from Beran's Hill."

"Let's hope they don't think we're attacking them," said Molly dryly.

"All two of us?"

Molly managed a half-hearted chuckle.

A few minutes later, both horses' heads came up, their ears perking, and they both looked to the left. Hava and Molly put hands on their muzzles again, to distract them. Horses, Hava knew, were not good at thinking of more than one thing at a time. Lightly stroking her animal's nose, Hava whispered, "At least one rider, close."

Molly nodded in the gloom, saying nothing.

As Hava had anticipated, a moment later the sound of

horses slowly walking could be heard. Then two more riders came into view, both looking into the woods.

"Damn," Hava muttered as one locked eyes with her. Without a word, she leapt onto her horse, with Molly a second behind her. Both slammed their heels into the barrels of their mounts, and the horses crashed through the sheltering brush between two trees. Hava had her right arm extended, her long knife pointed at the nearest rider.

A few seconds later, Hava heard the twanging of Molly's bow and saw from the corner of her eye the other rider lifted from the saddle by her arrow. That caused the first rider's attention to be drawn for a split second, at which point Hava flung herself from the saddle, grabbing the man's sword arm.

He lost his grip and hit the ground at the same time as his sword. Hava rolled over on top of him and drove the point of her blade into his throat, above the leather jerkin he wore.

It was over in seconds.

Hava's horse was cantering away, and the two riders' mounts were moving in the opposite direction. Molly rode up and extended her hand. "Get on!" she shouted.

Hava stuck her knife back in its scabbard, grabbed the fallen rider's sword, gripped Molly's outstretched arm, and swung up behind her. Molly urged her mount after Hava's horse.

A hundred yards ahead, Hava's mount had slowed to a walk, and Molly reined in so that Hava could dismount and get back on her own horse. Once seated, Hava said, "East!"

Molly nodded. "Hope the baron's close!"

They set off at a gallop, but another fifty yards down the road both mounts went tumbling, casting the women over their necks to slam hard into the ground. Hava had been trained all her life how to fall, and even she barely managed to tuck her chin, bring up her knees, and roll as she hit the ground.

Shaken, she managed to come to her feet, sword at the ready. Molly lay before her, stunned, unable to move.

Hava took a step toward her companion but then heard shouts from both sides of the road. One horse lay on the ground screaming in pain from a broken leg, while the other leapt to its feet and moved off at speed, its uneven gait revealing an injury of some sort.

Then everything happened at once. Men hurried out from both sides of the road, but rather than attack, they halted and a pair of them cast a large net over the two women.

Hava raised her sword to catch the net, but as soon as the point was caught between the netting, a shock ran down her arm. The net was weighted, and each strand of heavy cord had been coated with something that made cutting it difficult. The weight of it forced her to her knees and the sword out of her hand.

As two men reached to grab her, she heard a voice shout in that language she'd heard earlier, the one that was almost her native tongue, but just a bit off. "Do not harm them! We need more women!"

Hava turned to see who spoke, only to have someone grab her through the netting and place a pungent-smelling cloth over her face. She thrashed and turned her head away, avoiding the noxious rag, frustrating her attacker's attempt to subdue her. Suddenly, a sharp blow struck her head and she lost consciousness.

DAYLON DUMARCH SAW THE SCOUTS racing toward the vanguard just behind which he and Balven rode. A pair of riders galloped until the last possible moment, then reined in hard.

Daylon shouted, "What did you find?"

The closest scout said, "My lord, Port Colos has been sacked! The city is aflame and has been plundered!"

Daylon signed for his castellans to advance and shouted back to Balven, riding beside the sergeant commanding the infantry, "As fast as you can!" Within seconds the baron and his personal household guards were galloping toward the city.

When they reached the edge of the cleared land before the city gate, they saw a dead horse with a broken leg and its throat cut. It lay in the middle of the road, and they were forced to slow to go around it. As they reached the midpoint between the woodlands and the city, Daylon took in the vista.

The sun was rising behind him, and a warm grey light, tinged with rose colors, was driving away the night, but everywhere he looked he saw more blackened ruin. Port Colos was a trading center. There were no nearby farms and only fishing villages up and down the coast. No faubourg stood outside the walls, and only short towers flanked the gate. The gate had been thrown wide and through it Daylon saw only smoking ruin.

He slowed his company to a walk and they reached the edge of the city in minutes. There were still sporadic fires, small and burning themselves out, but producing enough smoke to choke anyone standing too near. It was clear that there was nothing of value left inside the walls.

One of his captains said, "Who is that, my lord?" He pointed to a man who had been nailed to the leftmost gate, apparently while still alive, given the amount of blood that had washed down the wall. Huge spikes had been driven through his wrists and ankles, leaving him spread-eagled.

Daylon rode closer, then recoiled. "That is the governor of Port Colos. I should say was."

A fifth spike had been driven through the governor's stomach to keep him secure to the gate. It had been a nasty death.

"What does it mean, my lord?" asked the captain.

"It means you send a rider to Balven and order the infantry turned around. We'll find no justice here. Whoever sacked Beran's Hill was not aided by the governor. Port Colos is no more." Tearing his eyes away from the murder before him, he looked at the captain and said, "Send a squad in to see if there's anything alive or intact in the city—I doubt it, but I need to be sure. Then have the men tend the horses and rest them before we follow the infantry. I doubt there's forage within a day or two from here now, so whatever grain we carry give to the mounts. We rest for a half day and leave at noon." The last thing Daylon expected was that the raiders would have abandoned the city. A chill hit the pit of his stomach as he feared that he and his army were in the wrong place.

The captain wheeled his horse and shouted orders, and Daylon calculated. If they left at noon, they would reach a clearing he knew of a little before sunset. They could make camp there and the horses would be fresh the next morning. That would put them back at Beran's Hill at midday tomorrow. Daylon dismounted and loosened the girth of his mount's saddle. He removed a bag from behind the cantle and unrolled it. He always carried an apple in it, which he fed to his horse.

There must be an unnamed player involved here, as he and Balven had speculated, for what he saw here at Port Colos, in addition to the destruction of Beran's Hill, heralded a threat from someone worse than Sandura. Lodavico, with all his allies, could not have sailed from his nation to Port Colos—certainly not through the Narrows—without Balven and his agents knowing, so taking Port Colos this way would be impossible. The governor had been Daylon's ally and apparently had stayed true to that alliance, and paid dearly for it.

This had been an assault from the sea, so this invading army had not come from anywhere to the east in North Tembria. But it was a massive force, powerful enough to claim the city, hold it while dispatching a major force to obliterate Beran's Hill, retreat, and completely raze the port. Daylon had no hint who might be able to pull off such a military exercise.

He stood silently, wishing by some magic he could be back in the security of his castle. Though he was uncertain just how much longer that castle would be secure.

DECLAN WINCED AS HE STEPPED down from the baggage wagon, and Bogartis said, "You all right?"

Biting down against the pain, Declan said, "No, but I'll live."

The old fighter got off his horse and handed the reins to a baggage boy. Without asking he moved the sling on Declan's shoulder aside and opened the collar of Declan's tunic to take a look at the bandage. He let go of the cloth and said, "You didn't tear anything, but there's still some seepage from the wound." His expression conveyed his opinion that Declan was an idiot to risk further injury by riding with Bogartis's company, but he had made that point before departure and apparently felt no need to repeat himself. "Someone needs to change that dressing."

Declan studied the old fighter's face for a moment, then said, "I'll live."

The baggage train had pulled over to rest the horses and change a few of the most weary with remounts. The baron's men were tired but fit. The mercenary bands that rode escort were a different matter. Some, like Bogartis's men, were equal to the forced march, but others looked out of it. Declan said, "You run a stout company. What about these others?"

"Sword for hire is a risky business. You get all sorts, and I am very particular about who I'll have at my back in a fight. Some of the other captains are less particular." Bogartis nodded toward a small knot of fighters who seemed to be arguing over something. "Some are not much more than scavengers, and some captains can't maintain discipline."

"I met a few of those," said Declan, thinking of the time he had had to fight to save Gwen. Then he shut that memory away. "Killed a few as well."

Bogartis frowned. "I saw how you fought and, as I said, I'd jump any wall with you at my side, but if you were with a band—"

"I wasn't," said Declan. "A small company caused some trouble at Beran's Hill some time ago and I sorted it out."

Bogartis's brow furrowed even more. "Which company?"

"A man named Misener, who was killed by a . . . I won't call him a man, an animal named Tyree. He . . . wronged people I loved, so I chased him down and, as I said, I sorted it out."

Bogartis nodded approval. "So, you're the one who killed the man who killed Misener." He reached out and gripped Declan by his good shoulder. "Misener was a legend of sorts. In his prime he was one of the best captains around. I never served under him, but when I was young I fought alongside his lads on more than one occasion, and I'm glad I never had to face him in battle. You eat the same dirt as the man beside you, you learn who he is. Anyway, Misener stayed too long, thought he could tame any man under him, tame him or kill him.

"Age will do that if you're not careful. It's why I'm thinking about turning this ragged lot over to someone new, so I can settle down before someone decides to take the company from me." He looked Declan in the eye. "If you've a mind to, you could be that lad. Stay with me a while and learn the ways of being a captain, then I'll take my leave and find a nice town to settle down in." He looked around at the resting soldiers. "Assuming this new war doesn't get us all killed."

"How bad is it, do you think?"

"Bad" was all the answer Bogartis gave. He was quiet for a while and then said, "Let's stretch our legs a bit. At my age, in the saddle isn't the best way to spend the night."

They walked past the lined-up wagons, while some horses were swapped out of traces for fresh animals. In the second wagon in line sat a young man, his face covered in bruises and cuts, leaning back against sacks of supplies, his eyes closed as he rested. His hands were bound, and a tether tied his wrists to a steel ring normally used to tie down canvas covers on the wagon.

After they passed, Declan said, "What was that about?"

Bogartis shrugged. "Apparently someone got very cross with the lad, and from where he's tied, I'd guess someone of rank wishes to talk to him about it."

At the head of the first wagon, two men stood next to their mounts. Declan caught Balven's eye and was waved over. Bogartis followed.

"Declan," said the baron's chief adviser. "It's good to see you've survived. Last time I saw you, you were unconscious on the ground." He neither acknowledged nor greeted Bogartis.

"I had to come, sir," said the young smith.

A shift of expression on Balven's face indicated that he understood. "Everything?" he asked.

Declan nodded. "Everyone."

Balven gave a sigh of regret, then said, "I'm sorry."

Declan gave a slight nod. "Thank you, sir."

"When you're recovered, I suspect we will need your skills."

The way he said it didn't reassure Declan that he might get any choice in the matter, and while he understood the need for good weapons if war was coming, he also wanted to find whoever was responsible for the destruction of his home and Gwen's murder and visit justice upon them personally.

A voice from the rear shouted, "Rider coming!"

Everyone turned as the sound of hooves reached them, and in a moment a rider came into view. His horse was lathered, laboring for breath, and he reined in before Balven. "Message for the baron."

Balven held out his hand and the soldier gave him a folded, tattered piece of paper. Balven unfolded it and read. Then he turned to the captain next to him and said, "As soon as we're done changing out the horses, we turn the baggage around. Give the men one more hour of rest, then we start back."

"Sir?"

"Copper Hills has fallen."

"Sir?" repeated the captain as if he didn't understand.

"The baron will no doubt be along this way shortly, and I'll wager he's already sent orders for us to turn around." He motioned to Bogartis. "Pass word to the other captains that I want them ready to ride." He gave the old mercenary a cursory inspection and said, "You're in charge. I want flankers on both sides of the road and scouts a half hour ahead."

Bogartis glanced at Declan, shrugged slightly, then replied, "As you wish, my lord."

Declan stood there dumbfounded. "Copper Hills is gone?"

"Apparently Baron Rodrigo managed to get out of the city with some of his family. He's holed up somewhere in the mountains and managed to get this out." Balven clenched the message. "He sends a plea for aid."

"What does all this mean?" asked Declan.

"It means this isn't a raid. It's an invasion."

Balven turned from Declan, walked to where a boy held the reins of his horse, and mounted. Without another word, he rode past and began personally overseeing every requirement of taking a large force of soldiers bordering on exhaustion and pushing them to their limit.

Declan was left alone. Invasion. It seemed too big an idea to comprehend. He hurried back toward the wagon in which he had been riding, trying to ignore the pain in his shoulder.

12

CHANGES ON FATE'S TIDES

Hava's wits returned slowly. Her head throbbed and her mouth was dry, with a bitter metallic taste. She tried to listen to voices and sounds, but they faded as she drifted slowly in and out of unconsciousness.

Sometime later she came fully awake, again keeping still and her eyes shut as she attempted to focus on her situation. She remembered that she had been captured, though the details of her capture were unclear. Her head still hurt, but what had been a hot, sharp pain was now an insistent, dull throb; however, she resisted the impulse to reach up and touch what she already knew was there: a massive knot raised by a blow. While struggling in the net, someone had hit her with a cudgel or truncheon, rendering her senseless. Fortunately, she conceded ruefully, it had been a glancing blow, or she would have been permanently injured, or even dead.

She took a measured breath and silently tested her limbs, wiggling her fingers and toes, tensing and releasing her arms and legs to see if anything was broken. Everything appeared to work, so unless some undiscovered injury manifested itself later, she should be able to fight. And she knew she'd have to fight, just not when.

Hava weighed the meaning of the sounds around her. She had no idea how long she had been unconscious, but at least enough time had passed for her to have been transported to a ship. The gentle side-to-side rocking of the vessel and the creaking of timbers and faint rattle of gear told her they were not yet under way, so most likely still at anchor outside the burning city.

The chill bite of metal on her ankles meant she was shackled, and the air reeked of shit, piss, vomit, and the miasma of fear. From the lack of breeze and the closeness of the air, she reckoned she was in the hold. Her wrists were tied with a simple cord, from which she knew, given time, she could escape.

Around her she heard breathing, weeping, moans, and bodies stirring as men and women tried to find some relief in their bondage. She realized she must be on a slave ship.

Hava remained motionless and continued to listen. A rhythmic groan of timbers and occasional banging led her to believe large cargo was being secured on the deck directly above where she and the other prisoners were chained. If the cargo was above them, that meant there must be three decks, and that she and the other prisoners were down in the lowest, with ballast and bilges just below. Slaves here, loot above, and then the top deck: she had accumulated some knowledge about ships since her first ocean voyage. She thought it was likely to be a well-manned vessel, probably a freight hauler, and long waisted enough to be a three-masted, deep-water ship.

A forecastle in the bow would hold crew bunks, and aft would be where the captain and mates would sleep. Depending on the size of the vessel, there might be a galley aft, or it might be up on deck.

Time to open her eyes.

A quick peep showed her just one crewman nearby,

turned away from her at the foot of a companionway ladder. She readied herself to feign unconsciousness should he look her way.

She glanced about. There was scant light from a single lantern hanging on the bulkhead to her right. She immediately saw this was a large vessel, and the ladder to the upper decks was actually stairs: she did not know why they were called ladders, but a lot of things about ships made no sense to her. That lantern threw a half circle of light to a few feet beyond where Hava lay.

She saw a dozen women opposite her with their feet toward her, all lying on mats, as she was. The ship had large vertical supports spaced about ten feet apart on each side of a slightly raised center walkway. Large iron rings had been attached at the bottom of each, and a long chain had been threaded through those loops.

Each woman had manacles with a smaller iron loop, through which that chain had been passed, set tight enough that the women could be packed close together. For Hava to escape, she would need to get that long chain freed from where it was locked at the end, probably attached to the stern bulkhead. She glanced and couldn't make out the end, her view blocked by the bodies that lay to her right.

A quick glance in the other direction left her without any clue as to the size of the hold in which she lay. She had been told pirates tended to favor small, quick boats, ones that could ambush coastal luggers and deep-water vessels slowly coming into the shallows. Swarm the decks, carry off what they could, then flee and hide—that was their way. Occasionally they'd kill the crew and seize the ship for a prize, then sell it to a buyer who did not worry about provenance.

That was how it was explained to her when she crewed for Captain Joshua under the stern tutelage of his mate

Daniel. She wondered idly what the ship was called now, for as was the habit in Coaltachin, ships in service to the Council changed names as often as most men changed their shirts. But whatever it was called, it had been a smaller ship than this, and one that could sail deep waters.

She chanced another quick glance at the guard, who was leaning back against the steps, half asleep, his face turned away. Taking advantage of his inattention, she lifted herself up and scooted slowly until her back was against the hull. Then she rose as high as the chain would permit, which was almost to a crouching position. The movement caused her head to throb more than before, but, upon examining herself, she discovered no other injuries beyond some bruises, scrapes, and one small cut on her left arm that had already scabbed over.

The light generated by the lantern next to the companionway prevented her from seeing much. It illuminated the guard and this end of the deck, but her view ended little more than a few yards beyond where she was chained. She saw shapes: bodies of other people she assumed were also chained.

Of those she could see, only women were chained nearby. She sought out Molly's face, only to be frustrated by the number of bodies turned away or features cloaked in shadows. She rejected calling Molly's name out, as caution overruled the impulse. The archer might have been killed, or have escaped, or, if captured, not even be on this ship. And while those chained up with her were moaning and crying, a shout would have gained the guard's attention.

Hava had no idea what lay in store on this journey, but whatever it was, she would not act rashly. The lessons she had learned in Coaltachin were predicated on a single foundation: first you survive, because dead you are of no use to anyone. After survival, escape. The last instruction was get back to Coaltachin, but given that she had no idea where she was going to end up, that might be problematic. She'd worry about that after she escaped.

She lowered herself back down and then extended her legs, trying to squeeze out whatever comfort the damp straw mat might provide. She let her head rest against the hull, content to wait, despite every fiber within her screaming at her to do something. Patience hard learned was a harsh master, but it was certainly less harsh than slavery.

She turned her attention to the cord around her wrists; after a moment she found an exposed ridge to her left provided by an ill-fitting joint of two deck planks and began, as quietly as possible, to start rubbing the cord against that edge.

DECLAN FLEXED HIS SHOULDER AND the sharp pain struck at the same time Bogartis said, "Leave it, lad. It'll heal, but slowly. If you keep testing that shoulder, you may do more damage."

Declan winced and nodded in resignation. "I thought you said I needed to move in order to stop the scars inside from binding up."

The mercenary captain rode at a slow walk next to the wagon on which Declan sat. "I did, but not every moment from the first day. Let it heal a bit first. And then move it gently, not like you're warming up for combat."

The sun was up and exhausted men and animals trudged toward Marquenet. Due to his injury, Declan was allowed to ride next to a wagon driver, while the more gravely injured lay in the wagon's bed, made as comfortable as possible for the journey. Bogartis rode next to Declan's wagon, and it was now clear to the smith that this captain of mercenaries was seriously interested in adding Declan to his company.

Declan still felt a numb void within, tinged with a seething anger that he couldn't quite bring to the surface. He knew that Gwen was dead, as were Jusan and Millie, and others: perhaps Molly Bowman, Hatu, and Hava as well. Yet despite what, by any measure, should be a crushing sense of loss, he felt little. It was as if he were watching someone else suffer from a distance.

He'd seen death in Oncon, even before he fought off the slavers with Edvalt and Jusan. As a boy he'd seen a couple of the old men taken by ague in the cold season, and Beck Linderman's son, caught up in nets and drowned before they could cut him loose and haul him back into the boat. He'd witnessed grieving but realized now he'd never truly felt it. Perhaps it was the wound, or as Edvalt would say it hadn't "struck him yet," but whatever the cause, Declan just felt empty.

"Lost in thought?" said Bogartis.

"Just wondering what the baron will have in store," Declan said, though this had been a thought from earlier in the day. He felt no need to share his emptiness with anyone else.

"Wondering the same," replied Bogartis. "There's a lot more going on than answering a raid, even one as brutal as Beran's Hill." He glanced around and added, "You don't suddenly turn this column around and head for home unless more's afoot than we're being told."

Declan nodded, though his curiosity was muted, like all his feelings.

"I don't know," Bogartis added quickly. "I've just served in too many tussles not to see what's in front of me."

A shout from behind and both Declan and Bogartis turned. There came the command, "Pull to the side!"

The driver glanced back to see the wagons behind moving to the left verge of the road and did likewise. As they came to rest as far off the baron's highway as was possible without ensnaring the wagon in deep mud, the sound of cavalry reached them.

A few moments later, Baron Dumarch and his company of castellans rode past at a canter. The horses were frothy and showing wide nostrils, and Declan knew that meant they were close to exhausted. As the baggage caravan had been turned around, Declan knew the remounts were ahead now, instead of behind, and assumed the baron and his honor guard would be changing mounts for the remaining distance to the city.

Declan glanced at Bogartis, whose expression said, "I told you so," without uttering a word. Declan nodded once in acknowledgment.

Bogartis looked back again as companies of the baron's cavalry brought up the rear at a trot, their horses also appearing to be in desperate need of rest.

It was halfway between dawn and noon, Declan judged, and from the state of the animals, the baron had ridden hard. "Some of those horses will be good for nothing more than fertilizer," he said quietly.

"That's the right of it," Bogartis agreed. He looked forward to where soldiers were switching mounts and said, "I need to ask something." He urged his horse forward and rode toward the head of the column, which was pulling off to the right side of the highway to rest the mounts.

Declan sat silently next to the driver, who was obviously relieved to get a bit of rest himself.

Bogartis pulled up next to a sergeant near the officer leading the column. They exchanged a few words, then the mercenary captain turned and rode back to where Declan waited.

"We're resting here for a while," Bogartis said to Declan. "My company and two others are guarding the baggage while the rest of the garrison is heading back to Marquenet." He glanced toward where the horses were being changed and said, "We'll need to lie up an hour or two for those animals to catch their wind a bit, and then it's a slow walk back to the city." He looked at Declan. "There's something I want you to consider, lad. If what's coming is as bad as I think it will be, the baron's going to decide he needs every armorer in the barony in his service. You won't be given a choice, and depending on how things fall out, you may be in service for years, and you won't be able to negotiate pay." He indulged himself in a bitter laugh. "Hell, you might even get killed in the process.

"If you seriously think you'd like to ride with me and my lads, once you're a member of my company the baron can't touch you. If he were to violate the rights of a captain's sworn man by, say, pressing him into his personal service . . ." He shook his head. "Word would spread and no other company would be willing to fight for him." Another glance toward the increasingly hurried swapping of horses, and the distant tread of infantry coming up the highway at a swift pace, emphasized the need for a quick decision.

"What do I do?" asked Declan.

"Simply swear to serve. Usually I take a man on for a year, unless I discharge him or have to kill him. Most of my boys have been with me four, five years. Sad to say the two youngsters who died up at Beran's were my two newest. It was a hard place to train for sword craft."

"So," said Declan slowly, "you seek to protect me?"

Bogartis laughed. "Hardly! I seek to take advantage of you before the baron does. If you're as gifted with hammer and anvil as you are with a sword, you're good as gold. You think on it for a bit. Now I'm off to spread the word to the other captains. Let me know what you decide when I return."

He rode toward the rear of the baggage train, and Declan

glanced at the driver, who seemed to have been entertained by the exchange. He gave Declan a slight tilt of his head, as if indicating that he approved.

Declan surprised himself with a chuckle, which in turn caused his shoulder to twinge. At least he could still feel something, even if it was only mild amusement.

He turned his attention to the head of the baggage train, where he could just make out the baron speaking with his brother, Balven, beside the first wagon. He experienced a passing curiosity as to what they might be discussing, then turned his attention back to considering Bogartis's offer.

"IT'S NOT SANDURA," REPEATED BALVEN. "You're certain?"

"This is beyond Lodavico's ability," said a clearly fatigued but agitated Baron Dumarch. "Rodrigo sends word he's fled his city while Port Colos is being obliterated. As soon as we change mounts, we're pressing on to ready our city for assault."

Balven shook his head in disbelief. Lowering his voice, he said, "Father spoke enough about our position and not needing to build new defenses . . ."

Daylon's face was a dust-caked mask of concern. "We can defend a third of the city if an attack comes. The rest is beyond the walls, with no defensive positions between the harbor and the castle walls. If those ships anchored off Port Colos set off now . . ." He closed his eyes for a brief moment, calculating. ". . . we'll have three, perhaps four days at most to ready a defense."

"Should we evacuate the city?" asked Balven.

Daylon was silent for a moment. Then he looked at his half brother and said, "If we get word of ships coming in number from the north, and we open the eastern gate and pass word for people to flee to Ilcomen, we'll have panic. If they do not come for us next, people will die for no good reason."

"And if we do nothing," added Balven, "and they come, more people will die."

"There is no good outcome," said Daylon as his horse was brought over to him. Mounting, he turned to look down at Balven and asked, "Any advice?"

Balven said, "There's a rumormonger named Blifen, at the Inn of the Purple Hen. I'll have him suggest to some people a plague—"

Daylon interrupted. "If you have a plan, save it. Then do it as soon as you're able." He shouted to a soldier who was about to mount, "Bring that horse over here!"

The soldier hurried to do his lord's bidding, and Daylon said to Balven, "You're coming with me." To the soldier he said, "Find a mercenary captain named Bogartis." He glanced at his brother who nodded his agreement: Bogartis was the most competent of the mercenaries. "Tell him he's in charge and get these wagons home as quickly as possible."

Then Daylon noticed Donte, sitting silently in the back of the wagon his brother had ridden in on. "And bring that man a horse. He's coming with us."

Balven nodded and went to take the reins from the waiting soldier.

A third horse was fetched while Daylon had Donte's bindings cut from his wrists. With a nod of his head, he indicated that the young man from Coaltachin should mount. Donte looked around and both Balven and Daylon assumed he was judging his odds of a safe escape, but seeing that the baron was accompanied by more than a hundred armed and well-trained men, his expression revealed he concluded it would be a useless undertaking.

Without another word, Daylon Dumarch, Baron of Marquensas, rode to the head of the column and signaled for his elite troop to move on up the road.

BERÑARDO DELNOCIO LOOKED UP FROM his reading as the hidden doorway between the bookcases opened. His agent, Marco Belli—known as "Piccolo"—entered, obviously in distress. He was covered in dirt, clearly nearing exhaustion, and barely able to stay on his feet.

Ignoring rank and protocol, Delnocio quickly rose, took Piccolo's arm, and guided him to a chair. "Water?"

"Wine if you don't mind, Your Eminence. I've had nothing to eat for three days."

The episkopos said nothing as he went to a side table and poured a cup of wine from a large flagon, returning to hand it to Piccolo, then sitting opposite him. "What happened?"

"I don't know, Master. Captain Stennis reached Beran's Hill a few days before me, and I already had other agents in the area. Stennis and I were in Port Colos, looking for the child. And suddenly the city was filling with outlanders and people who were strange to me; their fashion of dress and languages were like nothing . . ." He waved away his own words. "I'm rambling." He took a long drink of wine, then continued. "Port Colos was used to stage a raid on Beran's Hill."

Delnocio's brow furrowed as he asked, "By whom? After more than twenty years of depending on my counsel, Lodavico could not mount such an undertaking without me."

Marco Belli agreed with a nod. "He's not that clever and he needs our agents." He took another drink. "Stennis poked around in Beran's Hill before I got there, then together we questioned the locals about the Firemane child in an obvious enough way to draw out anyone who might be sheltering the boy . . . or girl."

"We think it's a son," interjected the prelate.

Piccolo shrugged. "Boy then."

"Young man by now."

"As it may be, master." Piccolo paused, collecting his thoughts. "The raiding party was massive, over two hundred men on horse, and it was done quickly, less than a day and night. From all reports, the townsfolk put up a stout fight, but except for a few who fled, the rest were put to the sword or given to slavers. The town was then fired and burned to the ground."

"Someone is sending Baron Dumarch a message, but who?" Bernardo waved his hand at Belli. "Continue."

"More raiders appeared, as more ships anchored off the shore, and started occupying every room in Port Colos, and when all the inns and lodging houses were full, they camped in the streets. My best guess is more than two thousand men were inside the city when the fighting started." He took another drink, wiped his mouth with the back of his hand, and took a deep breath. "I'm trying to sort through the confusion, Your Eminence. Stennis died: that I saw, and I barely found a way out of the fighting myself. My other agents?" He shrugged. "I stayed in the woods and kept away from the roads. For the longest time I could hear the sounds of the city being sacked and all night the skies above it were alight with the flames."

Bernardo rose, picked up the carafe, and refilled Piccolo's cup without a word. Belli nodded his thanks.

"I found a horse without a rider after dawn and kept moving east. I imagined with Beran's Hill finished, all the invaders would be behind me."

"Invaders?"

Piccolo nodded. "I skirted Beran's Hill by some miles, as I assumed by then Baron Dumarch's garrison from Esterly would be there. I needed to get here as soon as I could, so I took the safest route. On the road, I encountered men and women from Copper Hills. It also has been sacked, and Baron Rodrigo and his family have fled the city and are either dead or in hiding." He took a deep breath. "Copper Hills, Port Colos, and Beran's Hill, all taken within days?"

"Invasion," agreed Bernardo.

"From where?"

Bernardo was silent for a moment, then said, "I can only speculate some power of whom we are ignorant from Alastor. It can't be any force from Enast. We control most of them," he added, meaning the Church of the One.

"That leaves Alastor," agreed Piccolo.

"Unless there's a nation beyond it we've not heard of."

"You're better educated than me, Your Eminence. But even I know there are three small continents beyond Alastor, but some travelers have been there and returned, so we'd know if any threat was . . ." His voice trailed away as he saw a far-off gaze in Bernardo's eyes.

"I wonder," said the prelate softly. He looked at his man and said, "Eat. Rest. Tomorrow I want you to gather your best men here and return to the west. Put yourself at no risk for now: information is more valuable than gold. I'll pen messages to send to our 'friends,' to see if they have any information about these new invaders."

Rising slowly, his bones aching from fatigue, Marco Belli said, "I do not entirely trust our 'friends,' Your Eminence."

"They are a dark and mysterious race, the Azhante."

"We do not even know where they come from, Master. These Azhante . . . is that their nation or race? We know so little about them."

"And I do not trust those agents of Coaltachin we've employed before, so who better to see they behave?"

"There's something about the Azhante that makes me fearful."

"You, Piccolo? Fearful? I thought you feared no man."

"I fear no man I understand, and I understand most men, but not these men."

"Well, let us endeavor to use them, even if we don't entirely trust them. Yet it seems that as long as we have gold, they serve."

"That I do understand," said Piccolo with a faint, false humor in his voice. He bowed and departed.

Bernardo pondered what his best agent had told him and tried to gather his thoughts. First impressions led to flights of fancy and wild speculation, so he gave in to those impulses for a moment, before ordering his thoughts back to what was known. After a short while he conceded that very little was known, despite the enormity of the events.

The Azhante had been made known to him before the Betrayal, and while he knew King Lodavico of Sandura had employed agents from Coaltachin, Bernardo had secretly arranged his first contract with the Azhante and had used their skills several times since. Their services were costly but worth every weight of gold he had spent. He agreed with Piccolo as to their mysterious nature. He had thought himself clever, using spies unknown to Lodavico or anyone besides Piccolo. Now he wondered: Had he used them, or had they used him?

He turned to his writing table, took pen and paper, and began writing orders to be sent back to his allies in Enast, at the original cathedral of the Church of the One. He knew that within an hour or two Lodavico would request his presence, so he wrote quickly. He would have to return later to finish his messages, so that before Piccolo departed in the morning, messengers would be on their way. Above all he needed as much information as any of his agents could find about the people, nations, and armies of Alastor. And, he added, at some point he needed to discover what he could about these mysterious Azhante who had come into his service almost twenty years earlier.

HAVA USED HER TIME AS best she could. With no outside source of light, she could only guess it was nearing dawn. Her single clue was the tempo of movement above slowing, then stopping, which suggested the cargo had been loaded, so all that remained was the captain's order to weigh anchor and set sail on whichever tide best suited him. She assumed that most of the crew were eating or resting before the order was given. That was all she had to go on: assumptions. Yet she had come to understand some of what was happening around her from close observation. The few bits of information she had gleaned were logical.

She had worried at the bindings on her wrists enough that the cord was almost completely frayed through. It should take her only moments to finally break them. The first guard at the ladder had dozed, and she had considered, then rejected, the idea of freeing them completely, but the manacles on her ankles restricted her movement, and that meant he would have to be much closer for her to get her hands on him. Without her feet solidly under her, most of the hand-to-hand fighting she had learned all her life would be useless. Her preceptors had trained her in every dirty trick a woman fighting a larger, stronger man could use to quickly incapacitate him, but they all required her to be able to balance herself.

In the dim light the sailor didn't appear to be particularly big, and she had no idea of his age, but as a deckhand working on a deep-water ship, he was almost certainly fit and strong enough that he could easily overpower her with her ankles shackled.

After a while he had been relieved, first by a new guard, a small, thick-necked, and barrel-chested fellow who moved with more caution than his predecessor. Hava instantly judged him to be a far more dangerous foe than the first guard. He moved like a fighter.

Time passed as she studied the new guard, then three men joined him, bringing water to the captives. They unceremoniously kicked feet and shouted awake the sleeping prisoners. They moved quickly from one prisoner to the next, handing each a large ladle of fresh water, letting them gulp down a decent swallow before pulling away the long-handled dipper and moving to the next prisoner. A few captives protested but a sharp blow silenced them.

No one offered food, so Hava considered it possible they might not be fed until the crew was, and with this ship being readied to get under way, that might not be for many hours.

She experienced bouts of nausea, but she didn't know if it was the effect of the blow to her head or from not having eaten anything for quite some time. She also had a frustrating lack of new information since coming awake.

She planned. Taught since childhood that if captured, live, escape, and return to Coaltachin, she amended that to first she'd live, then escape, then find Hatushaly. She had no plan to speak of, just general concepts. She had to either slip away now—which was difficult, if not impossible, as she would need to free herself from the manacles around her ankles, steal up the ladder, and get over the side while still close enough to land to swim there before drowning—or wait until they reached their destination and escape then.

The problem with the latter was obvious: she had no idea where they were bound or what sort of reception the prisoners would receive. She had traveled while training to cities with slave auctions and knew from experience that slaves were generally delivered starved and hopeless, then given some food and rest before being put up for sale, so they would be more attractive to buyers. As a result, the guards tended to be a little more sure of themselves, but she certainly couldn't be the first captive plotting to escape, so she judged it unlikely she'd get away safely once the ship docked. She considered several plans, quickly discarding each as it arose, coming finally to the conclusion that she needed more information and, most of all, the means to free herself from the shackles and a weapon.

She lay back, attempting to think of some opportunity she had missed, fighting back rising frustration at being caught like an animal in a trap, her thinking clouded by hunger and her throbbing head. Then Hava felt a strange sensation, an odd moment of calm, as if the entire ship had paused, and three men entered the hold, coming down the ladder one after the other. The single guard stood away, and even in the dim light Hava could see he was intimidated by these men.

"No talking!" shouted the last man down, and instantly the murmur of voices fell away. He was dressed like a seaman, but the two who had come before him were not.

Hava felt the hair on the back of her neck stiffen slightly, and the skin on her arms prickled in what the matrons at the school called "chill bumps." The men were dressed in black. Their head coverings were familiar to her: they were called *shemagh, keffiyeh,* or *ghutrah,* depending on where the wearer hailed from. A cloth wrapped around the crown of the head, like a tight turban, rather than a hood, then drawn over the face, tucked into the other side, leaving only the eyes revealed. Unlike the sicari of her home island, whose headwear was little more than a skullcap of black cloth, these turbans were worn by people from a hot land. Also, these men wore loose tunics rather than close-fitting clothing, and the shoulders were exaggerated, suggesting padding or perhaps light armor under their tunics.

They also wore black enameled amulets, and the chains around their necks were blackened.

Hava sensed this was her first good look at the men about whom Hatu had spoken, the Azhante. She now understood what he had meant, that they looked a little like sicari, perhaps even Quelli Nascosti, "The Hidden," the elite assassins and spies of Coaltachin.

The leader walked toward the bow and the second man stood silently.

"All in order," said the last man to enter, and Hava took him for a mate or perhaps even the captain of this ship.

The two black-clad men moved forward toward the bow, leaving the others waiting, and after a short time, returned. With a heavy accent, one of the two men Hava thought of as sicari or Quelli Nascosti said, "Keep as many of the slaves alive as possible, for we counted them and we expect few losses. And do not trouble the women, for our master wishes them to arrive undamaged." He paused and, as if he felt the need to be specific, he added, "Not just the young pretty girls. *All* the women, especially those who can work." Again he paused, then asked, "Understand?"

"Perfectly," answered the sailor in charge. As he turned to go, the man who had spoken to him turned to his companion.

Hava's neck hairs rose again, because she understood most of what he said. His accent was strange, a few words were pronounced oddly, and some were unrecognizable, but she got the gist through context. She was certain he said, "Should more than ten die before reaching home . . ."—followed by something she didn't understand—". . . I will have his head on a spike."

The second man chuckled. "He is a dead man then. For surely more than ten will perish. Many have . . ." Another word that took a moment for Hava to understand, and then she realized it was *injuries*. ". . . that will see them dead, some before we depart."

The first man nodded, and his eyes were cold as he said, "He's seen too much of us and knows about the Heartland, so it is a good excuse to rid . . ." Again he slipped into a phrase Hava couldn't quite grasp, and finished, ". . . need a reason, or others like him will not serve willingly. His father was important, and he rests on that . . ." Hava assumed it was a term for *reputation*. "But still many heed him. The useful among the outlanders can become dangerous."

The second man nodded and they left, and the sailor who had first come down with water was the last to leave.

Hava lay back as comfortably as she could manage, her mind racing. Who were these men? She knew any hope of escape depended on avoiding a confrontation with them. And she fought hard not to fall into despair as she struggled to ascertain what this new information might give her as a means to get free of this slave ship.

13

PLANS AND CONSEQUENCES

———†———

Hava waited silently, considering her choices, discarding plan after plan. What was it Master Bodai had said? "Too many unknowns"? Of all the masters, he was the most insistent that no operation of any complexity was to be undertaken until it was clear that every possible issue that might arise had been accounted for, and even then there was always the risk of the unexpected. By comparison, Master Kugal was impulsive, even rash, and the other masters lay somewhere between the two.

At this point, waiting for the ship to weigh anchor and begin its journey to some distant land, Hava had a rough idea of what she needed to do, but the how was still eluding her. She had finally conceded that whatever plan she settled upon was going to be a bad one, but that would be better than no plan at all.

She'd worried the cord to the point where it appeared to the casual eye that she was bound, but she knew she could snap it simply by twisting her wrists; however, she still had to come up with an idea of how to deal with the iron shackles on her ankles. If only she had a nail and decent light she was certain she could pick the lock, but in the dark with only damp straw at hand, it was impossible.

So she waited and listened and eventually heard distant shouting from the main deck and saw two men come down the companionway. The first carried a torch, which caused Hava to look away for a moment, for the light was almost blinding.

At that moment the ship seemed to shudder and he looked behind him, and Hava felt every shred of hope she had been clutching to fade. For the second man to descend the ladder was a black-clad sicari.

The captured people in the hold started to stir and mutter.

The sicari spoke to the first man, the one who had seemed to be the mate in charge the last time he was down below.

The mate shouted, "Quiet! Listen! You will be given more water and food after we are under way. Anyone who causes trouble will be cast overboard to the sharks. Remain calm and live."

But this warning didn't stem the rising voices from the prisoners. Hava heard more female voices from the other end of the deck, nearer to the bow, as well as male voices coming from the other side of the hold. As the man with the torch came past Hava, she could see shapes moving between bars and realized that some of the men were caged.

Turning to look at the man she thought of as sicari, she saw him scanning the shackled women, and as his gaze reached her, Hava lowered her eyes. She didn't have to feign fear. There was no possible reason for him to think of her as anything more than another girl from Port Colos, yet she felt a sudden terror that he would somehow see her for what she was, a child of Coaltachin.

Her moment of irrational panic passed as the sicari continued his inspection of the women and then caught up with the mate; he spoke to him softly enough that Hava understood only a little of what he said, but she deduced that he was leaving the ship now and felt her hope return.

The two men walked back toward the companionway, but the mate turned to cast a last look at the slaves. For a brief instant he looked at Hava and their gazes locked for a moment. Hava gave the man a slight nod and then fell back as if exhausted. She hoped he was intelligent enough to recognize that she had something to tell him.

There was the faintest hesitation on the sailor's part, but he said nothing and followed the black-clad assassin up the companionway. Hava let out a long breath of relief: every move she made now was from a position of profound disadvantage and the slightest mistake on her part could quickly lead to death. She was quite sure that she wasn't ready to die: she needed to be free to find Hatu.

BARON DUMARCH FOUND THE CITY in turmoil as he rode in at the northern gate and moved down a side road, taking the fastest route to the castle, avoiding the more crowded streets of Marquenet. His brother, an honor guard, and the prisoner Donte followed him. The main force lay an hour behind them.

The postern gate to the marshaling yard opened as the baron approached, and by the time he was through, lackeys were ready to take his mount. Waiting for him were his two sons, Wilton and Marius.

"Your mother?" asked Daylon, removing his heavy gauntlets and handing them to a servant who had appeared at his side as a lackey led away his exhausted mount.

"She's getting the girls ready to travel. A ship is waiting to carry them to the island villa," answered Wilton, his eldest.

Daylon shook his head. "No ships. I want a fast carriage and light horse guard—just ten men. Pick them from those who remained here; the men who traveled with me are barely able to stand. Have them ready to leave for Ilcomen at a moment's notice. We should know by sundown if we are going to be attacked tomorrow. If they haven't landed men by then, they'll need tomorrow to stage. My family can be safely away before that."

Wilton was a man now, despite being young, and Marius was approaching manhood, his shoulders starting to broaden and a hint of a beard showed on his cheeks. They were both ready to stay and fight, but Daylon said, "I want you both to ride with them."

Wilton nodded, but Marius started to object. His father cut him off quickly.

"I need people I can trust to protect your mother and sisters," he said to them both, though he fixed his gaze on his younger son. "I trust no one more than you two." Then he gripped each lad by the shoulder and gave them a squeeze. "Now go ready yourselves for travel." To Marius he said, "Go to the armory and choose armor and weapons. It's time. You've earned it."

The boy's expression quickly ran from surprise to happiness, then to determination. "I will see that no harm comes to Mother or the girls."

Daylon gave his younger son a tired smile and said, "I know I can trust you. Now go."

As Daylon's sons hurried away, Balven approached. "They're like you were when you were young, anxious to be a grown man and to fight."

Daylon gave his half brother a brief nod. "I remember exactly how it felt, and that's why I'm sending them away. If what's coming is as bad as it seems, we're in a poor position to make a defense. I'm as guilty as Father, Grandfather, and all those who came before of relying on the Covenant and wealth and, after the Betrayal, assuming that any attack would come from the east."

"What do you want me to do with that lad Donte?"

Daylon looked to where Donte now stood calmly between two guards, his expression hinting at some odd humor. "Damned if I know right now," answered the baron.

"Toss him in a cell?"

Daylon weighed his answer, then said, "No, I'd like him a little closer than down in a dungeon. I want him feeling inclined to talk without having to waste days being beaten and starved. We don't have time.

"Put him under guard in one of the smaller rooms and see that he's fed. And if he smells as rank as I do, get him a bath and clean clothing. I need to speak to my wife and daughters and prepare the defense of the city, so I want you to question him for me.

"And before you eat, get word to the lookout tower at the north headlands. I need to know if that fleet is arriving any time soon."

"Done," said Balven, and he turned to instruct the guards where to take Donte, then hurried off across the marshaling yard to send a pigeon to the north headlands tower, more than a day's ride away. Daylon knew his brother would also dispatch a galloper in case the pigeon failed to reach the post.

For a brief moment the baron weighed taking a bath before talking to his wife and daughters. Linnet had coped with him being in need of a bath on more than one occasion, he decided, and tried to gather his strength. His wife was prone to histrionics, and being sent away with the girls would frighten her more than staying close to him, even if there was a battle approaching. But Daylon knew that he had to make sure his family was far from here so that he could focus on defending his city.

He signaled for his most senior sergeant.

The man hurried over. "Yes, my lord?"

"As soon as the troops arrive I want them fed and rested. The garrison, except for the castellans, will remain at the harbor and castle gates, but anyone else in the city is to be pulled back here. Understood?"

The sergeant nodded. "Yes, sir."

"Oh, and send word for those coming back to make note of how many people have already fled. I need to know."

"Sir," said the sergeant, then turned to carry out the baron's instructions.

Daylon Dumarch, Baron of Marquensas, took one long look around the marshaling yard as his castellans were unsaddling their mounts, helped by lackeys who would brush and water the horses. These were the premier soldiers of Marquensas. They would need to go to their barracks and eat and rest, but would it be enough? he wondered.

As he moved toward the entrance to the main keep, it occurred to him that he needed to have a serious talk with Wilton, who might be Baron of Marquensas far sooner than either he or his father would have expected. Such thoughts were probably the result of exhaustion, but still he couldn't push away the dread.

HATU STILL FELT SORE AND his mood bordered on rage, barely kept in check. He couldn't see the shore behind them, but from the angle of the sun he assumed they were heading on a south-by-west course, though without the aid of familiar stars in the sky he had no idea of where they were sailing.

Catharian stood at the stern but kept looking around. He motioned Williem aside and took the wheel. To the boy he said, "Get the others and grab what there is to eat for today. We'll be on this course for a while." He glanced at Hatu and said, "And we have someone who can trim the sails if need be." His tone was light, as if inviting Hatu into a better humor, but all he got for his troubles was a furrowed brow and a deeper frown.

At last Hatu asked, "Are you worried we might be followed? You keep looking astern."

Catharian nodded. "We got away from the coast as quickly as possible. The raid on Beran's Hill was part of a large assault and there were hostile ships everywhere. We were fortunate that this is a small ship and that it was night when we passed the invaders' fleet, since their attention was shoreward. I reckon some of them will be leaving on a similar course to ours, heading in the same general direction, but with luck we have enough of a head start that we can stay out of sight. The trouble is many of those ships will be much faster than us. If we see no sails astern by tomorrow, we should be safely away."

"Wonderful," said Hatu dryly. "I get abducted for whatever bizarre notion you have and may get killed at sea by people I don't even know, just because I'm on a boat that's completely unsuited for the high seas!" He was on the verge of yelling with frustration.

To find his way back to Hava, he would have to somehow overpower both Denbe and Catharian, decide what to do with Sabella, and convince the three lads that turning around and sailing back to their destroyed village—possibly into the teeth of a fleet that meant them harm—was a good idea.

Hatu realized that he was at the mercy of circumstances, so there was no point in losing his temper. He would have to put aside his ire in order to concentrate on opportunities for escape and return. Students from Coaltachin were taught one thing, which had become almost a reflex by Hatu's age: survive, escape, return.

Catharian had answered a few of his questions the day before but had appeared unwilling to elaborate on his earlier claim that magic would die with Hatu, saying only that there were those better able to inform him when they got to their destination. Switching topics in the hope of more information, Hatu said, "So who are these raiders who may be following us?"

Catharian looked at the young man for a moment, then said, "I'm not sure. There are . . . complexities in all this I know only part of, for despite being one who travels through many nations—much like your comrades and your masters—the less I know, the less I can betray."

Hatu nodded. He was familiar with the concept. Master Bodai called it "compartmentalization," a word that had at first confused then amused Hatu as a child. He remembered when he realized that it had to do with compartments, which was a considerable time later. Sometimes he felt quite stupid.

"What can you tell me?"

"Only that there are forces out there, both human and not, which are moving toward ends I certainly don't understand. All I know, and this has to do with what I told you about magic being at risk, is that we stand in opposition to those forces, and we are small and they are great."

"Wonderful," said Hatu mockingly. He let out an exasperated sound and then asked, "How long?"

Catharian looked at him. "How long what?"

"Until we get where we're going?"

"As long as it takes, depending on the wind. Then we'll get on another ship."

"To where?"

"That we will discuss later."

Hatu rolled his eyes but said nothing.

"Patience, my friend," said Catharian. "Anger and frustration will not get us where we are headed one moment faster."

As loath as he was to admit Catharian was right, Hatu knew that he was. One of the hardest lessons for him to learn, from childhood to the present, had been to let go of things over which he had no control. There was a part of his nature that longed for the power to simply wish for things to make them so. It was a childish desire, he knew, but it was part of who he was.

"Very well," he said grudgingly. "If this is where fate leads me, I'll come quietly."

Catharian laughed out loud. "Why do I think that will never be the case with you, Hatushaly?"

DECLAN WATCHED BOTH SIDES OF the road, as if expecting an attack at any moment, yet he knew his vigilance was not rooted in the moment but was a mix of sorrow at having been unable to protect Gwen and the others with unease about what might come next. He moved his arm testily inside the sling that confined it, for the umpteenth time being reminded it was there to stop him from pulling at the stitches in his shoulder. Which was why Bogartis had made him wear it, rather than for support.

Declan still felt little emotion, just a hollow space of cold alternating with a gnawing need to be doing something, even if he couldn't put a name to it, or at least any name beyond punishing whoever had taken his wife and friends from him. But what others might have called a desire for revenge was also muted. He had felt this way—dulled and displaced from himself—since awakening in Beran's Hill. He was almost exhausted just waiting for the pain of his sorrow and his rage to manifest themselves and had almost resigned himself to the idea that he might never feel anything again.

The closest he could remember feeling this way was while in battle, when that almost silent calm rose in him while everything around him slowed. He knew exactly what to do when facing an enemy. There was a sense of control, of complete certainty, and in a way he found it welcome.

But the feeling he had now was as if he had been rendered unconscious during the fight, and when he awoke, that calm and distanced stillness remained. Declan was not an introspective man by nature, but he admitted to himself that he might never truly understand himself, and about that he also felt indifferent.

One thing he did understand was that it would be foolish to think that alone he could avoid any desire the baron might have for another master smith in his service. By taking Bogartis's offer, he might still find himself pressed into serving the baron, but if the old mercenary captain's instincts were correct, it was the safer choice.

"How much farther?" Declan asked the driver, more a signal that conversation was welcome than out of any great need for information; Declan had driven this road enough times with Ratigan, Hatu, and alone to know the answer.

The driver was a man named Timmons, who was an affable, older ex-soldier. He had explained to Declan that he knew nothing but fighting along the borders of the Wild Lands and in the Northern Islands east of Sandura, but when he became too old to fight he had driven wagons for whichever army would hire him. Timmons glanced around. "We'll be in the city before sundown."

"Fine by me. Sleeping under the wagon with this aching shoulder is not restful."

Timmons nodded, though sleeping under the wagon was his usual billet.

Declan fell silent again. He was looking forward to finding better lodgings in the city. Then he remembered he had no coin of any sort. Whatever had been in his lockbox at the smithy was surely gone, either destroyed in the fire or pillaged by looters. He'd have to rely on Bogartis, which might once again leave him sleeping under a wagon.

Bogartis rode toward Declan's wagon, making a leisurely

inspection of the caravan. His routine was now familiar to
Declan. The old mercenary rode in the van for a while, then
turned and rode slowly to the drag, then slowly back again.
He had been seriously cautious at first, placing flankers on either side some distance out and a trailbreaker ahead—though
Declan thought that unnecessary with the entirety of the
baron's army marching less than a couple of hours ahead of
them. He seemed far more relaxed now that they were close
to the city.

Bogartis reined in and turned his mount to walk alongside the wagon. "We'll be in the city before nightfall."

Declan smiled slightly at the consensus.

"Have you decided?"

Declan looked at Bogartis for a long moment, then said,
"A year, you say?"

"In service?"

Declan nodded.

"At least, or until you're dead, or I throw you out of the
company." Then he smiled. "You can leave any time freely
after a year."

Declan said, "Then I'll join."

"I thought you would," said his new captain. "I'll see to
it that we sharpen up your weapons training. We're going to
need to use weapons soon, so when your shoulder is healed,
that's your first duty."

"I expected that."

"Good. Another week or so should do it, if you don't
get stupid and tear those stitches again." He shook his head
slightly. "I understand your impatience, but you must appreciate that wounds need to be cared for. I've seen more men
die from festering wounds and the fever than I have killed
outright by a blade or arrow. Remember that."

Declan nodded. "I will." He recalled those who had
suffered in Oncon. The practice of brining the wound, of

heating blades to cut out hooks and deep splinters—all was done for the reason that those who were treated without salt water or heated steel were more likely to sicken and die.

"Good." Bogartis put heels to the barrel of his mount and moved toward the head of the caravan.

Declan suddenly felt far more tired than he had before. As they crested a hill and he could see the distant smudge on the horizon that would grow into the city of Marquenet, he realized that making a life-changing decision after all the madness of the last week was exhausting.

HATU SIGNALED TO WILLIAM AND shouted, "Sheet in!" The eldest of the three boys, William had naturally fallen into place as their leader and was the one most likely to speak on behalf of the boys. The last few days especially had become difficult for them as the enormity of what had befallen their families and the changes in their lives had begun to finally sink in.

Having witnessed enough of the destruction to have a sense of their loss, Hatu was more patient with their failings than he otherwise might have been, given his own upbringing and harsh tutelage. He nodded his approval when the sail was adjusted as he wished.

He had been away from Coaltachin a long time, but although he'd been in Beran's Hill for only a relatively short period, he had come to appreciate that even if people seemed fragile and vulnerable, they had lives that were much harsher than anything he had endured. He'd been trained to be hard. He had discovered over the last few days that these boys and others like them were resilient by necessity and he genuinely admired that in them.

Catharian came up on deck and said, "Thank you for taking the helm."

Hatu chuckled. "What else could I do? Denbe is asleep,

Sabella can't sail, and you had to relieve yourself." He glanced at the agent of the Flame Guard, whom he still thought of as the "false monk," and said, "I suppose I could have watched you try to give the boys a quick lesson in helmsmanship."

Catharian returned the chuckle. "They might surprise us both. At least you allowed me time to clean up a little down there. It was getting rank."

"Getting? It was rank three days ago. Whoever thought of a privy that needs bailing out daily on a ship should be tossed overboard."

Catharian nodded. "It's acceptable for a coast-hugger, just doesn't work out at sea. If you're putting into shore each night, a bucket of seawater, open the trap, and you're done. Open the trap when the wind's in the wrong direction out here, you flood the lower deck."

Hatu laughed. "I've been on more than one ship where you just hang your ass out over the rail."

"I as well." Catharian moved behind the wheel as Hatu stepped aside. He checked the position of the sun and said, "On course."

"Well, there seemed to be no benefit to changing it. I have no idea where you're taking me, and wasting more time getting there didn't seem wise."

Catharian smiled. "We'll be at our destination soon."

"Do you mean Nytanny?" asked Hatu. "You and Denbe both keep avoiding the answer."

"Eventually, you'll be taken to the last bastion of the Flame Guard. It's the safest place in this world for you."

"You've said that before, but you've never explained that whole 'end of magic' bit or why my safety is so paramount to anyone beside myself."

Catharian could see Hatu's color rising and realized that Hatu's temper was returning. He sighed and said, "I can tell you only a part. But before we get there, we will visit an island where there is someone who will be able to give you a complete understanding, I hope, of all of this. As I told you, like most members of the Guard I am told only as much as I need to know."

Hatu's brow furrowed for a moment, then he nodded. "It's like that with the Quelli Nascosti. Your enemies can't torture information out of you that you don't have."

Catharian nodded. "What I do know is there was a very special relationship between your family and the Guard. The Firemanes were important in ways I barely understand, and much of it is wreathed in myth, exaggeration, even intentional lies. A great deal of what I was taught as I grew up in the order seemed hardly credible until the Betrayal. Not only were your family and most nobles loyal to your father murdered, but every member of the Flame Guard who stood exposed and many we thought were not vulnerable: all were hunted down and killed."

"By Sandura?"

"By Lodavico, certainly, but also by agents of the Church of the One."

Hatu nodded. He recalled that moment when he had realized that the two men, the Azhante, he'd seen with the agents of the Church of the One in Sandura were somehow related to Coaltachin. He was still enough a student of Coaltachin that he didn't tell Catharian, but he realized they were somehow a part of all the murder and ruin Catharian had talked about.

"In any event, it took us a few years to retreat, to regroup a little, and to establish ourselves in a stronghold. We're rebuilding as best we can, but as you've seen with Sabella, and perhaps with Denbe, it takes a special sort of person to first gain our notice and then successfully be recruited into our ranks."

"You recruited Sabella?"

"Those with the gift of sight are a little different, Hatu," answered Catharian as he checked the set of the sails and adjusted his course slightly, to maximize speed. He shouted to the boy Jenson, "Up to the top and give us a look!"

Being the smallest of the three, the little fair-haired lad could climb the mainmast nimbly without causing too much disruption to the course. Unlike larger ships, this vessel was vulnerable to small changes, like a large man climbing to the top of the mast. Hatu had wondered why, out of a choice of vessels, they had ended up on a boat designed always to be in sight of land.

After a pause, Catharian said, "When we find a girl like Sabella, we don't recruit as often as we . . . well, to be honest, we just abduct them. If we get them young enough, as we did with her, it's the only life they know. For others it can be very difficult." Bitterly, he added, "Often it does not work out for the best."

"Abduction rarely does, I'll wager."

"The gift is rare, so this happens rarely, but when it does and we find someone like Sabella, they become acolytes—"

"I don't know that word," interrupted Hatu.

"A follower, assistant, like your students in Coaltachin."

"Ah," said Hatu.

"The Flame Guard is . . . a little like a religious order, though we worship no gods or goddesses. Some of us hold to the old gods in their own way, and a few of us don't really care. But our leader is called the prior, which means 'first,' as he's the first among us, but we do not have the monks, priests, episkopos, and the rest of those offices you find in the Church of the One or other orders.

"We also have men like Denbe, experienced fighters who will kill or die if needed." Catharian took a breath, adjusting the course slightly. "You'll be told more when we get where we're going."

"And again, that's . . . ?"

"An island that goes by several names. I've only been there in transit. I'm sure those who live there call it something else, but to those of us in the Flame Guard, we think of it as a stopping place, somewhere to refit and rest a bit while traveling from one side of this world to the other, since our home is on the other side of Garn."

Hatu gave a smile of wry amusement. This island sounded like some of the ports in Coaltachin, known by many names to those who didn't reside there, in order to mask the true nature of the place. Especially the main island, Coaltachin itself, upon which many not of the nation had trod without knowing where they actually were. He said, "So we're only halfway there?"

"A bit more, but no worries. We shall leave this little vessel and as soon as possible be off on a larger ship, which is more comfortable and faster. Most of our journey will be over in half the time we've been at sea."

Hatu had almost lost count of the days but realized from what had been said that this journey, wherever it led, was just beginning.

14

REVERSALS

AND THE UNEXPECTED

Hava was dozing, not allowing herself to fall into a deep sleep as a habit from years of learning to rest in dangerous situations. Muffled voices brought her fully awake, and she opened her eyes in the gloom to see two sailors standing in front of the ladder.

"You know what they said," whispered one.

Hava judged it to be night, as everyone around her seemed to be asleep.

"Some of them are likely to be dead before we sail," said the other. "No one's going to notice if a girl was smothered before we toss her to the sharks. The ones who were sent ashore had all the fun; I haven't dipped my cock since we sailed for this twice-damned coast, and those black-clad thugs don't scare me!"

"Well, they scare me. If you're going to take one of these girls, I'm off. I'll come back when you've finished." With that the second sailor climbed the ladder and vanished.

Hava quickly decided this might be her chance. Before the man intent on rape could pass out of earshot she said,

"Hey!" in a whisper just loud enough to catch his attention without waking the sleepers.

The sailor glanced at her. Before he could speak, she said, "You don't want some farm girl. I know things they can't even dream of."

He paused, his thick eyebrows forming a single dark line across his forehead. His beard was untrimmed and flying off in all directions as if he hadn't washed it in weeks, and even in the stench of this hold she could smell his reek. "What do you know?" he hissed, moving toward her.

"I was trained to please a man," she whispered, although ironically she had been a very poor student at that. "I can show you things," she said, "in exchange for favors."

His grin split his dark beard and he stood appraising her. "You don't say?"

"Those girls will just lie there and some might scream."

While he pondered her offer, she quickly took in everything she could see, hoping a detail would reveal itself so that she might gain an advantage. He wasn't a particularly large man, but he was fat, big enough that if he got his weight on top of her she would be unable to push him off. She could see a bulge in his shirt that might be a weapon or perhaps a coin purse, and then she spied a tiny glint at the top of his right boot.

Before he could speak again, she asked, "What's your name?"

"Cho," he replied. "Cho of Erkkila. What do they call you?"

"Sabrina," she improvised. Giving her real name was something she'd been trained to avoid all her life. "Sabrina of Patmiat."

"Where's that?"

"Where's Erkkila?"

"Far from here," he said with a widening smile and keen interest in his gaze. "Where's Patmiat?"

"Far from here," she echoed, struggling to make her tone sound playful. She glanced to either side to see if anyone was awake. If they were, thankfully they were staying silent.

He chuckled softly. "So, what is the favor? To set you free?"

She gave a genuine laugh. "I know better than that. First, you leave me alive after, and second, you make sure I stay well fed on the journey. I know how this goes. Do that and I can keep you . . . happy throughout the voyage. Can you keep me alive and fed?"

He moved a step closer—as she had hoped. "I can do both."

She knew he was lying. He was a terrible liar, as his movements and shifty eyes betrayed. He might very well kill her if the word had been passed not to trouble the women, and he certainly wouldn't put any effort into getting her extra food. He knew if she complained to anyone else after the fact, he simply had to avow that she had lied.

Hava's mind raced. At worst she was going to have to endure unwelcome sex and perhaps an attempt on her life, but at best she might be able to create an opportunity to get off this ship before they lifted anchor on the next tide, which she assumed was only a few hours away.

He leaned forward slightly. "So, you going to be nice to old Cho?"

She sat up. "As if it was the last day of your life."

He leaned farther to put his mouth on hers. Hava appeared to welcome him, but at the last moment she twisted her wrists, breaking the frayed bindings. Quickly shifting her weight as much as she could to the left, she reached around with her right hand and grabbed him by the neck, yanking downward with all her strength. As she had hoped, he overbalanced.

By twisting she avoided most of his weight landing on her, though her legs were trapped from the knees down. She ignored the pain that caused and with one lunge reached to the top of his right boot with her left hand and found the dagger she had seen glinting there. Within a moment, she had the tip of that small blade planted just below his rib cage, not enough to injure, but enough to make its presence clearly known. "Say anything," she hissed into his ear, "and I'll slice your liver. You'll bleed out before a surgeon can heal you, if there's one aboard."

Cho started to pull back and she put more pressure on the blade, piercing his shirt to the skin beneath, and he froze.

"Good," she whispered. "If you want to live I need these shackles off."

"I can do that," he said, his voice trembling. He started to pull away and she grabbed hard, pulling back, preventing him from freeing himself.

"Do you take me for an idiot?" she demanded, poking the point of the dagger a bit deeper, drawing blood. "You're not going anywhere."

"But how—"

"Is there a lock on that main chain?"

"No," he whispered back, now almost quavering in fear. "A single eyelet with a lynchpin holds the chain. That's why there's a guard near it."

"When does the next guard relieve you?"

"Not until dawn. I guard you until then, maybe an hour before we raise sails."

"Roll to your left and get off my legs. Stay between me and the woman next to me, and if I feel you move in any other direction, I'll drive home this blade before you can twitch."

"All right," said the man, and suddenly the strong, pungent aroma of urine struck Hava and she realized Cho had pissed himself. She would have thought it amusing if her leg wasn't getting damp from it.

"Move," she commanded, and jabbed again, eliciting a yelp of real pain from the man.

Cho did as instructed, and while he was moving Hava did a quick pat on his waist, and besides coming away with a wet hand, she found the lump in his shirt was another blade, not a coin pouch. She pulled it free and said, "Wise."

"What?"

"Not trying to draw that second blade. I prefer you alive for the moment—it makes things simpler."

Cho scuttled back to where Hava had indicated.

"I know you're awake," she said to the woman on the other side of the sailor.

"Yes," said the woman, her voice quavering.

Hava peered over Cho and said, "Who is closest to the lock anchoring the chain?"

When no answer was forthcoming, Hava shouted, "Who is closest to the end of the chain?"

A quiet voice answered, "I am."

"Who are you?"

"I'm called Meggie, from Port Colos."

"Can you reach the big pin holding this chain in place?"

"I can try."

"Do so. Pull it out so we can free this chain."

Hava heard the sound of rustling as Meggie tried to move toward the lynchpin, then the sound of metal on metal. "It's hard," Meggie said in a weak voice. "My hands . . ."

Hava felt her tension rise even higher: she hated the idea of her fate literally being in the hands of someone else. There were few people in her life she trusted, and a stranger who was struggling to lift a simple lynchpin wasn't one of them.

Finally she heard a loud *clunk* and felt relief wash over her as she heard Meggie call, "It's free."

Poking Cho with the tip of the blade, Hava said, "Pull the chain through."

Now voices were being raised as those nearby started to speak, those nearest asking to be freed. Hava shouted, "Quiet if you want to live!"

She cast her gaze to the bottom of the ladder in the companionway as Cho began to pull on the chain. Stout, but not so heavy as to require great effort, the links slid easily through the loops on the shackles and the iron rings in the supports. It was only a few moments before the chain had passed through the ring on Hava's ankle shackles.

"Is there a key for these shackles?" she asked Cho. Should he not have it, she was prepared to pick the lock, but was fearful of the havoc that might ensue should she free herself and not the other prisoners.

"No," said Cho. "I need to take them off." He pointed to the shackle and motioned to ask to be allowed to touch it. Hava nodded. The man winced as he moved, and she realized that she had pressed harder on the dagger than she had meant to and that he was in real pain.

She withdrew the dagger point and he leaned over. Taking the ring through which the chain had passed, he turned it a half-turn and the shackles clicked open. "Clever," said Hava, understanding that with the chain in place the ring could not turn and the shackle would not release; this bit of mechanical ingenuity saved a great deal of trouble with jammed locks or those rusted frozen by salt mist in the air.

Her ankles were finally free. She moved and heard her knees pop as she felt them unlock from the long period of being forced into one position. She wondered how many people unshackled after a long voyage were even able to walk.

She told Cho to free the woman next to her while Hava got to her feet, looking forward to that moment in the future when she could take a long bath and do her best to scrub away the dirty feeling that seemed to have seeped into her very bones.

With one hand on a support to steady herself, Hava stretched her legs, which were tingling and throbbing. She chided herself for allowing her preoccupation with escape to cause her to forget a lesson taught while she was a student: to constantly flex confined muscles in order to keep the blood circulating so as to stay limber and be ready to move as soon as the opportunity presented itself. Every lesson she had been taught was valuable, but one in particular: Master Bodai had repeated one message over and over, that fear was the worst enemy, driving all other thought from your mind, and he had been right. She vowed never again to let that happen.

The woman who had lain next to Hava got to her feet unsteadily. With a fearful look at Hava, she said, "Thank you. I heard every word and you were—"

Hava cut off the praise. She flipped the second dagger over and presented the hilt to the woman. "What's your name?"

"Lydia."

"If necessary can you stick this up under his ribs"—she indicated Cho with an inclination of her head—"and slice his liver?"

An unexpected smile crossed Lydia's face. "I'm a farmer. I've gutted enough hogs in my day."

Hava felt a surprising impulse to laugh but pushed it aside. Turning to all those who were watching, she said, "If you have a prayer of surviving, of living your life free, remain quiet. If you do something stupid, you'll end up dead or in a brothel, a mine, or a fighting pit. Pass the word." She lifted her chin toward the bow. "And make sure everyone knows our only hope is silence and the willingness to fight when needed."

She stepped away from Cho and Lydia, crossed to the lynchpin on the opposite side of the walkway and quickly freed it. To the woman closest to the bulkhead she indicated she should start moving the chain forward, showed her how to twist the ring by feeling the shackles, and told her to pass instructions down the line.

Turning around, she was greeted by a round face with large, frightened eyes. The girl was barely more than a child, and she had tears running down her cheeks, though she was silent.

"Meggie?"

The girl nodded, and Hava inspected her. She felt a clutch in her chest when she saw blood across the lower half of the simple shift she wore and realized she had been raped before being brought here. Then she saw the girl's hands. Several fingers on both hands were dislocated, either as she struggled against her rapist or out of cruelty. Hava felt her eyes fill and blinked away the tears that welled up. Now she understood why lifting the heavy iron pin had been so difficult for the girl.

Leaning forward, Hava put one hand on Meggie's shoulder and said, "You are very brave." Glancing again at her hands, she said, "I have to do something and it will be very painful for a moment, but if I don't you will lose the use of those fingers."

Before Meggie could say anything, Hava slipped the dagger into her boot, grabbed the girl's wrist, and pulled on two dislocated fingers, popping them back into place. The girl gasped and then cried out, but it was a pitiful little wail rather than a full-throated scream. Hava knew the scream would not be heard two decks above and ignored it. She dropped that hand and gripped the other wrist, and quickly had three fingers back in place. The girl was gasping for breath and on the verge of passing out from the pain, and Hava pulled her close, holding her tight for a moment. When the child's trembling stopped, Hava said, "The pain will pass, and you'll regain the use of your hands."

Then she held Meggie away, looked into her eyes, and repeated herself. "You are very brave."

Meggie threw her arms around Hava as if holding on for life itself. Hava closed her eyes, breathing slowly and deeply as she calmed a rage that was building inside her. Someone would die for what happened to this child, just not yet.

After a while, Hava disentangled herself from the girl and said, "Sit here and rest." She turned to a young woman and said softly, "Go free the men in the cages and get to the slave beds on the other side, show them how to undo their shackles and warn them to stay quiet." The woman nodded and hurried off.

She walked back to Cho and said, "Remind me when the next guard is due?"

"As I said, at sunrise before we sail."

"One more question, are either of those 'black-clad thugs' you spoke of still aboard?"

"One."

Hava felt her stomach knot, but merely nodded. She had an hour or two to come up with a plan.

Others were now free and standing, and Hava said to those nearby, "If you can fight, stay here. If you can't fight, go to the bow and tell those who can fight to come to me."

Most of the women moved quickly toward the bow. She noticed Lydia hadn't moved and gave her a nod. The woman was perhaps middle-aged, stocky, and looked like no stranger to hard work. She smiled and said, "Now that I have my wits back, as I said, I've gutted more than one hog."

"Good. We may have only two daggers, and perhaps something else around here to use as weapons, but we are now going to survive or die."

"How?" asked Lydia.

With a grim smile, Hava said, "We're going to seize this ship."

THE THREE BOYS HAD BEEN attentive. Hatu judged them competent enough in their duties not to require constant supervision. They were briskly keeping the sails trimmed while Catharian manned the helm; they might turn out to be capable sailors.

In the days since Hatu had been on this small lugger he had rebuilt his stamina and strength despite the food being meager. His mood, however, was still close to explosive, his rage simmering just below the surface. Only a constant exercise of will—and a healthy respect for Denbe's combat skills—kept him from attacking Catharian. He also found it doubly vexing that the rare tranquility he had found after years of constant anger, when sailing the Narrows with Hava, was now gone.

He took a deep breath and locked his frustration and anger in a place in his mind he now thought of as a "thought prison." It was where he put those images and memories Hava chided him about as excuses to become enraged. They were, as she had taught him, things over which he had no control and dangerous to his well-being. He also pushed away his longing to see her again, as that was another fast way back to frustration and anger.

Taking another deep breath, he returned his attention to the present and took advantage of the rare quiet moment on this boat to study the false monk. The way Catharian watched the sails as he turned the ship's wheel reinforced Hatu's certainty that he was an experienced sailor and navigator. His guise might be false, but his skills were not. At least Catharian provided Hatu with a measure of how much he had come to master himself over the last few years; there had been a time nothing would have spared the false monk from his fury. Hatu thanked whatever gods might be paying attention for his "thought prison."

Denbe was below, almost certainly asleep, since he would take over the helm at sundown, utilizing the stars to set their course as he guided the ship through the night. Hatu assumed Sabella was below as well, as he had had no glimpse of her in the last hour.

Sabella was a mystery to Hatu, and he suspected she was part of the reason he had been able to maintain his composure. She had a palliative effect on him, which he surmised might be some sort of magic, if magic were real.

His discussions with Catharian on this topic had left him confused, which might be more a function of his inability to fully grasp the concept or of Catharian dissembling. Hatu felt there was a great deal of information not being disclosed by the false monk, but whatever the reason, Hatu just could not fully grasp the idea that he was some sort of key to the future of this world.

This world, he considered. Apparently, it was far bigger than he had imagined, even after traveling from Coaltachin to Marquensas. For a youth he had seen a lot, but the raiders attacking Beran's Hill had spoken languages he'd never encountered. Yes, this world was far bigger than he had ever imagined.

He took a moment to look around, taking in the horizon at every quarter. Not a hint of land in sight. He was resigned to being at sea, out of sight of land, with no idea where he was. It was the most compelling reason for keeping his anger under control. Once he made landfall, he'd reconsider his options. He hadn't ruled out killing Catharian and Denbe—though with the older fighter, he'd have to rely on wits and stealth, since he doubted he could best him in combat, but Hatu had been well trained in the art of assassination.

Sabella was clearly a party to his abduction, but as a willing partner, a useful tool, or under some duress? He had no idea. Moreover, being around her gave him a pleasant sensation. It was a little like being around Hava in the quiet moments when they didn't need to speak, or after making love just before drifting off to sleep. He found being around the young woman both reassuring and disturbing at the same time. He was drawn to her calming presence, but he was growing distrustful of his own feelings.

She was a pleasant enough looking girl, her brown hair a little lighter in shade than Hava's, but there was no other resemblance to his wife. Sabella was thin in comparison with Hava, yet Hatu found himself painfully aware of her body: the hint of the curves under her ankle-length dress when she moved, the arch of her neck, her quirky half smile. He found few women attractive compared with Hava, and even those he found pleasing to the eye didn't arouse him, yet there was this strange pull when he looked at Sabella.

Unlike Donte, who found nearly all women irresistible—to the point where they had joked that he had to be kept away from anything female—Hatu had never been truly smitten with any girl; but he now understood it was because he had always had Hava close. He could barely remember a time she wasn't in his life.

Yet there was something about this delicate young woman, an itch he couldn't seem to scratch. He was beginning to feel aroused by her, and that was a sensation he didn't particularly like or trust; if there was some magic at play, tying him to Sabella would make sense, as a way to keep him in line. It was another reason he was determined that as soon as this ship reached its destination, he had to get away from these people, whatever the nonsense they claimed about his family and his existence being vital to some great plan.

His best guess was that because the baron had named him as the son of some dead king, they might use him to gain some political advantage. Just thinking about this made the rage boil again and he had to quell it: all that concerned him was getting back to Marquenet and Hava, and if he had to kill everyone in his way, he would.

When Catharian called for a course correction, he glanced again at the three boys, wondering if his help would be required, but they seemed confident in their sail handling, so he settled down again, his thoughts returning to Hava. At least she had been spared the fate of Beran's Hill. He felt concern for the safety of Declan, Gwen, and the others, but at least he knew Hava was safe.

IT TOOK THE BETTER PART of an hour for Hava to get the prisoners under any kind of control. She was weary of reminding them to keep their voices down, until she had to start threatening a few of the men. Discord was hardly the way to organize a takeover of this ship, but a couple of the younger men seemed averse to taking instruction from her. Putting two of the more fractious young men on their backs in quick order stopped any more objections, or at least they were no longer being verbalized.

Apart from the dagger in her hand and the one Lydia held on Cho, the only other weapon was a crowbar one of the men had found under a tarp next to the cages where the men had been housed. It would make a more than adequate cudgel, and the man who now held it had once served in the Port Colos militia and seemed eager to repay the injury done to his homeland.

Cho now sat silently by the companionway, where he would be expected to sit for his watch, with Lydia just out of sight from the ladder, ready to gut the slaver if need be. He had fallen silent when he realized that cooperation was his only hope of leaving this vessel alive; he would certainly be held responsible by his captain and the black-clad sicari for the prisoners getting loose, so like it or not, his lot now lay with Hava and the slaves.

The bottom of the ladder, as the steps to the deck above were called, was set back behind a doorway, separated by a bulkhead. From rusted and empty hinges, Hava deduced a lockable door had once hung there, but she pushed aside any speculation as to why it was no longer there. The lack of a door gave her the advantage of seeing boots and legs appear at the bottom of the stairs before being seen herself for a moment, and she was going to take advantage of that.

The wielder of the crowbar, a large man named Jack, waited on the opposite side of the doorway from Cho and Lydia. Hava stood squarely in the line of sight of anyone reaching the bottom of the steps. The plan was simple. The second anyone appeared, Jack was to swing low and bring the target to the ground. Other men crouching just behind Jack and Lydia were told to make sure whoever came through never regained his feet; they were to stamp and kick the man to unconsciousness, even death, but he must not be allowed to regain his feet. Hava's task was to deal with any second person who might follow.

Hava felt the tension building in her shoulders as she stood ready. They were approaching the time when Cho would be relieved, and while she was comfortable waiting in ambush, she knew no one else was. There was a slowly rising tide of voices: Hava could sense if this ambush didn't happen soon, disaster was in the offing.

She was about to warn people to be quiet, but then heard

a boot on the companionway, the wooden steps giving a slight creak.

She nodded at Jack, and he readied his weapon.

A man came down, stepped through the doorway, and Jack swung low. The man howled in pain and Hava heard the crack of bone as his leg shattered. There was movement behind him, and with a jolt of alarm she realized she had almost missed the second man because he was completely clad in black. It was the sicari.

He came down the stairway and then through the doorway in a crouch, his arm raised to take any blow, and his short sword out of its scabbard. Hava saw him glance at Jack, and as he turned his attention in that direction, she jumped forward. The injured man lay screaming on the floor, and as Jack delivered another blow that silenced him, he almost struck Hava as she attacked the sicari.

Whatever training this man possessed, Hava assumed it to be equal to that of the black agents of the Quelli Nascosti. She knew almost instantly that this was a correct assumption. She lunged and tried to cut beneath the man's guard, but her blade encountered only air as he had moved out of the way as smoothly as a snake. She sensed more than saw his counterattack and tried to step away, but she tripped over the body of the man lying across the doorway and fell backward. The sicari's blade sliced through the air inches above her. Had she not stumbled he would have cut her in two. But that moment of blind luck was followed almost instantly by the certainty that she was about to die.

The black-clad man lunged after her. As he drew back his blade to thrust at her she saw a large boot strike the sicari in the side. He toppled over and fell next to Cho as Hava rolled away.

As the sicari got to his feet, Hava sprang up, grabbed an

overhead beam that gave her just enough leverage to pull up both legs, and kicked the sicari high on the shoulder, knocking him down. She dropped and saw Lydia kick the assassin hard in the head. As Hava stepped closer, Lydia kicked the man again and again, as fast as she could, in a frenzy that amazed Hava.

Half a dozen men and women came to surround the two men, kicking and stamping them without mercy until Hava said, "Enough!" She had to repeat herself before the attack ceased and she saw that both men were dead.

Picking up the sicari's sword, Hava realized it was a finely made weapon. Keeping the sword, she handed the dagger she'd used to a man nearby, then handed the sword to the man named Jack. He passed along his makeshift club to another large man and nodded in approval.

Hava found another pair of daggers on the dead sailor and asked Cho, "How well armed is the crew?"

He said, "There's no weapons locker, just some things in the captain's cabin. He has a sword, as does the mate. The rest of us . . ." He shrugged.

"How big is the crew?"

"Thirty or so. Had a couple of lads hurt in the raiding, and they're down in the forecastle."

Looking around the hold, Hava could see faces staring intently at her.

"Here's how we do it," she said. "I go first, Jack right after me, and we run as fast as we can up that staircase. I'll go right, Jack goes left, and each of you just go in the opposite direction of the person you follow. That should keep you from tripping over each other. Grab whatever you can use as a weapon—a bucket, belaying pin, heavy block on a rope, anything. Hit the first sailor you see and try to disable him, kill if you must. Act fast enough and they'll be unconscious.

If they drop a blade, pick it up. You may get cut, but we can sew wounds up, so just keep moving. If you don't, it's fairly certain you'll be dead by sundown."

She looked at their eager faces, then nodded once. "We go!"

Hava took the steps up the companionway and quickly reached the next deck. She had to loop around to the next companionway to the top deck, and as soon as she cleared the deckhouse, she turned to the right and saw a sailor tying down a line. He looked up and his eyes widened in surprise, but before he could react, Hava drove her dagger into his stomach.

She turned at the railing toward the stern, where she knew the captain would be, either still sleeping or just awake, getting ready to depart on the morning tide. The sky to the east was lightening with the rosy promise of dawn, and the entire deck was half lit, as the sky was now a thing of grey clouds with hints of light crimson and gold.

The crew was slow to react: an uprising from belowdecks was apparently the last thing they had expected. By the time those below started to appear on deck, armed prisoners were waiting for them.

Hava had just reached the door she assumed led to the captain's quarters when it opened and the captain stood with mouth agape and eyes widening as she drove her blade into his ample gut. His eyes rolled up into his head and blood gushed from his mouth.

Pulling out the blade, she looked into the dimly lit cabin and saw no one else. She turned as the sound of fighting diminished, and then there was silence.

Walking around a hatch cover, she saw the deck littered with bodies. A few were prisoners, but the majority were crew. She looked upward and saw no one in the rigging, then noticed movement along one of the yardarms.

"You!" she shouted, pointing. "Come down and you'll live."

The sailor in the rigging was obviously unconvinced. Hava saw him shimmy outward along the spar, then stand and dive into the ocean. Lacking a bow, she could only watch as the sailor surfaced and started swimming to shore. It was not a short swim, but if he was experienced and fit he would get there eventually.

Hava took a deep breath, trying to take in all that had just happened. She was alive and most of the prisoners had survived and they were all free, or at least as long as they could avoid being recaptured.

Loudly she shouted, "Dump the dead over the side!" Taking another deep breath, she added, "I want the surviving crew members over here." She pointed with her dagger to a spot close by.

A dozen men were forced to stand before her, many sporting cuts and bruises, one nursing a broken arm. "Any of you the mate?"

One man said, "I am."

"Name?"

"George," he answered defiantly.

"Watch." She said to Jack, "Go fetch that slug Cho from below."

In a short while, Jack and Lydia appeared with Cho, and Hava pointed to the rail. "Go stand there."

Cho did as instructed. His face was drained of all color and he was trembling. Hava saw the girl Meggie huddled next to an older couple, and when Hava beckoned her over, the girl slowly rose and approached.

"Is this the man who hurt you?" she asked.

Meggie said nothing but shook her head slowly. Cho's face relaxed slightly. "I never touched her," he said hoarsely.

"Good," said Hava. "That earns you a quick end."

With a quick slash, she cut his throat, and as he reached up to try to stop the blood, which flowed through his fingers, she put a hand on his chest and pushed hard so that he fell over the railing into the water.

Some of the onlookers gasped audibly at the brutality of his death. Others appeared pleased at this one act of retribution.

Hava turned and looked from face to face. "That man deserved worse. I want you to understand that I am willing to slit the throat of any man or woman who causes any trouble. Is that clear?"

A few voices sounded their acknowledgment, and others nodded their understanding.

"Listen," she said. "Any man or woman who wishes to return to that"—she pointed to the ruins of Port Colos off in the distance—"is free to go." With the sun only just up, the city stood delineated by stark contrasts: black ruins still shrouded in smoke and leaping flames where a few fires remained.

Hava looked to George. "Do you have a gig or longboat?"

"There's a gig off the poopdeck."

Hava nodded, then said to the prisoners, "There's a boat hanging at the rear. Any of you who wish to use it, do it now.

"Those of you who wish to stay and know how to sail, George here will give you your duties." She turned to face the mate and said, "You're now sailing master. You keep the job as long as you don't disappoint me. Are we clear?"

The man had a round face and an unruly shock of blond-streaked hair. He nodded. "Yes . . . Captain."

Hava couldn't help but smile. "Hava. My name is Hava. We'll talk about who's captain if we live long enough."

"For what?"

"To get away before those other ships weigh anchor." She raised her voice to address the crowd. "So that's your choice: get off now or work to crew this ship. If you wish to stay but don't know how to crew, we'll teach you, otherwise stay out of the way. Those who stay and want to leave later, we'll work something out."

She turned to George. "Are we all right?"

He looked around the deck, taking in the dozens of former prisoners who had been ready to kill him on her command, and with a bitter laugh said, "I think so, Hava."

"Where were you bound?"

"To the southwest, where we'd offload the slaves."

"Then that is where I want to go."

George's brow furrowed.

"I'm looking for someone, and if he was taken by slavers that's where he will be. How many ships have already sailed?"

"Two or three, perhaps, but this is the first slaver."

"Good, that narrows the search." She took a deep breath and realized that as her stress was flowing out, so was her ability to keep her thoughts coherent. "Clear out the captain's cabin, and if he's not been dumped over the side yet, toss him over." Softly she added, "I need some rest."

"Aye, Cap . . . Hava."

She looked to Jack. "Can you watch things here?"

He nodded. "Absolutely."

To another fit-looking man, Hava said, "Can you watch my door?"

"I owe you my life" was his answer, and he came to stand beside her.

As she moved toward the aft of the ship, she paused before Meggie. "No one will hurt you again, I promise."

Reaching the captain's cabin, Hava saw that his body had already been removed and someone had even roughly cleaned up the blood he had spilled. She stepped inside and shut the door behind her, realizing she didn't even know the name of the young man who now stood guard over her safety.

The cabin was a mess, with discarded bits of food and dirty clothing strewn over the floor. She'd endured worse, though, and fell forward into the welcoming bunk. As she began to quickly drift off, she thought, *Well, you said you wanted to be a pirate.*

DONTE SURVEYED THE ROOM HE found himself in. He had been escorted by two guards who had shoved him inside, locking the door behind him. He had already explored the one high window in this small but nicely furnished room and judged it impossible to wriggle through. With two armed guards outside the door, escape was unlikely, so he sat in a chair beside a small table and waited.

A little time later he heard the door latch start to move. Reflexively, he tensed, ready to fight, then realized that if the baron wanted him dead, he would have let Deakin garrote him.

The door opened and the man named Balven entered. Donte knew that he was close to the baron, therefore a man of importance, so he stood and lowered his eyes.

"Are you hungry?" asked the baron's adviser.

Taken aback, Donte hesitated before shrugging and saying, "Most of the time."

Balven chuckled. "I'll order food, but first I have a few questions." He motioned for Donte to sit down again.

Donte returned to the chair and waved a hand at his surroundings. "I'm surprised to be here," he said, then quickly added, "my lord."

"I'm nobody's lord," said Balven. "Balven will do." He glanced around the cozy little room. "This was the baron's father's reading room." He pointed at a bare wall. "There was a little bookcase there in which the late baron kept books to read in private. He was a man who adored read-ing." His tone was almost wistful.

"Reading," said Donte in neutral tones.

"I have a proper dungeon below with filthy damp straw and rats to share with, should you prefer."

Donte smiled. "No, m—Balven. This is a lovely room. I don't read much myself, but I'm willing to give it a go."

Balven laughed, then said, "You're a cheeky one, aren't you?"

"I'm Donte," said the younger man.

"Donte," Balven echoed. "You said you were looking for a girl named Hava, so I assume you know a lad named Hatushaly?"

"Yes, sir. The three of us . . . we're like brothers and sister."

"Really? They are husband and wife."

Donte laughed. "I heard that when I was at Beran's Hill."

"It's funny?"

"No . . . yes, I suppose so. He's been in love with her since we were children. He was the only one of us too stupid to realize it. I never knew she felt the same." Donte fixed Balven with a sharper expression. "But this isn't about their marriage, is it?"

"What can you tell me about Hatushaly?"

Donte cocked his head. "He's . . . my friend, and some-times he keeps me out of trouble, or sometimes I get him and Hava into trouble. I . . ." He tried to frame his story with truth, as he had no doubt this man could easily smell out a lie. "I was an orphan, in my grandfather's care, and he sent me to study where I met Hatu and Hava. They're, as I said, like my brother and sister. But Hatu was always the odd one, from some distant place, though he acted like one of us."

"Us?"

Donte paused, then said, "He's not really like anyone from my home—"

"Coaltachin, the Kingdom of Night," interrupted Balven.

The certainty with which the baron's adviser spoke again reminded Donte that he was a man not to be played, not to mislead. Shaded truth was his best choice in this circumstance, he realized. This would not be a choice of his by nature, but by years of training. He nodded.

"He was always odd, even as a boy. Had a temper like no one I know, and I have known some short-tempered people since I was a baby, especially my grandfather. But he was also fearless. When the bigger boys picked on him, he'd fight back no matter how badly he got beaten. We became friends, and he was always there with me. After a while no one would trouble either one of us, because no matter how outnumbered we might be in a fight, we could hurt people badly even if we ended up losing."

Balven nodded. "What else?"

Donte shrugged. "He was lighter skinned than most, and he had that ridiculous red hair he had to dye constantly."

"Why?" Balven leaned forward as if the answer was important.

"It's a strange color and made him too easy to recognize—" Donte stopped abruptly.

Balven's gaze narrowed. "I understand."

Donte wasn't certain what Balven understood about the role of agents of Coaltachin as criminals and spies, but he assumed he knew something, because even knowing of the existence of the Kingdom of Night in the first place made him rare among outlanders; but knowing about Hava and Hatu being from Coaltachin meant that this man knew more about things than Donte, and while Donte could be thoughtless, he was by no means stupid.

He took a breath, then continued. "Hatu's red hair is very

unusual in our homeland, so since he was a little boy, he's had to dye it to make himself look more like other boys."

"Let me make this easier," said Balven. He almost smiled. "You're acting as agents, or infiltrators, or criminals, so being easy to recognize is not a good thing. But we are spending too much time discussing what we already know. Let me focus my question. Do you know why Hatu is important?"

Donte shook his head. "Not really. He was treated as if he was special—that we knew from the beginning. Some of his training was . . . lighter?" He shrugged. "As if they wanted to ensure he wasn't seriously injured."

"They?"

"Our teachers." Donte was not about to volunteer the relationship between masters, preceptors, and students.

"He was treated more gently?"

Donte laughed. "I wouldn't call it gentle. He had his share of bruises, cuts, and once a broken arm." His thoughts raced quickly, not wanting to talk about the missions they had been sent on as boys, where Hatu always had the least risky assignment. He took a long breath, then said, "It's just they kept a closer watch on him. That's all."

Balven turned and walked slowly around the small room. After a moment, he said, "I am assuming that you really have little idea of his importance?"

Again Donte decided that a shaded truth was his best choice. "I don't know why he was considered special as a student, or why you might think him important, sir." He paused, his expression thoughtful. "He and I were on a journey, and we . . ." He considered how much of the truth he was prepared to share about the Sisters of the Deep and quickly temporized. "We ran into trouble and got separated. I was injured, and when I recovered, I spent some time . . . reclaiming my wits. I had no memory for a while, and when I regained it . . ." He closed his eyes, squeezing them tight as if recalling something painful, then opened them again. "Some things are still a bit muddied. I don't remember much since we were together on a ship bound for this city." He frowned. "Or perhaps it was another city?" He sighed. "It may come back to me one of these days." He pointed to his temple. "Got a serious bash to my head, they told me, and it scrambled things for a while." He reflected on the original question. "Except for what I told you about the teachers, I say again I don't know why anyone would consider Hatu special."

Balven nodded thoughtfully. "As I suspected. Now again, why are you so far from home and why are you seeking this girl Hava?"

Suddenly Donte again felt a slight pressure inside, as if two parts of him were caught in a struggle. One side was familiar, but the other was cold, angry, and frightened and felt as if it was coming from a long way away. He tried to consider his words, but they seemed to flow out of their own accord. "I was looking for Hava . . ." His eyes became unfocused and he stared into the space beyond Balven. ". . . because I knew she'd be with him, or know where he was."

Just as he was on the verge of recounting his voyage with Hatu and the Sisters of the Deep ensnaring his ship and the crew, he felt something snap inside him.

He shook his head as if clearing it, feeling somewhat astonished. Then he said, "I need to find Hatushaly."

"Need? Why?"

Donte's tone was almost cheerful as he replied, "I'm not certain, but I think I'm supposed to kill him."

15

APPRAISALS, GUESSWORK,
AND REPURPOSING

H ava awoke in an hour, hardly rested, but feeling as if
she would be able to endure whatever came next. She
took a deep breath, realizing that soon she'd have to find a
way to clean herself up. She couldn't recall a single moment
in her life when she'd been this filthy and smelled this rank.
Cho's stale urine on her trousers coupled with the stench of
her own fear-generated sweat, topped off by whatever other
muck she'd lain in below, made her feel the need to strip off
every garment and wash herself raw, even if it was with cold
seawater.

She opened the cabin door and found the young man who
had elected to stand guard blocking the entrance. Hearing
it open behind him, he turned and stepped aside. "Captain,"
he said.

"Hava," she corrected. "How long?"

"An hour, bit more, I reckon."

"Everything calm?"

"Pretty much, though some of the boys are looking to
take out their ire on the crew. That fellow George seems to
be keeping everyone from each other's throats."

"What's your name?" she asked, appraising him. He appeared to be barely more than a youth from his smooth cheeks and unlined forehead, but he was tall and powerfully built, with dark close-curled hair, dark eyes, and skin the color of tanned leather.

"I'm Sabien."

"You have a trade?"

"I was a mason's apprentice, almost a journeyman. I've cut stone since I was a boy."

That explained the size and muscles, thought Hava. He also had a skill. She considered that before she cut anyone loose, she might do well to see what other trades and professions had ended up on this ship. She didn't have any clear idea of what was coming, and knowing what resources were available might be useful.

She found the newly anointed sailing master, George, at the helm, watching the sails. "Captain—" He caught himself. "Hava."

"No riots while I napped?"

"We've had some moments, but I've managed to keep my boys in line, and that big fellow, Jack, he's done a good job keeping the rest reined in."

"Good," said Hava. "I think I'll find a place for him. See if he can learn. He probably knows nothing about sailing, but then neither did I until someone taught me."

George smiled. "Smart. He can keep an eye on the prisoners—or, should I say, former prisoners—and on me as well."

Hava nodded. George was not a stupid man.

"Now that I've had a bit of rest, a few questions."

George's expression was guarded but not combative. Hava had learned young how to read possible enemies, and she realized this man wasn't a committed foe . . . yet.

"How long before we reach our destination?"

"About three weeks, if the winds hold—maybe two if the weather is favorable, more than that if not."

"Do we have enough provisions?"

"If we fed the slaves as we planned, expecting a tenth of them to die along the way, yes. If we feed everyone equally, no."

"What do we do about that?"

"We could return to Port Colos, but there's nothing left there." He thought for a moment then said, "There are a half dozen small islands we usually bypass, but we could stop and do some trading. Fish is easily acquired as well as some breadfruit, coconut, a turnip common to the islands—the taste is nothing to celebrate, but it's nourishing—and perhaps some pigs and goats. I know how to salt the meat to make it last."

"We'll stop. I want an accounting of what we have aboard that we can trade."

"Aye, Captain."

Hava was about to correct him, then realized it was probably futile; if she was in command of this ship, she was the captain.

"And I never asked. What is this ship called?"

"*Borzon's Black Wake*. Borzon's some sea god," said George. "I've never heard of him or his wake. Supposedly it was some sort of terror of the ocean, a wake of horror or . . . ? And that is as much about it as I know. These old ships pass through a lot of hands," he added. "I reckon this was a trading vessel, but how it came to be a slaver is anyone's guess."

"How did you become a slaver?" she asked pointedly.

"I was raised on an island not too far from where we're heading. My father was a pirate and . . . I got into the family trade, you could say. I wasn't particularly happy with that life: no matter how good a raid, or how big a ship was cap-

tured, there was never a lot of money being passed around."
He shrugged. "Most of us would hit a port with our loot,
and within a few weeks we'd have spent it all, on women, on
gambling . . ." Again, he shrugged. "I had no idea where it
went. I left a crew in a town called Salvatia, another island
port, near starving when this ship turned up looking for a
crew, so I signed on rather than go back, not my best choice.

"The man you killed was a pig: no one will mourn his
loss. Half his crew had deserted. I had some experience, so
he hired me on as mate. By the time we got to Port Colos,
I was ready to jump ship. I would have, too, if the raiders
had left anything standing." He furrowed his brow. "The
captain seemed as surprised as anyone at the size of the fleet
that gathered. Most were already at anchor, and the fighting
started the day after we arrived." He shook his head slowly.
"If I'd known what was coming, I might have just stayed
where I was and starved."

Hava didn't know how much of the story to believe, but
decided to take the man at face value rather than suspect
him of some evil intent; he didn't seem the type, and as he
had observed, there were more people willing to protect her
than him, assuming any one of the remaining crew was of a
mind to protect anyone but himself.

Hava was silent for a long while, pondering her situation,
and George seemed content to keep his eyes on the sails
and heading. Finally she said, "This captain, what was his
name?"

George smiled. "He was also named George, funnily
enough, from Bouboulis. His father was a very famous pirate, and George was the biggest cockroach I've ever seen,
but that family reputation stood him in good stead, despite
there being little else to recommend him."

Hava said, "I like to know the names of the men I kill."
Then she gave a small laugh. "It really doesn't matter. Those

Azhante were going to kill him as soon as you got the slaves to port anyway. I overheard them. They said he knew too much about them."

George nodded. "Good to know." He paused, then added, "That means they were likely going to kill all of us. I'll pass the word your taking over has saved us from that. I know it wasn't your intent, but still, it may make a difference."

Hava said nothing. Trying to work out why people did what they did was never a major concern to her, though it seemed to drive Hatushaly as much as anything in life did.

Realizing he had returned to her thoughts now that she was out of immediate danger, she felt that emptiness once again. She desperately wished she knew where he was. This was a big ocean: he could be anywhere.

HATU HAULED IN A SHEET as the boat heeled over on a change of tack. The boys were knowledgeable enough that they didn't need to be instructed anymore, and Hatu found himself pleasantly surprised at that. He had never been particularly fond of children; he found them loud, annoying, and often in the way. He realized as he considered the pleasure he took from their progress under his instruction that he could one day be a teacher, like Master Bodai. He had labored to learn under the preceptors, but somehow Master Bodai had been different. The preceptors wanted the students to learn specific things, to master their lessons and know what to do in given situations, but Master Bodai had taught students to think for themselves.

Hatu smiled at that thought. He enjoyed knowing there was more than one way of approaching things.

It had made an impression on Hatu, especially when thinking about escape routes, how to avoid being followed, and other potential mistakes—what Bodai had called "being trapped by old habits"—because he knew many of those he had studied with had become predictable in how they did certain things. Hatu applied that wisdom to studying one's enemies and looked for patterns. He thought that was where Baron Dumarch had failed: he'd become predictable, and it had cost him dearly.

As the boat settled onto its new course, Hatu saw Sabella come on deck. He still didn't trust the feelings she aroused in him and was now convinced there was some sort of magic, for lack of a better word, involved. Perhaps a charm or potion? In any event, because he was now sure the effect she had on him was not natural, it made it easier to armor himself against it.

She saw him looking at her and nodded a greeting. She tended to stay below in a little screened-off portion of what had been the captain's quarters, while Denbe and Catharian occupied another section. Hatu had taken to sleeping on the deck most of the time, going below only if rain came, and on this voyage that had happened only twice, and both showers had been brief.

As he approached she said, "Catharian thinks we are safe from pursuit, because if any ship had sailed after us it would have overtaken us by now."

Hatu let out a small sigh. "He seemed concerned."

"You are still . . ." Sabella looked as if she was reconsidering her words. "I'm sure Catharian has told you," she began again, "that you were to have been fully trained by your age and returned to your family. There are things that I know, but only a tiny bit of what is yours to learn." She stopped as if uncertain she was making sense. "It's like . . . trying to explain color to someone who is blind. Or music to one who cannot hear." She sighed as if frustrated she couldn't explain more. "When we arrive at our first destination someone will meet us who can begin to teach you what should have been taught years ago."

He sensed that frustration beneath her words as well as a touch of regret. "Why does this bother you?" he asked.

She looked at him with troubled eyes. "I have touched your . . . how would you say, spirit? Your essential energy, for lack of better words." She gazed out over the ocean. "We searched constantly for years, but when I finally found you, you were burning brightly, Hatu, like a luminous star." She smiled. "I saw . . . blue, a blue fire in the heavens, in my mind, and I knew at once it was you." She lowered her gaze. "Since then I have touched you enough to have grown . . ." She looked uncomfortable. "I have feelings I was never taught to understand." She reached over and touched his hand lightly. "Part of what makes me feel this way is that I've come to care for you."

She saw the flicker of reaction on his face and quickly added, "And I completely understand how you feel about Hava. I've been . . . aware of you together occasionally." She seemed embarrassed by the admission.

Hatu frowned. "I'm . . . It's all right. You were merely serving your cause."

"I do care," she repeated, "and I know what comes next will be difficult, perhaps even painful, but I also know it is necessary. There are things about who you are—what you are—that require you to master yourself in ways you haven't even imagined. It just makes me a little sad, is all."

Feeling that this conversation was becoming more awkward by the moment, Hatu said, "Thank you for worrying about me, but I'm sure I'll be all right." He knew that the first chance he got to escape and seek out Hava, he'd take it, which made Sabella's concerns for his future suffering moot.

"I need to see to the sails," he said to her, though they needed no attention.

Hurrying away, he wondered if this journey would ever make sense to him.

DECLAN SAT BACK AGAINST A wall, his legs outstretched, resting as the day's heat took its toll on the workers. The baron had begun a rapid fortification, pressing any fit man who hadn't fled the city before he had returned into a labor force, and that included every mercenary under contract. Bogartis had been given a semiofficial position, a temporary captaincy, over all such companies and was away seeing to their deployment.

So far no word had come of any large movement of ships down the coast, but everyone felt certain it was only a matter of time before the invaders who had savaged Port Colos, Copper Hills, and Beran's Hill would arrive. The tension in the city rose each day. It was now the third day since they had returned, and apart from the work gangs, and a few women who had remained with their men in the city, Marquenet was empty. What Declan found most unexpected was the quiet, especially the lack of any children's voices. There must still be a few around—children of nobles, sons and daughters of merchants, urchins running around the streets—just not enough to be noticed. He suspected they were all staying, or being kept, indoors out of fear.

Declan was angry with himself. Bogartis had been right: he had tried to do too much too soon. He'd tried using a sword on a pell post, and his right shoulder had torn. Now his right arm was useless. He had grudgingly agreed to keep it in a sling, giving it a chance to heal properly. He could do little by way of heavy work, so except for helping haul some small sacks into the kitchen with his other hand, and herding chickens in the marshaling yard, which was now a makeshift barnyard, there was little for him to do but rest.

He looked up and saw a familiar figure approaching, a

young mercenary named Sixto, one of Bogartis's company. Declan didn't know him well, but he seemed an affable enough fellow, though he tended to keep to himself. He was carrying a scabbard in his left hand.

"Declan!" The young smith still hadn't quite placed his accent.

"Hello, Sixto," Declan replied.

"Bogartis said I should find you."

"Well, now you've found me."

The fighter gave a small smile. He wore his hair long, to the shoulders, and had a thin mustache and an odd little patch of chin whiskers below the center of his mouth but was otherwise clean-shaven. This was a fashion Declan had never seen before. As much as it was possible for a fighter who spent so much of his time on horseback, Sixto paid attention to his grooming, to the point where Declan thought him rather vain.

"Bogartis said I should train you."

Rising slowly to his feet, Declan said, "Train me in what?"

"The sword."

Declan glanced toward his sling. "It was Bogartis who scolded me for using my sword arm too soon."

Sixto tossed the scabbarded sword to Declan's left hand. Reacting slowly, Declan fumbled it and it fell to the ground.

Sixto said, "You're going to train using the other arm."

Declan retrieved the scabbard. "My left hand?"

"Makes you a better fighter and stops you from getting fat."

Declan clamped the scabbard under his right arm, then drew the sword with his left. It felt odd. Although the smith used his left hand a great deal in his craft, using tongs to turn blades and tools while forging them and pumping the bellows to keep the coals at the proper heat, holding a sword this way just felt wrong.

"I've seen you fight, and you're deadly, quick, and strong," said Sixto. "But if anyone were to study you long enough, they would see patterns, your instinctive reactions. That is a weakness."

Declan kept moving the sword around, trying to gain some sense of the familiar. Even with his shoulder restitched and his right arm in a sling, he felt an almost overwhelming desire to switch the blade to his other hand.

"I want you to block an overhand blow," said Sixto, and then he made a looping attack from above, not too fast, but not slow either.

Declan barely got the blade up in time and felt the shock of the blow run up his arm and his elbow bend with it.

"You want to fight as if you had your sword in your other hand," said Sixto. "You move as if it still was. But you can't do that. You must forget all you know and learn as a baby learns, by watching and repeating over and over. Now look at your wrist."

Declan did as instructed and saw that his wrist was exposed as his blade turned to his left. He nodded. "It's wrong."

"Yes, you turned the blade as you would in your right hand, but now you must point the blade to your right, so that the strong muscles in your arm can take the blow. Imagine you're in front of a mirror and then be the mirror. Again!"

This time Declan turned his blade so it pointed right and raised his arm to take the blow. Their blades clashed, and he felt the shock again, but this time he found he could turn his body and let the blow slide off his blade, thus exposing Sixto's shoulder and neck. He attempted to thrust that way, but the other man easily turned the blade aside.

"Good," said Sixto. "Your feel for the fight is sound. That's the right move, but you need a lot of practice because you're too slow and you had to think about it rather than just do it. Again!"

For nearly half an hour they repeated the same move and

countermove until Declan didn't have to think about it, just react. His left arm started to ache, which surprised him. A powerful man by dint of nature and his work, he still felt some discomfort from his muscles being used in a new fashion.

Finally, Sixto stepped away and said, "That's enough for today. Tomorrow we will try other attacks and ripostes. You learn quickly, my friend." He smiled. "Perhaps when your right shoulder is sound I shall teach you how to fight with two blades. It's a dangerous style of combat. If done badly it will get you killed; but if done well, it's deadly for the other fellow."

Declan grinned. "I look forward to tomorrow."

He fumbled with the scabbard and got the sword sheathed, then returned to his resting place in the shade with his back to the wall. At least the lesson had been a good distraction from his dark introspections. Now, unbidden, the emptiness returned and he wondered if he would ever feel anything beyond that hollow space where his heart once beat, now replaced by the need to find whoever was responsible for the raid that killed his wife and friends.

He watched as soldiers hurried about their tasks, sensing their urgency and even a hint of desperation. Out of boredom he considered how he would go about attacking Marquenet, and he realized that the city offered very little in the way of real defenses beyond the walls of the old keep.

This realization surprised him by being interesting. If invaders were coming from the nearest ports on the coast, villages and farms were all that lay between where they would land and the city. There were perhaps a dozen roads, but only three were wide enough to accommodate a large force. Those roads entered the city from the northwest and the northeast—the same road Declan and those traveling from Beran's Hill had used—and from the south, which served the nearest port on the border of Marquensas and the

Kingdom of Ilcomen. That southern route was the shortest, but the harbor there was at the end of a narrow bay, hardly large enough for a sizable fleet.

The northwest route was the most likely, Declan reckoned, and once at the city's edge, the invaders would be faced with a maze of streets and perhaps be trapped or prey to ambush.

The problem was becoming increasingly interesting. Declan decided to turn his full attention to it.

As the shadows of the day lengthened, Declan found himself lost in the problem, mentally assigning troops to various defensive positions and moving them around like game pieces, considering what resources might be readily available, what resources needed to be carefully guarded, and what might change in the heat of battle. The raid on Beran's Hill had taught him one thing: preparation was paramount, but you had to expect everything to change the moment battle was joined.

Declan barely realized it was almost sundown until he noticed squads of men moving toward the mess hall in the soldiers' commons and found that he was hungry. He got to his feet, feeling that his shoulder was slightly less tender than it had been this morning. He counted that a good sign.

As he walked to where the evening's mess was being served, he wondered how his plans for the defense of Marquenet might match up to the baron's.

BARON DUMARCH LOOKED DOWN AT the map. Balven sat opposite him and two of his most senior officers watched on.

Balven said, "Word from North Tower is that the ships are starting to move. Some are outward bound on a southwesterly course, but others seem to be coming down the coast in our direction."

Dumarch was silent for a moment, studying the map. At

last he said, "I can only assume they're using ships to attack us either from the northwest or from the south."

A captain named Renfroe said, "Boarding those ships again and disembarking just a short while later entails risks that would be easily avoided just by marching south from Beran's Hill."

The other captain, by the name of Markham, glanced at his fellow officer and nodded. "True." He paused. "Unless they are heading to the port at Yallu."

"Too narrow a harbor," said Balven. He looked at his brother and said, "If they mean to hit us from three sides at once, they could have forces marching south from Beran's Hill now, while some offload at . . . whatever the village is at the end of the northwest road."

"Tanarith," said Captain Markham. "Not much there, but it does feed the bigger road ten miles inland."

Balven continued. "So if they offload there and send their fastest ships south to Yallu, they could conceivably attack from all three roads at once."

"Or circle around and come at us from the east," speculated the baron. He looked from face to face. "In other words, we have no idea what they may choose to do."

Balven said, "There are too many possible threats; we can't prepare for them all. What is our best choice?"

Daylon was silent for a long moment, then said, "Keep doing what we're doing. Dig in. If anyone remains in the outer half of the city . . ." He crossed the room to a map of the city on another table and waved the two captains over. "I want every building in this city inspected. Anyone remaining in the outer half of the city"—he inscribed a circle over the map with his finger—"I want them moved into the area closest to the walls. I don't care if they object, just move them, and pass the word: anyone who is in the city by sundown tomorrow will be expected to fight."

Balven chuckled. "That should send a number of them out the east gate in a hurry."

"I want gleaning to continue as fast as it can, and every useful item in a home brought to the keep. Food, obviously, if they find any, but tools, clothing, anything left behind that might prove useful I want loaded into wagons and moved here by sundown tomorrow."

Balven said, "That's a lot of wagons."

"All the wagons from Beran's Hill should have been unloaded by now. Commandeer any others you find in the city."

"The horses should be rested," muttered Balven. "We'll work something out, my lord."

To Captain Markham, Daylon said, "Rest the troops that are most in need for one more day, just give them light duties. Then tomorrow morning we start building fortifications. I want a defensive maze in the city so that invaders will have to fight their way through traps and ambushes." He picked up the map and handed it to Markham. "After you get the men sorted out, I want you and your sergeants to sketch out your plans for defense on this map. Bring it back to me by supper and we'll go over it and make whatever changes we decide are necessary. Work will begin at dawn."

Captain Markham took the map, rolled it up, saluted the baron, and departed.

To Captain Renfroe the baron said, "I want pairs of riders sent to the coast west of here and south down to Yallu. Another pair to the east to see how the evacuation to Ilcomen is going and to bring back word of my family."

The captain saluted and left.

Balven put his hand on his brother's shoulder when they were alone. "You're doing all you can."

Daylon said, "It's the not knowing. If they're invading, why aren't they moving ashore and digging in? Even if we're in no position to counterattack, they should consider it a possibility."

Balven contemplated the question and then said, "Perhaps they're not invading."

Baron Dumarch shook his head. "What do you mean? The cost of razing Copper Hills, Port Colos, and everything north of our city is . . ." He spread his hands. ". . . incalculable. There just isn't enough plunder, including captives for slaves, to recoup a raid on such a scale. Occupying our land and taking it for their own is the only explanation."

"Perhaps not," Balven said calmly. "Copper Hills might as well not exist. We are crippled, and if everyone returned tomorrow, it would take months, years perhaps, for our people to recover, to rebuild the farms to the north and west, to reopen trade to the east. We won't see any fresh fish here for months to come." He shook his head. "I can't see a motive for an undertaking of this scale, save invasion . . . unless . . ."

"What?"

"If they want to plunder all of North Tembria, all they need to do is just keep sweeping across the kingdoms from Ilcomen to Sandura and launch raids into Zindaros and Metros . . ."

"No," said Daylon. "With that many fighters, they'd need to set up bases, start building encampments, and they'd do it north of us along the coast where they've driven us out. We have seen nothing in the way of camp followers: no commissary, no weapons makers, no tailors, none of the necessities of an army on the move."

Balven nodded. "You're right, which is why you are baron and I am not." He looked at his brother with admiration. "Father always said there were two or three things to be seen, and most men only saw one. I'm vain enough to think I am a master of two of them: the price of choices and the consequences of planning for the long term. There's a third element, the . . . extrapolation of possibilities, the anticipation of unforeseen consequences. I'm aware of them but I can't anticipate." He smiled ruefully. "You have that gift."

Daylon grinned at his brother. "You flatter me."

Balven laughed. "We've known each other too many years for you to think that." His expression became serious again. "I will attempt to find out as much as possible as quickly as possible."

"Information is vital."

Balven left, and for a long moment Daylon Dumarch, Baron of Marquensas, allowed feelings of overwhelming hopelessness wash through him. He refused to embrace them, realizing that to do so was to surrender. But he also knew that to reject that painful fear was a trap of denial. He took a deep breath and closed his eyes; this would pass.

After a few moments he opened his eyes and let the hopelessness fade, knowing that he would either protect his people or die in the attempt.

HATU HEARD JENSON SHOUT FROM the masthead, "Land!"

"Where away?" asked Catharian.

"Ahead!" came the answer.

Hatu glanced at Denbe and Sabella, both of whom were looking straight ahead. He knew his voyage to this first destination would soon be over, and he started to weigh all the possibilities he had imagined since being captured.

He had only a vague notion of where he was relative to Marquensas. His survival after fleeing the Sisters of the Deep had given him a clear understanding of just how far he could sail alone. He felt sure it would be too vast a distance for him to make it back on his own. He fought off any feeling of helplessness, but he knew his choices were limited and that he needed more information.

Catharian called to Hatu, "Let out the mainsail!"

Hatu did as asked, and while securing the mainsheet he saw the spot of land ahead grow larger. Soon he could see enough detail to judge it to be a fairly large island, as mountains shrouded in clouds and a wide, sprawling beach appeared. His interest was piqued: if it was large enough and if the port was busy enough, he might be able to hide, and then perhaps he could find his way back to Hava.

Catharian sailed downwind toward the island, then ordered a tack to the north, which took them away at an angle, apparently following a current. Then he tacked back on a southwest course that headed straight into a good-sized harbor.

As they entered the bay, Hatu realized the island was larger than he had expected, with an impressive lagoon that sheltered the harbor. From the size of a ship anchored just a short distance from the shore, it must be a deep lagoon as well. Hatu had seen a few islands like this near his homeland, but they were few and far between, and highly prized by the Council of Coaltachin. Such ports provided convenient sites for refitting, transshipping contraband, and other activities valuable to the Kingdom of Night. For a brief moment Hatu wondered if the Council might actually control this one.

They slowed as Catharian brought the ship around with a practiced hand: he obviously knew this harbor well. They headed past the ship at anchor, and Hatu saw it was clearly a deep-water vessel, with two tall masts and a long bowsprit. It was a ship he recognized as a brig, an ideal island trader, with ample room for cargo, yet nimble enough to deal with the tricky shoals of the islands.

Catharian shouted, "Prepare to drop sail!" and the boys responded quickly, while Hatu loosened his grip on the sheet holding the main boom. The small ship swung around hard as Catharian spun the wheel, and its forward motion almost halted as a slight swell moved it a bit sideways toward the quay, which was built on heavy rocks. Hatu wondered for a moment if this was a natural outcropping on an otherwise long stretch of sandy beach, or if it was man-made.

Harbor boys dropped large fenders—sacks filled with various materials to absorb the shock of the boat nestling against the quayside—and Hatu wondered if they worked for a harbor boss or expected Catharian to pay them a token, or tip as it was sometimes called. If so, they would be sorely disappointed, for in Hatu's experience Catharian never paid for anything.

Williem and Bowen tossed lines to the boys on the quayside, who tied off the boat, and two others ran forward, perhaps expecting cargo to be offloaded. Hatu concluded that everyone here worked for whatever they could get, as no one official looking was presenting himself. A crowd gathered, probably to see who had arrived and to break up the monotony of what passed for a day's work in this island community.

It was a lovely day with clear skies and a nice breeze cutting the heat. Behind the buildings of this small community, Hatu saw the mountains rising a short distance away. Denbe came up to him and said, "Wait here." The burly fighter leapt down from the gunwale to the quay. To Hatu's surprise, he produced a belt pouch and tipped the boys who'd made the boat fast.

Then Catharian and Sabella approached, and the false monk said, "We shall be parting company for a while, Hatu. Sabella and I have other duties, but we shall see you again, I'm certain."

Hatu saw the young woman smile slightly. She nodded but said nothing as she also jumped down unaided to the quay where Denbe waited.

"So do I simply wait here?" Hatu asked.

"No, there is someone you need to speak with, and he should be here any moment." Catharian motioned for Hatu to follow and hopped down from the gunwale, Hatu disembarking a moment later.

The crowd began to disperse when it was evident there was no cargo to unload, hence no coin to be earned, and as they drifted away Hatu felt a moment of cold panic stab his stomach as a familiar figure came through the crowd.

"Here at last," said Master Bodai. "We have a great deal to discuss."

He motioned for Hatushaly to follow him, but it took a slight push by Catharian to send him stumbling after the member of the Council of Masters of Coaltachin.

16

REVELATIONS AND SECRETS

Hava worked her way through the maze of cargo that had been stored on the mid-deck of the ship. She was half blind from inspecting crates, chests, bags, and heaps of goods covered in canvas lashed to the deck, but the amount of wealth she had discovered had her head spinning with ideas.

Sabien followed closely, taking his responsibility to guard Hava seriously. She didn't mind his instant loyalty, though she wasn't convinced it was fueled by gratitude and thought it might eventually fade.

She said, "Even sold to the most corrupt fence I've ever met, this booty is worth more than I can imagine."

Sabien shrugged. "I don't know its worth, Captain."

Hava was getting used to the title and the authority it carried. She said, "I traveled a great deal from a very young age. I've been in countless bazaars and shops, seen all manner of goods bought and sold." She reached over and picked up a plate made of silver, polished just before Port Colos was sacked by the look of it. "This cost more than a mason earns in a year, I'll wager."

"A master mason?" asked the young man.

She nodded. "There's both silver and gold and jewelry

mixed in with other cargo. Weapons in a chest back there." She turned her head and indicated a distant corner of the hold with her chin.

Sabien's expression showed his confusion. "I have never seen anything like this before."

"Neither have I," said Hava. "This ship was loaded with the pick of the plunder of Port Colos and with slaves . . ." She let the thought trail off. "That may be why one of the sicari stayed aboard."

"Sicari?"

"That warrior in black we kicked to death." Again she surveyed all the wealth assembled on this deck, then said, "Follow me."

Sabien followed Hava as she climbed the stairs in the companionway to the upper deck. George was at the helm with another man, a former prisoner, at the wheel. Hava had instructed George and the other sailors to train any fit man or woman who wanted to crew. Most apparently did, and Hava now counted more than one hundred people who were willing to sail with her.

She worked her way through those sitting forward in the ship, and as she neared the bow she spied a familiar face. "Molly!" Hava had been so preoccupied with the duties of commanding a ship that she had neglected to look for her friend.

Molly Bowman lay either unconscious or asleep next to two other women and a man who said, "She's been out since we boarded."

Hava said, "I was hit on the head and knocked from my horse, and after that I don't remember anything."

"She's been awake," said one of the women, "but she was rambling in her talk and passed out again quickly."

"What's your name?" Hava asked the woman who had spoken.

"Betsy."

"Look after her, and if she regains her wits let me know, will you?"

Betsy nodded, and Hava moved away. She was relieved that Molly was on the ship but concerned about her condition.

She returned to the afterdeck, motioned Sabien away and George to come to her. When they were out of earshot of anyone else, she asked him, "Do you know what's in the hold below us?"

He smiled and nodded. "I oversaw it being loaded. It's why I was not unhappy at your taking charge." He glanced around. "Most of the lads who are still here know a bit about the booty. The captain and those black-clad fellows had me rotate the loading so most of what the men saw was crates and boxes, sacks and the like, but these men aren't children; they've been at sea most of their lives."

"Where were you supposed to take it?"

George said, "I'm not sure. Captain George knew but never told me."

"I killed him a little too soon," said Hava dryly.

"None too soon for me," said George. "He was a pig, and I'm sorry I had to share a name with him."

"If you were to guess your original destination, where would that be?"

George let out a frustrated sigh. "One of the Border Ports, certainly, but I'm only guessing which one; it's where we were supposed to go."

"Border Ports?"

"What do you know of the Anoke Sea?"

"We're sailing on it," said Hava patiently.

"Do you know what is west of us?"

"A continent called Alastor?"

He nodded. "That's due west from here. It's not really a continent but a series of three really large islands, surrounded by dozens of smaller ones, and who knows how many tiny ones. But if you sail around the southern tip of Alastor, or between the lower two islands, to the other side of Garn, you come to . . ." George halted as if to gather his thoughts. "Well, that's the thing; those of us who live on this side of Garn don't really know what's on the other side of the world. It's a secret place and rumors abound about it— there are always rumors—and a few people claim to know more, but then people claim to know all sorts of things they don't really know about, don't they?"

Hava was tiring of the circuitous answer and said, "Border Ports?"

George continued to think for another moment. "Imagine a line . . . a line in the water, in the wind, from somewhere in the remote north, and that line passes through a string of islands west of here, to another distant point far to the south. If you are from this side of that line, you may not pass over to the other side."

"A border," said Hava.

George nodded. "And there are ports on those islands. Ships like this may offload, refit, stock up cargo, or whatever they need to do, but they may not sail any farther west."

"What happens if they try?" asked Hava.

"No one knows, as no one who has tried has returned." George glanced at the sails, then ahead to check his bearings, then added, "Or if anyone has, they don't talk about it. Lots of rumors, as I said, of course, and plenty of wild claims."

"Such as?"

"Those killers in black, they're the only ones who travel freely on both sides. Sometimes people claim to have overheard this or that when they talk. There are a lot of people who think there may be some large kingdom that is hiding itself from the rest of Garn." He raised his eyebrows. "But why would anyone do that? I suppose the answer to that is anyone's guess. Most places I've been, good and bad, well, they like to trade, make a bit of profit here, buy something rare there, and so it goes."

Hava nodded. "Seems that way to me, too."

"So the rumor is that this place is bigger than all the other nations of the world put together, which makes it being kept secret even less likely. But a smaller land that's maybe very rich, that would make sense. Their wealth would buy a lot of secrecy, if you see my meaning."

"I do," said Hava. She considered for a moment. "Speaking of wealth, if we weren't due at a given port, where would you want to offload the booty below?"

"That's tricky," said George with a smile. "A ship carrying this much booty without the protection of those black thugs is a rich prize."

Hava looked around. "With a fair number of people willing to fight."

"That is true," said George. "That may keep the small island boats away if they have their wits about them, and most do. You meet live pirates, and you meet stupid pirates, but not a lot of live stupid pirates, as the old saying goes."

"I've heard similar," said Hava, realizing she'd heard the same saying about student assassins: smart or dead were the two choices. "So back to fencing this loot. Where do you think we should try?"

"There are the Border Ports and a few smaller ones. The Border Ports have advantages, as a lot of trading goes on there. The men wearing black—"

"Sicari," interrupted Hava.

He nodded. "These sicari don't care what crosses the Border, except people, so there's really not much in the way of smuggling. I have no notion of what may be required to reach a port on the other side of the line, but I have a fair idea of where to go back there." With an inclination of his head, he indicated the course back to the twin continents. "All the trading with those from the other side of the Border is handled by merchants who live in the ports."

"All right," said Hava. "So if the merchants don't go east or west but stay put, only those sicari travel where no one else can go." An odd thought was forming, tickling at the edge of her mind, an idea not quite ready to clarify itself. She knew it would nag at her until she finally understood what it was but put it aside and turned her attention to more immediate concerns. "So we need a port that can handle some of this loot, then travel to another to sell some more. Not calling too much attention to ourselves in any one place."

"Smart," said George. "If we get too much attention and word gets out, we'll have to watch out for big raiders. The small island pirates, those with the fast little boats, they won't come after a big ship like this unless we get too close to one of their bases. I know how to get to the Border Ports without doing that. You get too close to where they live and they'll swarm over you like wasps.

"But the ships that are as big as this, but built for fighting, can have a crew of a hundred or more, and they'd take a ship like ours without hesitation. They're faster than we are, and unless we get lucky, we'll get taken." He glanced around. "Mind you, if they see this many fighters on the deck, they may veer off—more trouble than it's worth—unless they know we have most of a city's wealth below. Then they'd come after us for sure. Probably bringing some friends."

"Pirates work together?"

"Sometimes a captain joins with another or even two, and they go plundering together. Can last awhile if the captains don't get to squabbling. Most of the time it's just for a raid or two, though."

Hava looked hard at George. "I've been around a lot and, truth to tell, you don't strike me as a typical pirate, thief, or cutthroat, George."

"Thanks, I think, Captain. I've been a seaman long enough to know a few things. A pirate captain has to be a navigator and pilot—lots of these island routes can be treacherous—so I learned from my pa. I tried the honest trades for a while, but I've a weakness for gambling and fell in with some bad people. I got in debt and had to work to pay it off, and the man who I owed, well, he sold my service to Captain George. If you hadn't killed him . . ." He shrugged. "Maybe in a year or two he'd have counted my debt paid." He sighed and gave a rueful smile. "Probably not."

Hava smiled and echoed, "Probably not. I know how that debt game plays: you get charged for food and whatever, and you never quite get free of the obligation." She looked around the deck and saw most of those from below had taken to staying outside while the weather was good. Few had returned to the slave deck to rest. "I'll make you this promise, George. Once I get this cargo sold and those who don't wish to come with me offloaded, you're free of your debt. You can stay or go as you please."

"Thank you, Captain," he said, looking astonished.

"If you stay, when we part you'll either be dead or wealthy."

George laughed with genuine amusement. "We're all going to die sooner or later, that's a fact. So I might as well try for wealthy before then!"

Hava nodded. She returned to where Molly lay and saw that she hadn't moved. She wished there was a proper healer aboard, but none had appeared when the severely wounded had been brought up on deck.

Hava saw people looking at her as she walked by and

felt eyes on her from behind. She adopted a confident posture and smile as she moved back to the stern of the ship, wishing she were as confident of what she was doing as she pretended. Because she was relying on guesswork and intuition: she was going after Hatu with no idea of where he might be. But she'd be damned before she'd let these people know how uncertain she was inside.

HATU SAT ACROSS FROM MASTER Bodai at a small table, just outside the door of some sort of inn that was unlike any inn Hatu had seen in his travels. There was an open counter in the wall behind him, and people came and went, ordering food they carried off and providing their own cups and mugs to be filled with fruit juices or ale.

Master Bodai had told Hatu to follow him from the ship, along the waterfront, and to this table, which was flanked by two large, well-armed men who were clearly guards working for Bodai, although no words had passed between them. Bodai was silent as food and drink were placed on the table between him and Hatu. On the plate were two odd-looking items: something folded inside what appeared to be wrapped flattened bread. Rolled dough, Hatu decided, picking one up, having worked enough in his inn's kitchen to form a judgment. It had somehow been crisped, and it was hotter than he had expected, so he put it down again.

Bodai said, "Let it cool a bit longer so you don't burn your mouth."

"What are they?"

"Delicious," said the Coaltachin master.

Which didn't really answer Hatu's question. He waited, then finally asked, "Why are you here, with these people?"

Bodai let out a long sigh, as if releasing pent-up tension. "I am these people, Hatushaly. One of several tasked with ensuring you stayed alive while being trained by some of the harshest teachers in the world.

"The Flame Guard is an old and once very powerful order. They had agents like me secreted throughout all of Garn, or at least the parts of it you would recognize."

With a wave of his hand, Bodai indicated that whatever the food on the plate was, it was ready to eat. Taking hold of one, Hatu saw that the wrapping was folded over the top and he started to pick at it, but Bodai said, "No, leave it closed. Just eat it as it is." He demonstrated by picking his up and taking a large bite. Hatu saw juice start to drip out the sides, and Bodai wiped his mouth with the back of his hand. Then he closed his eyes for a moment as if savoring the food. He chewed contentedly for a long time, then continued. "As I said, the parts of the world you would recognize: there are parts of it you wouldn't."

Hatu was perplexed by this statement but decided to concentrate on the food, and he was delighted to be greeted by a savory concoction of what he took to be diced chicken, spices, a hint of tomato, some kind of pepper, and other flavors he couldn't identify but found delicious. The flatbread wrapping the filling had been fried and crunched between his teeth. He suddenly realized just how hungry he was.

He chewed, swallowed, then reached for his cup and was surprised to find that it contained a sort of wine diluted with a mixture of fruit juices, unexpectedly sweet, but a perfect complement to the food. Taking a breath, he asked, "What is this?" holding up the wrap.

"In the language of the people who created this delicacy, it's called 'little donkey.'" Bodai shrugged. "I have no idea why and probably never will; I'm just satisfied to have discovered it here on this lovely island."

Hatu looked around and then took another bite. "Where are we?" he asked.

"The island is called Elsobas," Bodai replied. "This small establishment is called a café, open only to feed passersby."

"So an inn without rooms," replied Hatu. "A kind of tavern?"

"A little less ale and . . . well, it's a café. The weather here is salubrious year-round, and people eat outside unless it's raining. Actually, even if it's raining and it's light, they still eat outside. Should I live long enough to retire, I can think of worse places to live."

"Retire?" asked Hatu.

"Masters who no longer command crews or govern towns, but just fish and watch sunsets—that's being retired."

"Master Facaria?" asked Hatu.

Nodding, Bodai said, "And Master Zusara, soon." Taking another bite, he talked around the mouthful. "It's better than ending up dead, which is what happens to most masters of Coaltachin."

Hatu ate quickly, finishing his food and drinking the last of his wine.

Bodai did likewise. "I imagine you have many questions, so let me tell you a few things to save us both some time."

Hatu nodded.

"You are the last remaining child of the Firemane line, which I imagine you know already. The baron must have told you?"

Hatu nodded again.

"He had no reason to keep it a secret from you, though it would be best if it was kept a secret from others."

"For a secret, quite a few people seem to know," said Hatu dryly.

"True." With a sweep of his hand, Bodai indicated the people nearby.

Hatu looked around and noticed that some were glancing in his direction, while others were actually staring at him.

"What?"

"When was the last time you put dye in your hair?"

Hatu winced. "Weeks."

"The sun brings out the gold-and-copper shine," said Bodai. "It's all right. We'll be long gone before the unique quality of your appearance alerts anyone who might potentially harm you."

Hatu felt little by way of comfort in that reassurance.

Bodai took another drink from his cup, then said, "Well, time is fleeting, so let me continue. I am a member of the Flame Guard. I infiltrated the gangs of Coaltachin when I was younger than you are now. It took long planning, and I took the place of the real Bodai, who was a son of a master . . ." He waved his hand dismissively. "I'll give you the full story some other time. I was a pedagogue, what you would call a preceptor, in other words a person who teaches, a teacher."

Hatu chuckled. "That is hardly a surprise."

"It was fortuitous that the real Bodai and I resembled each other and the father of the true Bodai was, shall I say, inattentive to his own children." He took another drink, and Hatu did as well. "By the time I reached Coaltachin, enough years had passed that those who knew the real Bodai well were either dead or . . . years fog the memory." He signaled and a woman came to their table and refilled both cups.

Hatu took a long drink and said, "I've had many different wines, but this . . . ?"

"The same people who call what we ate a small beast of burden call this 'blood of fruit,' which I guess is as good a name for mixing wine, water, and fruit as any." Bodai smiled. "In any event, by the time I reached Coaltachin I had learned to speak the language flawlessly, knew enough of the real Bodai to fool all but his closest friends—but they were conveniently killed when we captured him. Even his father accepted me, though I doubt he knew as much about his son as I did by the time we disposed of the lad."

Hatu was hardly surprised by any of this. Ruthlessness had been drummed into him during his training.

"From there it was merely a matter of working my way up from crew leader to gang leader, and eventually I took my 'father's' place after disposing of a pair of older brothers—the real Bodai had confessed to wanting to kill them himself, so I was merely carrying out his wishes, in a manner of speaking." He shook his head in mock regret. "The father . . . well, I would not be the first gang boss in the Kingdom of Night to arrange for my 'father's' demise.

"The rest of my story is of little concern to you, until the time when you were rescued from the battle known as the Betrayal. One of our agents used every gift at her disposal to flee the villa where the last Firemane king's family resided, and to the best of our knowledge no one else with a drop of Firemane blood exists. Your father and his father were both surprisingly devoted men who had children only with their wives. Highly unusual among nobles, I must say, but it's not completely unheard of.

"What was unexpected was that Baron Dumarch would arrange for you to be reared by the nastiest society of cut-throats, thieves, assassins, and thugs on that side of Garn." He spread his hands. "Still, it may have served. Without training, the power within you might have destroyed you, and though you were hardly trained as your father or the Flame Guard might have wished, at least the preceptors of Coaltachin beat discipline into you, and that prevented you from killing yourself and others."

Hatu felt a warm feeling starting to rise in him. He was not sure if it was emotion or a combination of the fruit wine and the midmorning sun. He said, "There were times . . ." His thought drifted away. It had been a long voyage and he was far more tired than he had thought. He glanced around as the warm feeling continued to rise and saw what Bodai had meant. It was very pleasant sitting here next to this tiny landing, with trees swaying in the breeze, seabirds wheeling above, and the sun warm on his face. "What about you? You're a master. Won't someone come looking for you?"

"I will not be the first master of Coaltachin to venture on a mission, never to be heard from again. Not often, but it has happened before. As far as anyone back there knows, I departed on a ship in a small port just across the Ilcomen border with Marquensas. If Denbe hadn't gotten word to me, the next day that ship would have been heading for Coaltachin. I sent a message home that I was returning north to see what was afoot with the raids, then got a smaller ship with men loyal to me and the Flame Guard, and here we are." He sighed. "The Council will get word of the assault on the western coast of North Tembria and will assume that at some point I was a casualty. And I may return to Coaltachin, if fate demands, with an enthralling account of my narrow escape and heroic survival."

"What next?" Hatu asked.

Bodai pointed. "See that ship?"

Hatu looked where Bodai indicated, taking notice of a ship resting at anchor. It was a much larger ship than the one he had arrived on, and it was anchored a short boat ride offshore. Hatu saw that it had three masts, twin foresails, and a large gaff spanker, all neatly furled. Several men were moving on the deck and in the yards, so Hatu assumed it was making ready to sail. He saw a large rowboat heading toward the dock.

"Denbe is already aboard and, along with the best fighters we have left, is making ready to start the last leg of your journey."

Hatu started to speak but really didn't care to, so he just nodded, then yawned.

"When the tide turns, we shall be on it. We will cross a stretch of ocean known as the Border to get you to the safest place on Garn. When we are under way I can answer all your questions and make you understand why it's vital we save your thankless hide. You may have been content to be an innkeeper—until the masters of Coaltachin decided to be done with you—but in truth you have a larger role to play."

Yawning again, Hatu glanced at the two men who stood slightly off and behind Bodai. "And these two large fellows are to make me go with you?" His eyelids were getting heavy.

Bodai grinned. "They're going to carry you to that approaching launch because you're not going to be able to walk once the drug I put in your wine takes hold."

Hatu tried to say something, but the words fled. Then he lost consciousness.

DECLAN PARRIED SIXTO'S THRUST AND moved to his right. He anticipated Sixto countering to that side and had his blade ready as a looping blow came his way. The clang of metal blades was one of many noises permeating the marshaling yard of the baron's keep, as laborers hurried to complete repairs and improvements at their lord's command. Everyone worked as if an attack was coming at any minute, so they worked from first light until dark and then by torchlight.

Declan felt his right shoulder loosening by the day but kept practicing with his left hand. He was growing adept at fighting with either hand now. He crouched, readying himself for a second attack.

As the sparring continued, Declan managed to hold Sixto

at bay, a considerable achievement compared to his previous lessons, in which he was usually smacked with the flat of a blade within a few minutes. Sixto had been a demanding tutor, barely giving Declan any measure of consideration, and the young smith had bruises all over his left shoulder, side, and back to show where he had failed to counter a blow.

Suddenly Declan became aware that something had changed. He stepped back and put his right hand palm out, indicating that he was disengaging.

"What?" asked Sixto.

"Listen."

Sixto paused, then nodded. Both men held on to their weapons and moved rapidly toward the gate to the keep. In the background, behind the cacophony of the workers, something in the sounds of the city below had changed: there was a swelling of distant voices, and the tone was one of alarm.

As they reached the gate in the outer wall, they could hear a rising tide of noise from the far side of the city moving toward them. After the relative quiet of Marquenet over the last week, with most of the city's residents having fled east, this was disturbing.

"What do you think?" Sixto said. "An attack?"

"No," replied Declan. "If it was, we'd have heard an alarm by now."

Moments later two riders came racing into view from the direction of the eastern gates. Both were mud spattered and one had bloodstains on his tabard, visible even from where Declan and Sixto stood. Their exhausted horses wheezed for breath as they raced past the gates toward the keep.

Soldiers ran from all corners of the marshaling yard shouting questions. The horses were wobbly legged, and Declan reckoned both were probably ruined by their headlong gallop.

"The east?" asked Sixto as the men hurried into the keep.

Sergeants restored order and the horses were led away, while Declan said, "They came from that gate, so yes."

"We'd better get ready," said the older fighter.

"Why?"

Sixto looked around and said, "Either an attack is coming or we need to go to where they came from."

"We?" asked Declan as he moved alongside Sixto to where the mercenaries had been housed.

Sixto glanced around. "The baron will certainly send someone should those who fled east be at risk. We aren't soldiers, so we won't be tasked with building these fortifications. But we are fighters and a fight is coming." He paused and put his hand on Declan's right shoulder. "I hope this is healed, because you will need both good arms very soon, my friend."

They gathered up their jackets from the ground where they had left them, and as they moved toward the barracks Bogartis appeared. He shouted to the men in his company, "Get ready. We ride in fifteen minutes!"

"You were right," said Declan. Then he said in a tone that didn't sound complaining, but just curious, "Why us?"

Sixto gave him a mocking grin. "Who else? We have fresh horses and we had a much gentler time returning from Beran's Hill." He paused, then added, "Of course, we were there during the fight, and these soldiers were not, but apparently that doesn't matter. Still, we did rest a bit while these lads are close to exhaustion from all the work." Declan conceded that there were few soldiers who hadn't been laboring from dawn to dusk in improving the city's defenses. He'd been impressed with how hard the garrison was willing to work for the baron. The mercenaries had been given lighter duties, mostly scouting and running messages, and Declan had spent a lot of time simply healing his injury.

Seeming almost pleased to be doing something besides

sitting around waiting for an attack, Sixto pulled his gauntlets from his belt and slapped Declan's chest with them. As he put them on, he said, "But mostly, my friend, we get paid to fight, and to die."

Declan had no response to that. He just followed Sixto into the barracks to gather up their gear.

17

VOYAGES AND DISASTERS

⸻†⸻

Hava moved to the bow to get a better look at their destination. After getting around to inspecting the previous captain's quarters and having all his clothing and most of his personal belongings either spread among the crew and former prisoners or thrown over the side, she had discovered a few very welcome items. Besides a badly hidden chest of gold coins and some gems worth more than any thief from Coaltachin could imagine seeing in one lifetime, she had found a rare and precious spyglass. The brass tube slid out to a length that allowed distant viewing, while compacting down again to fit in a pocket. She was using it now.

"What am I seeing?" she asked George.

"The port of Cleverly. The island is named Caladose, and this is the most likely port for a heavy trader like this one to put into."

"Odd name for a town," she remarked.

"I have no idea who named it," he replied, "but it's clever insofar as you have to be coming straight in as we are to land safely. Lots of reefs and shoals around here that can rip out the bottom of a deep-water ship like this. Most vessels this size will anchor offshore and use barges or longboats to offload their cargo."

"I wasn't planning on getting too close or offloading a large part of our cargo," she said. "Just enough to have a reason for being here and a chance to poke around and get some information. So this is probably this ship's original destination?"

George nodded in the affirmative. "*Probably* is the word. That much wealth below says this was a special shipment, intended for a very powerful and important individual or group. This is the busiest port in the northern reaches of the Border, and maybe we would have headed farther south." He shrugged and then added, "But I doubt it. Captain George would have been anxious to offload all these trade goods and collect his fees."

Hava laughed. "His fee was to have his throat cut and be tossed overboard."

George shared the black humor. "I suspect the rest of us are in danger of that fate as well."

"If someone is worried about one of your boys speaking about this booty, almost certainly. As I told you, the two sicari seemed concerned about Captain George knowing a little too much about where they came from. So, what can you tell me about Cleverly?"

George said, "I've put in here a few times, so I can suggest some people you can trust. Too many of those who claim to know things—"

"Tell you what they think you want to hear for a price," finished Hava. She realized again that the training she'd received had led her to understand how such scams worked. If George could cut down the time spent digging up possible information about where Hatu might have been taken, that was a gift from the gods.

"Yes," said George.

"Thank you. I'll take you up on that offer. I've got Sabien in the hold choosing what we're going to fence here. We're only selling enough to offer some explanation as to why we're here: actually I'm here for information."

George nodded. "I see that." He paused for a moment; then he said, "You've not told me what sort of information you need, or what exactly brings you on this sojourn to the Border Ports. If you don't want to, fine, but the more I know, the better I can help."

She glanced toward the island, which was now resolving into an image she could see without the spyglass. She collapsed it and stuck it into a pocket in her jerkin, a red thing embroidered with silver thread that she had found in the previous captain's trunk. Her first reaction had been amusement; then she had decided to keep it. By the time she'd finished taking over that cabin, she found she actually liked the gaudy garment. After a close inspection, she had discovered that not only was it a lurid fashion choice, but it was replete with useful hidden pockets—including a space inside to secret a pair of small blades—as well as numerous equally useful outside pockets.

"It seems keeping you alive was a good choice, George." Her first mate laughed. "I couldn't agree more, Captain."

Hava said, "What do you think of Sabien?"

"He's loyal to you, if that's what you're asking. He's a smart, strong man, and he seems to have no desire to leave."

"Good. That's why I made him third mate. How many do you reckon want to leave?"

"All of the oldest prisoners, which doesn't surprise me. They are not cut out for a life at sea. As for the rest, they have nothing to return for, unless they want to try to re-build their old lives out of the ashes, which they all seem too smart to believe possible." He sighed and shook his head. "When I was a young man I believed I knew all the answers, but life taught me otherwise." He stared off to-ward the island for a moment, then added, "And of course the very young, too; they're fortunate, as the older folks are willing to take them in."

Hava immediately thought of Meggie, who was barely old enough to be considered a woman. "What are they going to do if they don't come with us?"

"There are villages and towns scattered through these islands, so anyone who doesn't settle here can find somewhere nearby. This is a mixed community of people who were born here and those who have landed here and stayed. If you are honest and can work, someone will give you a chance."

Hava realized there were limits as to how much she could protect those who had fallen under her care, and she knew that fretting over those limits was futile. "Very well." She considered and then added, "Give anyone who leaves a few coins, enough to get them by, but not so much they become targets." She was surprised to find her eyes becoming moist. "Take a moment and advise them all about not revealing too much about their money."

"Aye, Captain." George left to carry out her instructions, leaving Hava alone with her thoughts.

She fought back rising anger, frustration, and a pang of guilt: torn between rage over needing to find her husband and a deep sorrow that she didn't even know the names of two of those three children she had turned her back on in Port Colos.

DECLAN FOUND THE RIDE EAST a relief in a strange way. He knew they were out courting trouble of the worst sort: unexpected trouble. The road from Marquenet to Ilcomen was supposed to be relatively safe to travel, especially with a large company of soldiers accompanying the baroness and her family, as well as a sea of refugees, while the invading forces were all supposed to be north of the city. Yet something unexpected had occurred, and he knew those riders hadn't raced back to the city because the baroness had forgotten her favorite dress. Still, Declan welcomed the change, as sitting around allowing his shoulder to heal, with only his fighting practice with Sixto to interrupt the monotony, was taking its toll.

Declan had been working since he could remember. His earliest memories were in the smithy with Edvalt, his fascination with the art of swordcraft awakened very early. He couldn't remember many days when he hadn't worked. Even on those days he wasn't in the smithy, he had gathered fruit, helped a fishing crew, or just done some other useful task. He was not the sort to lie in the sun for an afternoon nap.

Bogartis had recruited replacements for the men he had lost at Beran's Hill and rode ahead of a dozen of his men. That left another eight back in the city, and they would arrive in whatever time it took for them to join up with whomever else the baron was sending. Declan knew little of warfare beyond weapons and fighting so had no real sense of why things were being done this way. He considered asking one of the other men if he knew why the company was being split, but decided he'd wait for a calmer moment.

They had been riding for an hour and were now moving slowly past the straggle of citizens of Marquenet who had been among the last to leave, with their heavily laden carts and wagons and their animals already nearly exhausted. The people who watched them pass were silent, perhaps out of fatigue or fear.

A short time after passing the first refugees, Bogartis held up his hand and the column halted. They were in a clearing between two stands of trees, at the northwest end of a stone bridge, under which flowed a river Declan had once crossed in a wagon belonging to his friend Ratigan. Yet the entire scene was alien, and Declan didn't understand why it appeared so different today. Perhaps it wasn't; perhaps *he* was, he thought. His life had changed out of all recognition.

Declan looked past his captain and saw smoke in the distance. Trees blocked his view, and the road turned just a few hundred yards ahead.

Bogartis turned and shouted, "Sixto, you and Declan flank ahead, and hold up at the edge of those woods!"

Both men put heels to their mounts. Declan broke right and Sixto to the left. They passed the men in front of them, crossed the bridge, and rode swiftly to the indicated spot. Both were riding crouched low over the necks of their horses in case archers might be hiding inside the tree line.

Rustling ahead caused Declan to turn his horse toward the source of the noise and shout, "Someone's coming!"

As he made ready to take on an attacker, Declan was surprised to see a young man holding the hand of a little girl come running out of the woods. The child screamed at the sight of the mounted swordsman, and the man swept the child up into his arms and appeared ready to dash back into the woods.

Declan shouted, "I won't hurt you!"

The man stopped and looked at him.

"Who are you?"

"My name is Peter and we're trying to get back to the city."

"Back?"

"There was a battle on the road and we've lost our wagon." He glanced over his shoulder.

"Is someone pursuing you?" asked Declan, looking into the dark of the woods behind Peter.

"Yes!" shouted Peter, picking up his little girl and running away.

Declan waved to Sixto, pointing down the road. "I'm going to go look! People are fleeing back to the city!"

Sixto looked back and saw that Bogartis and the others had almost caught up. He shouted, "Be wary!"

Declan urged his horse to a trot. Each yard they advanced into the woods, the air grew heavier with the haze of smoke and the acrid stench grew stronger. He rounded a curve in the track and saw in the distance what could only be a fire of some size. He slowed his mount. He could hear people passing on both sides of the road: there was no attempt at stealth. These were citizens of Marquensas fleeing back the way they had come, off the road for reasons that became increasingly clear as he progressed.

Wagons and carts cluttered the road ahead, and horses, donkeys, and mules lay dead in their traces. The contents of the wagons were strewn in every direction: piles of clothing, boxes and trunks spilling kitchen pots and tools. For an instant, Declan recalled how he used to mend such items for the villagers at Oncon, and that felt like another lifetime.

Then there were the bodies.

Everywhere he looked, in, on, and around the piled-up wagons and carts, people lay bloodied and burned. Some had been cut down where they stood, others chased down from behind, and some had died from the flames they had run from. All had been left where they fell.

Declan waited there, taking in the grim scene, feeling empty, and in less than a minute Bogartis rode up, motioning the men behind him to hold and rest for a minute. "This is brutal work," the captain said.

Declan saw moisture in his eyes, but he didn't know if it was from anger or the smoke.

Looking at Declan, Bogartis said, "I dread what may lie ahead."

"Worse than this?"

Bogartis nodded, said nothing, and urged his horse on, motioning the men to follow as he slowly picked his way through the scene of savage slaughter. As he followed, Declan understood why those who had survived had run through the trees: this highway was a place of death to any who remained on it.

At last it became impossible to move forward. Bogartis signaled to his men to dismount and had the horses tied up.

On foot the carnage was even starker, as they had to walk carefully between the debris, trying not to step on human and animal corpses, and it wasn't always possible to avoid them. Declan knew that at one time he would have felt repulsed by this, but he again found himself without feelings. His only thought was not to join the dead beneath his boots.

They reached a clearing and saw that this had been the heart of the battle and was the source of the smoke. What had been a large fire of circled wagons and carts was now mostly smoldering, though a few small blazes were still raging.

"Damn," said Bogartis softly, and Declan instantly recognized the source of his frustration and anger. In the center of this defensive position, now reduced to burned wood, charred corpses, and dropped weapons, sat what was left of a single large carriage, the bodies of the animals that pulled it still bound to it by death after all tugs and straps had burned.

Declan recognized that carriage: he had seen it depart from the city only days earlier. Softly he said, "I thought them safely away."

Bogartis nodded. Then he said, "They were trying to come back."

The carriage and horses were facing Marquenet.

"They must have encountered something that caused them to turn around."

Bogartis waved with his sword. "This. They ran into

whatever army was plundering Ilcomen, and trying to get back they ran into this . . ." He shook his head. "Given the number of people on the road, I'm surprised they got back this far before being chased down from behind."

Declan moved a little closer and saw the burned corpses of the soldiers who had died defending the baroness and the baron's children. He didn't need to look to know that everyone in Baron Dumarch's family now lay dead in this small clearing on the road to Ilcomen.

He also realized that the army that had laid waste to Beran's Hill and Copper Hills and all the coastal villages must have another force to the east of here.

Declan looked over at Bogartis, and the two shared unspoken thoughts as they imagined the baron's reaction to discovering his entire family was dead. And then they wondered how any of them would survive with another massive army coming toward the city.

HAVA LED SABIEN THROUGH THE streets, looking casually into merchants' stalls and the open doors of buildings, chatting about trivialities. She saw a woman of advancing years who was selling charms, the sort many sailors wore for luck at sea, and crossed to that booth.

Sabien glanced over and Hava whispered, "Say as little as possible." He nodded.

"My friend here," she said to the tradeswoman, "is looking for your best charm to ward off evil at sea."

The woman's weather-beaten face split into a smile showing surprisingly white teeth against her tanned skin. She had a good look at the big young sailor she saw standing next to the oddly dressed woman. Hava noticed her take stock of her appearance and made a note to change that next.

"I have several, but this one"—she held up something

that looked like a poorly carved jade fish—"will ward off all but the direst fate."

"He needs it," said Hava. "He won't listen to me. Will you tell him it's madness to sail west?"

The old woman's eyes widened.

"He says he's been promised double shares or something."

"Are you mad?" the old woman asked Sabien, cutting off Hava. "Only those from the west can return there." She lowered her voice, apparently fearful of being overheard. "Few ships have ventured beyond this point and none have ever returned. The claims by some that they have been west and come back are full of tales of monsters, vast cities of gold, and the usual nonsense told by those cadging drinks from others at taverns."

Hava nodded. She'd come upon that practice many times.

Then the old woman leaned closer over her little table of charms. She whispered, "But if you are determined, you should have this trinket, one I have never offered to another." She reached under the table into a small box and pulled out a figure of a fat little man, carved out of black stone. "You should take both."

The haggling started, but Hava ended it quickly and moved away, thinking. The few hints here and there gleaned today led her to believe that there was a very powerful nation, or alliance of nations, that very much wanted to be left alone and that had the power and resources to ensure it was granted its privacy.

She wondered how this arrangement had come into existence: she'd come to believe that her own nation, Coaltachin, was unique in preventing others from knowing who or even where they were. Or that was what she had thought until now. But this appeared to be a trait shared with the Azhante. She wondered how they had achieved it.

She and Sabien finished walking through the market until they stood in front of a window bar on the outside of a building that the locals called a "cantina." There were small tables and chairs nearby where those who purchased food and drink could consume them. As a former innkeeper—albeit for a very short time—Hava found the concept fascinating. Obviously, it had to be somewhere with constantly clement weather, but she could imagine the idea of—

She cut herself off from thinking how she could incorporate this into the Inn of the Three Stars. It was gone. Beran's Hill was gone. Hatushaly was gone, and he was the only one of the three she might get back. A sense of nostalgia washed over her, but she refused to engage with it, so it passed through her instead. She would find her husband. She was determined.

She saw two men enter one of the many taverns dotted around the city of Cleverly, feeling instinctively that they were worthy of observation. "Wait here," she said to Sabien. The way the old woman had taken note of her sailor's togs made her realize she had been blind to the possibility of calling too much attention to herself. Her clothing choice was efficient, but it also made her look too much like what she was: a capable and dangerous woman. She removed her head scarf, handed it to the former mason, and then removed her sword. She'd taken to wearing a baldric, like most sailors who carried arms, as it was far easier to don or remove quickly aboard ship. "Put that on," she said to Sabien. He did as ordered and adjusted his own belt knife so that it sat on the opposite hip.

Hava hurried down the street to a stall she had passed earlier. Her blouse was nondescript enough, plain grey linen with puffed sleeves and drawstrings at the cuff so that they could be worn as high or low on the arm as the wearer desired. The problem was her work breeches and boots. She decided on a large blue skirt that swept the floor, which would hide both. The vendor, a stout man with a balding head, expected a haggle but was pleasantly surprised when Hava paid the first price he named. As Hava returned to where Sabien waited, she judged it more than likely the vendor was thinking he should have asked for more.

On the way back she glanced down to ensure her boots were indeed not visible, and if she was careful not to stride out too much they weren't.

She shook her hair out, then ran her fingers through it and returned to where Sabien waited.

"You're a sailor in port who's come off our ship," Hava told him, "and I'm some street whore you're trying to get drunk so you don't have to pay me."

He looked perplexed for a moment, then his face split into a smile. "We're mummers?"

"No masks, and we can speak, but yes, we are acting."

Sabien started to make a face and drop his shoulder, and Hava instantly realized the problem. "No," she said, poking him hard in the chest with her index finger. "You're trying to get *me* drunk, because you don't want to pay me. I'm drinking; you're only pretending to drink. Soon I will shout at you and you'll get angry and get up and leave." She glanced up and down the street. "Wait for me at that corner down there, at that big blue building. Understand?"

The sudden red staining his cheeks indicated that he did understand and was embarrassed. "Yes, Captain."

"And don't call me Captain in there."

"Yes," he replied, and she could tell he bit back the word *captain* only at the last instant.

She led him into the tavern and saw the two men sitting by a rear door, both watching the room. She laughed and wobbled a bit, then turned and pulled Sabien's head down

as if kissing him on the cheek, whispering, "Get two drinks
and meet me at that table." With a flick of her wrist, she
attempted a giggle, which to her ears sounded forced and
unconvincing. If only she had paid more attention in her
studies with the Powdered Women.

She half walked, half staggered to the empty table on the
other side of the door where the two men sat. One glanced
at her for a moment, so she smiled at him seductively. He
looked away.

She sat down and leaned back and waited for the two
men to speak. Her frustration grew slowly as Sabien came
over with the two flagons of ale. She nodded and whispered,
"Sip slowly." Then she made a show of taking a deep gulp
while not actually swallowing any. The taste that lingered
told her this was not a particularly savory brew.

She affected speaking to Sabien, but all her attention was
on the two men. She was certain now that they were agents
of some kind and that their purpose in this tavern had nothing to do with either drink or women.

While she and Sabien pretended to negotiate the price of
her virtue, a few patrons passed through the curtained doorway between her table and the two men's. By the amount
of traffic, Hava assumed that must be where the privy was
located.

After spilling most of her drink and judging that one
ale wasn't having much effect on Sabien, Hava dispatched
him to fetch another round. When he did so, she noticed a
change in the attitude of the two men. They were no longer
scanning the entire common room of this tavern but were
intently watching the door as if waiting for someone.

Hava had been trained since childhood not to dismiss
these subtle changes in those being surveyed. She felt a returning pang, missing Hatu, not only for the obvious reasons, but because out of all the students at their school he

had been the best at noticing the sorts of almost impercep-
tible change she sometimes overlooked.

Time passed slowly, and Hava decided it was time to pro-
voke a response. She spilled her drink again, then shouted at
Sabien, "Look what you made me do, you lout!"

The young man was surprised enough by the unexpected
outburst—despite having been warned about it—that he
looked genuinely taken aback. As he started to stammer,
she shouted, "You're trying to get me drunk to avoid paying me! Get out!" She slapped Sabien just hard enough to
bring tears to his eyes from the sting, but not hard enough
to injure him.

The blow caused him to leap to his feet, almost falling
back over his chair, and as he blinked away the tears and his
cheeks reddened both from the blow and from embarrassment, he said, "Fine!" He started to say something more,
but a widening of Hava's eyes told him to stop, so he just
nodded and yelled, "Fine!" a second time, and stalked out
the door.

Hava made a show of adjusting her blouse and skirt, then
took a deep breath and looked around the room slowly, until
her gaze landed on the man closest to the door at the table
she had been watching. "You boys looking for some fun?"
she asked in a slurred voice.

Neither man graced her question with a reply. The one
nearest to her simply held up his hand and made a shooing
motion, not taking his eyes off the main door.

"Well," she said with mock indignity. "I have to go piss
anyway."

She stumbled through the doorway and immediately
moved to one side, so that she was separated from the two
men only by the cloth curtain. She glanced around and saw
that the outhouse was where she expected, a dozen yards

away on the other side of an alley so that the stench wouldn't reach the main room of the tavern. She would go down the alley to meet Sabien.

It was quiet enough that she should be able to hear the two men speak. She hoped it would be soon: she was eager to get rid of this ridiculous skirt. After what seemed an eternity, but was almost certainly less than ten minutes, she heard a chair scrape and one of the men said, "Well?" The hairs on her neck and arms stood up, for he was speaking the Azhante tongue.

"It's the *Black Wake*."

"What's it doing here?" asked his companion.

She had no idea which voice belonged to which man.

A third voice said, "This is not where the . . ."—then a word she didn't understand—" . . . is supposed to be. Did you see the captain?"

"I didn't go to the ship but watched from a shop across the wharf."

A few words were uttered in tones too low for Hava to catch, and then the voice of the man who had been last to join the table said, "One boat left, but I couldn't see who came ashore. A big man and a small man, I think. The small one wore a red jerkin, so perhaps that was the captain. If betrayal was in play, I did not want to place myself at risk before being certain."

"The captain probably came here to skim some booty for his own purse before traveling to Elsobas. That's where all slaves were to be delivered." There was a moment of quiet, then he added, "Perhaps because he's early. He's not due there for another two or three days."

Some more muttered conversation was exchanged, then Hava thought she recognized the voice of the last man to join the table. "All the slaves were to be routed there, and then the rest of the *Black Wake*'s booty brought to . . ." She heard the word, but it was the name of a place she didn't know. But at least she knew where to search next for Hatu.

"Send men to check every brothel in the port for that fat pig of a captain; his first duty was to follow instructions. I will not endure the wrath of a pride lord because of him. Kill him and put someone else with as many sicari as we can spare aboard the ship in the morning and sail it to where it needs to be. Once there we can dispose of the rest of the crew."

Hava didn't wait a moment longer but glanced around to see if anyone might see her, rid herself of the annoying skirt, and hurried down the alley toward the blue building where Sabien waited.

HATU CAME AWAKE WITH TWO thoughts in his mind: first, that he was tired of waking up on strange ships with his head throbbing, and second, that he just might kill everyone who'd had a hand in his abduction. He got to his feet and found that his breath was a little short and his legs a bit wobbly. He assumed these must be the aftereffects of whatever drug Bodai had put into his drink.

He looked around the cabin and decided that at least they had chosen nice quarters for him. He worked his way to the cabin door, the tingling in his arms and legs fading and his strength returning with each step.

By the time he reached the main deck, the afternoon sun and strong wind helped to revive him, though he felt an unexpected thirst. He moved to the water barrel, pulled off the wooden cover with one hand, and plunged the iron ladle into the fresh water. He pulled it up and took a long drink. The iron-tinged taste of the water reminded him as much as anything else that he was aboard a ship, and that fueled his anger.

Hatu climbed the steps to the quarterdeck and saw Bodai at the wheel. He was watching the sails one moment, glancing to port and then starboard every few seconds. He took a step toward his former master, and a sailor moved in front of him. "He needs to be left alone. We're in treacherous waters."

"Why is he at the wheel?"

"Few know the true way, and he is the only pilot who can get us safely free of these reefs."

Hatu watched carefully as Bodai steered.

A lookout at the bow shouted, "Blue water to port!"

Hatu saw Bodai correct the heading slightly to port and looked back at the sailor. The seaman said, "You can tell the depth by the color in many places among these reefs and islands. The darker the color, the deeper the water." He blew out a breath that was almost a sigh, as if he had been holding it in. "On the right day, when the sky is clear. When the sky is overcast or too cloudy . . ." He left the thought unfinished, but Hatu took his meaning. This was a dangerous place.

"Why this route?"

"The Nytanny people do not patrol here without a reason."

Hatu had no idea who or what the Nytanny were and turned to ask a question as the sailor walked away. Resigned to leaving that question unanswered, Hatu watched Bodai. He still found it unbelievable that this man was not a true master of Coaltachin but in fact an agent of the Flame Guard, a group he still knew so little about. In just the same way that Catharian was not a true monk of the Order of Tathan, working on behalf of the Church of the One. Hatu found it almost comical, the irony that everyone who claimed they were trying to protect him was actually living a lie.

He could just about understand the logic, but given his upbringing, trust was rare and hard-won, so he'd bide his time, rein in his anger, and wait to see what the future held. He had a rough idea of the course they had taken from

Elsobas. Should the opportunity present itself and he came upon a large enough boat stocked with provisions, sailing from anywhere along this string of islands and keeping to a course of east by northeast would eventually take him back to North Tembria. All he needed was a chance.

He shook his head as if waking himself. It was a fantasy, an idle dream of escaping and returning to North Tembria, making his way back to Hava, ignoring all these claims of his legendary status . . . He ached to be with her in their little inn. But this was the height of folly: it was wishing for the impossible.

Hatu moved to the rail and glanced down. The water was clear enough that beyond the ship's wake he could see glimpses of coral and rock. Taking a deep breath, he felt the fog in his brain continue to lift. The wind was a relief, for the sun at this latitude was harsh. Standing in the shade was pleasant, but the ship's constant changing of direction kept putting him back into direct sunlight.

He looked around, for a moment wondering if he should lend a hand, but decided to wait until he was asked, for any disruption in the smooth operation of the ship in these waters was dangerous, even if it was well intentioned.

The sun continued to lower, and perhaps two hours before sunset Bodai handed the wheel over to the helmsman. He worked his shoulders a bit as he walked toward Hatu, as if they were stiff from steering the ship.

Hatu said, "We're a long way from anywhere I know."

Bodai nodded. "We're a long way from anywhere. This is perhaps as empty a stretch of water as you're likely to find." He glanced at the sails out of habit, to check if they were properly trimmed, then said, "I've visited more islands than I can remember, on both sides of this world. But here"—he waved his hand in a circle—"we're two days' sail to the nearest inhabited island and three days beyond that to a port of any size. And still we are more than a month away from reaching our destination."

Hatu said, "So you'll have time to explain all of this?" His tone left little doubt he had no trust in these people.

"Most of it. Some of it will wait until you've finished your studies."

"Studies?"

"Yes," said Bodai with a rueful expression. "You were to have come to us, like the other Firemane boys, for special training when you were a toddler and returned to your family after ten years."

Hatu's expression was doubtful. "But I've been—"

Bodai interrupted. "Your training in Coaltachin proved useful up to a point: it kept you alive. The training I speak of, the training you were supposed to have undergone as a small child, should have been over before fuzz appeared on your cheeks."

"What sort of training?"

"How to use the power within you, without killing yourself or others."

"Power?" said Hatu. "I have no power." But as soon as he said this he remembered that night aboard the ship with Hava as they passed through the Narrows, when he had first kissed her and she had told him that light had come out of him.

"You have power you haven't even become aware of, boy," Bodai said. "If you use it without training, it could be disastrous."

Hatu said nothing while he thought about this. As much as he wanted to deny what he had just been told, to turn his efforts toward finding Hava, he knew there was some truth to what Bodai had said.

DECLAN WATCHED IN SILENCE AS the rest of the troops from the city arrived, the baron in the lead. Daylon Dumarch's face showed a cascade of emotions: shock, disbelief, horror, and then grief—all within seconds.

One of the sergeants who had been set to guard the site by Bogartis said, "My lord, I don't think—"

The baron pushed past him and moved to stare at the smoking rubble that once had been his personal carriage. Declan had already seen what the baron now inspected with horror. Twisted husks that had once been people lay contorted, both inside and outside the wagon. The burned bodies of soldiers who had died defending his family lay in a circle, and almost certainly two of those bodies belonged to the baron's sons. Within the wagon Declan had seen three corpses, two of them small: the baron's wife and daughters. His entire family had been destroyed in a single day.

Balven dismounted and ran to his brother's side, as Daylon emitted a cry, a wail that began in the pit of his soul, ripped through his heart, and erupted out of him.

Declan watched on and wondered why he had never felt that way when his own wife and friends had been butchered.

18

CHOICES, CHAOS, AND CHANGE

D onte followed the soldier from the room in which he had spoken with Balven, aware that something serious was going on: everywhere he looked servants were hurrying. He passed through pantries where food was being prepared for storage or for travel, he didn't know which, and through a large scullery where dishes and cooking utensils were being cleaned before being packed away. They walked down a series of halls in the keep, past rooms he assumed were servants' quarters, since they were all belowground.

Turning a corner, Donte saw another hallway off to his right that led back to the kitchen, pantry, and scullery; past that, they climbed steps and went through a doorway into a barracks. It was currently empty, for every soldier in the keep must be busy elsewhere. Donte had no idea what was going on, but judging by the commotions that had been occurring throughout the day, he knew it was something momentous, possibly an attack. As he glanced toward the far door that led to the marshaling yard, the soldier said, "That bunk in the corner is yours."

"Do you know what is going on?"

"We're at muster," said the soldier. "I was told to bring you here and wait until someone relieved me."

"And I'm to just wait here, too, I guess."

"I was just told to keep you here," the man said, placing his hand on the hilt of his sword. He looked like a seasoned soldier, and Donte noticed a small castle emblem on the left side of his tabard, indicating that he was one of the baron's household guards, the best soldiers here. There was a small chance that Donte could take away his sword and overpower him, but it seemed unlikely, besides which the castle was teeming with more like him and, beyond that, the city streets would hold hundreds more, and he doubted he could kill all of them.

Donte looked at the indicated bed: a thin mattress filled with what he assumed to be straw on a wooden frame strung with rope that held it up off the cold stone floor. He walked over to it and sat on the bunk, and the soldier moved off to stand nearby.

Donte turned and lay down on the bed and stared at the ceiling. He'd slept on worse. Far worse. He closed his eyes. There was nothing to do but wait, and over the years Donte had learned time seemed to pass quickly if he slept while waiting, plus he was better off rested, in case something nasty came his way.

Given the uproar on all sides, Donte suspected something very nasty was coming his way.

HAVA ASKED, "ARE WE READY?"

George nodded and said, "Yes, Captain."

"Then let's get under way."

George passed the orders, and Hava observed how her crew was falling into place. She had ordered as quiet a departure as was possible, given that she knew the sicari ashore were looking for Captain George and she did not want them raising the alarm any sooner than was necessary.

She had returned to the ship by as circuitous a route

as she could improvise, having Sabien navigate a stolen dinghy while leaving the ship's gig tied to the dock. She hoped whoever might be stationed in the harbor would be watching that boat, waiting for the captain's return, rather than watching the *Black Wake,* but she knew she would have only minutes once she ordered the sails raised before someone ashore noticed they were departing. There was no ship in evidence nearby that could overtake hers, but that didn't mean something faster wasn't anchored off another part of the island. Just because Cleverly was the hub port didn't mean it was the only port.

She hoped her precipitous departure wouldn't endanger those who had elected to stay in Cleverly. They would probably be questioned about her possible destination if they were identified.

Again she took in the unfolding routine of a ship's crew that knew what it was doing. Two of the previous crew had elected to leave, but the rest remained, and more than thirty of the freed prisoners had sailing experience. Others were apprenticing, at least until they decided what their next choice in life might be.

George turned to his captain and said, "Elsobas is about two days' sail to the north of us." He tilted his head as if thinking about something. Hava was coming to trust his knowledge of this region. She had little choice, after all, since she knew next to nothing about this part of the world, though she was learning quickly. Besides, George might have been a degenerate gambler, but otherwise he seemed a reliable sort, and Hava had spent most of her life around people who were anything but reliable. She glanced to the rear of the ship where Molly Bowman lay, recovering from her injuries, which had been more severe than first judged. Molly had regained consciousness the day after Hava found her, but she had quickly fallen asleep again. Hava had tried to speak to her, but each time she had found the young woman sleeping. She hoped Molly would regain her health soon. Hava had a feeling she'd need the tough archer before this journey was over.

Hava turned to see George still lost in thought as he steered the ship away from Cleverly. "George?"

"Captain?"

"Elsobas. Why there?"

"It makes sense that is where the slaves from the Twins would be brought. From there past the Border Ports, it's rumored that several different lanes of travel exist to . . . whatever destination lies to the southwest."

Hava knew "the Twins" was how he and others on this ship referred to North and South Tembria.

"And there is a lot of business done there that bears watching," George added, "so expect agents, those working for the black-clad—I mean the sicari—to be watching." He again looked as if he was dwelling on something. "Also, it may be where the sicari are most vulnerable. The stories say if anyone was trying to slip by those sicari, that's the island they'd choose. I've never ventured beyond, but tales suggest that from there you can run through a string of islands that are almost completely surrounded by nasty reefs and shoals, through a channel that only a few know, and you end up at some . . ." He smiled and spread his hands for a moment, palms down, before grabbing the ship's wheel again. "Treasure, secret places, the usual." He was silent for a moment, then said, "But sometimes there's a nugget of truth in stories, and if anyone could be smuggling past the Border Ports, that would probably be their chosen course."

Hava nodded. "Then Elsobas it is."

Silently, she prayed to whichever god or goddess chose to listen that she was making the correct choice, that Hatu had been taken there by the monks, or whatever they truly were, and that she'd arrive in time to find him.

DECLAN RODE BETWEEN SIXTO AND Bogartis. It was clear that everyone in the company needed to talk, for none of them had to be a military expert to know that Marquensas was verging on total chaos. The surrounding lands in all directions were under threat of being attacked at any moment.

Behind the column, refugees were appearing, swarming out of the woods on both sides of the wide road that led back to the city. Some of the soldiers at the rear of the column had shouted questions to them, and word had been passed up to those in the vanguard. Bogartis's company was first of the mercenaries, which put it in the middle of the long column, and what Declan heard painted a grim picture.

Apparently, a force had marched up through the Covenant, near Declan's home village of Oncon, and swept westward along the highway into Ilcomen, slicing through the lower half of the kingdom. The baron's family, faced with a wave of refugees fleeing ahead of the invaders, had been forced to turn and attempt to go back to Marquenet, only to be slowed by the clog of people around them.

Raiders had come at them from the south, and the combination of a stout defense and panicked refugees had kept the fight going for hours, until the attackers had simply cut brush, set it on an abandoned wagon, fired it, and pushed the wagon into the midst of the defenders. Declan could imagine the rest.

He knew the baron had been so overcome by his loss that his brother and two soldiers had had to steady him enough to get him back onto his horse. Dumarch and Balven were now far ahead of where Bogartis's company rode, and Declan had no inkling of whether the baron had regained any shred of composure.

Shouts from behind them caused Declan, Bogartis, and the rest of the company to look to the rear. Instantly Declan realized that those coming up from behind were not refugees but a company of horsemen.

"Wheel and ready!" shouted Bogartis, as the companies behind his started to engage the attackers. He signaled for his company to follow him as he charged into the fray.

Declan flexed his right shoulder and felt no discomfort. He drew his sword and drew a long belt knife with his left hand, ready to employ the two-handed fighting technique Sixto had taught him.

For a brief instant he was startled by the appearance of the warriors who came charging at him out of the tree line. They were short and broad chested and had arms that seemed unusually long for their frames. They wore what looked like animal furs, and their bodies were covered in paint, mostly green, but with streaks of red and yellow. Their heads were uncovered and their black hair was tied up on top of their scalps in a large knot, and they carried swords and cudgels: only a few were archers. They screamed and shouted, and Declan couldn't understand a word of their language, but when an arrow sped by, missing him by inches, his shock was short-lived.

"Take out the archers!" he shouted instinctively, put his heels to his mount's flank, and charged. He swung his sword down at a nearby swordsman, slicing into his shoulder, and had his horse knock over a second as he reached the closest archer. He reined in just enough to guarantee a solid blow and heard the bowman's skull crack with that strike.

Almost oblivious to the dangers around him, Declan found himself once more in that strange calm that he'd experienced in battle before, that detached awareness of everything around him, so that when a blow was directed at him, he could counter it reflexively. He worked his way through attackers with relative ease, his horse's reins in his teeth, using leg pressure to guide the well-trained horse while he sought out and killed every archer he could find.

He lost all sense of time and was completely focused on fighting, the rage he had held within after the murder of his wife and friends not flaming up but seeming to provide a steady flow of strength. He cut down attackers one after another, and none of them came close to landing a blow. The long rondel dagger he held in his left hand felt slightly cumbersome: he'd already decided that, when time permitted, he could improve on the design should he find a forge and metals.

When the baron's company turned and joined in, the battle was quickly won. The attackers who remained vanished into the trees like ghosts, followed swiftly by half the baron's company.

While Bogartis rode over to speak with the baron and his officers, Declan leapt down and cleaned his blade on a dead man's shirt.

Sixto rode to where he stood and asked, "What were they?"

Declan shook his head. "I've never seen their like before. Savages of some kind."

"I've traveled widely and I've never come across them," Sixto said, staring at the body of a fallen invader.

Declan came to stand over the dead warrior. Up close he looked like most men, save for his very short torso, broad shoulders, and long arms. His skin, where it showed under the paint, was darker than Declan's, but no darker than a lot of the men who fought today, and not as dark as some. Looking around at the battle site, Declan noticed that every fallen invader had dark hair. At last he offered, "Some tribe from across the sea?"

"Fair guess," said Sixto.

Declan remounted and moved to wait next to Sixto. The rest of Bogartis's company gravitated to them so that by the time their captain returned, they were already grouped together.

"We have a new commission," Bogartis declared.

He took a deep breath, and instantly Declan knew the men were not going to like what they heard.

"We're now contracted to serve for a year." In and of itself that wasn't necessarily bad news, except that every man in the company knew Marquensas was under assault and it meant they were now an adjunct company to the baron's army, and probably going to be subject to the orders of his officers and sergeants, something no mercenary cared for. Before anyone could voice an objection, Bogartis added, "At double our normal pay."

That caused the men to stay silent, and Declan glanced about to see a few of them even smiling. Depending on the fighting, that could be a nice year. Often weeks, even months, could pass without a company being paid.

Bogartis said, "Two things, now. First, I'm naming Declan my second-in-command." Immediately several of the men who'd been with Bogartis for years asked why or grumbled. Bogartis held up his hand. "You've seen him fight! And he's the man who killed the man who killed Misener." At that they all fell silent again. Declan looked at Bogartis, his expression conveying that he hadn't asked for this. Bogartis gave him a slight nod, then said, "The second thing is we leave here tonight."

The men began to mutter again, and Bogartis added, "The baron's leaving whatever provisions his men have here for us, and we'll forage as we go."

"Go where?" shouted one of the men.

"Everywhere," answered their captain. "We're to break up into groups of four, and I'll give you specific destinations in the morning. We'll be moving east through whatever's left of Ilcomen and Ithrace to the border of Sandura. Some of you are going to find boats and cross the Narrows to Zindaros, Metros, even as far as the Border Tribes."

"To do what?" asked another man.

"You'll be recruiting. If the southern kingdoms have been raided as well, there will be a lot of soldiers without masters and free companies for hire. You will promise them whatever they ask to get them here." He paused, then said, "Baron Dumarch is opening wide the treasury of Marquenet, and he has only one purpose now. He intends to find out who is responsible for the death of his family and he will visit destruction on them.

"He is going to build the largest damned army Garn has ever seen."

MOLLY BOWMAN HELD ON TO the rail, finding her sea legs. "How are you feeling?" Hava asked.

"When I was young, I walked behind a mule who didn't take kindly to it and woke up the next day with my da looking over me." Molly shook her head slowly. "My head didn't hurt half as bad then. That's how I felt when I first came to."

"You landed hard. Didn't know if you were ever going to wake up," said Hava. "I got bashed, but it must have been a glancing blow because I came to soon after. You've been out for many days. They must have cracked your skull. Could have killed you."

"I'll take it as luck then," Molly said with a rueful smile. "Mostly all I have now is a dull ache, as if from too much ale." She rolled her neck and then her shoulders and said, "Something to eat might help."

"We've got provisions down below. There's a galley of sorts in the crew space and plenty of dried fruit, jerked meat, and salt pork. Should be some fresh food, though not much left." Hava smiled, relieved to see Molly returning to her old self. "Some ale's left, and some wine in skins."

"Water will do."

"Buckets of it. We managed to take it on board before we fled from Cleverly."

As Molly turned to find her way to the galley below, Hava added, "And if you head down to the second deck and go forward, there's quite a nice collection of weapons, including what look to me to be some well-made bows."

Molly paused for a moment, then said, "I'll check those bows first, then eat." She picked up her pace and hurried to the companionway below.

Hava laughed, and some of the nearby crew turned to look. Molly was going to be just fine.

Hava strolled to the aft rail and scanned the horizon for any hint as to whether they were being followed. As time wore on, her concerns were lessening.

After a while, Molly returned to the quarterdeck, chewing on a large slab of salt pork. "Is there something wrong with thinking this tastes good?" she said around a mouthful.

"No," said Hava with a chuckle. "It means you're hungry."

"I am," said the archer. "My trousers feel a bit loose, so I guess I lost some weight while I lay around."

"It happens," said Hava.

"Last I remembered was you getting surrounded as someone threw a net over me, then . . . here." She took another bite of salt pork. With a half-full mouth, she asked, "So, you stole a ship?"

Hava grinned. "Pretty easy, actually."

"Crew and all?"

"Sort of." Hava spent a few minutes filling in her friend and finished by saying, "If we're going to find Hatu and the others from Beran's Hill, it looks as if this next port, Elsobas, is our best bet."

Molly looked dubious. "You really think there's a good chance of that?"

"Didn't say good chance, just best." Hava shrugged. "That's what I heard at our last port, that all slaves from the coast would be run through this Elsobas. So that's where we're heading."

"You're the captain." Molly grinned.

"You're free to get off at any time."

Molly actually laughed, spitting out some chewed pork. She put her hand over her mouth and said, "Thanks, but I think I'll stay aboard for a bit." Looking at Hava over her upheld hand, she pleaded, "Don't make me laugh like that. I'll choke."

"Let me know when you feel up to some duty."

"What do you have in mind?"

"We're going to need more than two archers if we get into a fight." Hava remembered being in the rigging with Hatu before and how effective that sort of advantage could be. "Talk to the people we freed and see if any of them have any skill with a bow."

"That's a good supply of weapons below," said Molly. "And some of the bows are finely made. More arrows than we'll ever need. I'll start asking around now. It'll do me good to move around and stretch myself a bit. All that sleeping wears a body out."

Hava laughed at the incongruity of that statement, but she understood what it was like to recover from an injury. "Good," she responded, and Molly set off from the quarterdeck to start talking to the hundred or so former prisoners.

She turned and saw that George was holding firm to their course and felt a glimmer of hope return. Turning back, she saw that Molly had started a conversation with a small group of men on the deck. "Six," she said to herself. "We need six really good archers."

HATU FELT THE SHIP ALTER course abruptly and left his small cabin. He'd been given some privacy, which he appreciated, but the boredom had driven him to working in the rigging occasionally. He had just finished a watch and lain down to rest and was on the verge of sleep when the sudden wallow of the ship as it heeled over snapped him alert.

He reached the deck and climbed the ladder to the quarterdeck and saw what had caused the abrupt change in direction. In the distance a ship had appeared, and it was bearing down on them quickly. Hatu turned to Bodai. "Who are they?"

"Someone we do not wish to deal with," came the reply as the former master of Coaltachin centered the wheel and the ship came onto a new heading. "We're in a deep patch of water, so we have a ways before we return to the shoals and reefs," he said. "That's why they picked this spot, so they could cut us off rather than chase us."

Hatu said, "Those Azhante we ran into in Sandura?"

Bodai nodded.

"They knew we were coming?"

"They suspected it," said Bodai. "They have enough resources that they can leave ships out here for a long time, resupplying them as needed." The old man shook his head. "And there are still so many things you do not understand. Like Sabella, they have people who can sense your presence." Bodai pointed his finger accusingly. "Mainly when you lose your temper, and you've done that a lot lately."

Hatu felt his anger rising again. "With good reason!"

As the ship drew closer, Bodai said, "We can only stand a chase for an hour, then we're back in dangerous waters."

"Turn and fight?" suggested Hatu.

Bodai nodded. He gauged the wind and then shouted, "Arm yourselves!"

Down on the main deck, Denbe raised one arm in acknowledgment of the order. Hatu had been avoiding the large fighter since they left Elsobas, still harboring resentment over being taken by him and Catharian. Still, if there was going to be a fight, Hatu was now grateful the powerful soldier was aboard.

Everyone in the rigging at once dropped to the deck while others ran below and returned minutes later to hand out weapons. Soon, archers were ascending the rigging, and Hatu said, "I've fought from the yards before. I should get a bow."

Bodai shook his head. "You're the last man on this ship who will fight. If you die, everything we've done for years is wasted. Every man and woman of the Flame Guard who has died will have been lost for nothing."

Hatu felt his temper rising and fought back the coming rage. He took a deep breath and then said, "I need to do something!"

Bodai said, "Steer for a moment," and stepped away from the wheel.

Hatu stepped into the space Bodai had just vacated. "What heading?"

"As she goes," said Bodai as he hurried down to the main deck.

He returned a few moments later with a sword and buckler shield. Denbe followed, and it was clear to Hatu that the old fighter had been given the responsibility of guarding him.

"At least let me defend myself!" shouted Hatu as the other ship drew slowly closer.

Bodai glanced at Denbe, who nodded.

Stepping in to take the wheel again, Bodai said, "Go get yourself a sword, just in case. You know where the weapons locker is."

Hatu hurried below and found the locker almost empty. A decent-looking short sword and a few bows were left. He selected a bow and a hip quiver loaded with arrows, slung the bow over his shoulder, then grabbed the sword and returned topside.

Denbe motioned for Hatu to stand behind him. Hatu unshouldered his bow and said, "Don't get in my shooting line."

"Shoot over my shoulder, if you must," said Denbe. "Just don't do anything stupid."

The ship took a tack to starboard and brought the pursuing ship clearly into view. Hatu's eyes widened and he shouted, "We have to take that ship!"

"What?" cried Bodai.

"Remember when I told you and the other masters about what happened, when Donte and I were taken? About the three ships that chased us? That's one of them, I'm sure of it."

Bodai said, "They're Azhante, and they must have been tracking you as we were." He glanced at Hatu. "Just be grateful we found you first."

Denbe looked back at Hatu. "They will sacrifice every man on that ship to kill you." He moved to where a small buckler shield had been hung from a belaying pin, so that it was close to hand.

Hatu said, "I understand." He felt a strange lurch in his stomach, as if he had taken an unexpected step down, and a moment later, his stomach felt hot, as if he had eaten extremely spicy food. He wondered why his stomach should be acting up at a moment of grave danger. He'd heard stories of men who had shit themselves in combat, but Hatu had been in fights before and never felt this way.

"Get ready!" shouted Bodai, and he hauled hard on the wheel, while sailors quickly trimmed the sails. Suddenly they were heading straight for the oncoming ship.

Hatu looked around to get a sense of where everything was. In the yards above, where he wanted to be, archers were taking aim. He knew they'd target archers aloft on the other ship, as well as any exposed men on the decks. The sails of both ships would offer ample cover, so the art would be shooting through the gaps in between.

"We'll sail past," shouted Bodai, "then let them turn and chase us. If I can get us back into the channel I might get them to run aground."

"We're going to be dodging arrows," said Denbe to Hatu. "Stay behind me."

As the ships appeared to be headed on a collision course, Bodai steered slightly to starboard, bringing the Azhante ship squarely up to the port side. Hatu could hear arrows being loosed, but none struck near where he stood on the quarterdeck, and the sails prevented him from seeing if any of the men on his ship were hitting their targets. As the distance between the two ships closed, he felt the burning sensation in the pit of his stomach increasing in intensity. His mouth was starting to water and to fill with a bitter taste, and he felt as if he might vomit.

As the Azhante ship started to pass, the rate of arrow-fire increased, and Hatu held his bow at the ready in case he saw a target. He heard a dull *thunk,* and then a man on the main deck shouted, "Grapples!"

"Cut 'em!" cried Bodai, and was almost knocked off his feet as the ship lurched.

"This is madness," said Denbe. "Both ships will swing around and neither will have any control."

"Yes," said Bodai, fighting to keep whatever position he could while his men hacked at the lines on the grappling hooks.

Hatu saw figures in the yards above on the other ship and took aim, unleashing an arrow, but the flapping sails blocked his view so he didn't see if he'd hit his mark. Molly or Hava wouldn't miss! Anger surged through him as that thought crossed his mind.

He heard fighting from the deck below but had trouble getting a good look, as he was trapped between the stern rail and Denbe. He loosed another shaft over Denbe's shoulder at a black-clad figure in the yards directly opposite the quarterdeck and saw his arrow take the man down.

The sound of fighting intensified, and Hatu could hear men getting closer to the quarterdeck. He saw Bodai give up on keeping any control of the ship. Bodai quickly lashed the wheel and swung his sword out of his baldric.

Denbe turned, forcing Hatu to turn with him. Being shoved, even for his own well-being, caused every muscle in Hatu's body to tense as if he were about to strike a blow. He felt his jaw clench and his eyes open wide, and pain built in his stomach: he knew he'd vomit in a few moments if this continued.

Men in black swarmed up the ladder toward them, and Hatu saw Bodai expertly parry a blow and slash a deep wound across the first man to close with him so that the sicari fell with blood fountaining from his mouth and chest.

Denbe stepped forward to block a sicari from attacking Hatu, who now had dropped his bow and held his sword and small shield ready. Both were hot to the touch, as if they'd been left in the sun too long. Hatu felt a moment of confusion: he had only just fetched them from below.

Denbe dodged to his right to block an attack and suddenly another man appeared to his left, attempting to step around the warrior to attack Hatu.

Without hesitation, Hatu stepped to his left and thrust over Denbe's shoulder, forcing the attacker to retreat a step. The sicari shifted his footing and lashed out at Hatu, missing and inadvertently dragging his blade across Denbe's shoulder as he stepped away.

The old fighter groaned in pain and took a half step to his right, and Hatu slashed at the head of the sicari. His blow missed his opponent but forced him back another step.

Denbe's opponent now seized the moment to plunge his blade into the chest of the big fighter. He was repaid by Denbe returning the blow, and died with a sword point in his throat.

The second attacker flailed at Hatu, who kept his wits about him enough to parry it and then deliver a thrust that sliced open the man's cheek. Like the others, the man wore the strange headgear Hatu had first seen in Sandura, similar to the uniforms worn by sicari from Coaltachin. The cut caused the attacker's head cover to fall away, and Hatu saw in his face that he was clearly intent on killing him.

Hatu had never been this close to someone who wanted him dead, and the bile growing in his stomach rushed up into his throat. His thought at that moment was that vomiting was probably going to get him killed, but he couldn't seem to stop it.

The wounded man reeled back, and Hatu stepped around Denbe, who was staggering from his wound, and cut hard across the sicari's chest. Suddenly there was blood everywhere, and Hatu knew his attacker was dying.

He turned to Denbe. The old warrior looked up at him and tried to say something, but was unable to make a sound. His chest was wet with blood, and a moment later Hatu saw Denbe crumple and die at his feet.

A raw heat rose up inside him. Dragging his gaze from the old fighter, he saw that more black-clad attackers were swarming up the ladder. One kicked the still body of Denbe aside and raised his blade to deliver a killing blow to Hatu.

Rage erupted within Hatu. The sensation of needing to void his stomach turned into another sensation that he'd never experienced in his life. He saw the blow swinging toward his head and put up his left hand reflexively. He felt the blow glance off the buckler and the shock of it run up his arm, and suddenly the world around him exploded into red.

The buckler dropped away. Hatu put his hand out and he saw the attacker right in front of him. When he opened his mouth, rather than void his stomach, a scream unlike anything Hatu had ever known tore from his throat. It was not merely a sound, but a wave of something Hatu could put no name to. As the sicari's sword slashed downward, a blast of flame erupted from Hatu's hand. It engulfed the sicari's sword hand and within seconds reduced it to a charred nub. Hatu watched as the sword fell to the deck with a clatter, and the sicari shrieked in agony.

Hatu thrust his hand out again, and a narrow line of fire shot out and wrapped around the man's head and shoulders. With a flash of clarity, he felt rage turn into purpose. He walked forward and each sicari before him fell away in agony as they burst into flame. No weapon touched Hatu as the flames rose around him. It was as if he had become another being, a demigod shielded by unimaginable energies. Both his hands now shimmered with fire, and waves of heat preceded him. He found his mind retreating into a place of calm observation, as if someone else had taken over command of his body, and he was only a witness.

Within moments, the victory by the Azhante was turned into defeat, as screaming enemies burned all over the ship, and his own crew fell back in awe. Hatu moved to the side of the ship and turned his hands toward the Azhante vessel, and long lances of fire seemed to explode from his palms. Within moments, flames raged across the deck and up the masts as the sicari vessel's sails caught fire.

"Cut her loose!" he heard someone shout.

Hatu felt his vision shift and his knees begin to shake. Turning, he saw frantic crewmen fighting the flames on his own ship, spreading from the men he had burned, and others furiously hacking at the grappling ropes that bound the two ships together. He felt dizzy, and then suddenly there was darkness.

WHEN HATU OPENED HIS EYES he found himself back in his quarters and saw Bodai sitting on a stool beside his bunk. He tried to sit up but discovered he was desperately weak, his body aching and every joint protesting as he tried to move. When he attempted to speak, he could barely make a sound, for his throat and mouth felt as if they had been filled with hot sand, and his head ached beyond anything he had ever known.

Bodai was pale, his upper body wrapped in bandages. He reached out and put his hand on Hatu's chest. "Don't try to sit up."

Hatu lay back and with a hoarse croak asked, "Denbe?"

"Dead," said Bodai, which confirmed Hatu's memory of the assault. He felt sorrow, despite his previous anger at being abducted by Denbe, and a shock of relief that Bodai still lived.

He tried to frame another question, but Bodai shook his head. "You destroyed the Azhante ship. We lost a lot of men, but we survived. We are back on course."

Tears shone in the old man's eyes as he said in a harsh whisper, "Now do you understand why you must be trained?"

19

BETRAYAL, ACCEPTANCE,
AND PIRACY

B ernardo Delnocio sat in shocked disbelief as the reports came in, by the hour now. Every agent in his employ had sacrificed every carrier pigeon they possessed to send him dire news.

He sat in stunned silence at the last one he had opened, from Levar, his closest ally in Brojues, his eyes and ears on the Council of the Episkopos, and he had read the three words repeatedly.

The secret passageway began to open, and at once Bernardo laid his hand on the dagger at his belt, which he kept discreetly out of sight until needed. Marco Belli slipped into the private chamber, their usual meeting place. The most deadly and trusted agent in Delnocio's service looked haggard and near exhaustion.

Delnocio held up his hand, indicating that they should not speak. Removing a key from a pocket in his cassock, he inserted it into the lock of an ornate trunk that sat against a wall and opened the lid. Bernardo Delnocio quickly stripped off his clerical garb and donned a well-made outfit designed for travel: sturdy trousers and tunic, leather boots in place of his ornate slippers, a cap with ear covers, and a dark green cloak, which he folded over his arm.

If Marco Belli, the man many called "Piccolo," was surprised by this exchange of regalia for common garb, he did not show it. Last from the trunk, Delnocio removed a small box of plain wood and quickly opened the lid to inspect the contents. Satisfied that all was as it should be, he nodded once and led Belli back into the secret passage, waiting as the spy-assassin closed the entrance, which masqueraded as a bookcase.

Once they were deep into the tunnel, Delnocio asked, "What did you find?"

"Chaos everywhere, Eminence. The butchery began along the coasts, from the Covenant and running west. Nothing east from there, but that's Ithrace, already in ruins."

"Come. We'll talk as we ride. You have horses?"

"Fresh mounts are nearby, as always, against need, but you're leaving Sandura?"

"I must."

"A ship arrived as I did, from Enast. It bore the banner of the Church Adamant."

Delnocio nodded. "That makes sense. That would be Lord Marshal Bellamy, with at least three hundred soldiers."

"Bellamy, here?"

The episkopos once tasked with taking control of all of North Tembria for the Church was now being hunted by that very same Church. He motioned for Belli to lead on. They wended their way through narrow passages, part of a secret network even the king was ignorant of, a relic of his ancestors' needs to come and go unseen.

They came to a small stable, as far removed from the royal quarters as possible. "We have food and water?"

"Enough for a few days," answered the assassin.

"We'll have to find more as we travel. How many men have you here?"

"Six who will be with us in minutes, ten if we can wait two hours."

"We cannot wait. We leave now."

"Where are we bound, Eminence?"

"Marquenet."

For the first time in all the years he had employed Belli, Delnocio saw open surprise on the man's face. "To Marquensas?"

Both men knew that meant a punishing ride across the Sea of Grass and through Passage Town. Belli's expression turned calculating, and Bernardo knew he was now thinking of what they would need on such a journey. "Marquenet," whispered Belli, shaking his head.

"I must speak with Baron Daylon Dumarch."

"To what end, if I may ask?"

"Sanctuary."

Now Belli looked absolutely shocked. "Sanctuary," he echoed in a tone of disbelief.

"The Lord Marshal has undoubtedly arrived to burn me at the stake on some trumped-up charge of heresy, and his small army is to make sure no one objects too vigorously." Bernardo paused for a moment, then said, "And the absence of another episkopos suggests that King Lodavico and his family may stand on the pyres in my stead: the Church taking direct control of the kingdom makes things so much more efficient in the face of this massive chaos sweeping across the two continents." He took a deep breath. "I received a message just before you arrived. It was carried on the same ship as Lord Bellamy, I assume, and probably released as soon as we were close enough for the pigeon to survive its flight. It is from Episkopos Levar."

"What did it say?"

"Just three words: *We are betrayed.*"

"By whom?" asked Belli, now openly confused. Until this moment he had assumed Bernardo Delnocio was the single most powerful man in the Council of the Episkopos, the rulers of the Church of the One.

"By forces very few on this side of the world are even aware of, my friend."

Belli entered the small stable, then turned and said, "Wait a few moments, Eminence, while I fetch the others and whatever I can take from the kitchen."

"Be quick," said Bernardo. "Bellamy will seal off the castle, then the city, within the hour. We must be gone."

"We will," came the answer; then the wiry killer vanished around the corner.

"We are betrayed," whispered Bernardo Delnocio to himself. He could hardly believe it himself.

HAVA HEARD THE CALL FROM the top of the foremast: "Land!"

She looked to George, who said, "Elsobas."

"I want to keep things locked down here, but everyone is getting . . ."

"Sea happy," finished George. "I've sailed on voyages that took months, but most of our people here are not experienced sailors. Some are in serious need of getting their feet on dry land for a day, at least."

"Pass the word then," said Hava. "Sabien and I will go ashore, and if we don't find trouble, or it doesn't find us," she added quickly, "I'll signal and you can send those ashore who need it the most. Do it by watches, but let everyone know if we need to get out of here, we will need to do it in a hurry."

He nodded. "As much of a hurry as this ship is capable of."

Hava was painfully aware that the *Black Wake* was many

things, but fast was not foremost among its qualities. It was steady, and stout in bad weather, but any ship of speed would be able to catch it unless it had a very good head start. "Get everything ready for a quick departure while you wait for our signal."

"Yes, Captain," he said.

The ship routine was becoming smooth as the newcomers to sailing either mastered their tasks or got out of the way. Hava was convinced she had a core crew now of close to eighty men and women, twice the number needed to sail this big ship. That allowed George to have more watches and each member of the crew to have more leisure time, if learning fighting from Hava, Molly, and others who were skilled with weapons could be called "leisure." Hava had hoped Molly could find six good archers. Molly had found eleven men and women with some familiarity with a bow and had judged four of them to be good and the rest trainable.

Hava did not wish to face any company of experienced fighters with this crew, though she reckoned they were willing to fight to the death rather than face capture again, but determination was no match for murderous efficiency and experience. Still, there was something about that determination that made Hava confident that each passing day narrowed those gaps in experience.

She glanced over to where Sabien was sparring with four other men. From the look of things, they appeared to be fighting in earnest. Apparently, the young mason had a reputation in Port Colos as a brawler; certainly he hadn't been shy with his fists as a youth. He didn't look the type, Hava thought, but until you see a young man drunk in an inn, arguing over a woman or accused of cheating at cards or dice, you really didn't know how quickly an amiable lad could turn into a belligerent scrapper.

"Order the gig to be made ready," said Hava, and George called to a deckhand below and relayed the command.

The ship slowed as its sails were reefed, and Hava noticed the improvement with a sense of approval. She recalled the first time she had climbed the rigging to learn how to be a sailor, and even remembered her banter with the mate who had said the only women who sailed were pirates. She smiled at that memory.

The anchor was dropped and the ship held fast. As Hava and Sabien moved toward the gig that was to be dropped over the side, George approached. "We might be in for a bit of weather." He lifted his chin toward the west; Hava looked and saw little difference.

"What am I seeing?" she asked.

"There's a slim line of darkness at the horizon. Could be a storm heading our way."

"What do you propose?"

"If we batten down, that will delay us offloading cargo if you want to fence more of the loot. If we don't, we could be in a mess if it's a bad storm and we have a lot of unskilled hands trying to make everything watertight."

Hava looked at her first mate in silence for a moment, then said, "You know these waters and I don't. Back home I wouldn't have noticed that line of darkness. What's your advice?"

"I'd wait," said the first mate. "If it's darker and closer in an hour, then I'd set the crew to working."

Hava nodded. "Then that's what we'll do. In the meantime Sabien and I will poke around." She took stock of the village near the shore. "This the only port?"

"There are anchorages all over this island, which is why it would be a smuggler's delight, if there were any smuggling to be done. Those sicari, if they're looking for someone to break past the Border, are likely to have a ship or two lying in a cove on the other side of that headland." He pointed.

Hava looked where he was indicating, then said, "Give me a minute."

She took off her boots and sword and, making for the nearest ratline, shimmied up the mizzenmast. Scrambling quickly to the top yard, she reached into her waistcoat pocket, pulled out her spyglass, and surveyed the area.

The small town had deep water on this side, as evidenced by several deep-draft boats moored alongside the quay. A single long pier extended from the northeastern point, and the beach on the other side rolled west, then curved around to form a tidy lagoon, beyond which was the headland George had indicated. If time permitted, she'd climb to that promontory and see if there were ships lurking on the far side of the island.

She regained the deck quickly and crossed to where the gig was being lowered. "This is our last boat," George reminded her. "If we could find one to buy . . . ?"

"I'll keep an eye out," Hava said. She had left the other small boat tied to the dock when escaping the sicari in Cleverly. They had one longboat, which was lashed to the center of the deck, over a main hatchway, but it required six men to row and one to steer, and had enough room for several trunks or smaller crates.

She had thought that she might move to the end of the pier and simply offload cargo there, but if she could find a large enough boat, or even two, ferrying goods to sell here would reduce unwelcome scrutiny of the ship. She was uncertain as to how much of a head start they had, but the sooner they were out of here with the least amount of attention, the better.

As Sabien rowed toward the quay, Hava felt an unexpected pang. She had been feeling near-elation at how well things had gone since her escape and taking over this ship. People had died, but that was something she had seen all her life, and the momentary stab of regret for the loss of people she barely knew had passed quickly. Nor did she mind the sense of duty that came with being in charge; she knew from her years of training that those who had the most authority bore the greatest responsibility, and she'd seen crew bosses severely punished for the failures of those under their command.

She had escaped, and Molly had survived, and while Hatu was missing, and terrible things had occurred at Beran's Hill and in the barony, she had prepared herself to face whatever news might eventually reach her.

Now, however, that near-elation was suddenly chased away by a rising foreboding that this might be her last opportunity to find Hatu. If he wasn't among the slaves who had arrived here, where would she look next? If a fleet of sicari arrived and her command of *Borzon's Black Wake* was revealed, all might be lost. She willed aside her feelings, for long ago she had come to believe that her best choice was always to move forward with confidence. The only thing she could guarantee was failure, so she would proceed as if she wouldn't allow failure to happen.

The town, also called Elsobas, was delightful, thought Hava. A few taverns lined a broad walk beside the quay, and she could see other buildings spreading up a slope leading to the headland she had seen from the ship. She wandered here and there, deflecting a few questions from merchants who wanted to know if she was from the ship that had just put in and what cargo it was carrying, as they anticipated the possibility of getting an early advantage should a profitable trade be in the offing.

It took less than half an hour for Hava to determine that the town seemed to be free of sicari agents, or at least to accept that any who might be lingering were far more adept at hiding than she was at discovering them. She returned to where the gig was tied up and picked up a large white cloth, a piece of material used to repair sails, and waved it back and forth until she saw a response from the ship: another cloth waved. That meant crew would be coming ashore.

"Take the gig back to the ship, Sabien," she instructed. "It will hasten things. I'm going to go look for another small boat."

"Yes, Captain," he said, untying the gig and quickly boarding.

Hava moved away from the busier section of the quay-side, from the brothels, cantinas, and taverns, looking for signs of a boatyard. A street boy was watching her and she smiled. He was either a pickpocket in training or a lookout for a gang of urchins sizing her up.

She walked slowly in his general direction, and at the moment he tensed, anticipating the need to bolt, she stopped. "A question," she said to him.

He looked quickly around to see if anyone else was nearby and assessing his safest avenue of escape. She took a leisurely step in his direction, and his hesitation was his undoing. By the time he had chosen his route, she was on him, grabbing his tunic with her left hand but not drawing her weapon. He raised his arms high above his head, so that he could slip out of his tunic and run, but she put her foot against the wall between his legs, and when he dropped, he landed on her shinbone. She heard the breath go out of him with a *whoof*.

Tossing aside the now-empty tunic, she grabbed him by the throat but didn't squeeze. "No obvious weapons, so you're a lookout. The 'eye'!"

His eyes widened, and he tried to sound fearless as he shouted, "My boys will be here in . . . soon! You'd better run!"

Hava tried hard not to laugh. "I was an eye, a stall, a cutter, and a bag before you were born, boy." She glanced from side to side to see if anyone was watching. "I bet your crew is halfway back to whatever hole you use as a hideout."

The boy's face was a mask of terror, despite his attempt to look brave. He was thin, had dark skin and black hair, yet his jutting lower jaw and willingness to fight reminded her of Hatu. She said, "Give me answers and you won't die."

He seemed unconvinced, but said, "What questions?"

She smiled. He really was very much like Hatu at his age. "I need a small boat. Where would I find such a thing?"

He pointed to her left, farther down the road from the quay. "Faluke. He won't cheat you."

"I doubt he could," she answered. "Now, a more important question. Of whom here should I be wary?"

"I don't understand."

She leaned a bit closer and said, "Reach for that blade you have hidden in your boot, and I'll make you eat it."

He slumped against the wall.

"There are men, and you know the kind of men I mean, who anyone wise would wish to avoid. Are any of that sort in this town today?"

He feigned ignorance. "I don't know."

She leaned even closer and whispered, "Quelli Nascosti."

Only her firm grip on his throat and her leg between his kept him from collapsing to the ground. "Oh, mistress, you will see us all dead."

"Not if I can help it," she said cheerfully. "Are there sicari in Elsobas?"

"None today that I know of," he said.

"What is your name?"

"Surya."

"Stand still," she said, and took her hand away. If he had had any notion of fleeing before, her use of a term in her own language, which was close enough to Azhante to terrify the boy, kept him motionless.

"Surya, are you part of a crew?"

His confusion instantly reassured Hava that he was not a member of some distant crew run by either Coaltachin or the Azhante, but of an independent gang. She suspected he was the "eye" by dint of being the youngest member of his crew.

"Do you have family?"

He shrugged. "Ma died when I was born. Da is a drunk who beat me, so I ran away."

"Here?"

"A couple of islands over, and it took a while to get here."

Hava calculated. "How many are in your gang?"

With unexpected bravado he said, "Many, and they'll be looking for me soon!"

She shook her head, trying not to smile. "Let's try again. How many in your gang?" For emphasis, she reapplied a bit of pressure to his throat.

He gasped. "Six." Tears were forming in his eyes.

She loosened the pressure and asked, "How would you like to make more silver today than you've ever seen in your life?"

His eyes widened. "Truth?"

"Truth." She let go of his neck, and while he craned it in relief, she reached into her belt purse and pulled out a silver coin. His eyes widened at the sight of it. She tossed it into the air and his hand shot out and grabbed it with remarkable speed and accuracy.

Hava gripped his wrist so he couldn't flee with the coin.

Surya struggled slightly but then gave up. Looking at her with eyes still moist from fear, he said, "What do you want?"

"How many deep-water coves or practical anchorages are there on the other side of this island?"

He seemed confused by the question, so she said, "How many places can a big ship anchor on the other side?"

He thought about this, then said, "Four for really big ships, a couple more for smaller ones. The rest of the coast is too rocky."

She let go of his wrist. "I need a smart lad like you, and a few others as smart, to go over to the other side of the island and come back to tell me what you see. Can you do that?"

He tried to resume a casual air. Before he could come up with whatever ridiculous plan he might concoct to gain silver without doing any work, Hava said, "Find your mates. Spy out those deep-water anchorages and meet me . . ." She thought for a moment, then said, "At the cantina at the far end of the island, near the pier. Be there before sundown and you'll get a second silver coin, and your mates will each get two as well."

She could see him calculating: he was as devious as any boy she had ever trained with. Forcing herself to stop being both amused and annoyed by that, she said, "I am looking for something specific. Bring me the best information you can. If there are any ships anchored, I want you to be able to describe them." She poked a warning finger into his chest. "And tell your little gang of thieves I'll know if any of you are lying. I was a better pickpocket than you are before I was half your age." She knew no self-taught street urchin could match those trained in Coaltachin. "And if everything goes as planned, there may even be some gold in it for you."

At the mention of gold, the boy's features became animated. She had him now.

"Surya?"

"Before sundown at the cantina. Yes, we'll be there!"

She reached down, picked up his tunic, and tossed it to him. Then he was off.

When he was out of sight she chuckled. He would have fitted right in at her school, she thought. Might have been friends with Donte, Hatu, and herself at the same age. She stood up and looked around, taking a deep breath. Time to go and look at boats.

By midafternoon Hava had inspected all the vessels that Faluke had in his boatyard. He had been working on a commission, a large fishing smack, aided by two apprentices. The yard was a prosperous-looking enterprise, and Hava extrapolated from this that there must be many communities scattered around these islands that produced enough trade to create a strong economy, making fishermen wealthy enough to commission what appeared to be a very finely crafted vessel.

Faluke also had half a dozen shallow-draft boats and a few smaller rowboats of varying condition, at least four of which might suffice to replace the boats the *Black Wake* had lost. Sabien had returned from his quick trip to the ship and caught up with her while she was inspecting things; he observed while Hava haggled a bit over two rowboats that would be taken back to the ship.

Leaving the yard, Sabien said, "That didn't take long."

"No," agreed Hava. "I paid a bit too much, and he was in a hurry to get back to finishing his commission. That smack is almost ready and probably will fetch him a good living for a few months."

As they rounded a corner, Hava halted for a second, and Sabien walked past her. He turned to see what was happening, then stepped back as Hava took off at a full run. By the time he turned she was already halfway up the quayside. Sabien dashed after her.

As he gained on her, he saw Hava running straight for a man whose back was to her. She lowered her head and threw her shoulder into his back and took him straight to the ground. The man twisted, producing a dagger from some-where on his person and slashing at her.

Hava rolled to her right, deftly avoiding the cut, but was forced back, enabling her opponent to ready himself for her next attack.

Hava had her dagger out and was about to attack from her knees, when Sabien rushed over and kicked the man, aiming for his head but striking his shoulder instead. The man's dagger went flying, and Hava leapt forward, pinning the man to the ground with her forearm, her dagger pointed at his throat.

"Where is my husband?!" she shouted.

From under her arm, Catharian could barely speak. "Kill me and you'll never find him, Hava," he choked out.

"I can find ways to not kill you that will make you wish I had!"

She stood up, and Sabien grabbed Catharian's arm and half yanked, half helped him to his feet. "I dare say you might," said the former false monk.

"Now, are you going to tell me where Hatu is?"

"Certainly," said Catharian. "Telling you where is not the problem. Getting you there is. But first things first."

"What?"

He grinned. "Buy me a drink, as I am currently lacking funds."

DECLAN FINISHED EXPLAINING WHAT BARON DUMARCH was proposing to a company of men, some of whom wore the tabard of Ilcomen, others who were trained mercenar-ies, and some who looked like craftsmen or farmers, but all of whom were young, strong, and willing to fight. Declan lost count of how many men he'd talked to, but at least a hundred were now making their way to Marquenet.

A large wagon carrying men passed and Declan heard

someone call his name. It was a very familiar voice, and he wheeled his horse around as the wagon slowed.

"Ratigan!" he cried, happy to see the face of the pugnacious teamster.

The wiry little man leapt down from the wagon as Declan dismounted. They embraced and, for the first time since the destruction of Beran's Hill, Declan felt a slight stirring inside, like a tiny sigh of relief. "You made it."

"Barely," said Ratigan. "It was a close thing." He looked over and saw other wagons slowing because he was blocking the road. "I'm heading for Marquenet with everyone there."

"Remember that inn where we stayed the first time we rode together, before I settled in Beran's Hill? Half the city is empty, so you should be able to lodge there. I'll come find you," Declan said. "What about Roz?" Rozalee had been his first lover, and now was Ratigan's business partner.

Ratigan shook his head. "I don't know. It was complete madness when Ilcomen was attacked. We grabbed everything worth anything, threw it in a couple of wagons, and headed this way but got separated." He heard people start to yell and said, "We'll catch up when we can. I'd better stop blocking things."

He began to turn away, then turned back. "Oh, a few wagons back! Someone you should see!"

Declan mounted his horse as Ratigan urged his rig forward and the other wagons slowly began to follow him. Declan moved down the line of wagons, glancing into each as he passed. When he came to the fourth wagon back he was shocked to see a familiar face, one he had doubted he'd ever see again. "Edvalt!"

His old master looked up, stared at him, then slowly shook his head with an expression of wonder on his face. "Declan!"

"Wait here." Declan rode quickly to where his three

companions from Bogartis's company stood. He reined in and said, "I'm going back to Marquenet with these wagons. You lads want to go on without me or go back?"

A young fighter named Lassen said, "Back. Word is spreading that there's nothing ahead but more frightened, angry people, and we're nearly out of food." The other two nodded.

Declan said to Lassen, "You take the front wagon." He directed the others to head back a little farther, though it was probably an unnecessary precaution. Whoever had attacked these miserable refugees was undoubtedly miles away.

Trotting back to the wagon Edvalt rode in, he asked, "Mila?"

Edvalt's sunken eyes gazed upon Declan with barely disguised pain. "No."

"You were with your daughter's family—" Declan began.

"All gone," Edvalt interrupted.

Declan took a deep breath and felt his feelings once more curl up inside him, a hard shell of cold indifference quickly surrounding them. Mila was the closest thing to a mother he had known, and he had loved her as a son would.

"You're a soldier now?" asked the master smith.

"I'm a mercenary, riding with a captain named Bogartis."

"I've heard of him. What of your smithy?"

"Destroyed."

"Jusan?"

Declan shook his head. "He was betrothed, and they both died." He paused for a moment and added, "With my wife. On our wedding day."

Edvalt closed his eyes briefly, then said, "Who does he serve, this captain of yours?"

"Daylon Dumarch," answered Declan. "The baron is building an army."

"To what ends?"

"His own family was lost. He has no wife or heir. He is building an army to find who did this monstrous thing and destroy them."

"There's some black humor here, Declan," said the old smith as the wagon bumped along. The other men sitting around listened attentively, but none spoke. "It was by not taking service with the baron that I came to Oncon, and there I was when you were brought to me. The baron wanted me to serve and I refused, but now it looks as if I am going to serve him again."

"Willingly?"

"Eagerly," said Edvalt, his expression turning dark. "If he wants to destroy the people responsible for the loss of all I loved, and he's building an army, that army is going to need weapons." He looked at Declan and said, "Shall we make swords for Baron Daylon Dumarch together, Declan?"

Declan was pretty sure Bogartis would have no objection to this. "Gladly, Edvalt. And we shall make the sharpest, strongest blades any army has ever seen."

"That we will," said Edvalt Tasman. "That we will."

HATU STOOD AT BODAI'S SIDE, ready to take the wheel when the old man grew fatigued, though Hatu was forced to admit he was a lot stronger and tougher than he appeared. Even so, after the fight they were shorthanded, and the waters were still difficult to navigate, so Hatu had been working all the time since. Every man had, catching short naps when he was able to.

"We'll be out of troubled waters in a few minutes," said Bodai. He had answered a few of Hatu's questions since he had regained consciousness. Every man aboard had witnessed Hatu's sudden command of his fire and how he had visited destruction on the Azhante, though not one person had said anything to him, and many now watched him fearfully.

Bodai scanned the horizon. "We're clear of the reefs now," he said. "And should we not see another sail for the rest of this day, or, more properly, should another ship not see us, then we will be on a free leg to the Sanctuary."

"We've not spoken about what happened."

"That is true."

"No one here has spoken of it."

"I suspect it's because no one here has seen anything remotely like it."

Hatu reflected for a moment, then said, "This Firemane power—"

Bodai held up his hand. "None of your ancestors possessed abilities like yours, Sefan."

"Hatushaly."

"If you prefer."

"I do."

"Your two eldest brothers had been trained, as had your father, as your next oldest brother was about to be, when the Betrayal ended all of the Langene line but you." He paused, as if gathering his thoughts. "Elmish, our prior, can tell you so much more when we get to the Sanctuary."

Bodai fell silent again, studying Hatushaly's face as if trying to read something. At last he said, "You will soon begin to understand your true place." He gave out a contented sound, as if a great burden was lifting from him.

Hatu studied him in return and said, "If you're not a true master of Coaltachin, who are you?"

"Me? As I told you, before the happy accident that put me in place of the true Bodai, I was a pedagogue."

Hatu actually laughed. "I always thought you gave the longest answers of all the masters." He paused, then added,

"I meant what sort of a man, because until now I saw you as a master of Coaltachin, a member of the Council, and you did nothing to make me think otherwise. I guess I wish to know how you managed to gull the other masters."

"I was never raised and trained to be an agent like Catharian. I was supposed to stay in the Sanctuary and teach our young, and the Firemane children when they arrived. The opportunity to infiltrate Coaltachin was too tempting, and we had other pedagogues, so I chose to go and pretend to be Bodai." He sighed. "I've been him so long I can hardly remember my true name." Before Hatu could ask, he said, "I was Zander, but Bodai serves me well. Staying improved our oversight of Coaltachin, vital after the Betrayal, when most of us were murdered.

"One false master could know what fifteen lesser agents in the field might discover, and those of Coaltachin are wary of strangers. So I stayed.

"Apparently, I was fated to be your tutor, one way or another," he said with a chuckle. "Ten years you would have tutored under me, and you would have left with . . ." He took a deep breath, clearing his thoughts again. "We've always known there was a power . . ." He shook his head. "Elmish will be able to explain it all." Then he laughed bitterly. "I was supposed to be a teacher, not a master of thugs in a nation not my own. Denbe had retired as a soldier. He was a scholar, a man who read incessantly, who penned comments that other scholars would use to guide their own research. He donned armor for the first time in more than twenty years when we found you." Softy, he added, "He gave his life for you."

Hatu didn't know what to say. He knew all this, yet his life as a student in Coaltachin made self-sacrifice an alien concept. Loyalty was exacted through fear and a fierce desire to rise in power. He had been the odd one out, the different one, and now he understood why, yet he still felt in his bones the things that had been taught to him.

Finally he said, "I just wish . . ."

"What?"

"I wish I was back in Beran's Hill, at my little inn, with Hava."

"I wish Denbe was studying his scrolls and books, and I was teaching your older brother and never had to spend my life among murderers and thieves. We rarely get what we long for. At least Hava was a wise choice."

"Choice? For what?"

"Even as a baby you were difficult." Bodai shook his head as if regretting something. "We had an agent who saved you from Lodavico's murderers. Everyone in your household was put to death. Children were thrown from cliffs onto the rocks below just in case they might have a drop of Firemane blood."

Hatu had heard the tale before but said nothing.

"She spirited you away," Bodai continued, "and found her way into Baron Dumarch's tent, using every skill the Flame Guard had taught her." He laughed humorlessly. "She died trying to make her way back to us, and we received only a short message from her.

"We knew you were with the baron but assumed he'd raise you as one of his own, or give you to some noble family or perhaps some wealthy merchant . . ." Bodai shrugged. "We never would have dreamed in a thousand lifetimes he'd hand you over to the care of the masters of Coaltachin.

"I was supposed to spend a few years as the false Bodai, then fake my death, returning to the Sanctuary and the Flame Guard. But once Facaria took you into his care, my instructions changed. Everything I did besides run my own crews was to keep an eye on you and ensure your safety. Word of your temper and difficulties reached me—"

Hatu interrupted. "Is Facaria one of the Flame Guard?"

"No, but with his attitude toward duty . . . he views a contract as a religious document," Bodai said with a deep chuckle. "If we had planned that it couldn't have turned out better."

"And Hava?"

"Facaria said something to me once when she first came to his attention. He realized there was something rare about her. I arranged to be there when he tested her and sensed at once what you now know as truth. I knew that she also had a special kind of . . . magic, for lack of a better word. The sort of magic we find in people like Sabella, but of a different type from that possessed by the other acolytes.

"If you were this untamed wild force, she was a calming force: she would keep you grounded, stop you from destroying yourself. Perhaps she was put on this world to prevent you from becoming a danger to all of Garn. Without her, you would probably have died years ago, and possibly a great number of people with you. For that reason alone, she may be the most important person on Garn. If we can, we will find a way to bring her to you."

Hatu looked at Bodai and could think of nothing to say.

HAVA TOOK A SIP FROM the cup before her and made a face. "What is that?"

"A local drink made from wine, fruit juice, and water." Catharian gave a slight shrug.

"It's terrible," she said, pushing the cup away from her.

"Having tasted the wine you served in your inn, I think you'd find the local wine without the fruit juice even more disagreeable." Catharian looked over his shoulder at Sabien, who stood behind him, ready to ensure he didn't leave his chair without permission. "Does he have to hover over me like that?"

"Yes. Now, I'm not killing you at the moment because I want to know where my husband is, so let us not linger over discussing what we like to drink, all right?"

"Fine," said Catharian, moving his shoulder a bit to alleviate the massive bruise left by Sabien's boot. "As I tried to explain, I am serving an order that is committed to protecting Hatushaly from harm."

"So you say."

"He's on his way to the safest place on Garn for him to be."

"Again, so you say. Where is that?"

"A place known as the Sanctuary."

"Fitting name, I guess," said Hava. "Where is it?"

"That's the hard part. It's not on any known map, or at least not any I've heard of, for reasons of secrecy." He tapped his head. "I know the way, as do others of my order, but it's a difficult route and I happen to lack a ship."

"I have a ship," said Hava.

"I was curious as to how you got here and found me," admitted Catharian. He glanced around and saw only one big ship in the harbor. "Yours?"

She nodded. "*Borzon's Black Wake*."

Catharian's eyes widened and he almost spat out his mouthful of wine. "The slaver!"

"The same."

"Gods of all ages, girl, do you know what you've done?"

"I have a pretty fair notion."

"That's the Golden Pride's treasure haul."

"Who are the Golden Pride?"

"People none of us wish to meet, ever." He waved his hand quickly. "No, tell me at another time how you stole it. Right now just tell me that other ships of that fleet are not behind you."

"We were the first to leave Port Colos, and we put in for

a day and a bit in Cleverly, then sailed here. We arrived a few hours ago."

Catharian's brow furrowed as he thought. "Then we still may have time."

"For what?"

"To get that ship as far away from here as possible before a fleet filled with Azhante cutthroats arrives and nails us to the walls of these shops as a lesson to any who might annoy them in the future. They will happily kill you, and every person who ever knew you, and even anyone who just saw you on the street once. That's the sort of monsters they are."

"We can leave shortly," said Hava. "I have a ship, and you know the way to this Sanctuary."

Catharian shook his head. "Not in that wallower."

"Why?"

"The way is through reefs and shoals that will rip out that ship's hull three times over. We need something of shallower draft, and far more nimble."

"See anything around like that?"

"Not today, but there should be at least a dozen here in the next day or two, when the other ships from the raid start turning up. Unfortunately, most will be crawling with fighters."

Hava looked at Sabien and said, "Start getting our people back aboard. Looks like we may be leaving sooner than we wished."

"Captain," Sabien said with a nod. He turned and left.

Catharian echoed the title. "Captain? There is a story to tell, isn't there?" He shifted in his chair as if he might stand up.

Hava instantly pointed a dagger at him, motioning for him to stay seated. "*Hun-hu*," she said quietly, and he sat back. "So we need a nimble ship."

"Yes, and a solid crew."

"That I have."

The boy Surya appeared, with three others behind him. Hava glanced up at the sun and reckoned she still had a couple of hours of daylight. "You're early," she said to them. "I thought you said there were six in your crew."

Surya looked away with a sheepish expression. "Four."

"What did you find?"

"There is one ship anchored on the other side of that headland."

"Show us," Hava said, standing up. A single look at Catharian told him she meant he was coming as well.

Hava picked coins from her belt pouch and passed two silver pieces to each of Surya's companions. She put her hand on Surya's shoulder and said, "Lead the way." To the others she said, "Go get some food." The three scruffy-looking lads ran off laughing.

Surya said, "Follow me." He led them through alleyways southwest of the pier, where after a while the town ended and a path up to the headland began. "Sometimes people go up here to look for signs of weather or maybe incoming ships. Most of the time there's no one around."

A third of the way up a smaller path diverged to the north and the boy led Hava and Catharian along it. This path wound its way through shrubs and low trees until they came to a small ridge. Here the boy fell to his stomach and crawled upward until he could look over the edge.

The two adults followed suit until, popping their heads over the ridge, they saw the ship. It was a two-masted vessel, slender compared with the *Black Wake,* but large enough to carry a decent cargo or companies of men.

"Does that look nimble enough, Catharian?" Hava asked.

He gave a chuckle. "More than enough. That's perhaps the most feared Azhante warship. It has at least thirty killers as crew and can outrun almost any vessel in Garn, and if there's one it can't, it can outfight them. See that ballista mounted on the foredeck? The jibs are dropped, the bow-sprit removed, and that ballista mounted and manned in minutes if the crew knows what it's doing, and that crew most certainly does. That, dear Captain, is the *Queen of Storms*."

"I like the name," said Hava with a grin.

"If we leave now," Catharian said, "sail around the south-west tip of the island and stay on the western shore and don't get caught, we could—"

Hava interrupted him. "No. The *Queen of Storms*. I'm going to take her."

Catharian looked appalled. Finally he whispered, as if fearful of being overheard, even though the ship was a mile away, "Take her? When?"

"Tonight." Hava gave Catharian's shoulder a reassuring pat. "We will take that ship tonight and be on our way to the Sanctuary by dawn."

Catharian could find no words.

20

PLANNING AND RESOLUTIONS

———◆———

Hava pulled Catharian back down below the ridge as the boy Surya ran off with her message for Sabien.

"Are you mad?" asked Catharian. "That's the finest ship in the Azhante fleet. They must have put in just after Bodai and Hatushaly left."

She grabbed his collar and yanked him close. "Bodai?" She searched his face. "You've abducted a master of Coaltachin?"

"No," Catharian shot back, "of course not. He's one of us. He's one of the Flame Guard."

Hava was speechless. Not just a master, but a member of the Council? She finally forced herself to speak. "We'll speak of this later."

"If there is a later." Catharian gestured toward the ship. "The *Queen of Storms* is the most dangerous vessel on the seas. When I first saw it, years ago, it had just destroyed a trio of ships trying to sweep past the Border. No matter how often word spreads through the Border Ports, there's always some band of fools who think they're smarter, tougher, or—"

"In other words, stupid men," supplied Hava.

"In a nutshell. Now, how do you propose taking a ship crewed by trained assassins?"

Hava took a moment to organize her thoughts. "These Azhante are not that different from my people."

"More than you know," Catharian interjected.

"Not every sicari in Coaltachin is Quelli Nascosti. We are feared because of our reputation as much as our skills. Rumors as much as results . . . Reputation wins fights as often as strength." She laughed. "As Master Bodai would say.

"Every sailor on a ship of Coaltachin is a fighting man, true, but the Hidden Ones are too valuable to waste on all but the most serious missions. When we took the *Black Wake,* there were no more than two Azhante before we sailed, and after they set sail, only one aboard, whom we killed.

"So," she asked, "how many Quelli Nascosti do you think are on that ship?"

Catharian shook his head. "I can only guess." He considered her question silently, then said, "If their seers sensed that Hatushaly was anywhere nearby, they probably put all the assassins on that ship." He calculated. "There would perhaps be a dozen scattered throughout these islands under normal conditions." He gave an audible sigh, as if realizing that talking Hava out of this madness was a waste of breath. "Six or eight, I should think. But the rest—thirty or forty of them—will all be fighters. So twelve assassins and forty warriors. All Azhante, and the fighters are just as dangerous as the assassins."

"And I have perhaps twice their number of fighters."

"They're not all trained warriors!" Catharian's rising tone was evidence of his disbelief.

"I gave every prisoner their freedom: everyone who remained is there by choice." She looked him in the eye. "They would be slaves or dead if not for me." She paused, then said, "They would die for me." In that moment she knew that was true. Strong feelings started to rise up in her and she pushed them back down, locking away this unimagined combination of pride and responsibility.

Hava crawled back up to watch the ship as the sun lowered in the west.

Catharian moved up next to her. After a few minutes he asked, "What are you watching for?"

"I'm planning" was all she would say.

As THE SUN STARTED TO go down over the island, Catharian asked, "Are you going to stay here all night?"

"No. I think I know how to take that ship now."

Catharian raised his eyebrows. "Good. I don't welcome walking back down that trail in the dark."

"I'll protect you," she said mockingly, slipping below the rim and standing up.

"Can you protect me from a broken ankle?" Catharian shot back as he followed her.

"Watch your step."

He couldn't see her grin as he groaned audibly.

They reached the edge of the village with little difficulty, and when they got back to the cantina they found Sabien waiting for them. "I've got everyone back aboard the ship and the gig is ready to take us back." He cast a questioning look at Catharian.

"Oh, yes," Hava said. "He's coming with us."

The three made their way down to the quayside where the gig waited. Another sailor and Sabien rowed them to the ship, and when they were aboard, Hava asked Catharian, "How far is it to the other end of the island and around to that cove?"

"Quite a distance. The other side of the island has fewer hills, but more inlets and lagoons to walk around."

"By boat?"

"A day, maybe more if the winds aren't favorable. It's why

the pier is at this end and most departures are from this end of the island. To the west is a northwestern tack, then a southwestern leg through the shoals and reefs. To the east, it's a straight run to the northeast to get back to the Twins." He looked at her in the fading light. "What are you thinking?"

"I need to get that longboat"—she pointed at the boat lashed upside down above a forward hatch—"on the other side of the *Queen of Storms* at dawn."

"Too far by three times to row," said Catharian. "But there's a narrowing, between two inlets, about two hours south of the town, a dip in the hills, and you could carry the boat across the island there."

Hava seemed to weigh this option, then said, "That longboat is too big to port for a long distance at any speed. We need . . ." She calculated. ". . . three smaller boats." Her expression brightened. "And I saw three serviceable boats sitting in a yard not too far from here.

"Sabien, I want eight men to come with me to buy some boats and carry them down to the beach." She glanced at the sky, seeing that it was almost sunset and she'd have to hurry to get to the boatyard. "Then get everyone who can fight to shore after dark. Try to do it unseen, down the beach a way." He nodded. "Leave just enough crew aboard to sail the *Black Wake* around the headland."

She saw Molly standing a short distance away and waved her over. "Of the archers you've tutored, who's your best?"

"I've got a couple who aren't bad."

Hava nodded. Turning to Catharian, she said, "I assume none of those sicari are in the town, or they'd already be crawling over the deck looking for a reason why this ship is here and not going where it's supposed to be going."

Catharian nodded. "Everyone on the *Queen of Storms* is probably waiting for someone to try to head out to the west," he said. He didn't mention Hatushaly, but Hava took his meaning. The Azhante had arrived just a day too late to see him leave.

"You're coming with us," she told Catharian. "But I want you to stay with the second company. You will wait until we have control of the deck and swim over to join us. If we have to retreat, I don't want you dead. You're the only one who can get us to the Sanctuary."

Dryly, Catharian said, "If you have to retreat, getting to the Sanctuary is the least of your problems."

She made a face, then shrugged. Turning to the others, she said, "So I've seen the strong points of that ship, and I know something of the men on it, so here's what we'll do . . ."

DECLAN FOUND RATIGAN IN THE nearly empty inn he had suggested. Someone had taken it over, for the floor was covered with fresh straw, and a woman in her middle years stood at the back of the room watching over her customers. Ratigan shook Declan's hand and said, "They have some bread, hard cheese, and a bit of ale."

"That's all right," Declan said, sitting down. "So, tell me what happened."

Ratigan said, "I was on a wagon, getting ready to roll out a cargo from Ilcomen to here, and Roz was watching them load up a second shipment that was heading north, then looping around to here—we were going to meet up in a few days and take a double load of freight back to Ilcomen." He shook his head. "Suddenly we hear there's an attack coming from the west, and the next thing people are running and shouting. Before they could finish loading the second wagon, the workers dropped what they were doing and joined a panicked mob rushing east." His expression was resigned. "I just told Roz to get a shake on and follow me.

"It was pandemonium. I made it through the gateway of our freight yard to the boulevard. Roz followed, but if she got out of the city, I never saw her. The mob between us just got too large for me to drive the mules through and I got swept along with it. Once through the gate, the mob spread out and I started making decent speed. That slowed when the forests became too thick to pass through and people returned to the roadway. I don't know what's become of Roz . . ." His voice trailed away.

Declan nodded and said nothing.

"A day later I ran into people fleeing the other way, from the fighting on the other side of the Covenant, and . . ." He let out a long sigh and got to his feet. "I think I'll have a mug of that ale."

Declan sat back and said, "Make it two."

Ratigan returned a moment later with two full mugs, shaking his head in disbelief. "This had better be the greatest ale ever brewed, given what they're charging."

Declan grunted. "Prices are going to be dear for a while."

Ratigan took a long swallow of ale, making a face that communicated his lack of enthusiasm over its quality. "I've had better."

Declan took a drink and said, "But we've both had worse."

"There is that," said Ratigan, putting the mug down. "Where was I? Yes, I started dumping freight and picking up wounded men. By the third night at the side of the road, Edvalt and others from the Covenant caught up with us. We chatted and I found him a seat in another wagon, as mine was full of wounded. Edvalt won't complain, but his age was catching up with him and he was limping.

"From what he said, there had been raids along the coast to the border of Ithrace. We went on until we saw smoke on the horizon that told us Ilcomen was in flames. East of that? No one knows. So we turned around and headed west again, but it's clear to me as daybreak that we're all being herded toward Marquensas."

That caught Declan's attention. "What makes you say that?"

"From what we were hearing, people behind us were being harried. Not major assaults, but sniping by bowmen, riders coming up from behind ridges, a few people killed, but little loot being taken.

"As soon as the fight that killed the baron's family was over, the attacks stopped and—at least from what I was told—the attackers fled south. I guess they had a ship waiting for them at the coast. Until I ran into you, all I had seen were refugees."

Declan considered Ratigan's words and nodded. "I think I need to ask my captain about this."

"Captain? So, what happened to you?" asked Ratigan.

Declan relayed his loss during the destruction of Beran's Hill, and when he finished, Ratigan said, "I'm so sorry. I really liked Gwen, and Jusan and his girl Millie, too." His expression grew dark. "Now that I'm here, everything is beginning to sink in." When he looked at Declan the smith-turned-mercenary saw there was a sheen in his eyes. "It's not just losing my business . . ." Ratigan took a deep breath. "I've had nothing before, and I can start over. At least my wagon yard and the house are still here.

"I should go there soon. That's where Roz and the others working for us will go if they're still alive . . ." His chuckle was bitter. "I agreed to meet here because I was afraid after I put up the horses, I'd find everything in my home gone." He sighed. "I was right. Anything worth having was looted. Some people." Standing up, he put a hand on Declan's shoulder. "I'm truly sorry for your losses, my friend."

"Thanks," said Declan, also getting to his feet. He drank the last of his ale, though Ratigan had left his unfinished.

"I'll send word, but I think the baron will have tasks for all of us."

"I hope so. I had a little pouch of gems and coins stashed away where the looters didn't find it, but most of what I owned was with Roz in Ilcomen. I don't know if she grabbed anything . . ." The words trailed off.

Declan reached out and squeezed his friend's arm. "I've known her longer than you. If anyone is tough enough to get through this, it's Roz."

Ratigan nodded, though he didn't look convinced.

They left the inn and Declan began to walk back toward the keep, while Ratigan took the other direction toward his freight yard, both men lost in thought.

HAVA SAW THE SKY BEGINNING to lighten in the east and knew sunrise was less than an hour away, as her crew rowed quietly around the coast toward the ridge that sheltered the lagoon where the *Queen of Storms* was anchored. George had shown them how to muffle the rowlocks with rags, since noise traveled well across water, especially on a night like this one, with the weather calm and clear.

It had taken some hours for her crew to carry the three small boats across the island. They had had to stop twice for a short break; when they reached the breakers on the far side, they had rested for an hour. Now the men and women of the raiding crew were both tired and anxious, but ready to fight. Hava was impressed by the determination spending time in the hold of a slave ship had engendered.

For a few minutes she had been torn over where exactly she should place herself. She was probably the best archer in the crew apart from Molly, but she judged that Molly was better able to lead the five other archers she had sent up to the ridge above the lagoon. They would be in place before Hava attacked the ship.

Hava had been clear with Molly as to her plans. She was anxious, but she also trusted Molly to change the plan if the situation warranted it. She had finally decided to lead the boarding party: she was the only one who could understand enough of the Azhante language that she could comprehend orders they might shout out, and she had more training than anyone else in close combat.

Hava motioned for the other boats to hold back and wait while she took her boat to the shore first.

When she'd scouted out the lagoon from above the day before, she'd noticed a small breach in the rocks, just wide enough for her crew to carry the boats through. She used hand signals to ensure they remembered that making any sound would mean their deaths.

Her little crew picked up the boat and carried it silently through the gap. Hava kept her eyes on the *Queen of Storms* and trusted those behind would follow her example, Sabien in the second boat, and Jack, her second mate, in charge of the third. She looked for movement on the ship and saw none, but that didn't mean there was no watch posted. A motionless man in black in the dark could seem invisible when only a few feet away—something she had learned early in her childhood.

Dawn was coming. If all was going to plan, George would have the *Black Wake* under sail and should be coming around the point of the headland just as the sun was about to appear over the horizon, which would give the archers on the ridge above enough light to see the deck of the *Queen of Storms*. With its sails furled, the deck was more exposed, and Molly and the others had a single instruction: *If you see anyone wearing black, shoot him.* No one in Hava's crew wore black.

The other two boats were ready and Hava beckoned them through the gap, then made a motion with her palm down, communicating "Wait."

The minutes dragged by. The crews of the three boats crouched silent and motionless as the sky continued to grow lighter with each passing moment. They all knew their orders: everything depended on surprise.

Now came the riskiest part of the attack.

Hava signaled, and her boat was the first to move out. As quietly as possible, she had her crew row up beneath the port side of the *Queen of Storms,* had the men on the side closest to the ship raise their oars and let the boat drift against it. Makeshift fenders of cloth filled with sand were quickly inserted to keep the sound of wood striking wood to a minimum.

Hava looked behind and saw Sabien's boat nestle in and Jack's boat behind him. She needed to give no order for silence, for everyone with her was holding their breath. She listened.

This was the most maddening part of her plan, for she could see nothing above on the deck. The sky overhead was getting lighter, but all she could see was the rigging and black spars against the greying sky. Two men held ropes equipped with grapples. Hava slipped a short bow over her shoulder that wouldn't trip her up, then a quiver with a tie to hold the arrows in place. She had a short blade on one hip, a dagger on the other, and another blade in each boot top. She tried to stay alert without being overly tense. Childhood training once more came to the fore, ensuring that when she had to move she wouldn't uncoil like an overtightened spring. She forced her breathing to slow.

More minutes slowly passed, and then Hava heard a shout from above. She held up her hand, indicating that her raiders needed to wait. In her mind she imagined what was happening: whoever was on watch above them had seen *Borzon's Black Wake* turning hard into the lagoon as its sails were reefed. She hoped the bigger ship would lose enough speed so that if it actually struck the *Queen of Storms* minimal damage would be done to both ships. George's only job was to distract and block the *Queen of Storms,* keeping it at anchor. Under way, the smaller vessel might be the most dangerous ship on the water, but stuck in an anchorage, it was just a floating trap.

A few other voices could be heard above now. She imagined men hurrying around up on deck, taking up their defensive positions.

Suddenly she heard the *thunk* of an arrow striking and the sound of a man hitting the deck. Molly was adhering perfectly to the strict orders Hava had given her. As soon as *Borzon's Black Wake* appeared, alerting those on the *Queen,* anyone wearing black was a target. The arrows started raining down, and she heard a man scream and more arrows hitting the wooden deck, bouncing off harder surfaces struck at an angle, and she waited for another moment.

She knew the Azhante would be briefly disoriented by the sight of the ship appearing at their bow and a sudden assault by archers from above and aft. She also knew that as more Azhante came up from below, things could quickly get out of hand.

"Now!" she shouted, and her crew threw the ropes with grappling hooks up over the side of the *Queen of Storms.* Hava leapt and grabbed a rope, yanking hard to make sure it was secure, then shimmied up it as fast as a spider.

Reaching the top of the rope, she vaulted over onto the deck, landing lightly on her feet. As she crouched she unshouldered her bow, pulled the restraining cord off the arrows, and had one nocked in seconds.

She studied the deck. Three bodies lay with arrows in them, while another half dozen arrows protruded from various parts of the ship. Two black-clad Azhante had taken cover, one crouching behind a mast, the other lying behind the main hatchway covering. Neither saw her: their attention was trained upon those on the ridge above who were shooting down at them.

She knelt and quickly loosed two shafts, the first taking down the crouching man and the second, the one behind the hatch. She stood up slowly, glancing in all directions.

An Azhante fighter came up from below, half dressed, holding a sword, and Hava had an arrow in his chest before he could take in what was going on. Two more tried to rush out only to be shot, one through the neck, and the other in the shoulder, and he was taken down by Hava's crew. A shout came from below that Hava barely understood, but she took it to mean a warning to those still down in the lower deck that there were enemies on the main deck.

Hava motioned for her crew to station themselves on either side of the entrance to the companionway and said, "Kill anything that tries to come out."

She used her bow to indicate a rear companionway that needed to be guarded and stationed men at both hatches: the smaller one before the mainmast and the main hatch aft of it. Both were closed but not battened, so it might be possible for those below to quickly push one open and try to swarm out. She positioned men at the fore companionway, but even her limited experience suggested that provided easy access to the rope and chain locker, perhaps to the fore portion of the hold, so she expected any rush topside would be from the rear companionway.

Within a minute all was eerily silent. Hava hurried up the short ladder to the foredeck, where she could get a better view.

Borzon's Black Wake sat mere yards away, slowly rocking with the gentle waves in the lagoon, and she saw George at the helm. She waved once, then pointed past him. George was to take the massive ship out of this lagoon under reduced sail, to anchor just off the point.

George waved back, indicating that he understood.

Hava turned to survey the deck, counting eight dead Azhante. A quick scan of the yards showed none of the enemy in the rigging, which meant that the rest of the crew was still below; no doubt they were planning a way to get up on deck and kill everyone.

Catharian and the second contingent of Hava's forces started climbing up onto the Azhante vessel, dripping wet but looking determined. Hava quickly sent them to support those already waiting for the Azhante to come up from the four exit points.

Catharian came to Hava's side. "No fighting?"

"No," she said quietly. "They lost eight trying to get up here and were smart enough to pull back."

"Smart," said the agent of the Flame Guard. "They took the same advantage as you. You pick them off if they come up; they pick us off if we try to come down the ladders."

"How long do they think they can hold out down there?" she wondered aloud.

Catharian laughed, a short bark. "They've got enough food and water below for a four-month voyage with a full crew. There are perhaps as many as another hundred Azhante and a few thousand allied fighters due to start showing up when the fleet arrives . . ." He glanced at the brightening sky behind the ridge to the southeast. "Today, perhaps?" He nodded once to Hava. "No later than tomorrow."

Hava said nothing but pushed past him and went to the stern. She waved her bow above her head, the signal for Molly and the other archers to descend the hill as best they could and get to the boat.

Returning to Catharian, she said, "Then I guess we need

to end this as quickly as possible and be gone before that army arrives."

"What do you have in mind?"

"I don't know, but give me a minute."

Laughing dryly, Catharian said, "Take all the time you need."

DECLAN HELPED LIFT A WALL stone to the two men on the step above, then turned to take another being passed along by a line of workers. At the other end of the line stood a massive dray that had been pulled by a team of ten mules, bringing stones down the hill across farmland from an abandoned quarry a day's ride away.

The baron had quickly brought order to the city and surrounding countryside by a simple edict: everyone works. No matter what skills or lack thereof people had, they would find something for every able-bodied person to do. Even the elderly gleaned in the fields, the woods, and through the abandoned villages, and children were sent to run errands or set to watching the infants as their parents worked.

Food was being made available, as stores in the castle were distributed and hunters were sent out to find game. Sheep, goats, and donkeys were rounded up and organized into flocks on abandoned farms and fields near the city. Small herds of cattle were now guarded in meadows and pastures nearby, and fishermen were again working out of the coastal villages.

During the first couple of days after their return, the baron had waited for an attack that never came. His lookouts along the coast had reported ships sailing from the north, passing by vessels still anchored offshore. When there was no further visible activity, scouts were dispatched and discovered that the ships at anchor had been abandoned, put there apparently to keep the baron and his troops buttoned up inside the city. Daylon Dumarch had them towed to the largest harbor in Marquensas, ordered dredging to begin as soon as feasible, and declared that he would begin building a fleet. The abandoned ships would be refitted and returned to full service as fast as possible.

Declan placed another big stone in his new wall with the help of Tarr, another of Bogartis's company, and had just turned to receive the next one when Sixto appeared and shouted an order for them to fall out. As they did so, two other workers stepped in to take their place.

Sixto said to Declan and Tarr, "The captain wants us all."

Declan grabbed the shirt he had left on a post, because the work was hot, and donned it while following the other two men. The area around the castle was a vortex of activity, for the baron had commanded everything be done without regard to the time or costs involved. He was paying a good wage to people he could simply have commanded to work for nothing but food, but instead he was providing enough that people might rebuild their lives once the current crisis had passed.

If it ever is going to pass, thought Declan as they reached the keep.

Edvalt Tasman stood next to Bogartis, and Declan saw the rest of his company gathering. When all were present, Bogartis said, "For those who don't know this man, his name is Edvalt, and he is, by reputation, the finest weapons smith of our time. The baron has ordered him to forge swords for the new army he is gathering." He turned and looked at the old smith.

Edvalt said, "There is a means of making steel few know, but I know it, and I taught Declan. We are going to break a time-honored practice of keeping the means of fashioning jewel steel secret, because we need the finest weapons that can be fashioned by the hand of a man, so that when we find the home of those murderous dogs who've raped and butchered people we love, and pillaged and destroyed our homes, we will have superior arms and armor." He glanced at Declan, who simply nodded once in agreement.

Bogartis said, "The refitting of one of the abandoned ships will be completed in a few days. Once it's ready, we will sail it to . . ." He looked at Edvalt.

"South Tembria. Past the range of the Border Tribes, to Abala, on the edge of the Burning Lands."

"Why there, Captain?" asked one of the mercenaries.

"Because that's where we've been told to go," said Bogartis. "I'll tell you what you need to know when you need to know it. Now get back to your tasks. I'll send word when the ship is ready and a crew is aboard."

Declan lingered, and Edvalt said, "You have no problem, then, with betraying the secret?"

Declan's laugh was bitter. "None of these lads knows the first thing about a forge, Edvalt. Our secret's safe with them."

"We will be training other smiths."

"I don't really care." Declan gave a dismissive wave of his hand. "I don't care about gaining wealth by making jewel-steel blades for nobles who don't know how to use them anyway. I just want to find those who killed our loved ones and see them dead. If better weapons will do it, I have no problem."

"I feel the same." Edvalt put his hand on Declan's shoulder. "We've both lost everything, except each other, and for a time, that will have to be enough."

Declan's expression was unreadable. He just nodded, turned, and started back toward the wall he had been rebuilding. As he walked down the slope from the castle he could see other fortifications being constructed at an equally furious rate farther off in the city, in places where no defensive positions had existed in an age. He knew that Baron Dumarch had sent companies to Beran's Hill to begin construction of a fortification there and another to Port Colos, which he was claiming and would be rebuilt as a port for his navy and no longer a haven for traders and smugglers.

Declan had no way of judging, but he suspected that should the baron finish all the tasks he had ordered, Marquensas would arise not as another barony, but as a new kingdom as powerful as any in the history of North Tembria.

HAVA AND HER CREW WAITED on the main deck, but after half an hour there had still been no attempt by those below to break out onto the deck. Finally she looked at Catharian and Sabien and said, "We've got to tempt them out. If we try to breach that hatch or go down either of the companionways, we will be slaughtered."

"So what are you thinking?" asked Catharian.

"Have you ever had to smoke out an animal?" She looked at both men.

"Once," replied Sabien. "When I was a boy, we found a badger holed up in an underground den between blocks of stone we needed to use." He thought for a moment, then said, "I don't think it was my da—I was pretty young—but another man who did the smoking out."

Catharian was nodding, looking interested. "Say on."

"Badgers can be vicious, and I remember my da saying it was best to steer clear of them, but we had to get that animal out of there. So they lit a fire, found some rags, soaked them in . . . oil, maybe? Then we used some boards and built this . . . sort of tunnel, so the badger only had one way he could run. Got the rags smoldering so that they gave off this awful stench, picked them up with a long pole, and stuck the pole into where the badger was. We all stayed out of the way and that animal came racing out through the wooden tunnel and ran straight up the hill, back into the woods."

Hava nodded. "I saw a skunk under a house sent off that way." She looked around. "So we need to smoke them out."

"And how do we do that?" Catharian asked with a wry smile. "By burning the ship?"

Hava grinned. "No. I like this ship. I'm going to keep it." To Sabien she said, "Take one of those boats over to the *Black Wake.*"

The other ship was now anchored just off the strip of land that divided the lagoon from the sea to the northwest of where they sat. "Get down below and find what you can—clothing for rags, poles, oil or anything that will make enough smoke to get those Azhante to come up or to pass out from it, I don't care which."

"Suffocating them down below would be my preference," said Catharian.

"I have no doubt," replied Hava.

Sabien hurried off, and Hava looked around to make sure every man was paying attention to his task. She noticed a young man near the wheel on the quarterdeck was watching her and the others rather than looking aft and waved to him to turn around. As he did so, an Azhante fighter vaulted over the stern rail, kicking him with both feet he came down. The young crewman slid past the wheel and was momentarily stunned.

Hava had an arrow nocked in her bow and was already drawing when the Azhante fighter was struck from behind and propelled forward, falling on top of the young man he had disabled. Protruding from his back was a hunter's shaft, and Hava said in relieved tones, "Molly!"

She indicated that everyone should stay where they were, but Catharian and two other men hurried to the stern, where they found the youngster wriggling out from underneath the Azhante's corpse.

Hava and Catharian looked over the stern railing and saw a large hinged window being quickly shuttered as several arrows now protruded out of the ship's stern.

"It seems our friends are more impatient than we had anticipated," said Catharian.

Hava looked out to the beach and saw Molly and the other archers standing at the shoreline. "That was a shot of damn near a quarter of a mile." She shook her head in admiration. "You have to love Molly Bowman."

"Well," said Catharian, "if they're eager to come up and fight, she'll keep them inside, and there aren't any other windows big enough for them to climb through." He looked around. "I'm thinking the next best choice for them would be that main hatchway."

He and Hava climbed down the short ladder to the main deck. "It's big enough that if they can move it quickly, they can swarm up out of it."

"I wish we knew how many were still down there."

"As do I." He quickly counted and said, "I make it nine dead, so that cuts it down at least."

"What's your guess?"

"The smallest crew on this ship would be around thirty, ten on a watch, or more in bad weather." He calculated silently and said, "But as a raider, it's probably got fifty or so."

"So we may still face a good forty very dangerous men."

Catharian nodded.

Hava counted quickly and realized she had almost ninety able-bodied men and women on the deck, though more than half were inexperienced fighters. In low tones to Catharian alone she said, "We have the numbers, but a lot of these people will die if we have a stand-up fight."

The false monk nodded and whispered back, "Let us hope your lad returns with something that can gain us an advantage."

Hava could only nod.

HATU TOOK A TURN AT the helm, simply to break up the monotony. The crew on board this ship was perhaps the most efficient he had seen and was well able to deal with the losses resulting from the encounter with the Azhante. He could tell that to a man they mourned the loss of their fellow Flame Guards, especially Denbe. Hatu had thought of him only as an old warrior, but after speaking with a few of the crew he had begun to understand more about what Bodai had meant by Denbe having been a scholar. Several of this crew had studied under him. They also seemed, if not afraid of Hatu's sudden powers, respectful enough to keep their distance. Their reluctance even to chat with him contributed to his boredom.

The tedium he endured caused his thoughts to turn inward, to a darker place than he wished. He was worried about Hava, and he hoped that the others at Beran's Hill had survived that attack. Having been spirited away at the height of the battle with no one to tell him the final outcome had caused him a low-level but constant worry. But since Hava had been with the baron's garrison coming from the city, the entire barony would have had to be gutted for her to be at risk. He smiled as he thought of her waiting at the inn for him to turn up. He was determined that once he reached the Sanctuary, he'd insist to Bodai that word be sent to her, and perhaps even arrangements could be made for her to join him.

He was now more than a little curious to see this Sanctuary, just as he was growing more curious about his upcoming training. He was still unsure as to how he felt about the explosion of power he had unleashed when pressed to fight for his and the others' survival. He experienced equal measures of excitement at the thought of taking control of that power and fear at what such use of power might cost him: what he might gain was offset by what he might lose. He realized that one lesson he had learned from Bodai as far back as he could remember rang true: do not obsess over that which you cannot control. If it was his power, he would learn to control it.

21

TRIUMPH AND ESCAPE

H ava kept a careful view of any possible point of exit by the remaining Azhante. Sabien and his crew had been gone for the better part of an hour, and the Azhante below seemed content to play the waiting game. At one point, a few minutes after Sabien had left, the main hatchway had lifted slightly, raised by poles Hava suspected, just enough for someone to peer out, to check out the disposition of her force. A quick arrow through the gap caused the hatch to drop loudly, and although no scream of pain ensued, Hava was pretty sure she had scared the Azhante trying to look out half to death.

The mood was tense. Hava spent much of her time cautioning everyone to stay steady. Those with previous combat experience she knew understood her warning and were reassured by her calm command of the situation. She might still be a youngster compared to many, but she had been through more blood and pain than most of them combined. It was the ones who had never fought before whom she worried about. They might flail around, harming themselves or their comrades, or fall apart completely, dive over the side, or simply cower until an Azhante blade ended their lives.

Movement on the other side of the ship told her that Sabien had returned and a rope ladder was lowered. Items were handed up, and soon the large mason was standing before her, beckoning to the other men who had traveled with him to bring over their cargo. "We found something," he said.

"What?" she asked as a bundle the size of three large hams, or a small side of beef, was set before her. The package was covered in a large sheet of heavily waxed canvas and tied with several lengths of cord. Despite this, she caught a whiff of what could only be called an outhouse odor.

Other men unrolled a bundle of fine daggers and Sabien said, "Not everyone here is armed for close fighting."

She nodded her approval. "Good." To another man she said, "Pass these out to anyone who doesn't have a knife or dagger." She surveyed the deck quickly to make sure everyone was attending to their duties. When she locked eyes with a few gawkers, they quickly got back to their task of keeping watch against an attack.

"But here's the best thing," said Sabien. He called to a short, barrel-chested, balding man nearby. "Henri!"

The man's face showed deep lines, and his hair was so grey that Hava judged him old enough to be her father. But she saw something in his manner and bearing to count him likely to put up a good fight if it came to that.

Henri knelt down and cut the ties around the large bundle. As soon as the wax-treated cloth fell away, such a stench rose from it that Hava took half a step back and felt her eyes begin to water. "Gods, what is that? It reeks."

Henri grinned. "I was trained as an apothecary, a chemist, and later became a perfumer. Believe it or not, this is ambergris, a very valuable product in making extravagantly expensive perfumes."

"Perfume?" said Hava. "It smells like shit."

Henri laughed. "Because it is—or vomit, depending on which end of the whale it comes out of."

"Whales?"

"It originates in the stomach of whales, and it is exceedingly rare and valuable."

"Why, for the sake of reason?"

"It is a perfumer's secret," he began, and one dark look from Hava had him instantly adding, "but I will tell you, Captain.

"It is found on the shore, or sometimes in the shallows or in the gut of the sperm whale when it's been harvested, and yes, it does stink to high heaven. But as it ages it becomes less pungent and eventually has a very faint aroma. The secret few know is that when you mix it with alcohol and, say, lilac, or any other sweet essence, it causes that scent to linger." He smiled like a child explaining to an adult something he had just discovered. "The rarest and most valued perfumes sold to nobles and wealthy ladies contains a drop of that mixture in each bottle, so that the fragrance doesn't fade. That way a bottle of perfume will last a very long time. I sold my scents to merchants all over Tembria and to the islands beyond."

For an instant, Hava wondered if his little vials and bottles might have ended up with the Powdered Women and Mistress Mulray. She might even have used some herself during that period of her training. She pushed the thought away and returned her attention to Henri.

"This," he was saying, pointing at the stinking lump of gold-tinged spew, "is enough ambergris to last a master perfumer a lifetime and keep his children in comfort for their entire lives! When I used to buy it from traders, I would buy a lump half the size of my fist. I could save for years and not be able to own half that much." His thumb and forefinger framed a small gap. "A drop is all you need to make a large vial." He stood back with a look of amazement on his face. "That small bit I would buy cost a bag of gold. This is worth thousands of times more." He looked at Hava with regret etched in his features. "And now we're going to burn it?"

Hava gave him a tight smile. "So it smells bad," she said. "How does that help us?"

Henri motioned for another man to bring over a large jug. "This is lamp oil. If we knead the oil into the ambergris, it will burn like fury, but without flames. It will smolder, and the fumes will sicken those who do not flee. If they are foolish enough to linger it will cause them to pass out. If they pass out and no one moves them, they will suffocate."

Hava smiled with satisfaction. "How long will it take to prepare this concoction?"

"Only a few minutes, Captain."

"Do it!"

She turned to Sabien. "How do things stand on the *Black Wake*?"

"Everything is well in hand, Captain. George awaits your orders and the crew is ready to go where you wish."

She turned to Catharian. "Is there somewhere not too distant where we can leave that floating treasure trove and have a decent chance the Azhante don't find it until we return to strip more booty from it?"

Catharian paused, thinking. Slowly he smiled. "I know just the place. It's a small island about fifty miles northwest of us, which puts it just outside the normal course of travel by ships going west and absolutely on the wrong side of the Border for ships heading to the Twins." He narrowed his gaze. "Leaving it abandoned or with guards?"

"Why?"

"With guards you'll need provisions, and there's not much there—some breadfruit and coconuts, and of course fish if that's what you wish to do all day, but nothing else for food, no wild pigs, no goats. Just monkeys, and the word is the flesh of those monkeys is tainted."

Hava calculated. "And if we abandon it there?"

"If we dress the ship with enough netting and hang palm fronds and other plants in the weave, I'm almost certain no ship would pass close enough to notice."

"Almost?"

Catharian chuckled. "What in life is certain?"

She nodded.

When Henri had finished creating the concoction, he looked around and said, "I need a large piece of metal, a shield perhaps?"

"There's one up on the quarterdeck," said Hava. She motioned for a crewman to fetch it.

"Interesting," said Catharian.

"What's interesting?" asked Hava.

"That's the royal crest of Ithrace," Catharian said, indicating a design on the shield of a small crown above the stylized red flame on a silver background. "That was carried by Hatushaly's father when he was betrayed."

Hava shrugged. Hatu seemed to have had very little interest in his true family's history, and if Hatu wasn't interested in it, why should she be? "So?"

"It's interesting because it means that booty from the Betrayal made its way through the Narrows all the way here."

"Why would a royal shield of Ithrace be on an Azhante ship?"

"I can speculate, but that's all it would be. Still, it's a very interesting question."

Henri flipped the shield over, revealing the plain metal side. He placed the large ball of oil and ambergris on it and said, "Once we light this, I'll need that hatch cover lifted for just a moment."

Hava nodded. She knew the warriors below would be prepared against an attack from above, so she expected arrows to come speeding out of the hold once the cover was lifted. "Get six oars!" she said to Sabien, who hurried to a longboat and got men to move it so they could pull the oars out from under it.

"We only have four," he said.

"That will have to do unless we have some pole arms around?" She saw none and said, "Four it will be."

The handle on the hatch cover consisted of rope threaded through holes, so that the deck crew could simply reach down and pick it up. The Azhante would assume that was how it was being moved if she tried to come down that way, so any man close to the edge of the hold invited an arrow. She pointed at the two closest corners and said, "There and there. Lever up the cover, and the moment the smokeball is through, drop it!"

She was still for a moment, then motioned over two of her crewmen and said softly, even though it was unlikely that anyone below could hear her. "Move to the other side, and when I signal, grab the ropes and move it up a little bit as if you were beginning to lift it on that side."

They hurried to their indicated positions. Even if the Azhante looked in that direction for only a second, it just might mean the difference between getting the smokeball into the hole or not.

Sabien had gotten hold of a brand, which he and another man now set ablaze with flint and steel, and when it was burning fully, he looked to Henri. Henri judged the position of the shield, then nodded at Hava.

She pointed to the two crewmen on the other side of the hatch, who leaned over and started pushing on the hatch cover, as if trying to lift it. She counted to three silently, then signaled Sabien, who set the torch to the ball of oiled ambergris. It quickly caught alight, but rather than bursting into flames it showed embers on the surface and produced a prodigious cloud of smoke. Even on the open deck, the reek was causing eyes to water. She signaled the men on the oars and they leaned on the oar handles. The hatch cover lifted. When the aperture was just wide enough, Henri tilted the shield and the ball rolled through. Hava didn't need to tell the men on the oars to drop the hatch: two Azhante arrows came shooting out, barely missing them, and they quickly fell away, the hatch falling back into place loudly.

Hava stood with her hand on the hilt of her sword, waiting.

A few seconds later she could hear the muffled sounds of alarm from below. Catharian moved close to her. "Good thing that ball didn't land on a barrel of lamp oil."

Hava's eyes widened slightly, welling with tears from the smoke. "I hadn't thought of that."

"They're usually stowed in the fore part of the hold, secured to the wall, so any shifting cargo won't break loose and crush them."

"Good to know," she whispered.

"What now?"

"We wait."

BALVEN LOOKED AT DONTE, WHO was sitting on the bed of the former officer's room in the barracks, where he was under guard. "What shall we do with you?"

Donte shrugged. "Things have seemed very busy around here since we arrived, sir. I could work."

Balven smiled. "I know where you're from. Should I trust you?"

"Probably not," answered Donte with a grin. "But I have nowhere to go, it seems. From what I hear, the last place Hatu and Hava were seen has been burned to the ground, and I wouldn't begin to know where to look for them.

"Besides," he added, craning his neck a bit, "I'm bored, and I have this odd notion that someday they'll return to Beran's Hill or maybe even here."

"Based on what?"

"Nothing, really. Just a feeling, sir."

"Like the feeling that you're supposed to kill Hatu?"

Donte spread his hands slightly. "It's a puzzler, for certain. He's my best friend, yet . . . it's like a whisper. I ignore it most of the time, but every once in a while, just as I'm falling asleep, waking up, or just sitting here, I can almost hear it.

"It's one of the reasons I'd like to do something. I don't mind the free food, scant as it may be, and this bed is comfortable compared to just about anywhere else I've slept, but just sitting here is wearing a bit thin."

"Very well," said Balven. "We'll find some work for you. Do you have any particular skills?"

"Like most boys from my home island I've been apprenticed to a fair number of trades. A little smithing, carpentry, a bit of masonry. I'm a fair hand with horses and dogs, and I can work in the kitchen."

"Come along then," said the baron's closest adviser. "I think I know a good place for you to start. We're losing some men working on the walls, and if you know a bit of masonry, that will come in handy."

Donte followed Balven out of the barracks and down to where the new outer wall was being erected. Donte saw a company of mercenaries, a few of whom looked familiar from his short time in Beran's Hill, riding past.

"My brother is sending them on a mission, and until today they were building this wall. I sent a few more to replace them, but I could use more workers." He waved over the foreman and said, "Take this strong lad and put him to work."

"Yes, m'lord," the foreman replied as Balven departed. He looked Donte over and said, "What do you know about stone?"

Donte smiled. "It hurts a lot when you drop it on your toes."

The foreman chuckled. "That it does. What else?"

"I can cut from the quarry if someone shows me where, and I can trim to fit."

"Trimming to fit it is then," said the foreman. "I have lads who can only lift heavy stones and put them where I want, but trimming stone to fit well, that's useful."

As they neared a makeshift pavilion with a planning table set up inside it, Donte looked past it and saw a familiar figure on top of a completed portion of the wall. It was the soldier named Deakin who'd tried to garrote him. He grinned.

"What's making you so happy?" the foreman asked.

"I've been cooped up. This is going to be fun."

"Strange idea of fun," said the foreman, handing him a large, flat-bladed stone chisel and a heavy wooden mallet.

"You have no idea," Donte said softly, his eyes fixed on Deakin.

"THE SANCTUARY," SAID BODAI.

"Where?" asked Hatu.

"Behind that wall of clouds. We're about to pass through another string of shoals and reefs scattered among tiny islands, some no bigger than this quarterdeck."

Hatu stood mute, astonished by what appeared to be a solid wall of grey stretching from one side of the horizon to the other. As they neared, he felt the humidity in the air rising and the temperature falling from very warm to cool.

"The coming together of currents, cold and warm, and the specks of land that stretch for literally a thousand miles or more create this mist. Many ships were lost on those reefs, I suspect, before a way through them was found."

They entered the mist and quickly all visibility fell away.

"There was a time," said Bodai, "when I would have had someone on the bow tossing out a line and calling out the depth. But over the years I've learned there's only one turn we must make." He stopped speaking, and then Hatu saw him moving his lips in a silent count. This went on for almost a minute, then suddenly Bodai called out, "Hard aport!" and moved the wheel quickly, counting again before centering the helm once more. "There," he said to Hatushaly. "Now it's straight through to . . . well, you'll see." He shook his head slightly with a satisfied expression. "You could lash the wheel and, if the wind didn't change, head straight to the Sanctuary on this bearing."

Hatu nodded. The ship was now engulfed in mist that was almost as thick as fog, but there was a light breeze. Still, the ship seemed to be moving faster than it should. "Are we in a current?" he asked.

"Yes," said Bodai. "It's probably what carved this channel through the reefs and shoals. Wait."

"Wait for what?"

"A few minutes more."

Hatu waited curiously, wondering what was coming next. As time began to drag, the entire seascape brightened abruptly and it was as if they had stepped out of a dark room into vivid daylight. "Amazing!" Hatu said in hushed tones.

"Isn't it? Once in a while, when the wind is blowing almost due south, the mist lifts through the islands, but I would guess that on ninety out of every hundred days the barrier of mist remains. Over the centuries, most ships have just come to avoid it. There's little on this course for any to seek out but those who serve the Flame Guard. Now, see that speck on the horizon?"

Hatu squinted, peering between sheets and sails over the bow, and saw a tiny smudge of darkness on the horizon. "Yes," he answered.

"Watch it."

Hatu glanced at Bodai, then moved down from the quarterdeck, across the main deck, and up the ladder to the forecastle, where he stood to the right of the bowsprit. He watched the smudge on the horizon grow larger. Soon it was clearly an island or the tip of a peninsula. He became mesmerized by the emerging image, as details began to resolve themselves, and after less than five minutes he could see distant columns and larger structures behind them.

As they approached, a vista of former grandeur began to reveal itself. The columns he had seen were cracked and broken, surrounded by fallen stones. He had been apprenticed to stonecutters long enough to recognize that a massive outer ring of columns had once risen high on both sides of what he could now see was a harbor, with an enormous edifice rising behind: colonnades of arches that must once have been splendid but had now fallen into neglect and ruin. What must this place have looked like before whatever destruction had visited it? It must have been breathtaking, Hatu thought.

Bodai came to stand at his side and said, "Once the majesty of this place shone like a brilliant flame to rival the sun."

"I can imagine," said Hatu quietly. "What happened?"

"Well, we left. The Flame Guard is an ancient order, one of the oldest in the history of Garn, but our mission evolved over a long time. Some of your training will explain the history of our order and the protective role we have played.

"When the Firemane line rose in Ithrace, we began to send more of our people there. You'll be taught more in due course, but for now let me just say it became vital for us to be there. The Firemane succession was far more important than simply that of a line of kings and their families; it was the holder of one of the elemental powers of this world.

"After years passed, only a few remained here to train people like Sabella and Denbe and to care for our archives and library. There were never a large number in our order to begin with; at our height we had perhaps two thousand spread across the whole world. At the time of the Betrayal there were only six hundred, and most died in the sacking of Ithrace, including your family's slaughter at Betrayer's Field.

"A hundred or so years ago an earthquake caused most of the visible damage, and we lacked the resources in both workers and wealth to carry out the necessary repairs." He took a deep breath as they approached the island, and Hatu saw that a single dock that looked a bit makeshift was their destination. A small ship was anchored a short distance away, making room for their vessel.

"You mentioned Sabella. I haven't seen her."

"She left before we did, after I had you brought aboard this ship. She arrived on that ship over there, to bring word to the prior that you're coming. She also brought those three lads Catharian rescued."

"Really?"

"Again, as you study, you'll understand why we need to repopulate this place." Bodai waved his hand in a sweeping motion at the massive ruins ahead.

A small group of men on the dock made ready to catch lines and make the ship fast. Hatu glanced over his shoulder and upward to see the expert crew furling the sails. "Well, if you need orphans, the world's full of them," he said. "Especially after the slaughter at Beran's Hill."

"I wonder. Rumors were flying around Elsobas that something much bigger than a raid on one town in Marquensas was under way. People from other islands sending word . . ." Bodai shrugged. "Rumors are always flying around the Border Ports. That's why Catharian is going to return to Marquensas on the first available ship."

As they settled in next to the dock, snug against the fenders, and the mooring lines were secured, Bodai said, "Who knows? He may very well be on his way there now."

Catharian said, "They've been quiet for a bit."

Henri looked at Hava. "They're either puking their guts out or unconscious."

She appeared dubious. "I know the sort of men they are better than most. If there was any way they could avoid that, they will have devised it." She let her gaze sweep over all the men around her. "We go in hard and fast. Any man who has never fought before stays back. I don't want you accidentally sticking a blade into one of our own, or yourself for that matter. Your duty is to kill anyone trying to climb out of that hold dressed in black. Understood?"

Several of the men and women nodded, but no one spoke. She could smell the fear of people who had been ripped from their homes and seen mothers, fathers, children, sisters, and brothers killed before their eyes, then endured captivity and worse. Still, each seemed willing to face that fear, and for that she was thankful.

She pointed to those who seemed best prepared and motioned them to step to the fore. "First in," she said. Then she motioned with her hand to those not selected and said, "Second in. Wait and then come in ready! Let's do this thing!" she declared, hoping her own fear wasn't evident.

Four men lined up on the fore and aft sides of the hatch cover. Hava indicated that they would need to lift and move the hatch cover to the starboard side of the deck in a single swift motion. Two men were ready with heavy gloves, and Hava picked up a piece of a cut-up shirt and tied it over her nose and mouth. Others followed her example. When the cover was moved, no arrows shot out, and all was quiet. She nodded to one of the two men and jumped over the edge and down into the hold, hoping she didn't land on anything that would trip her or, worse, break her bones. As Master Kugal had said several times to her, Hatu, and his grandson Donte, "Sometimes you just have to leap into something on faith." Or as Master Bodai had said once, "I'd rather be lucky than good."

She struck the deck below with her knees slightly bent and her legs took the shock easily. She'd jumped from greater heights. The smoke that filled the hole was blinding, and now it began to blow up from the open hatch. The man with the gloves landed next to her a moment later and looked for the smoldering source of the smoke, locating the still-burning ball of oily grey ambergris at the rear of the deck, where it had probably been kicked in an attempt to get it as far away as possible.

The gloved man grabbed it and heaved it up through the hatch to the deck above, where the second gloved man would toss it overboard.

Hava crouched, sword ready, as the smoke began to clear. She saw bodies sprawled everywhere. She quickly counted, engulfed by the stench of vomit and shit.

She took a moment to steel herself and knelt next to the nearest body, while others from above jumped down carefully one at a time. The man she examined was dead by suffocation. By the time Catharian arrived, she had counted twenty dead.

"With the eight we killed on deck, then one Molly shot, is that a full crew, do you think?"

"I doubt it." He looked around. "I said maybe thirty at the least, but we need to search every inch of this ship, because at least one will be trying to escape and carry word back. Sometime today, or tomorrow at the latest, this island will be swarming with Azhante and their companies of killers and mercenaries. This ship is the jewel of their fleet, and they will come looking for us as soon as they know it's taken."

Hava nodded. She instructed some of her crew to fetch ropes and haul up the bodies and dump them in the lagoon. She had no doubt the local sharks and crabs would make short work of them. "Search them first. Anything that looks like a message comes to me. Weapons and valuables are for anyone who wants them."

Rope slings were quickly fashioned while Hava led a thorough search of the hold. Bodies were stripped of weapons and some coins, but the only jewelry found were the black lacquered pendants she had observed before.

One of the men approached her. "We've checked every corner here, Captain, but there's a forward bulkhead with a door. Thought it best to tell you before anyone opened it."

"Show me."

He led her past barrels and crates lashed to the sides of the ship, probably provisions that could be supplemented with fresher food from the local markets. If it hadn't been for the horrible gas concoction devised by Henri, those twenty men could have hunkered down in here for a month, she thought. And, at best, she and her crew had one day. A fleet of ships, many with Azhante aboard, would be arriving soon.

She reached the door and got down on her knees to look under it. She took out her dagger and tried to slip it under the doorway, but immediately felt it hit something that gave just a little. She stopped pushing.

Standing up, she motioned her men to step away and whispered, "It's battened."

"And we have no idea how many men are on the other side," Catharian said.

"More than one, I'm guessing," replied Hava. "That's the crew quarters or I'm a fool, and if you say this ship has a crew of thirty or more, it'll hold hammocks or bunks for at least ten men. There could be a full watch of killers waiting in there."

"Maybe we could block the doorway and starve them out?" asked Catharian in a joking tone.

"Even if the Azhante fleet wasn't arriving, I suspect they have a scheme to get off this ship. Chew through the damn hull, maybe." She thought for a moment, then added, "If they come out it's going to be bloody, as they know what they're doing and most of us don't." She looked at Catharian.

He nodded. "I've been in my share of fights, but only street brawls and the like. Serious combat, no. I've seen these Azhante a few times, and they are lethal."

"Street brawls . . ." she said slowly. "Perhaps that might be the thing."

"What have you in mind?"

"When we took the *Black Wake,* I simply had everyone trip up a single Azhante and rush him. Someone kicked the Azhante in the head before he knew what was happening, and he was dead shortly thereafter."

"I doubt you can trip however many are in there as they come out," he said dryly.

"I need to get up on deck," she said. To the first men in the hold she encountered, she ordered, "If anything comes out of that door, kill it. Don't think; just kill it."

The rope slings used to haul up the bodies were still dangling, and using one, she quickly climbed to the deck. The men still on deck began to question her, but she held up a silencing hand and hurried forward. As she had suspected, the bulkhead at the fore of the hold aligned with the entrance to the cabin that supported the foredeck. She climbed the ladder, estimated the distance to the bow, and then returned to the main deck. Two young men who looked both anxious and determined were watching her and she motioned them over. "Stand by the ladder, and if anything comes through that door, kill it."

One of the young men said, "I don't see a ladder, Captain."

"The little stairs," she said impatiently. "Stairs on a ship are called a ladder. I don't know why, they just are."

They positioned themselves as ordered, which gave them a clear line of attack should anyone come out, as the door's hinges were on the opposite side to where they waited.

She returned to the hold, slid down a rope, and hurried to the bow of the ship. "I have an idea," she said to Catharian, taking him aside. "That bulkhead rises to the rear of the foredeck, and I have no idea what is in the cabin above, but there might be a hatch between the two."

He pondered this. "Most ships don't, but a few do. If this one does, that might put our cornered rats up there, rather than behind the door."

"Or both," Hava added, "if we're especially unlucky."

She moved back to beneath the open hatch and shouted, "Molly, you up there?"

"Here, Hava," said the archer, leaning over so Hava could see her.

"Keep an eye on that forecastle door, and if it opens, just shoot anyone who comes out."

"Already ahead of you," Molly said, brandishing her bow. "I got ready the moment I heard you tell those two boys what to do."

"Get me another bow and drop it down here."

Within a moment, a bow and quiver were lowered down to her and Hava sheathed her sword. She looked around and pointed to a pile of battening and two large hammers. "Get those," she instructed two of the largest men nearby.

She moved until she had a clear shot at the door, knelt down, and took aim. Without a word, she just nodded at the two men, and each took one side of the door, then the man on the right took a hard swing.

The hammer was iron wrapped in heavy cloth so as not to damage the hatch cover when it was pounding in the battens to render it watertight. So rather than the expected crack of wood, the sound was more like the striking of some massive drum, a dull thud that echoed and reverberated.

The two men began beating in rhythm, and Hava could see they would have the door down quickly. After the fifth blow, the door began to splinter and buckle a little.

A tiny hint of light at the bottom of the door warned Hava that the batten had been yanked away. She barely shouted, "Stand away!" to the two men with hammers before the door was yanked back. Fortunately for the two men, the banging on the door had warped the wood slightly and it protested for a moment before shooting open.

Hava sent an arrow through the entrance to the crew quarters and was nocking a second as two men dived out the door at waist height, hitting the deck with a roll, ready to turn to deal with the men with hammers. One Azhante died from Hava's arrow before the other could turn to see where his closest opponent might be. But the other assassin immediately did what Hava knew you should do when facing a bowman, which was charge at them to get close and render the bow useless, and as she had feared, half the men with her were transfixed by the suddenness of the attack or trying to distance themselves from the black-clad killers.

Another Azhante fighter rushed out, followed by others. Hava tossed aside her bow, drawing her sword as she rolled to her left, just avoiding the charge of the first man.

He turned and found her lunging at him and barely avoided her attack. With each passing second, Hava grew more grateful for all the training she had endured in school, for this Azhante was as challenging an opponent as any she had ever faced.

He took a wicked swing with a sword that might have removed her head from her shoulders if she had stepped forward, but she had guessed right and moved a step back. Suddenly she saw the killer's head jerk forward and his eyes roll up as he collapsed, revealing Catharian standing behind him holding a bloodied sword with which he'd slashed the back of the man's neck. "Street brawl," he said, puffing a little.

Hava scarcely had time to acknowledge him, for she could see that the only advantage her force held was numbers, so she just pointed at the next assassin and charged.

The next Azhante sensed her threat from his blind side and turned, allowing the cowering laborer he had faced to thrust his sword blindly at the assassin, nicking his side. The Azhante's reflex as he swung back gave Hava the advantage she needed. She cut him down before he could refocus on her.

Seeing three Azhante dead seemed to inspire those who had been rooted by indecision and they rallied, swarming over the remaining three assassins.

Suddenly it was over.

Hava looked around and saw two of her men facedown on the floor in pools of their own blood and another half dozen holding their hands over gushing wounds. The victory had come at a price, albeit a lesser one than she had feared.

She hurried to the crew quarters, stepping over the body of the man she had first shot, and saw with some relief that there was no hatchway to the cabin above. Catharian followed. From behind her he said, "That doesn't mean there aren't more of them up there."

"I know." She passed him and climbed quickly up a rope

to the deck. Yelling back down, she shouted for them to get the new corpses up and over the side.

She hurried over to Molly. "I'm too damn tired to be cautious," she murmured, reaching for the door handle to the forecabin. She glanced at Molly, who already had her bow drawn. Pushing slightly at the door, she stepped away and, after a moment of silence, saw Molly lower her bow.

Sticking her head inside, she saw a tidy cabin with two bunks and a chest of drawers. Otherwise it appeared empty.

A wave of relief washed over her as she realized the battle was over. She took a moment to catch her breath, fighting off a sudden urge to cry.

Catharian and Molly reached her and she took another deep breath. "Here's what we do—" she began.

"I need to go back to Elsobas," interrupted Catharian.

"Why?" asked Hava.

"If ships have arrived, I need to talk to people who know what happened after I left."

Molly was shaking her head in amusement as Hava said, "You're an idiot. Look around. You've got more than a hundred people who can tell you what happened. I can tell you Port Colos was razed, Beran's Hill burned to the ground, and every fishing village from the south tip of the west coast to the port was raided." She paused. "Oh, yes, and Copper Hills was overrun."

Catharian's eyes widened and he seemed lost for words.

"We've been a little busy, and you never said you needed information. There are also rumors of fleets sailing south, among other things. Just ask the people around you!" She shook her head and repeated, "You're an idiot. As I was saying, we will transfer all provisions from the *Black Wake* to this ship, since we'll be ferrying more than a hundred people in a ship designed for perhaps fifty. Then we'll hide the *Black Wake* where you suggested." She took another deep breath, trying to stem the emotions that threatened to well up.

Just as she was about to speak again, Molly tapped her on the shoulder, and she turned to see the boy Surya and his friends scampering over the stern. Surya ran to Hava, screaming, "Ships. Many ships are arriving!" He stared at her with blind panic. "Take us with you, lady! The men in black will find out we helped you and we'll be killed."

Hava was silent for a brief moment. Then she said, "Fine." Turning to Catharian, she said, "We're going to take this ship and find my husband. Starting right now!"

EPILOGUE
REUNION AND DARK HARBINGERS

1

Hava looked anxiously toward the approaching island. The journey of weeks had frayed her patience and her nerves. She understood the risks now, having seen how hard it had been for Catharian to navigate through the shoals and reefs. He had been correct: the *Black Wake* would surely have had its hull gutted had anyone tried to make their way through with a boat that deep-drafted.

She had also come to appreciate how wicked the *Queen of Storms* was. On those occasions on which she could take the helm to give Catharian and George a rest, she had found it to be the most nimble ship she had ever been on. She had spent some time inspecting the fitting for a ballista on the foredeck and the device itself. This was not a defensive weapon. This ship was a predator. With some practice the crew was able to take in the jibs, dismantle the bowsprit, and install the ballista in less than half an hour.

She and Catharian had shared what they knew about the raids as well as information from George and the others, and between them they had put together a picture of utter annihilation. Catharian had said destruction on such a scale appeared to be a prelude to invasion, but the raiders had withdrawn and were somehow involved in the very strange trade that began and ended at the Border Ports, which Catharian seemed to understand only slightly better than George or Hava.

Hava was also working to wrap her mind around the discovery that Master Bodai was an agent for the Flame Guard. She just couldn't grasp how anyone could infiltrate Coaltachin and reach the level of crew boss, let alone a master, and a member of the Council at that.

All of this swirled in her mind as the ship neared the dock, and her emotions caused by months of separation and fear threatened to boil over. As they drew into the harbor she saw two other ships anchored at a distance.

Catharian came to her side. "It looks to me as if Hatu made it . . ." His words trailed away when he saw Hatushaly standing on the dock next to Bodai.

Hava didn't wait for the ship to be tied up but jumped onto the railing and leapt down to the dock. She was risking considerable injury if she misjudged the distance, but she landed safely, and with two steps had her arms around Hatu, squeezing him so hard she threatened to break his ribs. Hatu held her tightly without saying a word, and then, after a long moment, he laughed.

In strangled tones he said, "I've missed you, too, but I can hardly breathe."

She let him go, cupped his face between her hands, and kissed him hard. Then she stepped back and slapped him hard across the face.

His eyes watering from the blow, he said, "What was that for?"

"For what you put me through!" She felt tears welling up, but she didn't care. "You should not have let that man"—she pointed at Catharian—"take you. You should have fought and stayed for me!"

Hatu's cheek throbbed from the blow, but he grinned widely. "It wasn't as if he took me captive all on his own. I'll tell you about it all later."

Bodai said, "We all have a great deal to discuss." He looked at his former student. "Many, many things, but not right now." He smiled in an almost fatherly way Hava had never seen before. Now she could begin to believe that he was not truly from Coaltachin.

He turned and led Hava and Hatu into the Sanctuary, and they followed with their arms around each other's waists.

2

Toachipe watched for the light of dawn, his eyes scanning the eastern horizon as the lightening sky hinted at the coming first rays of the sun, as it was his duty as Hour Marker of Akena to wake the city, the capital of Nytanny. On most days this was simply a call to service, to the opening of shops, to the departure for work, or to the other prosaic duties of the populace.

Today was different, for it was the celebration of a great victory, to the glory of the Golden Pride and the realm. The great celebration was to begin at noon, and it was his duty to awaken the rulers of the Pride.

A runner appeared at his door, and he held up a hand, which silenced the messenger before he could speak, as Toachipe continued to stare toward the east. He had held this position of honor for twelve years, and this duty was one of the few that no one, not even a ruler, could interrupt.

At the precise moment at which the sun sent its first rays of light over the peak of Itabu Mountain to light the golden spire atop the Palace of the Rulers, another day in the annals of Nytanny would begin. Scribes who had woken when Toachipe rose would now be in position to record every significant fact and detail of the day, from the most mundane to the momentous.

Without any conscious thought, as if a time device existed within him, Toachipe looked above him from his position on this open deck and waited. No matter the weather, from scorching heat to freezing cold, not one morning in twelve years had the Hour Marker missed his duty. Now he saw the first glint of light off the golden spire, and immediately he struck a small gong.

As the sound echoed through the halls, servants instantly began to move with purpose, for all rulers had to be awakened and brought to their duties. Toachipe motioned for the runner to deliver his message.

Toachipe read the report, but his eyes could hardly make any sense of what he read. He read it for a second time and gave a deep sigh at this news. He would have to choose a messenger to take this missive to the Lord of the Golden Pride, and the man selected stood a reasonable chance of being killed outright for being the bearer of bad tidings.

Somehow someone had captured *Borzon's Black Wake,* which carried as its cargo the personal tribute to the leader of the most powerful Pride in the nation. This was bad enough; but even worse was that someone, perhaps the same group, had taken the *Queen of Storms* from the Azhante.

Despite it being a day of celebration, this was not going to be a good day, Toachipe reckoned. And even deeper inside he felt the terrible suspicion that there were not going to be many good days coming in the future.